KEVAN MANWARING is a novelist, poet, storyteller and teacher (MA Teaching & Practice of Creative Writing, Cardiff University). Originally from Northampton, he studied performance art and film on the Fine Art Degree in Coventry. He has been performing his words for over a decade in venues across the South West, as well as further afield. In 1998 he was awarded the Bardic Chair of Bath for an epic poem based on a local legend. With **Fire Springs – Storytellers of Bath** he has co-created and performed in several shows. In 1999 he won the Writers' News Ghost Story competition. He has been running creative writing and performance workshops for all ages since establishing **Tallyessin** in 2000 with a Prince's Trust Loan. In 2003 he edited *Writing the Land – an Anthology of Natural Words*, after receiving a Reading Families Millennium Award. He has written 7 collections of poetry and 3 novels. He runs **Way Of Awen Development** and teaches fiction writing for the Open University. He lives in Bath, where he has led ghost walks. He loves rambling, real ale, folk music and celebrating the spirit of the place.

The Long Woman

by

Kevan Manwaring

Awen 2004

First published by Awen Publications 2004
7 Dunsford Place
Bath BA2 6HF
awen@tallyessin.com

British Library Cataloguing-in-Production Data
Data available

ISBN: 0-9546137-5-9

Cover by Steve Hambidge copyright 2004
www.crookedkm.co.uk

Book production by Robert W. Palmer at
Tuff Talk Press, Bath, England
robertw.palmer@tiscali.co.uk

Funded by the Arts Council of England

Printed and bound by Antony Rowe Ltd,
Bumpers Farm, Chippenham,
Wiltshire SN14 6LH
England

ARTS COUNCIL
ENGLAND

Thank you to: Cathy Williamson for her inspiration, support and undying love; Moyra Caldecott for telling me to write the book I wanted to read; Anthony Nanson for his expertise at Wordsmith Communication; Kirsty Hartsiotis, Inga Bryden, Peter Alfred Please and Lindsay Clarke for their feedback; Geoffrey Breeze and Toby the lurcher for sharing their love of sticks and walks; Derek at the Eastbourne Lammas Festival, who first told me the story of 'Dru the Windsmith', which he had read in *Green Man: Companion and Gazeteer* by Ronald Millar, S B Publications 1997; *Anthem for Doomed Youth,* Jon Stallworthy, Constable, London, 2002 published in association with the Imperial War Museum exhibition; *Life in the Twenties*, J Madders & G Horseman, Cottage Publishing, Devon 1993; *The Coming of the Fairies*, Arthur Conan Doyle, Pavilion, London 1997; *The Old Straight Track*, Alfred Watkins, Abacus, 1974; *The Candle of Vision*, AE, Prism Press, Dorset, 1990; and to all the poets whose work I have quoted.

CHAPTERS

Dedicated to my Mother and Father

THE ANGEL OF NO MAN'S LAND

The darkness crumbles away.
It is the same old Druid Time as ever. '
'Break of Day in the Trenches', Isaac Rosenberg

23rd August, 1914, Franco-Belgian Border

Wind keened like a banshee around the biplane. The dawn air numbed cramped limbs; smoke and sweat half-blinding both pilot and passenger. Sitting in the rear seat designated for observers, navigators and bombers, Isambard Kerne, Officer of the Royal Flying Corps, lifted smeared goggles and wiped them with a cotton handkerchief, tracing with fingerless leather gloves the monogram his wife had embroidered on the corner. For a moment dark eyes lingered on the initials. From the edges of his flying helmet, his clipped black hair was showing grey — like flecks of cloud in the fleeing night. He thought of Maud back home, brushing her teeth, boiling an egg, or taking Nubi for a walk on the Downs.

Reality rattled around him, breaking his rêverie. Vision cleared, he checked the box-camera fitted into the floor of the passenger cabin — an innovation of his own, safer and more stable than sticking his head out over the side and getting it blown off. And then he tested the telegraph attached to the outer rim of his cockpit, sending a message to the radio operator:

Approaching frontline. Visibility good. Merlin out, Kerne tapped in Morse code.

All was ready for the surveillance shots they had orders to take — Intelligence needed enemy positions and numbers. The gun batteries would use the information to place their shells. He tried not to think about the consequences. 'Just follow orders and keep your head down,' they all said. That's all he could do. He wasn't a soldier by nature, but he'd had to enlist — before he was called up. It was the honourable thing to do, his brother, veteran of the Boer War, had insisted. Archibald would have never let him live it down otherwise. It was his turn to do his duty for King and Country. *Dulce et decorum est pro patria mori* and all that John Bull. Archibald had survived.

Surely Isambard would too — the Kerne luck had to hold.

This is not the way for a forty-four-year-old to go about life, Isambard reflected. His peacetime occupation, as a railway surveyor, was a far more sedentary affair — except for the odd wrangle with awkward landowners. It gave him time to pursue his main interest — his research into ancient alignments. Yet his lifetime obsession with prehistory had been overwhelmed by the present.

They'd soon be at the target zone. The spotter plane spluttered along at barely seventy miles an hour but it felt too fast for him. Kerne produced a silver hip flask from the breast pocket of his fleece-lined flying jacket. His gloved fingers brushed the GWR engraving on the side — a gift from his work colleagues. He debated about offering some to the pilot — then thought better of it. Harry 'Mad Duck' Mallard was probably still reeling from last night's session. And the G and T he always had before take-off. Kerne took a shot of brandy, feeling the slow fire burn through him, taking away the chill and steadying his shaking hands. Slipping it back into his breast pocket, he set to work.

Peering through the view-finder, Kerne surveyed the flat world below — trying to focus, ascertain the depth of field, the correct exposure. Features emerged from the morning mist, but no discernible landmarks. Not like dear old England — every hill and vale distinct. Yet surely to a Belgian even such a monotonous landscape must have character, evoke strong memories, associations, nostalgia — like Logres did for him, as he thought of his England, using the Welsh name of his mother's native tongue.

Dawn cast its pallor on the unfamiliar world beneath, the lights of farms snuffed out. 'All over Europe ...' murmured Isambard. 'We shall not see them lit again in our lifetime.'

The daylight was as cold and stark as a surgeon's lamp, revealing the vulnerable flesh of the land. The virgin fields of Belgium spread out below — roads, ditches, hedges, brakes of poplars, lines intersecting like the cables between the wings. The BE-2 buzzed slowly over all, its thin membrane catching the morning sun like a dragonfly in a pool of light. It was mid-August — the crops were high, but would go unharvested. Every available man was at the Front. The women would eventually take over the farmwork, but for now the ears of wheat stood tall and silent, catspawed in the warming breeze, poppies swaying.

The biplane passed over the broken bridges of the Mons-Condé canal — recent target of Royal Fusiliers saboteurs. The map of Europe was being rewritten.

They were passing over Mons itself. Kerne recognised the slag heaps of the mining town, checking the Ordnance Survey chart attached to the side of the cabin in its glass case. He tapped Mallard on the shoulder and pointed downwards. This was their spot for today – 'a bit of photography and back for lunch at the base', as Mallard had said. *Tickety bloody boo.*

Mallard gave the thumbs-up and grinned – his Viking eyes gleaming with berserker fanaticism. He took the plane down a couple of hundred feet with a sickening lurch.

He's loving this, thought Kerne. It's all a game to him, like a bloody pheasant shoot.

At first he though they were cattle. Then glints of rifles, insignia and pale faces showed them to be rows of mounted officers waiting in the twilight fields, like redundant chess-pieces.

'Allenby's cavalry,' shouted Mallard over his shoulder. 'Waiting for the Boxing Day hunt by the looks of things. Tally ho down there!'

They passed lines of British troops digging in with dogged solemnity. Noticing the biplane, they waved, or saluted with two fingers, that ancient insult of the British archer. They wouldn't do that to General Smith-Dorrien, Isambard thought, the General who was leading the 70,000 strong infantry corps of the British Expeditionary Force east and west of Mons on a fifteen mile front. The living lines of soldiers stretched like ants on the African plains Archie had described to him. No difference between the Allies or the enemy from the air, mulled Isambard.

The biplane sliced through shrouds of smoke. The pounding started, audible even through the din of the engine. Howitzers punctured the sky. Explosions flamed all around them like burning eyes. The fuselage shuddered and groaned. Kerne held on tight to the delicate camera equipment – prayed that it would survive, that they would survive.

Below, a rent in the clouds revealed a new hell. A quagmire of tangled carnage. Amid shattered trunks and twisted limbs, the whistle and boom of shells, strikes that vomited mud like geysers, old craters filled with muddy water and bodies, the death rattle of machine-guns carried like Morse code. Isambard's head buzzed. He blinked and looked again. How had the flat fields of Mons been turned into such a Hades so soon? The battle had only just begun. Yet already it looked like it had been raging for years.

The arclight flickered around them – licking the edges of the wings. Between the shreds of smoke the scene below alternated between a late summer of burgeoning wheat and the wasteland of winter, like the flickering kinetoscope of a train window. Was he seeing things? Certainly, seeing the land from the air was a disorientating perspective. Kerne had spent his adult life measuring solid earth. Aerial surveillance was a new science and they were the guinea pigs. Yet he'd rather be in the sky than down there any day. He spotted a soldier crucified in a skein of wire – half his face missing. Hard to tell if he was British or German.

I'm like the Recording Angel, witnessing history, he thought. *The evil that men do.* Quickly he covered his head with the black cowl, focussed by sliding the bellows along their rails and clicked. There but for the grace of God, brooded Kerne. Shaking his head out of the hood, he went to reload.

A shell burst directly below a wing, making the biplane buck. Cursing, Kerne fumbled with the icy photographic plate. In slow motion he watched it shatter. Frozen shards showered the cabin.

In front, an explosion ripped a tear in the smoke and mist, revealing a vast horde of German soldiers.

'Christ, there must be twice as many Huns!' Mallard shouted back. 'Kluck's got us outmanned! We haven't got a snowball's chance!'

Frantically Kerne started tapping out a warning message. His hand couldn't stop shaking. He tried to concentrate as the bombardment increased.

Light flashed off the biplane's wings. Then the air seemed to peel away like flayed skin.

Mallard was screaming at him. 'Eyes to the front! Twelve o'clock, twelve o'clock!'

The enemy fire coalesced before them into an otherworldly vision. In the flak Kerne thought he saw flashes of archers, a knight shining, raising his sword ...

Time dilated, Kerne felt detached from his body, from the events. In a pattern-recognising part of his brain, not frozen by fear, he thought distantly an avenging angel with outstretched wings, holding spears ... He breathed a prayer to the sky, yet the heavens seemed empty. Then it struck him. 'Like the long man!' he shouted into the void, the wind stealing his words.

'Hell's teeth!' spat the pilot. 'It's Saint George himself!'

Inspired by the vision, Mallard gunned the engine and swooped down.

Christ! He's going for a bombing run, thought Isambard. Just drop them over the side – no problem. Except he might lose his head. He braced himself as the biplane plunged and accelerated over the battlefield, the engine's whine, thrum of wires, and Sturm und Drang of cross-fire deafening.

A sense of doom tightened Kerne's stomach. If they were hit there was no chance of baling out: no parachutes were issued, to stop them from doing so.

'Cry God for Ha-aagckkk!' shouted Mallard, his battle-cry cut short by a bullet in the throat from below. Gurgling blood, he let go of the controls to clutch his spurting neck. The BE-2 plummeted. Cables screamed, snapped, as the flimsy machine nose-dived.

Pitched forward, Kerne fell towards Mallard. He reached over to grab the pilot and thrust his handkerchief against the wound. The wind sprayed blood over him, smearing his goggles with a red mist. Mallard's hands flailed about, trying to staunch the flow. The controls moved by themselves. The intense light obliterated their features, like a series of camera flashes. Flying blind, the biplane tumbled drunkenly across the blasted charnel house of No Man's Land, straight into the cloud of fire.

Letter addressed to Maud Kerne, Eastbourne:

25th August, 1914

Dear Mrs Kerne,
It is my painful duty to inform you that your husband, Flying Officer Kerne, is missing in action, presumed dead. He was on aerial reconnaissance during the battle of Mons, Belgium, on August 23rd and did not return. It is extremely unlikely that he will be found alive after 48 hours, so we must presume the worst. Officer Kerne was a gallant gentleman and it is a great loss.
I am to express to you the sympathy and regret of the Army Council at your bereavement.
Any application you may wish to make regarding the late officer's effects should be addressed to 'The Secretary, War Office, White Chapel, London, SW' and marked Deceased Officer's Effects.

Yours sincerely,

Captain Arundel-Hatt, RFC

1

THE DEAD OF WINTER

The pallor of girls' brows shall be their pall;
Their flowers the tenderness of patient minds,
And each slow dusk a drawing-down of blinds.

'Anthem for Doomed Youth', Wilfred Owen

31st December 1922, Paddington Station

Maud Kerne sat down in the waiting room, an hour early as always for the 10.30 a.m. London to Penzance, as she had done for the last nine years. Like a scratched '78' of her sister's, nine times she had taken the journey, always at the same time of year – the limbo between Christmas and New Year's Day. Time to kill in the hangover of the twenty-fifth – the glamour of the season faded with the false sentiment, smiles dropped like pine needles on the carpet. She could stomach no more cold turkey, the anticlimax of it all, and was glad to be on her way. Staying with Constance, enduring her noisy twins and, worse, the attentions of Archibald, her brother-in-law, was always wearying. Not that she was ungrateful to be taken in at this time. In fact, it had become something of a tradition. Tradition: one of those ridiculous things people mindlessly adopt, she thought, because it has happened before.

Yet wasn't that what she was doing? Playing the dutiful widow. And she did not even know if her husband was dead. The body had never been found. *Missing in action* – the words haunted her. Against all reason she held on to the shred of hope that he had not been killed. That one day he would turn up again. Yet nine years had passed and there had been no sign of him. So she had to face the unpleasant choice: either he had survived and deserted her, or he *was* dead.

Her life had been in limbo. Unable to grieve, unable to move on.

In the aftermath of her husband's official death she had appreciated the support of her sister and brother-in-law, the only family she had left, but now it seemed like a chore. All Yuletide she had yearned for the solitude of her annual journey. Even in swarming Paddington she felt more alone than in the forced intimacy of a semi-detached in Eastbourne. Life roared around her, but it seemed far away. Like a gas lamp turned low, she had withdrawn into herself, and if the others waiting to depart were not so preoccupied or torpid, they might have been unnerved by the sullen statue in their midst. She was a pariah. A woman alone. Yet the first time she had taken the journey she had not been.

Was it nearly quarter of a century since that first trip with her future husband?

Maud Kerne needed a holiday. That was what her work colleagues all said. And her sister, her brother-in-law, and Maggie, her best friend. Anybody would think they were trying to get rid of her. 'Maud – take a holiday,' they insisted. And so here she was, waiting for the Holiday Line. Yet was it the beginning or the end of the line, this terminus?

The sounds of the vast station echoed around her, volume modulated by the opening and closing of the frosted door. Through the window of the waiting room she saw the cathedral-like iron arches that reached overhead like a tree canopy or cage, an iron cage. A wonder of its age they had called it, or perhaps the belly of the whale for all the lost souls on life's road. But not Maud – oh no, she knew exactly where she was going. She should do: it was a journey she had taken many times before, in honour of her husband – commemorating their first trip to Glastonbury in 1900, when he had proposed to her on the Tor. It was her pilgrimage to him, her way of remembering; not that she had ever forgotten. The events of that summer in 1914 were engraved on her mind like the hot metal of a press.

A man with a walrus moustache rustled a copy of *The Times*. She snatched a half-read headline: 'Mussolini cr— his Rubicon ... marches to Rome.' *The Tatler* gave an office-worker a glamorous face. Another paper veil, another wall of privacy. A poster for the new magazine *Good Housekeeping* showed a beaming housewife advertising a 'miraculous' labour-saving device called a vacuum cleaner. Just what Maud needed – something to cleanse the void inside her. Her empty life. So hollow without her Sammy. Like this echo chamber, she thought; Narcissus long vanished, announcements distorted on tannoys, some higher authority issuing incomprehensible dictums, conducting chaos.

She pulled her rabbit fur trimmed coat around her. Shades of brown, like the rest of her. She was a study in brown. Hair, eyes, shoes, stockings, skirt, jacket, hat. Her skin was wan, its pallor not artificial, like those modern girls all made-up. Bold as brass, a young lady applied lipgloss in the mirror above the waiting room mantelpiece, to the withering looks of the matrons and the admiration of the stiff-collared men. Long legged, a slimness exaggerated by the long tight dress, her hair in waves. 'Is that a shingle?' someone wondered. 'A dead ringer for Louise Brooks,' murmured a man to his friend. Thoroughly modern like Maggie, Maud's would-be flapper friend, whereas Maud tended to blend into the background. Fine. Maud did not want life to notice her any more, but she already felt like a ghost. The phantom of platform five, that's what they should call her.

There was a chorus of coughing. Maud's skin crawled at the thought of all those winter germs and bad habits, the room reeking of pipe tobacco and cough sweets. The air swirled with smoke, highlighted in the shafts of pale winter sunlight. Like the Athena auditorium, Maud thought, *or a chambered barrow at midwinter*, she could imagine her husband saying. He never liked the pictures. Preferred long walks in the countryside. Preferred his own way in many things. Even death, it seemed.

Maud's gaze wandered. Plain walls were given a touch of reflected glamour by film-posters advertising the latest releases. Fritz Lang's *Metropolis* depicted a woman encased in metal, trapped, like Maud, in the city, in her life, in herself. Yet the pictures offered her escape. She enjoyed the Saturday matinées. After evenings of marking essays she needed to do something less cerebral, although nothing could match a good book — her first and deepest love. A heavy tome awaited her in her hand luggage, a Christmas present, but it could wait. She wanted to savour every page on the train, when it felt like lying in the arms of her Sammy, reading in bed, rocked gently to sleep.

She looked at the time on the wall and recalled 'a pair of glasses and a smile' Harold Lloyd in *Safety Last* hanging on to the clock-face, as it buckled under his weight, as if melting in his hands ... And, oh, how she would melt into Valentino's gaze in *The Sheik*. He would hypnotise her and she would be completely in his power, like Lil Dagover carried away by the spectral somnambulist Conrad in *The Cabinet of Dr Caligari*. Yet looking around her at the sleepy torpor of bodies, Maud wondered, aren't they all sleepwalking through life?

And what was this around her except smoke and mirrors?

From the counter in the corner of the room, steam billowed out from a brightly polished silver urn. 'Tea's ready,' said the dour maid, and people began to queue up. Like pilgrims for their ointment, thought Maud. Here, in this new temple of modernity — where modern-day pilgrims flock. A Canterbury for iron horses. All around her, relic seekers returned home with their pieces of a saint — Saint Nicholas.

A red-faced porter grumbled into the grate, attempting to stoke some life into the fire.

'It doesn't seem to want to get going this morning,' he said, half to himself.

Nothing does, thought Maud. The world had ground to a halt. Frozen solid. Dead still. *Like her life.*

She caught her reflection in the mirrored door as an old lady entered — forgetting to shut it, to a tirade of complaints about the draught. Maud looked long-faced and thin-lipped. She had never been beautiful, but her summer had turned to autumn all too quickly, and winter was in the wings.

Her life had been whittled away by teaching. The faces changed, but the roles remained: the bully, the swot, the shy one, the trouble-maker. Set texts and set in their ways. No room for innovation at the Lewes Grammar School for Girls — to which she had commuted from Eastbourne for the last twenty years.

Time dilated as she daydreamed ... The faces of the past rose and receded before her, like waves breaking. Where had all her friends gone? They had got on with their own lives, moved away, settled down, had families. All she had was Nubi. Her neighbour was looking after the lurcher for her — her sister would not tolerate him in the house. He must be missing her dreadfully, the great soft oaf. A pang of guilt went out to him. He had been her constant companion through these troubled years — she must take him on a long walk when she got back home.

9.49. The large clock clicked on, relentless. Forward, it seemed to shout. Forward! A speeding locomotive, unstoppable. Forget the past! Think of the future! Look! Look! *Yet we exist on a knife-edge*, Maud observed with the clarity of an outsider. *The split-second that is now.*

Maud checked her own pocket watch — a large station-master's one. A memento of Sammy's — a gift from the railways. The only thing of his she kept with her at all times, though it was too heavy 'for a lady'. It looked like his compass — yet she had lost true North. It had proven false. No higher authority. No guiding goodness. How could there be, for the Great War to be allowed to happen? For her husband to be 'killed' in the first month? To Maud, C of E, it was God who died that day. Mere anarchy was let loose, and she was left on the naked shingles of the world.

She held the watch and imagined her husband near. Imagined him setting off to work. The lines he surveyed for all of these people to travel on ... like his namesake, Brunel. He had followed in the footsteps of that great man – and now she followed in his. Yet so many branch-lines had become dead-ends, failed attempts. But in his explorations he found older routes ... Renegotiating the conversion of Isambard Kingdom Brunel's safer, smoother broad-gauge to Stevenson's narrow wasn't Sammy's magnum opus, his research into ancient alignments was to be ... *But we are all tram-lined in one way or another*, thought Maud bitterly. What choices had she been offered? As a woman she had few, as a widow even less. Yet she would never regret having chosen Sammy – one thing in her life she had got right.

Maud caressed the watch's smooth silvery surface like a talisman. She traced her kid-gloved fingers over the lovingly polished copperplate engraving on the back:

To Isambard Kerne, surveyor for the GWR
For excellence in performance of duties
Godspeed
MCMXIV

It should have been given to Isambard when he retired – but he'd never reached retirement age. The Great War saw to that. The surveyor's skills were needed in the skies above Belgium, where the average lifespan of an airman was seventeen-and-a-half hours, she'd remembered reading once: a little bit of trivia masking so vast a tragedy. And so it had been given to his widow as a keepsake.

As if it could ever compensate for the lost time.

The bells broke her rêverie. At the ten o'clock chimes, Maud rose, smoothing her skirt. Time to make her way to the platform edge. A middle-aged veteran in a medalled red jacket opened the door for her, puffing out his chest like a rooster. She smiled weakly and passed.

Outside the waiting room, life swarmed like the restless pigeons – trapped inside the iron cage like the rest of them. One of the bedraggled grey birds hobbled on a rotten leg. As she strode by they rose into the air with a bustling indignation, like WI members being told to move their meeting. To the staccato of her heels, the rustle of her fur and false silk, Maud passed through the crowds, the luggage trains, in a dream, in a daze.

Omnibuses pulled up, disgorging their contents. All stations were desolate places, Maud thought. Everybody wanting to be somewhere else.

She recalled holding her husband's hand — shy smiles, the excitement of that first trip — their first time away, she still a student of English literature in her final year at Somerville College, Oxford. The innocence of the new century awaited them. Anything was possible. That was nearly twenty five years ago. Since then the century had been steeped in too much blood. It seemed tainted beyond redemption.

Around Maud, daily life continued as if 'The War to End All Wars' had never happened — soldiers and flower-sellers, gentlemen and their sweethearts, dowagers with tiny dogs, businessman in bowler hats, salesmen with carpet-bags, families saying farewell or being greeted, children being told off. The hue and cry was deafening — shrieks of steam, slammings of carriage doors, blowings of whistles, trundling trolleys, puffing porters. The hustle and bustle was like a tea dance to which Maud had not been invited, the dance unknown, the music provided by a drunken orchestra.

Beneath a banner of 'Blood and Fire', a Salvation Army band were playing Christmas hymns on a collection of brass and wind instruments. They had just launched into a dour rendition of 'Silent Night'. A black-uniformed woman rattled a tin at onlookers. Then a squeaking made Maud look down: on a make-shift cart a man with no legs, dressed in a soiled threadbare uniform, but with a medal on his chest, wheeled his way in front of the crowd, wielding an empty tin cup in his teeth. He dropped it in his lap and caught her eye. 'Spare a penny, missus?' Most tried to ignore him, but an enraged gentleman, whose wife was in tears, asked the guard for the beggar to be removed. Maud dropped in a ha'penny to scowls and carried on. 'God bless you, lady.' She did not look back.

Feedback pierced the hall, then a metallic voice on the tannoy announced, 'The 10.30 Penzance Express is now boarding, platform 5.' There was a sudden movement of people — but she was already there, at the head of the queue forming behind her. Maud flashed her pass at the ticket inspector. He smiled, knowing she was 'one of them', a staff dependant. She bridled at his knowingness — she detested all forms of familiarity. Indignantly, she passed through the gate on to the platform.

Porter's trolleys rattled past. Her luggage had already been sent in advance – a trunk sewn into canvas. All she had with her was her hand luggage. So efficient, these thoroughly modern times, as Maggie kept reminding her. Everything moving faster and faster – to where? Where did that sacred cow Progress get them? Mechanised warfare. The wholesale slaughter of a whole generation. ... *for these who die as cattle.* Only poetry gave some indication of the full horror of the so-called Great War. The poems of the doomed had gripped her like dispatches from the Front.

The flower girl shivered by her dried blooms. Maud walked through the station like a ghost. No one could hear her in this dumb show, which had become like a silent motion picture to her, flickering in black and white. The train hurtled towards her. The damsel on the tracks. No one to rescue her. Her husband had been tied to his job, and she to him. Yet the Suffragettes on the railings had not wanted rescuing. Had all their efforts been in vain? Now she had to pay her own way, or it was the poorhouse for her. Her parents were gone, and she was too proud to ask for her sister's charity. She could imagine the smugness of Constance – it was bad enough that she gave Maud her cast-offs. How skew-whiff, for the oldest sister to be living off hand-me-downs! Yet, she had been living in someone else's skin all her life.

Maud could feel a migraine coming on. The scene diminished as if she looked at it from the wrong end of a telescope. She saw the newly-deads alighting, or queuing up for their next life. The carriages brought fresh arrivals, singly or in pairs from disease, assaults or traffic accidents, to whole villages from massacres and disasters. Confused and lost, with questions on their brows – 'There's been a mistake on my ticket ...' 'I got on the wrong train ...' 'How do I get home?' 'Where's mummy?' An old lady called out for her husband – on a different train. The guard could not stop the train, would not let her get on; panicking, forgetting decorum, she ran along, crying, until she fell, sobbing. Her husband placed a hand against the window, his breath misting the glass. Maud's mind whirled. She steadied herself against a girder. Did death lead to rebirth? New destinies, new lives? Yet nobody could choose their destination. They had already been enrolled in their next life lesson. It had been decided for them, according to their grades.

Maud had to sit down for a moment on a pile of cases. A gang of grubby children hung about there, waiting for their beleaguered parents to finishing loading their luggage. They danced around in a circle, singing over and over again:

In Fleet Street, in Fleet Street,
The people are so fleet;
They barely touch the cobble stones,
With their nimble feet.

The lads run like a windy day,
The lasses run like rain,
From Temple Bar to Ludgate Hill,
And then run back again.

Recovering a little, and concerned that people would notice, she pushed past them, irritated. Maud hated to be late. To have to rush. She had got there in good time. Had it all planned to perfection. Life ran like clockwork until people got in the way.

From unheated Third Class blue-faced passengers stepped from the open carriages. Everyone knew their place on God's Wonderful Railway. It was a cast-iron caste system.

On billboards, pastel seaside posters for the 'Holiday Line' promoted the golden delights of the Cornish Riviera. Yet the colour was drained from the land, and from the people beginning to feel the pinch of hard times. Thin shaped women, thin faces, thin lives. It was a threadbare world. From a dog-eared and mouldy poster, Lord Kitchener challenged with his pointing finger: 'Your Country Needs You!' How many had bled for that patriotic call to arms?

Disgusted with its lies, she hurried away and bumped into a tall smartly-dressed man. The impact made Maud drop her purse. It fell at the feet of the stranger.

'I'm terribly sorry! Here, let me help you.' Immediately, he leant down to pick it up.

Flustered, Maud snatched back the purse, all composure gone. She offered a polite but icy 'Thank you' and, before the man could speak, she scuttled on. The shock of intimacy had unsettled her more than the accident. He had looked right at her!

Ever since her husband's vanishing, she had been twitchy around men. She lived her life half-expecting one to tap her on the shoulder and say, 'Maud, darling, it's me – your Sammy. I'm back!' So jumpy had she become of the opposite sex, she had acquired a reputation in her small social circle as something of a Suffragette.

Maud tried to regain her composure as she approached the platform. The gleaming engine was resplendent in the GWR livery.

She had to get on that train before any more unexpected encounters!

There was a scurry of movement towards the carriage – its doors gaped open, ready to eat. As the throng swarmed down platform 5, there seemed to be a commotion holding everybody up. First the purse, now this – it was one of those mornings! Cursing under her breath, Maud pushed past – and then she saw what gripped the bystanders' ghoulish attention A young man was having a turn. He was dressed smartly enough, Maud thought – he couldn't be a derelict. It looked as though he was having some kind of fit – twisting, frothing at the mouth, holding his head, staring wild-eyed at the people around him.

Then he screamed: 'Heads down! Heads down, lads! Heads down! Hunhunhunnn. Nuhnuhnnunnnn.'

Bystanders stared at him like at a freak show, or an exhibit in a medical museum, talking about him as if he wasn't there or was some kind of dumb animal.

'One of those shellshock nutters, by the looks of things.'

'The noise must have triggered it off.'

'Shouldn't be allowed in public.'

'Cowardice – that's what it is. Not a real man. Should take it on the chin. My Albert did.'

'It's just an act.'

'Why isn't he in a home?'

'Electric shocks – that's what he needs.'

'Walk in the country.'

'A good woman.'

The soldier looked at Maud. Stared into her soul. She blanched.

Don't. Stop. I didn't mean to live, forgive me, his eyes implored.

Then he spoke to her. 'It's a long way to Tipperary. Got a light, mate. Got a light?'

Maud's eyes widened. She was transfixed, as if her deepest desire or terror was displayed before her.

'I – I don't smoke,' she said.

'Light?' he pleaded.

'Sorry – I'm so sorry.'

He noticed her response. She was not mocking or shouting at him. Sensing some rapport, the man walked quickly to her, stumbled on to his knees, reached out, whining, drooling. Maud flinched, horrified.

Children screeched with laughed, teasing, dancing around him, singing:

The lads run like a windy day,
The lasses run like rain.

To their terror and delight he joined in, slathering, swaying, clapping hands out of time.

The station clock read 10.27. Out of time! Maud had to get on that train, but the onlookers blocked the platform.

'Ring-a-ring-a-roses ... We all fall down, we all fall down ... All the king's horses, all the king's men ... Couldn't put Humpty together again ... He marched them up to the top of the hill ... All fall down ... Jack fell down and broke his crown ... And Jill came tumbling after. And Jill came tumbling after ...'

Maud recoiled, distraught. She had to get away. She had to get on that train!

And scared Miss Muffet away.

With a final effort she stumbled onto the carriage, heart pounding.

And Jill came tumbling after.

Men grabbed him, but he pulled free, and lunged at window, screaming. You're different he seemed to say with his eyes; *you understand.* Steam screamed from vents like ghosts in the machine. Shafts and pistons shifted, spat. The juggernaut groaned to life. A whistle blew. A police constable had been called over.

'C'mon, laddy. Straighten up. You're upsetting the ladies. Pull yourself together.'

'*Pack up your troubles in your old kit bag,*' he sang.

An attempt was made to grab him. There was a scuffle. The constable's hat was knocked off. The crowd watched on, amused. Faces leered from the carriage windows.

'Mummy, why is that man silly?'

'Because he was in the war, Berty.'

'Right, I am arresting you. Name?' said the red-faced policeman. 'Name?'

'I don't know.'

'He's the Unknown Warrior,' someone joked – but it died.

The guard blew his whistle, then jumped into the brake van. The engine let out a burst of steam. There was a shunt, as all the carriages fell in line – then slowly, ponderously, inexorably, they moved off. Well-wishers waved at the departing, or blew kisses, determined to play out their own script regardless of disruption, deliver their rehearsed lines, against a backdrop of heckling.

Suddenly, the man broke free and lunged at the window, pressing his face against the glass. Bloodshot eyes fixed Maud in the corridor of the carriage. *He could be my lover, wishing me goodbye. My Sammy.*

Then he was grabbed by policemen and dragged away.

Shaking, Maud reached for her watch. It always reassured her in times of stress. She stared at the frozen filigree hands. They had stopped. In a stupor, she checked the time again: 10.01.

It could not fail – it was her only anchor! She had only wound it that morning, as she always had. Must have been the collision with that gentleman, she thought, with sickening realisation. She held the watch tightly, pressing its cold metal against her skull.

The train creaked west.

A sallow-faced ticket inspector asked where she was going with a West Country twang to his voice. Where was she going, indeed?

'To Glastonbury,' she curtly replied. *To Avalon*, she thought, remembering her husband's fey comment when they had first made that trip, *the Isle of the Dead*.

Maud wanted to cry but nothing came. She had not been able to cry since her husband had vanished. People thought her callous. But every grey hair upon her head spoke of the tears she had not shed. She hid her face behind her hands as the rain began to fall.

The face of the soldier haunted her mind. She could still see him, pressed against the window screen, like a portrait of anguish – *The Cry* of Munch made flesh. And in the rhythm of the carriage and the rain's drumming, she heard the taunting echo of the children's song:

The lads run like a windy day,
The lasses run like rain.

2

HOLLOW HILL

Come, heart, where hill is heaped upon hill,
For there the mystical brotherhood
Of hollow wood and hilly wood
And the changing moon work out their will.
And God stands winding his lonely horn,
And Time and the World are ever on flight,
And love is less kind than the grey twilight,
And hope is less dear than the dew of the morn.

'Into The Twilight', WB Yeats

1st January, 1923, Glastonbury

The frost-covered hill rose to the gunmetal sky. Between the spikes of frozen grass the gritted footpath snaked upwards to the tower. Maud's ankle boots crunched on the salt crystals. She gulped down the icy air, letting it burn away the worries in her breast.

The face of the man in Paddington had haunted her all night. She had been in no mood for joining in the town's New Year celebrations, but fortunately the guest-house she always stayed in was a peaceful place. Mrs Middlewich respected her desire for privacy — the lilac-draped spinster had seen the state Maud had been in when she'd arrived from London and simply brought some hot sweet tea to her room as she unpacked. The landlady was used to seeing her guest forlorn, for she knew the nature of her visit, but she was surprised at Maud's distressed demeanour this time. Yet she let the magic of the place do its work, and by the morning Maud had regained her composure and appetite, if not her social skills.

After a quiet breakfast, she wrapped up and set off, filled with the energy of that special day — the importance of the New Year to her overshadowed by the significance of one nearly a quarter of a century ago — the day of their engagement.

Isambard had kept his plans secret, persuading Maud to accompany him to Glastonbury 'to celebrate the new century'. She knew he looked forward to visiting the Tor, Chalice Well, Wearyall Hill, and the ruins of the Abbey – he'd be making notes and measurements all the time for his damnable journal, she thought – the one he never let her read. Yet he had an ulterior motive that surprised and delighted her once romantic nature. She had always been a fan of Tennyson and the Pre-Raphaelites and so the Arthurian associations of the town thrilled her. She loved seeing the grave of Arthur and Guinevere – the lock of golden hair said to have been found amongst the bones set her imagination alight. Isambard had been sceptical for once, saying it had been a hoax to draw in medieval pilgrims – but she would not let him shatter her daydream. And even he had to admit the place had an unmistakable enchantment.

Seeing the famous Glastonbury Thorn in flower made the mystery seem immanent. The gnarled tree bloomed with white blossom in the middle of winter – a living symbol of rebirth in a barren landscape. Isambard said it was believed to have been grown from the thorn tree that sprouted from the staff of Joseph of Arimathea, plunged into the spot where he first set foot on soil after his long journey from the Holy Land. Her husband was more interested in the idea that this was an early example of geomancy – that Joseph was 'fixing the spot', the earth energy of the place, with his rod.

Her Sammy had loved his sticks. Maud had borrowed one from the guest-house, to steady her as she ascended the Tor. The ground was treacherous underfoot in places, and the exertion of the climb made her concentrate upon every step – like a devout pilgrim, with head bowed.

Yet the divine spark had gone out. She was left with the burden of existence, with a mundane world devoid of divinity. When her husband had been taken from her, God had died in her heart, and all hope of an afterlife. She carried the whole weight of her mortality up the slippery steps. *This cursed body*, she thought. *I'll be glad when its journey is over.*

The bitter morning air found every gap in her clothing, despite thick stockings, gloves, and fur-trimmed coat buttoned up to the neck, with a russet scarf looped around and over her felt hat to stop it being whipped off by the strong gusts that spiralled around the Tor.

The ascent began to warm her bones a little as she applied herself to climbing the curiously shaped hill, which stood out like a ship on the green sea of the Somerset Levels.

She remembered her husband's comments when they had first climbed here – how he loved to extrapolate!

'At one point it would have been all under water,' he had said, gesturing around them at the flat expanse with his field glasses, 'and the Tor would have indeed been an island – Ynis Wytrin, the Isle of Glass, as it seems to us now in the ice of winter, or Avallach, the Isle of Apples, in fecund summer. It was thought of by some as the Isle of Avalon, the Celtic land of the dead.'

'Where King Arthur was said to have been taken to heal from his wounds inflicted by Mordred his son!' Maud had chipped in.

Isambard's dark eyes had widened at this, then he had squeezed her hand – pleased to find in her a kindred spirit – someone with whom he could share his hidden passion.

The ash stick tapped out her progress up the ancient stone steps worn smooth by countless pilgrims. Her breath grew shorter as she climbed the five hundred odd feet in as many steps. She forced herself not to stop and enjoy the view – she would wait until she reached the top, as her Sammy would have done. The wind increased around her as she gained height, its freezing force making her eyes water – but she would not let it steal tears from her. They belonged to her husband and she carried them for him – frozen inside her like diamonds.

Bulky shapes shambled around the summit, cows silently steaming, nosing for tufts of grass. Apart from them she was alone on the Tor. One noticed her and lowed, a foghorn in the mist still clinging to the Levels. Reaching the brow of the hill, Maud emerged into the stark light of a new year.

Up ahead loomed the hollow tower like a stone needle. Through the eye of its empty doorway threaded the wind. As she reached the flat summit the wind hit her in full force, making her gasp. The north wind stripped away any sense of self. Maud clutched her hat. Using the stick to steady herself, she made for the weathered walls and stood against them for support, glad of their solidity. In the lee of the tower she had some shelter. Catching her breath, she looked out over the view of the town and the white Levels, spread out like unleavened bread in the weak winter sun.

They had stood in that same spot two decades ago, hugging one another for warmth. It had been the dawn of a new century – she was about to turn twenty, Isambard thirty-one. It had all seemed so perfect. They felt it was *their* time, the future belonged to them. It was as if they could see the map of their life spread out below them. Maud planned to get a teaching job in the south when she graduated from her Oxford College the following year; Isambard had begun work for the GWR. They wanted a house on the coast. Only one thing was left out of the equation – the most important of all.

When she had opened up the small velvet box he had presented her nervously and saw the ring gleaming there, it was as if a new world was encapsulated within it. Her reply had been drowned out by a roar of wind – he misheard and she had to shout it out, shout it to the sky.

At the same time he gave her the ring, Isambard had a flash of inspiration – his gaze fixed on the horizon. 'The shining roads!' he had murmured in awe.

The perfect moment had been almost ruined by his obsession. Isambard had become very excited for the wrong reason, talking about a network of ancient tracks that criss-crossed the country. He recalled passing Dod Lane on the way here. The Dod men, he had explained, were the ancient surveyors of the land, usually seen with the two staves of their sighting poles, one in each hand. Like a chalk figure, he couldn't remember where.

Maud went inside the ruined tower – empty now, doorless, a square of sky above her head. She had tried not to cry back then as she had faced the wall – feelings fluctuating inside her, of elation and disappointment. He had finally followed her, after his rêverie, as if he had just remembered her. Flustered, he apologised and kissed her in a corner out of the wind.

She warmed to him once more – forgot his thoughtlessness. It would not be the last time.

They toyed with the idea of scratching their names into the stone but were too conscientious. But then they had noticed somebody had already done so with what looked like their initials: MA + IK. Soon, they would have the same surname. *No more Maud Arkwright.* They had laughed with nervous delight, but his feathers had been ruffled, as though he'd climbed a mountain to find a flag already there.

The tower acted as a kind of wind tunnel, yet in the centre you could stand in the eye of the storm and be kept upright by the current. She remembered him holding her there, telling her to close her eyes and *trust*. Then he let go and she floated in the hollow of the wind.

She felt foolish trying it now but was compelled by memory. It was part of her ritual of remembrance. She felt so much older, heavier with life. Surely the wind was not strong enough to carry her now. But the wind whispered to her – *let go, let go, let go*.

She closed her eyes and held out her arms.

The wind howled about her but she felt strangely still and calm. She felt as if her husband was near and would catch her if she fell. A warm glow swept over her that made her shiver. Was it voices she heard in the wind or whispers in her head? She found herself singing, *singing*, for God's sake! When was the last time she had done that?

'The lads run like a windy day
The lasses run like rain…'

Suddenly she felt she was not alone. She opened her eyes, just as she lost her balance.

And that's when she saw him.

He was *thin* – more defined by what wasn't there than what was. Yet there was a power that emanated from him: *a dark energy*. He stood taller than a tall man, as though stretched. A foggy cloak seemed to smooth his contours, made them blur, flicker. A staff he held in one hand alternated with the other, as if she were seeing him from the front and back at the same time – or as though he held two. He seemed to walk towards her, looming larger. His face was shadowed by his hood, but she caught an impression, no more, of his gaunt face. Dark orbs glimmered like distant stars. They called to her from across an unfathomable divide. He reached out to her, imploring. An icy hand brushed her face. She screamed in terror, her cry amplified by the tower. It shattered the visage like a stone cast into a pool's reflection. There was a sudden blast of wind and he was gone.

Maud crumpled on to the stone bench in shock. It was as if the world she knew had suddenly lurched, no longer as solid as she thought. As though a little bit of her memory had been lodged free, she suddenly remembered something about an earthquake that had destroyed the church that had once stood here, leaving only the tower. *An earthquake on the Levels!* It was hard to imagine but it had happened. She gripped the cold stone and gulped down the colder air. What had she seen? The wind must have made her giddy. Indeed, she was feeling light-headed. She should descend and get herself a sweet tea and a snack, her sensible voice was telling her. She had to pull herself together. Other sightseers were starting to arrive up the steps. Maud did not want them to see her in this state! The need to save face and avoid unwanted attention gave her a sudden burst of speed.

Smoothing her skirt and adjusting her hat she got up and, gripping the cane tightly, briskly walked down the hill, acknowledging the visitors' 'Happy New Year' salutation with a polite but thin smile.

She passed a grey heron on the way down – keeping sentinel over the Somerset Levels, perpendicular in a flat land. Silently, it took flight, stretching out its wide wings and gliding into the white.

Maud sat in the Assembly Rooms on the High Street – the only place she could find open – trying to sip her cup of tea without rattling the crockery. She was shaken but did not want to show it. Holly, ivy and mistletoe festooned the walls. Two portly ladies prepared lines of teacups and slices of cake behind a counter. Otherwise, she had the place blissfully to herself – though not for long.

There was a talk on in the main hall, a meeting of the Chalice Orchard Club, something about the 'Glastonbury Zodiac' by a Katherine Maltwood. Sounded cranky to her. People were spilling out now and as the café area began to fill up she was glad she had got a seat early. They were mostly middle-class middle-aged ladies, chatting animatedly about the lecture. As they queued Maud over-heard some strange conversations about giants in the land, earth mysteries, leylines, astrology and alignments – not unusual topics in a town with more than its fair share of 'mystical' types, as she had found over the years. Normally she'd be derisive of such talk but after what had happened it made her feel somewhat queasy.

'You've had a loss recently haven't you?'

Maud's mouth pursed. She went ashen. Oh no, she'd been spotted.

'Are you alright, dear?'

A stout but fey looking woman, with a violet scarf about her face, looked at her concerned. She had strong cheekbones, a proud nose and a firm mouth. Make-up softened a fierce darkness about her eyes. Her accent was a strange mixture of northern, Welsh, and West Country.

Maud tried to put on a brave face, but her bluster was strained.

'Oh, I'm fine. Just felt a little giddy, up on the Tor.'

The woman nodded emphatically.

'It has that effect on you if you're not used to it. It bowls me over sometimes and I'm an Avalonian now.'

Maud looked puzzled. Normally she'd be instantly sceptical but nothing was certain any more. 'What do you mean?'

'Oh, I've moved down here from London. May I?' The woman motioned to sit down.

'Oh, sorry, of course. I'm not myself this morning.'

'I hope I'm not disturbing you, but it looked like you needed a chat. My name's Dion. I'm an author.'

'Pleased to meet you.' That last remark caught her attention. 'I'm Maud. English teacher. Written anything I know?'

'Not likely. They're quite specialist. Esoteric. Niche market. Not everybody's cup of tea. I'm working on a book now about a – friend of mine.' She paused, pursed her lips.

'It's a kind of eulogy and extrapolation of his ideas. Like you, I've lost someone I've loved. He was High Priest of our Order?'

Maud's empathy turned to discomfort. 'Good heavens!'

'They're occult but not anti-Christian. Pagans aren't Devil worshippers you know. Although they do honour the Horned God. Not Satan. Different kettle of fish.' She waved with a Bath Oliver, before taking a bite of it.

'I see.' Maud studied her tea. Around them, similar conversations took place. Was she surrounded by witches or lunatics? Eccentric theories seemed to be a staple diet in Glastonbury. She was starting to think of excuses to leave.

'Look, Maud, I'm no crank. I might be able to explain what happened to you. I'm very familiar with the mysteries of this place. I've taken it to heart, or, rather, it has taken me in to its heart. What did you see up there?' Dion held her hand across the table and looked at her with concern.

Maud squirmed. She did not want to appear a fool, but she need never see this person again. What did she have to lose?

'I saw a man.' She stopped, shook her head. 'It must have been a trick of the light.'

'No, please go on. Give me the facts and let me decide. You could say I'm on expert on these matters.'

Maud gave her a hard look. Dion looked sympathetic, sincere. She seemed to genuinely want to hear. Maud stirred her tea and spoke, not looking up. 'He, he was tall and thin, wearing a cloak – perhaps holding a staff – or two. Oh, this is ridiculous!'

She cast down the teaspoon.

'No, carry on,' implored Dion.

Maud sighed, struggling to express the experience. 'He turned, pointed and, and...' She mouthed the word 'vanished' and shuddered.

Dion placed both her hands over Maud's and reassured her with a gentle voice. 'You're safe now. It's alright now. Drink some tea, dear.'

Taking a deep breath, Maud carefully sipped her tea, trying not to show her trembling. Dion's presence was strangely soothing. She felt a sisterly connection. She could trust this woman. Perhaps she didn't have to carry it all herself, keep it all in. Her shoulders lightened and she nodded determinedly, shoring herself up.

'That's better. You're being looked after Maud. You were meant to be here. You were meant to meet me. It's what the Swiss psychologist Jung calls "synchronicity". Glastonbury is one of the green roads of the soul. Pilgrims have been coming here for centuries for healing and revelation.'

Maud looked uneasily into her tea. She had come here out of simple remembrance, hadn't she? Then why the cold ache inside that this woman threatened to crack open?

'Let me tell you about the Tor. The local belief is that it's the entrance to the underworld, the Celtic land of the dead, as ruled over by Gwynn ap Nudd, the Hades of the West Country. He's said to ride across the sky with his Gabriel Hounds, gathering up the souls of the dead.' Dion stared at her. 'I believe you saw him.'

Maud shook her head in denial. This was getting out of hand!

'This is remarkable. I need to write this down – if you would give me permission.'

'No, no – definitely not!' Maud stood up defensively. 'I – I don't want this mentioned. It didn't happen, you understand. None of it ever happened.' She made a dismissive gesture, knocking over the tea things with her sleeve. The china, milk and sugar went flying, smashing on the tiled floor in spectacular fashion. The room quietened around them, absorbing the shock. All eyes were upon them.

'Maud, it's alright, I promise. Just sit down please. Calm yourself – you've had an encounter with spirit and need to ground yourself. Please.'

Maud wavered, seeing the mess at her feet, the milk running down her skirt, as though upon a stranger's body.

'You were meant to meet me. *Deo non Fortuna.* "By God, not by chance." Our family motto.' Dion suddenly looked vulnerable. Her voice cracked. 'I know what you're going through.'

Maud felt like she was looking into a broken mirror. No! The madness had to stop here. She gathered up her things, looking in dismay at the mess she had caused. She hated scenes. She tried to pick up the fragments but it was no good. It was as if she had broken the chalice itself. In a terrible fluster she left the room, feeling the gazes of the ladies burning into her.

She had to leave Glastonbury and never come back. The phrases of the violet lady rang in her ears. *Green road of the soul, land of the dead, Gwynn ap Nudd, Gabriel hounds, By God, not by chance* ... But God was dead.

She would show them. She would outrun them all.

3

A SÉANCE IN EASTBOURNE

The Sea of Faith
Was once, too, at the full, and round earth's shore
Lay like the folds of a bright girdle furl'd.
But now I only hear
Its melancholy, long, withdrawing roar,
Retreating, to the breath
Of the night-wind, down the vast edges drear
And naked shingles of the world.

'Dover Beach', Matthew Arnold

The terrace house in Bradford Street stood cold and empty in the backwaters of Eastbourne's Old Town. Maud twisted the key in the lock of her front door. The frost made it stiff, and she was weary from her journey home. It was tea-time and it was dark already. She needed a bath and something hot to eat.

Nubi was hungry too – he was looking thin, she was sure of it. 'Hasn't Mrs Mulligan been feeding you properly, poor baby?' The wiry lurcher rubbed up against her legs, threatening to knock her over in his excitement, all tail and tongue, leaving grey hairs on her skirt and coat, but Maud didn't mind – it was so lovely to see her Nubi again.

The first thing she had done upon her return was to go straight to her neighbour's house and pick him up. He had nearly bowled her over, leaping up to lick her face.

The lock gave and the door strained open. The wood must have swollen slightly in the freezing damp, she thought, a draught of dank air reaching her nostrils from the passage. She had only gone for three days but the house felt like a tomb – icy and unwelcoming. The walls were bereft of decorations – she never bothered with them, since she usually spent Yuletide at Constance's and in Glastonbury.

She shivered when she thought of her journey now – the Paddington incident, the apparition on the Tor, the scene in the Assembly Rooms. The shock of it all was still sinking in.

Turning on the passage light, she bundled her trunk inside and deposited it with a sigh. Nubi wagged around her, skidding on the linoleum. On the mat there was a single letter. She picked it up and recognised immediately her sister's handwriting. Dropping it and her keys on a little stand, she took off her coat and hung it up. Rubbing her shoulders, she walked through into the gloomy kitchen and set about getting a cup of tea on the go. While the kettle boiled she filled Nubi's water bowl and poured some dog biscuits into his dish. Pulling on her favourite cardigan – an old one of Isambard's with no elbows left – she sliced a couple of doorsteps from the fresh loaf she had bought on the way home to put under the grill, and sat at the old kitchen table, feeling the cooker slowly heat up the room, the delicious smell making her stomach rumble.

So here she was back home again. Be it ever so humble, there's nothing like it, she thought. It was her sanctuary – here she could escape the world. The kettle stirred on the hob, Nubi slurped up his water, panting between gulps and grinning at Maud with dribbling jaw.

'What would I do without you, hey?'

The lurcher cocked his head then trundled over to her, putting his sleek head on her lap, big liquid eyes looking up at her. She stroked his wiry grey fur and muttered sweet nothings to him.

They had bought him in 1909, when it became obvious they were never going to have children – Maud had been diagnosed with an ovarian cyst. Isambard had been devastated for her, but she had just felt numb. Barren though it was, life had continued.

And life had a way of compensating. Her girls at Lewes Grammar provided a channel for her maternal feelings – exasperating though they were. But Isambard needed someone to dote upon, and it was he who one day came home with the lurcher, not more than a clumsy puppy then. Isambard had called him 'Anubis', in his typically sententious manner. The lurcher soon became known as 'Nubi' though – naughty Nubi usually. She had been annoyed with him at first – his making a mess of everything, but soon found herself spending more and more time attending to his welfare. He breathed new life into their marriage as they began to go on walks together, up on the Downs. Isambard loved that dog, and for Maud he had become her one true companion. Yet at fourteen years he was on his last legs – although he seemed healthy enough, albeit a bit slower and immovable in his tics of character. What would happen if he died, she dreaded to think.

The kettle boiled and she made herself a pot. As she sat down with her mug and a slice of buttered toast the telephone rang.

'Never a moment's peace,' muttered Maud. She'd only put the phone in at the insistence of her sister. What if she fell, or became ill? Living all on her own, it was best to be on the safe side.

'Hello, this is Maud speaking.'

Her frosty façade melted when she recognised the Irish brogue of her best friend.

'Maggie! Lovely to hear from you. How was your New Year?'

Maggie had gone to a wild party in Brighton, she confessed in a racy tone, where she had drunk champagne and Charlestoned all night. She was still recovering from a 'cocktail too many', but it had been 'one helluva bash' and she'd acquired the number of a Rockefeller from the Big Smoke.

When she had finished her breathless précis Maggie asked about Maud's 'pilgrimage', as she always referred to it in a teasing manner. It had been 'fine', and 'refreshing'. Maud did not mention her experiences – it was still difficult to talk about them, even to her closest confidante. She was still trying to understand what had happened herself.

Maggie asked her what she was up to that evening. Maud had no plans, except quiet ones. But her friend would not let her mope about the house on her own – she knew her too well. She was going to come around at seven, to take her out. There was something on that would be 'right up her street' – a séance. 'It would be a hoot!' Maggie promised. Maud wasn't so sure, but she was unable to dissuade her friend, or curtail her infectious enthusiasm. Before Maud could think of a good excuse, it was all arranged and she was left holding the droning receiver.

The windows of the church hall glowed in the icy winter's night as Maud and Maggie approached, arm in arm. Maggie was dressed in a new maroon coat with a befeathered cloche hat, beneath which her boyish pretty face shone out, rouged and roguish.

'Don't worry – it'll be fine,' she reassured, as they reached the well-scrubbed steps. 'Come on, it's too cold to dilly-dally!'

The door was ajar and they gratefully entered the foyer, where people were stamping their feet and rubbing their hands, greeting one another and chatting excitedly. Everyone seemed to know one another.

Maud knew this was a mistake.

'Hello, come in, come in. Would you like a cup of tea?'

A benevolently smiling crone had spotted them lingering in the doorway.

Too late.

'That would be lovely,' beamed Maggie, nudging Maud in the ribs.

'Yes, please,' she responded woodenly.

They were ushered into the main hall. At the back of the room filled with chairs was a table where old ladies served tea, like witches over their steaming urns and pots. Cakes mushroomed around them, as more were offered by the arrivals – each one more elaborate than the last, and greeted with critical comments and praise.

'How many sugars?' asked the old lady.

'Two for me,' said Maggie.

'None, thank you.'

'First time here, is it?' the old lady asked as she poured them both tea.

'Yes,' replied Maud, feeling guilty for saying it.

'I've been once before – sometime ago,' said Maggie, ignoring Maud's nudge – who knew she was lying. 'Used to go to them in Lewes.'

'Well, you've come on a good night – we've got a marvellous medium tonight: Sylvia Jenkins. Have you heard of her?'

The two friends shook their heads, but it seemed they had passed muster. They said thank you for the tea and set about 'blending in'.

The gaggle of ladies milled about, thawing out with tea and hot air.

Maud and Maggie exchanged sardonic looks and whispered comments.

'Look at us, like a couple of grannies!' laughed Maggie.

'Don't!' Maud hissed, subduing her laughter. Maggie always had a knack of making her have giggles.

Yet they weren't the only younger ones there – there was half a dozen their age, and an embarrassed but curious couple even younger, in their late twenties. There was also an older gentleman who seemed to be holding court among them. Dandily dressed and effete in his gestures, he had a scarf about his neck and was that blusher about his cheeks? Maggie giggled, trying not to stare. He was extemporising on esoteric matters with flamboyant declamations, as if privy to knowledge beyond the affairs of mere mortals.

Maud soon wearied of his rambling theories and wanted to sit down.

'Come on, let's get a good seat!' enthused Maggie, sloping off with tea and cake in hand.

Many of the ladies had already reserved their seats with hats or personal cushions. Maggie and Maud ensconced themselves on the end of the second row, and immediately realised why it was empty – due to a nasty draught from the high window. They kept their coats on and slurped down the tea for heat. Maggie polished off the cake like a schoolboy, and went to get some more.

'Do you want another slice?' she asked. 'That Battenberg looked yummy!'

Maud shook her head, rolling her eyes as Maggie sauntered off to help herself to seconds. Maud sunk into her seat, feeling like her accomplice. Yet she had always admired Maggie for her brazenness. Cocksure, that girl. All that Maud was not – yet it was good to be around her. She warmed herself around her friend's sunny disposition.

Maggie got chatting to some of the regulars, leaving Maud alone with her thoughts. What was she doing here? She should just get up and leave. *Right now.* Yet ladies thronged about the doorway – it would be very difficult to escape without causing a stir, as she had done at the Glastonbury Assembly Rooms. And it would upset Maggie – she appreciated what her friend was trying to do. Get her 'out of herself', or out of the house at least. And bringing her to a spiritualist meeting was her way of trying to help her – Maggie was one of the few people who knew what Maud was going through. Maggie had helped her in the first few difficult weeks. Although Maud had said everything was fine, and insisted on carrying on teaching, Maggie had seen her deteriorate, become unresponsive, sullen. 'Walking dead,' Maggie called it.

Everyone began to make their way to the hard wooden seats – Maud understood now why the regulars brought their own cushions and blankets. It was chilly, even inside the hall. The wind whistled through the rafters and rattled the window-panes.

The dandy mounted the stage to a light ripple of applause.

'Ladies, I hope you are warm and well. We have a very special guest tonight. She has been acclaimed as the seer of Scarborough – please give a warm Sussex welcome to Sylvia Jenkins!'

From the back of the hall, from between simple drapes appeared the rather plain looking woman – dour even, with the austere air about her of an Amish wife.

'Ladies of Eastbourne, it is a privilege and pleasure to be here tonight. I thank you for your hospitality and delicious cakes. I see some of my sisters back home may have competition.' There was a wave of self-congratulating laughter — the crowd did not take long to warm to her. Her plain northern manner was a breath of fresh air to their prim and proper world. 'Tonight I hope to channel messages for you, if the spirits are with is. Now, let us see who's out there.'

She sat down on the chair in the middle of the stage, the lights were lowered and she began — closing her eyes and furrowing her brow. She began to sway back and forth and utter low moans, then stood bolt upright and walked forward. Some feared she would fall but she stopped and opened her eyes — although a different person looked out.

She scanned the room — her audience in rapt silence.

'Speak! Who need to hear from beyond? I am ready to receive.'

Several hands shot up.

The medium pointed to one of the younger ladies, who stammered out her question.

'Is my Johnny at rest? I want to tell him — tell him I love him, one last time.'

The seer's eyes rolled up. She swayed and began to groan.

'I see a meadow. Full of light. He is walking through it. He looks well, but lonely. He turns — calls out your name. Cries, 'I love you and always will. I will be waiting for you — but don't come before your time. Live life for me.'

The young lady sobbed. Others comforted her.

One by one the requests were answered; reassurances, demands, apologies, questions, confessions.

Then the medium turned to Maud.

'There is someone in the audience who is in pain.'

A murmur of empathy.

'Someone who is in need.'

Another sigh of agreement.

'Someone who needs our help but will not ask.'

The seer's eyes bored into Maud's.

All eyes seemed to be upon her. She squirmed in her chair. Maggie held her hand, but her gaze seemed to reinforce the others. There was no escape.

'What is your name?' demanded the medium.

Maud looked around — was she speaking to her?

'Your name!'

'Maud,' she muttered.

'Speak it so everyone can hear it!'

'Maud,' she emphasised, flushing with embarrassment. She hated be noticed, to be singled out from the crowd.

'Maud, Maud, Maud,' the medium chanted, then snapped to attention.

'You have suffered a great loss.'

Hasn't everyone here, thought Maud.

'You have suffered immensely. I see a husband ... sent to war ... who did not return. You have honoured his memory. Done all a widow should. But the mourning has not stopped. You have to let go – he wants you to forgive yourself, Maud. He wants you to stop blaming yourself. You couldn't have done anything. You couldn't have stopped it from happening – you must believe that, Maud. Only then will you find your answer. What you seek is on your doorstep. I see a study ... The words ... Behind the mirror.'

This was too much – how *dare* she speak of her husband!

Maud stood up and shouted, 'No!'

There was a shocked gasp. The medium snapped out of her trance and nearly lost her balance on stage.

'Don't speak about my husband. Don't speak –' Maud's words dried on her tongue.

An appalled silence. Everybody looked at her, shocked.

'Don't you see? They're all dead. *Dead!* And there's nothing we can do about it. Nothing will bring them back.'

There were sounds of consternation and disgust. Someone was crying. Chairs scraped back and the lights flickered on.

'I think you should leave, madam,' said a steel-haired dowager.

The dandy was patting his temples with a handkerchief.

'It's alright ladies, it's alright. Don't worry. Don't worry.'

The medium stormed off stage and began arguing with him, complaining about the conditions.

There was a terrible commotion. Maggie grabbed Maud by the arm and practically frog-marched her out of there, apologising all the way, as they passed through the stony-faced crowd, looking down their noses, looking in disgust.

The cold night air slapped them in the face. The door was slammed behind them.

'Won't be going back there, then,' commented Maud.

Maggie stared at her in disbelief in the blue light of a gas lamp.

'What on earth has come over you, Maud?'

'I, I had to say something. That woman started to talk about my husband – how dare she! *How dare she?*'

'That's the whole point, Maud!' Maggie sighed. 'Folk go to hear good news from their lost loved ones.'

'But she was making it up!'

'Whether it's true or not, it doesn't matter. If it makes them feel better – that's okay isn't it? Well, apart from you.'

Maud realised what she had done. She had upset many people – people bereaved like her. Even made someone cry. The tears turned in her now and she collapsed on her friend, shaking but unable to exorcise her grief.

Maggie held her for a long while, then gently guided her home. She wanted to come in for a cup of tea, just to check Maud was alright, but Maud was insistent they just parted.

'I need some time by myself. I need some peace.'

Maggie, happy-go-lucky Maggie was for once put out.

'I was only trying to help! I though it would be comforting. Maud – you don't let people help you. You don't let people in. You've got to let go, or you'll snap. Oh, you're insufferable! See you in school.' Maggie stormed off.

'Maggie, don't – go.' Maud called out, choked by self-loathing. 'Good night,' she sighed and let herself in. The front door closed with a sickening finality. As she drew across the bolt it seemed like she was sealing herself into her tomb. I close the door upon myself, she thought. Perhaps I am better off with the dead.

Parting on poor terms with her best friend deepened the disaster of the night and her depression. Nubi came bounding up and she stroked him absent-mindedly. She caught her reflection in the hallway mirror, and turned away from it, repulsed. She could not bear to see herself, a grim mask in the stark hallway light.

The clock on the stairs ticked. Nubi panted at her feet. The human silence of the house pressed down upon her. Was this the peace she wanted, the peace of the dead? Then the message of the medium came back to her – rising from her subconscious, insistent, like waves on the shingle down by the pier:

The words behind the mirror.

Maud looked up the stairs, to the darkness. Beyond, in the spare bedroom, lay her husband's study, or rather, her shrine to him – for he had never used it in Bradford Street. She was frightened of the secrets it held. Did she want the dead to speak?

4

THE WORDS BEHIND THE MIRROR

So when I'm killed, don't wait for me,
Walking the dim corridor;
In Heaven and Hell, don't wait for me,
Or you must wait for evermore.
You'll find me buried, living-dead
In these verses that you've read.

'When I'm Killed', Robert Graves

Maud scrubbed and scoured. The house was spotless, but dust was always accumulating − decay was always encroaching. She could never rest because her enemy never did. She had to remove every iota of dust. She had to keep things clean and orderly. Her hands were raw from the detergent, her knees numb.

The radiogram was on loud. She hummed to herself, half listening to the news, the plummy tones of the broadcaster. 'Britain recognises Nepal's independence ... The Turks continue to fight ... Ireland joins the League of Nations.'   The mantra of chatter was soporific, reassuring, keeping her company in her solitary home life.

It was the morning after her return. Sour sunlight trickled through the open window. The cold clean air disinfected the room − the smaller of the two upstairs rooms, which she had dedicated as her husband's study. She always kept it immaculate − ritually cleaning it every day. Tenderly she polished and dusted his escritoire, the cases of leather-bound books, the cabinets of files, the framed maps. In one corner was his cartographer's table, with compass, rulers, charts in tubes stored underneath. She could still see him labouring under his sallow oil lamp late into the night.

'I'll be along in a minute, dear,' he would always say as she brought him his evening cocoa. Yet he seldom got to bed before she had already gone to sleep − another night's intimacy neglected.

What had preoccupied him so? His antiquarian hobby of charting old trackways. She knew no more than that. She knew better than to ask. He always grew uncomfortable, awkward, as her sceptical gaze bored into him while he tried to explain about his fanciful theories.

The radiogram burbled on: 'Prince Albert and his blushing bride, the Duchess of York, on one of her first state functions, launched the *Flying Scotsman* today in Doncaster. The new engine looked splendid in its apple green livery, a locomotive setting a new standard for public transportation. Now we can all travel like royalty.'

Sammy would have loved to have seen her, reflected Maud on the radio broadcast. He loved to travel by rail, taking the train to different parts of the country to go on walking holidays – his field trips, where he took copious notes in those hidden journals of his.

And back in his study he would write them up – always in private. It had been his hermit cell. To set foot in it was an unspoken taboo. Yet the study Maud cleaned was a simulacrum. It was a smaller replica of the one he had in their Gudridge Park house – their home before his 'death'. After he had failed to return from the war Maud had been forced to move into the humbler dwelling in Bradford Street – the only place she could manage on her teacher's wages. The move had been a humiliating and traumatic one. It had been bad enough with the burly men manhandling her life piece by piece into the pantechnicon for all to see, but when her husband's dresser had been dropped on the staircase it was as if her very soul had shattered around their feet. They had been struggling with it down the stairs and had not unfastened the heavy gilt mirror – confident they could cope with the weight. But it had been surprisingly top-heavy and halfway down the stairs the mirror slipped off its supports, coming crashing down the uncarpeted wooden steps. The sound had been extraordinary – one of those noises that suck up all others, leaving a vacuum of silence in its aftermath.

Maud had turned purple but was unable to speak her anger. While the workmen stood on in embarrassed indecision, she had gone to the shards and had begun to pick them up with her hands.

'Careful, luv – sorry, Mrs Kerne.'

Yet Maud was more fascinated by what she discovered among the fragments than any glass cut. Notebooks – bound in oilskin, bearing the initials 'IK' and a Roman numeral. Fifteen of them she counted. She picked them up one by one, blowing off the glass filaments, and piled them up neatly. Her hands had trembled and bled from tiny splinters.

When the move had been completed, Maud had looked once more at the notebooks, each one the size of a hardback novel. She could not bring herself to read them − fearing a Pandora's Box of guilty secrets that would desecrate the cherished memory of her Sammy. Instead, with typical sang froid, she placed them inside the escritoire and locked it. And for nine years they had gone unread.

Then the suggestion of the medium came back to her again as she cleaned the study:

The words behind the mirror.

It was impossible for the stranger to have known about the notebooks, and yet the coincidence was uncanny.

Perhaps she had put off reading them for far too long. After all that had happened to her recently she needed some kind of explanation − any kind of reason for why life had turned out for her the way it had.

And so she took the little key for the escritoire from around her neck and unlocked the desk. The lock clicked and she pulled the writing desk open. It folded out flat, revealing the ink well, trays for correspondence, drawers for writing paper − and a small shelf for books. And there they lay − where she had left them nearly a decade ago, untouched.

For a while Maud just sat in her husband's old study chair and looked at them. Why had he hidden them? What had been so secret?

Maud was certain, with the deep instinct of a woman and wife, that her husband had never had an affair − he was too much of a workaholic, and obsessed with his 'studies'.

If the notebooks contained secrets, they were beyond anything Maud had the powers to guess.

Taking a deep breath, she slipped out each tome and wiped it free of dust, turning them over in her hands − feeling them, weighing them. Then, placing them in numerical order, she pulled on the thong binding of the first one − it resisted at first, then the tight bow-knot unravelled. She opened the cover. The yellowing paper cracked apart. She immediately recognised her husband's meticulous hand-writing. 'Journal One − 1900.' Over the page she read the subtitle: 'Research − the cursus and other green roads'. The last phrase made her shudder. *Green roads.* The strange woman in Glastonbury had mentioned something; what was it? 'One of the green roads of the soul' − that was it! What that meant Maud did not know. There was only one way of finding out. She began to read:

The Journal of Isambard Kerne

6th January 1900

My intention is to record research in this journal concerning the lost roads of England – for my own reference, and perhaps for posterity, not that I make any claims about the value of what I record, beyond the fact that it fascinates me.

The vision I had on the Tor of the 'shining roads' has stayed with me – like a candle flame on the retina. It troubled me and caused me many restless nights. Yet I could not make sense of it until this evening. My intuition was groundless without solid evidence. And tonight I had stumbled upon some.

I am fortunate to have access to several Ordnance Survey maps as part of my new post with the GWR. I have to pore over them for new routes and to check land rights. Rights of way are a thorny issue. We have to be careful when developing or expanding new lines that we don't block any of these. Some of them go back to the Stone Age, such as the Neolithic Ridgeway. I have to respect earlier 'waymakers'.

It was while so engaged in my work that I made what may turn out to be a remarkable discovery. It came to me in a flash as I was working late on a railway map. My eyes were getting tired. My mind was wandering. I was beginning to tire of my work, and I started to ponder upon the ancient trackways that so interest me. I browsed over the archaeological survey map showing the ancient monuments of Somerset. I was glancing over at it, upside down. I was seeing things from an unusual angle. Without a familiar point of reference, the eye sees things as they are, rather than as we expect them to be. I was looking at an inverted England, my world turned on its head.

Then suddenly, like an optical illusion, it came to me. I saw how the monuments and ancient sites seemed lined up with amazing regularity. Excited, I took a ruler and, placing one end at Glastonbury, rotated it 360 degrees. I was amazed to see how many instances of alignment occurred – west to the Polden Hills, north to Brent Knoll, Brean Down and the many barrows and camps of the Mendips, north-east to Stony Littleton long barrow and Avebury, and due east to Stonehenge, and south-east to Cadbury Castle. Following one alignment, I noticed along it churches, Roman settlements, clumps of trees, wells, springs, earthworks, standing stones and notable hills They all fell into place. Before me were the ruins of some great act of terrestrial engineering. Why were so many features in alignment? What were these ancient lines on the land for?

Shaking, I checked other maps. Similar alignments emerged. I checked and checked. More lines appeared. The land was criss-crossed by them! And where they intersected major monuments could be found: Avebury, Stonehenge, Stanton Drew (Aubrey & Stukeley were on to something). I must visit these places with my surveying equipment and do some field studies. This could be the discovery of a lifetime!

How long has this secret been hidden beneath our feet?

Browsing quickly through the yellowing journal Maud saw pages of neat handwriting, hand-drawn maps and topographical features, lists of numbers, cryptic notes. She scanned the spines of the others. A book for each year of their marriage. A parallel life they had not shared. Maud closed the cover, her hands shaking. How long had this secret been hidden indeed! Why hadn't he told her about this? Why had he kept something so important to him secret from her? Was she so scathing, so sceptical? Had she really crushed his precious beliefs? She knew he was more 'spiritual' than her, but it seemed to complement her own practical attitude. Maud felt deeply hurt. She knew he had this secret world, but never realised its depth. It was as though he had another life that he hadn't shared with her. Where he felt more at home. She felt jealous. The thought flashed through her mind of burning all the blasted journals right now – just throwing them into the grate and be done with it. She clutched Volume One tight in her hand as the emotions raged within her. Her breast was rising quickly, deeply. Then it struck her – she hadn't felt so alive in ages! She could feel her husband there, could imagine the argument ensuing, his apologetic tone, pacifying gestures.

'You can keep your secrets, you silly man!' she said out loud, then sobbed silently in the empty room, her eyes stinging but dry. All she had of him were these words.

The clock chimed in the hall. Nubi barked for his dinner at the bottom of the stairs. She pulled herself up, and decided there and then: *I will journey with you, husband.* She would read his precious journals! It was a way of reclaiming some of that time of which he had deprived her in his selfish privacy. It had been her marriage too and she wanted the missing pieces back.

5

A PLEASANT SURPRISE

Glad from a world grown old and cold and
  weary,
Leave the sick hearts that honour could not
  move,
And half-men, and their dirty songs and dreary,
And all the little emptiness of love!

'Peace', Rupert Brooke

When Maud had finally opened the letter from her sister the following day, she found it contained an invitation to tea – Constance had 'a pleasant surprise'. Sounded ominous. Maud hated surprises, or any disruption of her carefully orchestrated but fragile equilibrium. Still, she had to oblige – Constance had gone ahead with the plans, assuming Maud would have no other social options – and the date was that very afternoon! Irritated, she rushed through her chores and got ready after lunch.

Maud left her two-up two-down in Bradford Street and walked from the Old Town to the sea front – thinking about the style she and her husband used to live in, in the large house by Gudridge Park. Her sister always resented her for that, and it seemed she had spent the last decade determined to better herself and beat Maud. Constance had hunted down a hardworking but docile husband, and with his money she had furnished a smart house behind the Burlington Hotel, just off the promenade, that they could ill-afford, what with two children to look after: the twins. Constance could not have planned a better revenge – she had proved herself 'better' than her sister, and now Maud was forced to go to her for charity, for hand-me-downs, though she was the elder by three years. Constance loved helping Maud: she became the embodiment of the middle class charity-giver: well meaning, patronising and smug.

Maud had learned to dread these afternoon teas, but though she hated to admit it she was in need of some human company after the disturbing events of the last few days — she'd had more contact with the afterlife than this one.

The streets were desolate in the rain. Out of season Eastbourne was a desperately sad place. A beggar sat huddled in a doorway — an increasingly common sight along the high streets of Britain, so the letter pages of local papers complained.

Maud emerged on the seafront, where the memorial for the Second Royal Sussex Regiment stood sentinel in front of the pier. A biting wind whipped in from a sea ruckled and surly. Maud pulled her rabbit fur collared coat tighter about her, her hair a tight bun underneath her hat. She had made an effort, but always looked underdressed compared with her sister.

Passing the plush fastness of the Burlington, Maud made her way along Elms Avenue past the pretty three-storey houses.

Long ago Maud had got over the bitter irony that her sister had done so well out of the war while she had lost her husband and ended up living in a terraced house, struggling to make ends meet on her teacher's wages and husband's pension — alone, except for Nubi. Constance couldn't abide the dog in their house. 'We have to think of the children' was her excuse for any demand. 'It's a health risk.' She seemed unaware of the pall of cigarette smoke that made Maud cough and her clothes reek whenever she visited. There was no telling Constance — in fact, it was difficult to get a word in edgeways. One just had to sit and be spoken to, like an admonished schoolchild. Yes, that was it — Constance spoke to her like Maud spoke to her pupils. No wonder it irritated her so.

Yet even Constance would be a pleasant distraction at the moment, after the disquieting events of the last few days. What the 'pleasant surprise' would be Maud had no idea. The thought of it made her slightly nervous. Previous 'surprises' had generally involved embarrassment and seemed designed to make Maud 'ever so grateful' — gifts she could ill-afford or use; grotesque ashtrays from one of their holidays, mangy furs, or shoes for a ball she would not be going to. The houses sat primly in a row, white gabled, respectable, with a chaste palisade of balconies. Number eleven had a bay tree growing by it, and a neat garden — ready to burst into colour come the spring. Molly the maidservant opened the door.

'Hello Molly.'

'Mrs Kerne, how do you do?' Molly said, curtseying. 'Can I take madam's coat?'

Maud hated all these airs and graces, but she liked the plain-faced maid, and played along. Molly took her coat and hat and led her through to the sitting room, where she was forced to sit and wait like a tradesperson.

'Mrs Thorpe will see you now.'

'Thank you, Molly,' said Maud through clenched teeth, silently infuriated. Who on earth does she think she is, treating her like this? She was ready to give her a piece of her mind when she reached the top of the stairs, where Constance stood, waiting in a light afternoon pastel dress, looking elegant in a seemingly effortless way. Her dour Arkwright features softened and enhanced by make-up, she was all that Maud could be 'if she made an effort' – but was not. Her sister's eyes twinkled with mischief.

'Maud, hope you didn't mind waiting – all the best surprises are worth waiting for. Look who's here to see you ...'

Constance kissed her cheeks, and squeezed her hands, before stepping aside to reveal –

'Archibald!' Maud gasped.

Her brother-in-law appeared from the parlour, arms outstretched to hug her. Seeing him always made her start – it was like looking at an older version of Isambard, although the brothers could not be more unlike. Archibald had always been the more ebullient of the two; a sportsman, hunter and natural soldier, though his energetic enthusiasm tended to be on the bullish side. Even his infamous war wound had not softened him. He liked getting his way, like Isambard – but he went about it in a far more direct manner. Any refusal of his wishes was like a red rag to him. And it was hard to refuse him. There was no doubt he had charisma, and was in good shape for a man in his mid-fifties, broad chested, with thick well-groomed grey hair and a waxed moustache. As usual, he was dressed as if he were about to go on a game shoot.

'Maud, dear sis – long time, no see! How the devil are you?' He embraced her too tightly, smelling of cigars and brandy.

'Archie, please – mind your language,' Constance gently chided, looping her arm through his.

'Sorry, Connie. Bad habit of mine. I'll mind my p's and q's while ladies are present. Not in the barracks now, hey?'

Archibald liked to mention the Boer War as often as possible, much to Isambard's annoyance. Archibald had never let his brother forget how he had served his country.

'Come along, dear sister. Let's catch up over tea. I'm sure you to have a lot to say to each other.'

Maud was finding it difficult to say anything, caught between the two of them and reeling from the reappearance of her brother-in-law. What on earth brought him down to Eastbourne from London this time? He was usually after something.

Molly brought in a tray of tea and sandwiches.

They arranged themselves strategically around the parlour, taking their favourite seats.

The ladies politely nibbled while Archibald tucked in. 'I'm ravenous!'

'Oh Archie, you're worse than the twins!'

They talked of the worsening economy, the rising unemployment. Hard times were ahead – they all had to tighten their belts. Maud mentioned the beggar she had seen.

'Bloody loungeabouts,' grumbled Archibald from the couch. 'The Council should do something about them.'

'You're right, Archie. They put off the daytrippers.'

What did they want, to sweep them away like old leaves? Such talk left a bad taste in Maud's mouth – not that she joined in, but it was as if by listening she was complicit with their prejudices.

Yet she realised they were all avoiding talking about something – a matter of great importance. Had Archibald fallen on hard times? Was he looking for someone to bail him out, or perhaps, and Maud went cold at the idea, to halve his living costs? She knew he lorded it up in London. He had a good job in the War Office, but frittered away his income on his bachelor lifestyle – gambling, drinking, smoking, hunting, partying.

Constance often said he needed a 'good woman' to sort him out.

What were they plotting? Maud squirmed, feeling she was being interviewed. A sinking feeling. They weren't thinking of ...

Then the nurse brought in the twins. With the fair hair of their father but the grey eyes of their mother, they made a striking pair – Daisy in a pink fairy dress and Ramsey in his favourite sailor suit.

'Auntie Maddy!' Only the twins called her that, and it made her flutter every time. Their size surprised her as usual. Though she had only seen them recently, she couldn't get over how big they were. Surely she had not looked that old at nine? Daisy was growing into a little lady, and Ramsey, well, he had always been big for his age. They had arrived on Armistice Day – although they brought with them anything but peace. Maud had been terrorised by them when they were younger – she had no control over them like her own pupils. She had no leverage or authority in Constance's domain, and so they ran all over her. They landed on her and took her breath away.

She hugged and kissed them both.

'Have you been enjoying your Christmas presents?'

They looked sheepish.

'Ramsey's broken the wooden train set you got him and Daisy's bored with her doll already,' Constance explained.

'Come over here and say hello to your Uncle Archie!'

Cheering, they ran over and leaped on him. Archibald bounced them – one on each knee.

'Children, mind Uncle Archie's leg!'

'Keep that up and you may shake the shrapnel out!' he laughed.

'Tell us a war story! Tell us a war story!' they demanded.

'Not while ladies are present, children.' He winked at Maud. The twins groaned with disappointment. 'You two are like Romulus and Remus – do you know who they are? No? They don't teach you anything at school these days. They were wild children who became the founders of Rome. They were found in the wilderness where they had been suckled by wolves!' Archibald growled like a wolf – and with his salt and pepper mane he looked the part. He played rough and tumble with them, until it became too rough – Archie as over the top as ever.

'You don't play fair!' Ramsey pouted.

'Fair? Who told you life was fair, lad? Life is not kind to losers. Only winning counts.'

Daisy began to cry.

'Come here, princess – what has that big brute done!' Constance gathered Daisy into her arms, casting a scolding look at her brother-in-law.

Archibald shrugged and pulled out a cigar to light, moving to the balcony to do so.

'They're getting tired – I think it's time they went to bed. Now say goodnight.' But the two were sullen and silent.

'Goodnight darlings,' said Maud.

'Goodnight, wolflings,' teased Archibald, baring his teeth in a broad smile.

Amid protestations and tears the nurse took them away, to the general relief of all.

Constance lit a cigarette, but forced Archibald to stand on the balcony to have his cigar.

'I don't want the house reeking like a gentlemen's club,' she explained. 'What would the master think when he comes home?'

'Whatever you tell him to, Connie!'

'Oh, you are a one, Archie!' she guffawed.

Maud began to cough. Their flirtations were tiresome. What *did* Freddie think of her sister's relationship with Archibald? All week long he slaved away to support Constance's lifestyle, while she enjoyed the company of that scoundrel. Perhaps Freddie preferred to be cuckolded by someone he knew. Never the most interesting of men, at least he was reliable. He had no racy tales of war with which to regale his children, who found Uncle Archibald 'far more exciting than Daddy'. The poor man had a heart murmur that kept him out of the Great War. Instead he held down a comfortable and reassuringly unstressful post in the Civil Service, 'counting numbers'. He seemed resigned to his lot. Whether he was happy Maud had no idea – he was seldom seen in the hours of daylight and neither particularly enjoyed evening dos.

The conversation rattled on without her – the words meaningless sounds.

Maud instinctively reached for the pocket watch – then remembered she had taken it in to be mended. Irritated, as though by an itch she could not scratch, she gazed at the clock on the wall instead. Time to go. It was starting to get dark outside already.

'I have to go.'

Her comment went unheard, so she stood up and repeated it. Connie and Archie looked up from their cabal, surprised, and made noises of disappointment.

'So soon? You've hardly been here an hour.'

'Let me walk you back,' Archibald insisted.

'Oh Maud, being a party pooper already?' said Constance, pouting.

'It's quite alright – I can walk back by myself. I don't want to stop your chat.'

'It's too late for that, sister. But we can't have you walking home by yourself – not with all those unsavoury types out there. Archibald will be delighted to escort. You couldn't be in safer hands.'

'It's no bother at all, Maud. I could do with a stroll', he belched, 'to walk off all that cake! Got to keep trim.' He patted his stomach and winked at Constance, who smiled demurely back.

Molly was summoned and fetched the coats. The sisters kissed at the top of the stairs. Maud thanked her for tea. Constance gave her an unfathomable smile – she always made Maud feel a fool. Archibald said he'd be back for supper, winking.

Outside, the light had been drained out of the sky and a cold drizzle was falling. Maud popped open her umbrella, but Archie took it to hold over her and offered his arm. 'Allow me.'

She had little choice unless she wanted to get drenched.

The walk home would normally take ten minutes, but her brother-in-law took his time as if it were a Sunday afternoon stroll.

Maud noticed how his 'war wound' got better or worse depending on his mood – or who was there to see him. He now wielded his cane like Fred Astaire, twirling it about.

He seemed to be immensely pleased with himself – yet if he had good news, he delighted in delaying it.

Whenever the two were alone the conversation inevitably turned to Isambard in some form – this was Maud's defence against her brother-in-law's advances. Ever since Isambard had introduced his new fiancée to him, Archibald had set his mind on wooing her – not because he wanted her, she was certain, but out of brinkmanship towards his brother. As the eldest and a war veteran he felt he should have the 'hero's portion', as befitting the warrior of the family, and resented any success Isambard claimed for himself – his academic and professional achievements. Archibald thought of his brother as a 'useless dreamer', a liberal who represented everything he loathed.

He asked after Maud's trip. She passed it off as a 'refreshing excursion', knowing what he thought of her annual act of homage to Isambard's memory. And all the time she forced herself not to mention the journals – yet the more she tried to subdue that subject, the more it seemed to want to be spoken off.

'Three days in some cranky West Country town, remembering your dearly beloved doesn't sound like much fun to me.'

'It was a most memorable journal. Journey.'

They had both heard the slip of the tongue. Her brother-in-law looked at her curiously.

'Did you say "journal"?'

'No, yes. I meant journey, of course. It's probably because I kept a diary.'

Maud looked away. Fool! If Archibald found out about the discovery he would be around in a shot. She knew her husband wouldn't have wanted his brother to see them. Maud wanted to treasure them for herself. They were preserved moments from her husband's life. She did not want them mocked.

'Bet that makes racy reading!'

She gave him a sour look.

'How about having something really interesting to write about?'

She knew this was the news he was bursting to tell her.

'I'm going to Paris on a business trip – and wondered if you would like to come along for the ride. The ferry, the hotel, the meals – everything's on the house.'

'I cannot make it,' she said sharply – flustered at his suggestion.

Archibald took the refusal as a challenge.

'Why on earth not?' he said, as if to say 'What could you possibly have planned that's more interesting than going to Paris with Me?'

Maud knew he would not rest until he had a solid reason. She had to think fast!

'Well?'

'I can't come because – because I'm visiting Blackwardine for the anniversary of Isambard's birthday.'

Only as she said it did the idea, dormant until then, fix itself in her mind. Yes, that was what she would do – pay a visit to Isambard's mother, Martha. She was the sweetest of ladies and Maud had always got on well with her. The birthday of a lost son must be a sad occasion – but the sharing of memories would lighten the sorrow.

'Why the blazes do you want to do that?'

'Because,' rejoined Maud, annoyed at his tone, 'I want to remember my husband. Your brother.'

'But you've already been on your cheerful trip to that cranky place. Why follow his ghost around?'

'Because I want to honour his memory. I want to – retrace his journey.'

'What an odd idea – he hardly blazed a trail. Stayed in England all his life –'

'Until he died in France.'

'Ah, yes. Damned shame, that.' Avoiding her eye, he lit a cigar. 'But … life goes on.'

The darkness had claimed them. Only the cigar's glow was visible. Maud's eyes reflected the burning.

She might have screamed at him then, but the moment was disturbed by the silent figure of the lamplighter on his rounds. One by one he had been igniting the gas along the street, bathing them in blue.

'Goodbye, Archie.'

'Aren't you going to invite me in? It's getting freezing!'

'No. The house is in a terrible mess. And besides, you know you don't get on with Nubi.'

Archibald shrugged, hiding his disappointment. Placing his cane under his arm, he inspected his cigar and tried to relight it, but his matches were damp. Giving up, he just let it droop from his mouth. As Maud put the key in the lock he went to turn away.

'You know, neither of us is getting any younger,' he said, leaning on his cane. 'We shouldn't be alone at our age.'

Maud stared at him, an old man with his stick. She almost felt sorry for him – but sorrier for herself as her own misery was mirrored back to her.

'If you ever get lonely – just give us a call, hey. I'm only human, though you may think I'm a monster at times.' He waved with cigar in hand and walked off. 'Goodbye, Maud. Take care. Keep in touch.'

Maud shut the door firmly and sighed deeply. The 'pleasant surprise' had been an ordeal.

Nubi came loping up. She fussed him, thankful for his reassuring presence. No one would touch her if he could help it.

Maud felt like a trapped animal, with the hunter closing in – but she would slip through his grasp. Archie could keep his Paris trip and his 'life goes on'. She had the whole past to explore. Isambard's journals waited for her – at the top of the darkened stairs.

6

THE COLD PROPHET

And felt the hillside thronged by souls unseen,
Who knew the interest in me, and were keen
That man alive should understand man dead.

'Biography', John Masefield

At first, it was awkward seeing Maggie again after what had happened, but the old friends quickly made up. Maud tried to make amends – treating them to a night out at the Athena. They went to see Chaplin in *The Kid*, but even that did not lift Maud's spirits.

'Sweet Mary, your heart is heavy if that cannot make you laugh,' observed Maggie.

'And still you hang out with a miseriguts like me.'

'Don't be daft; you're a friend.'

Despite the weight she carried, Maud busied herself with the new term. Life continued in a blur of lesson-planning, marking, reports. Yet time had stopped inside her.

A month after her return Maud decided to collect Isambard's watch – wondering why she had not heard from the repair shop.

'I'm sorry, Mrs Kerne – I have tried and tried, but I cannot mend it. It won't budge from 10.01. I'm completely flummoxed.'

The short-sighted watchmaker, who Maud thought looked like Albert Einstein, scratched his corona of hair and said he did not know what was up with it. He apologised. She took it anyway. She felt vulnerable without it. It was her talisman.

Maud put off seeing her mother as long as she could, but she knew that before she set off for Herefordshire she had to pay her respects. And so on a freezing February morning she took Nubi on a walk to the cemetery. A thick sea fog shrouded the skeletal trees. The ground crunched underneath with frost as she walked through the lych-gate and up the yew lined path. From a swaying branch a solitary raven cawed and flapped away. Nubi gave a defiant bark, then set about the undergrowth between the ivy covered stones.

In loving memory of Agnes Arkwright
1834-1907
wife of Joshua Arkwright
mother of Constance and Maud
who miss her dearly.

Mottled by lichen the grave was a modest affair − plain and hard like their mother. Maud knelt and cleared the withered flowers from the stone vase, then replaced them with the three lilies she carried − one from each of them, the sisters and their father, although he had been driven to the grave long before his wife.

Maud had never forgiven her for the way she had treated her father − depriving him of his dreams, cutting him down to size. Maud had seen him shrink during her childhood, from Macclesfield cotton mill baron to middle-class Banbury bourgeoisie. He had to compromise so much he became a broken man. The mill had never been the success it should have been − technical faults aside, he lacked the goodwill of the locals. He sickened for his native soil and lost the will to live − dying at the age of fifty-two of 'drowning', from drink. He had been found floating in the canal one morning and had been buried back in his beloved Macclesfield. They had moved to Eastbourne shortly after that − her mother moving in with Maud and Isambard at first, much to the latter's annoyance. Then Constance had taken her in when Maud moved house. She had seemed unrepentant to the end, an interminable battle-axe − 'Boadicea of Banbury' they used to call her. Maud hoped she hadn't inherited her mother's worst traits − or any of them. She was proud to think of herself as her 'father's daughter'.

Nubi came loping along, and she had to stop him cocking his leg up the grave − although she did hesitate for a fraction. 'Come on, you terror! We don't need you to water the flowers.'

Maud nodded to her mother − who had never given her any useful advice, and wasn't going to start now. Maud had got herself into a fix she was going to have to get out of alone. She clicked Nubi on to his lead and walked away without looking back.

The Malverns had loomed like a dark wave on the horizon as Maud approached Herefordshire on the train from Bristol, and now she ascended them, to the tiny village of Isambard's birthplace,

Blackwardine. A horse-drawn coach had brought her the last few miles from the nearest station, and, reaching her journey's end she was sore, weary and chilled to the bone.

Luckily, she always received a warm welcome at Rose Cottage, and it certainly looked inviting to her – with its curl of smoke rising from the chimney, the patch of thawed thatch around it, heavy eaves like frosty brows drooping over bright deep set windows.

As the carriage drew away, Maud found herself smiling as she opened the creaking gate – still skew-whiff on its hinges – and walked the last few steps up the garden path, hauling her case with both hands. With a sigh she dropped it in the porch and knocked on the door. Almost immediately it opened and there was Mrs Kerne, beaming and bosomed, as round and brown as a nut, a woollen shawl around her shoulders.

'Maud, dear! I knew it was you. Come in quick – before all the warmth goes out. Here, let me help you with that.'

Maud protested, but the old lady was healthy for her seventy-three years. Must be that country living.

A smell of cats, cabbages and washing wafted out. The low-beamed living room was simple but snug – herbs hung to dry from the rafters, side by side with copper pans. Sepia family portraits and horse brasses adorned the walls. Two chairs were pulled up close to the range, and a black kettle puffed on the hob. Half a dozen cats lounged about the furniture. A ginger tomcat slinked towards her, but thought better of it when it scented Nubi upon her.

Was this how she was going to end up? A crone surrounded by cats?

'Here, you sit yourself down there and let me pour you some of my broth – you must be chilled to the marrow. How was your journey?'

'Oh fine, the trains ran on time – I got all the connections.'

'My boy did a good job, he did. Just like his father.'

Martha Kerne attributed any efficiency of the railways to her son's surveying. She was fiercely proud of him, of both of her sons – although she had doted upon Isambard, as her last child: much to Archibald's chagrin.

Maud watched her mother-in-law as she ladled the steaming mixture from the iron cauldron into a bowl. She admired Martha's independence – three-quarters of a century old and looking after herself after losing her beloved husband a decade ago. She got some money from her husband's railway pension, and Archibald sent her

some now and again, but she earned her own pin money by taking in
the villagers' washing, and baking.

She was a fine cook, that woman, and Maud's stomach looked
forward to the meal later. At home, Maud seldom made the effort –
unless she had guests, which wasn't very often. She could cook well,
and had done so when Isambard had been around – but didn't bother
now, happy with simple fare, the quickest thing she could rustle up.
Martha delighted in her culinary concoctions, and savoured the
whole process. She hadn't lost her zest for life. How did she do it?
What kept her going?

Over the steaming bowl of broth Maud related the latest news from
Eastbourne: Constance, the twins, Archibald, the Christmas lights.
She talked about everything except herself.

'But what about you Maud, how are you?' asked Martha, looking
worried. 'You have the look of hiraeth about you?'

'Hiraeth?'

'It's a Welsh word – means "longing". You look like you're
sickening for something.'

Maud sipped at the broth. It was good – its warmth slowly thawed
out her bones, making her shiver in lessening waves.

'I'm bearing up. The trip to Glastonbury took it out of me. It's been
a difficult few days.'

Martha's gaze did not flinch. She would not be fobbed off with
small talk or euphemisms.

Maud stirred her soup.

'I guess I've been thinking about Isambard a lot – I miss him.'

The old lady held Maud's free hand. 'I know, I know – so do I.
It's always this time of year. His birthday brings it up every time. I
start moping about and I'm no fun to be with – you just ask my
neighbours!'

Maud managed a smile. 'Thank you.' She let out a little laugh. 'I
came to comfort you and found myself being the one in need of
sympathy.'

Wiping the corners of her mouth with the cotton napkin, she
thanked Martha for the soup, and went to wash up.

'You leave that alone, girl – I'll have no guest of mine washing up.
Go and settle in – I've aired your room and warmed your bed. There's
a fire in the grate, clean towels and plenty of hot water if you want a
wash. Make yourself at home and do as you please – read, have a nap
or keep me company; I mind not.'

Maud kissed the old lady on her plump cheek. She had been more of a mother to her than Agnes had ever been. Taking her things up to the little room she always stayed in – Isambard's old room – she felt a delicious fatigue wash over her. 'I'll just lie on the bed for a moment,' she said to herself, slipping off her shoes. But as soon as her head hit the pillow she was overwhelmed with a weariness stretching back years – yet it made her too tired to sleep, as it stirred in her long dormant, long suppressed feelings. The bed might as well have been a rack, what comfort it brought her. Then Maud heard the sound of Martha singing down below with her Welsh lilt:

The wind doth blow today, my love,
And a few small drops of rain;
I never had but one true-love,
In cold grave she was lain.

'I'll do as much for my true-love
as any young man may;
I'll sit and mourn all at her grave
For a twelvemonth and a day.'

The song continued, slipping into Maud's subconscious as sleep finally claimed her – deep and dreamless.

Next morning Maud awoke feeling peaceful and rested. After a breakfast of porridge with Martha she walked up to Croft Ambrey hill fort, fancying some fresh air. And on that sharp February morning fresh the air certainly was. With relief she took deep draughts of late winter. Frost still lay on the ground – but some fragile snowdrops poked through, hopeful and defiant. Her breath froze before her in ghost-like clouds. The sky was clearing, revealing an almost electric blue.

With determined strides, she hiked up the hill. Thoughts of her husband rose to the surface. It was the anniversary of his birthday, 11 February 1869. She remembered when Isambard had brought her there for the first time – with great reluctance to reveal his "humble origins", yet Maud had reassured him with her own. She had a miller for a father and was proud of it. She had hit it off with Martha straight away – but she recalled his father, Harold, being distant. He seemed always to be looking at some absent horizon, or to have his head buried in the newspaper, puffing on a pipe.

A tethered horse munched in its nose-bag at the foot of the fort. A visitor? Maud firmly gripped the walking stick she had borrowed from Martha. It could deliver a good crack to the skull if necessary. A single woman had to be careful, as Archibald had pointed out.

Especially of people like Archibald, she thought.

A man appeared in silhouette on the ramparts. He seemed to be setting up a camera tripod. She was annoyed to see another walker on the hill. Maud wanted it to herself and she did not want to speak to anyone. Yet she had to visit the top – to stand where she and Isambard had done all those years ago. How many? Was it twenty-three? Yes, just after he had engaged her – he had brought her to meet his parents, after much persuasion, on his annual trip back for his birthday. He had proudly introduced his new fiancée to them and showed them the ring he had bought her – the ice crystals underfoot reminded her of its glittering stone.

Maud pulled her walking coat tightly around her and strode confidently up the well-worn path that went straight past the man. She resolved to remain calm and act unafraid, but what she saw when she finally reached the brow of the hill completely threw her.

Gasping, she saw that the gaunt figure held two staves. The sight alarmed her and she stumbled on the track, feeling faint.

The figure stepped forward and asked her in a firm voice what was wrong. He was a man in his late sixties, dressed plainly but smart in a thick riding coat and trilby, gaiters around his trousers. Putting down his sticks, he reached into his jacket. Maud flinched.

'It's alright, miss. I've got some brandy in here – it looks like you could do with some. I'm sorry if I gave you a fright.'

He produced a hipflask and offered her a sip.

'Alfred Watkins at your service.' He tipped his hat and revealed a face thin and frosted by a trim white beard. A pair of round spectacles perched on his nose, attached by a cord around his neck. He seemed a straightforward fellow and Maud felt she could trust him.

She refused the brandy politely, but accepted his hand. Watkins helped her up to the top of the rampart – where a footpath circumnavigated the entire fort. She saw the instruments he had with him, and immediately recognised the apparatus on a tripod.

'Ah, a theodolite.'

Watkins peered over the rims of his glasses. 'So you know what I'm up to, do you?'

She nodded. 'My husband used to use one.'

'Oh yes?'

'He was a surveyor for the GWR.'

'A professional. Well, I'm just an amateur – Mrs ...?'

'Kerne. Maud Kerne.'

'Kerne … Now that name sounds familiar.' Watkins scratched his head under his hat.

'Probably because my husband was from these parts − down there in fact.' She pointed to the hamlet tucked in the fold of the valley.

'Blackwardine − interesting … Not many people come from there these days, Mrs Kerne. It's dying out, that place − the young folk have moved away, leaving only the old 'uns to count their days.'

'Like my mother-in-law.'

'Begging your pardon, I meant no offence.'

'None taken, although I don't think Martha is idle in her autumn years.'

'And I don't suppose I am neither, come to think of it − I have my hobbies to keep me amused.'

'They look like more than hobbies, Mr Watkins.'

'Well, nice of you to say so. You could say I'm something of an inventor and discoverer. If I may blow my own trumpet for a minute, I am the man behind the pin-hole camera.'

'Really?'

'Yes, and I'm working on a light meter to boot, but don't worry if you don't know what one does. It's a bit technical.'

'I'm impressed. But what about the sticks? They're what really intrigue me.'

'Those are my sighting poles − I use them for surveying, just like your husband does.'

'Would have − he's no longer with us.'

'I'm very sorry to hear that, Mrs Kerne.' Watkins looked genuinely upset, taking the hat from his head in respect. 'Was it the−'

'War, yes. His surveying skills had been needed in the skies.'

Watkins gazed into the blue yonder, pondering the possibilities of aerial surveillance.

'From the air − imagine! I hear a chap named Crawford has begun taking photographs from above and finding all sorts of things invisible from the ground, crop-markings and the like. Lost treasures of our ancestors. But forgive me − my ramblings are no doubt in poor taste.'

'Not at all − carry on, Mr Watkins. It pleases me to hear you. It reminds me of my husband.'

Watkins furrowed his brow at this, uncertain whether he wanted to sound like a dead man. But when he saw the encouragement in

Maud's eyes he continued.

'I've lived in these parts all of my life – I'm a Hereford man, born and bred. As an outrider for my father's firm of flour millers I've had to do a lot of travelling – I've criss-crossed this part of the world for the last fifty years and know it like the back of my hand.' Watkins pointed to the landmarks on the horizon, although some Maud had to imagine, since they were indiscernible to her untrained eye. 'Going clockwise from the south – the Black Mountains, Radnor Forest, Longmynds, and Clee Hills; the Malverns we stand upon, and, round by May Hill, the Forest of Dean heights, to the Graig and Skirrid Mountain – a broken ring of heights, looking inward over lesser wooded hills and undulations ... My field of work.'

Maud took in the view, the anonymous panorama coming alive to her with his knowledge.

'You certainly know the lay of the land.'

Watkins smiled into his beard at this. 'You could say that, missus. In fact, it's funny that you should.'

'Why's that?'

'Because,' he licked his lips. 'Because 'leys' are what I'm surveying. In fact, this was where I found my first one!'

'Ley?'

'My term for alignments ... although originally it was Anglo Saxon for open ground.'

Alignments! There they were again.

'I first found a clue a couple of years ago when on my rounds there stood revealed to me the original sighting pegs used by the earliest track makers in marking out their travel ways.'

He checked to see he hadn't lost her and continued.

'I held in my hand the key plan of a long-lost fact.' Seeing Maud's fascination develop, he warmed to his subject: 'Vexed for weeks, I was unable to solve the riddle, until it came to me in a flood of ancestral memory one summer's day while out riding across the Bredwardine Hills. I pulled up my horse on the brow of the hill to check my map and get the lay of the land, as you so aptly called it, when I saw it all in a flash – a grid of glowing wires criss-crossing the landscape. Imagine that!'

Just like Isambard describes in his journal! Maud thought, imagining all too well what Watkins had described.

'After the flash of inspiration came the field-work. I had to test my theories. I am not one for idle conjecture, Mrs Kerne. I dream, but I make my dreams real. A visit to Blackwardine led me to note on the map a straight line from Croft Amebury, lying on parts of Croft Lane past the Broad, over hill points, through Blackwardine, over Risbury Camp, and through the high ground at Stretton Grandison, where I surmised a Roman station. I followed up the clue of sighting from the hilltop, unhampered by other theories, found it yielding astounding results in all districts, the straight lines to my amazement passing over and over again through the same class of objects. I had found my first ley!'

'Forgive me if I cannot follow all of your reasoning, Mr Watkins − I am merely a − ahem − lay woman.'

'Very good, Mrs Kerne, very good. Forgive me if I've rambled on − but once you're on a ley it's difficult to stop!'

'It's quite all right. It's been fascinating in fact. Most illuminating ...'

Watkins was somewhat abashed at this, and went off on a tangent to hide his embarrassment.

'You've hit the nail on the head again. "Leye" is an obsolete word for flame or fire.

Beacon hills, where they lit the bonfires, would have been early ley markers − along with the ponds and streams that reflected them at night.'

'The shining roads...' murmured Maud, remembering something her husband had said on the Tor.

'Hey, what's that?'

'Oh, nothing. Something my husband said once.'

Seeing Maud gaze sadly away, Watkins changed tack.

'You should come along to my next lecture − I gave one last year to the Woolhope Club in Hereford. I turned my notes into a pamphlet, *Early British Trackways*. And I'm now turning that into a book − that's why I'm doing extra field research, to expand upon my notes, double-check everything, and take photographs for it.'

'You're writing a book? Do you have title?'

'Not yet.'

'What you've been talking about reminds me of Kipling's 'The Way Through the Woods' − do you know it?' Watkins nodded. 'Perhaps that would make a good title.'

'Perhaps,' he said, rather circumspect. 'Thank you for the suggestion.'

'Sorry if I'm being forward − I'm sure you must have your own ideas. It's uncanny though – my husband was on to the same thing, or something very similar anyway.' It was the first time she had talked about her husband's 'hobby' – but if anyone would be sympathetic then it had to be Watkins.

'Really?' He stroked his trim beard. 'It would have been fascinating to have met him – I'm sure we would have had a lot to talk about.'

Maud detected a slight testiness in his tone. Academic rivalry? Yet Watkins had nothing to worry about – whether Isambard had 'discovered' the same thing or not did not matter. Watkins had published his findings, and that was all that mattered to posterity.

How many other visionaries, poets, inventors and artists had been engulfed by the Great War? What potential treasures had been consigned to oblivion?

Maud gazed over the frozen world, and the two of them stood together in companionable silence as Watkins tinkered with his apparatus.

After finishing his reading, the old man jotted in his notebook.

'Forgive me for being rude,' he said. 'Have you come far?'

After mulling over the wisdom of disclosing her home town, she decided the man was pretty harmless and told him she lived in Eastbourne.

'Ah, in sighting distance of the Long Man of Wilmington,' nodded Watkins. 'You know, I believe he was a surveyor, a Dod man, with his two sighting poles.'

His words found an echo in her mind: *I held in my hand the key plan of a long-lost fact.* The Long Man! The chalk giant had been on their doorstep all along, striding over the South Downs, overlooking the Weald – a vast symbol of Isambard's craft. It would appear others had walked the lost roads that so obsessed her husband. And now she walked them – and where they would take her, she did not dare imagine. But she was not alone.

Maud shook the old man's hand.

'Thank you, thank you – it's been so nice to meet you!' Maud enthused. 'You don't know what this has meant to me.'

She bid farewell to the curious man, who watched her go – all the way down the hill. Even when she reached the bottom he was still looking on, and gave her a final wave before she turned the corner of the track. A far-sighted old man.

7

WIND SMITH

I will gather and carefully make my friends
Of the men of the Sussex weald;
They watch the stars from silent folds,
They stiffly plough the field.
By them and the God of the South Country
My poor soul shall be healed.

'The South Country', Hilaire Belloc

Maud sat on the train back to Bristol and reflected upon her visit to Blackwardine.

The encounter with Watkins on the hill fort had been eye-opening but had left her with more questions than answers. First the incident at Paddington, then the visitation on the Tor and the scene in the Assembly Rooms, the séance and the discovery of the journals, and now this meeting with Watkins. Too many coincidences ... What did that Dion woman call it? Synchronicity: that was it. *By God, not by chance*, as the Fortunes' motto ran. In a world without God? Yet even without a 'captain at the helm', or a Christ on the Cross, it was beginning to feel as though serendipity was becoming predestination. Her path seemed set. Then where was this journey leading her? What about free will – she could just turn around, couldn't she?

These 'experts' she had met – who were they to say what must be so? However fascinating they were, they had smacked of the autodidact. None of their theories would withstand an academic onslaught. They were self-taught fanatics, engaged doggedly in painstaking solitary pursuits – drafting their own maps of the universe.

Just like her husband had been.

Maud had brought his fourth journal with her – to read on the train. She pulled it out of her handbag. The gentleman opposite her in the compartment had nodded off – his head swaying slightly on his shoulders in rhythm to the carriage's motion. Ridiculous that she should feel self-conscious reading the journal in public, but it was like exposing her dreamlife to daylight.

Pulling open the cord-tie, she scanned the pages recording Isambard's research in 1903. She was sure that was the year they had visited the Long Man of Wilmington, of which Watkins had reminded her on the hill fort. Yes, she was certain she held the very journal it would be in. What a stroke of luck! Again glimmers of memories re-emerged. It had been high summer — she flicked to the middle pages. There, in July! Eagerly, she began to read:

From the journal of Isambard Kerne:

31st July, 1903

Ever since catching a glimpse of the Wilmington giant from the main road between Eastbourne and Brighton I had intended to explore its mystery further. I recall the first time I beheld it from a carriage: appearing through the gaps of the trees, as though striding down Windover Hill with his two great staves. It sent a shivering thrill through every fibre of my being – the recognition of a long lost mystery. Surely the staves were sighting poles, and the Long Man was a Neolithic surveyor? Who else laid out the lines of ancient monuments that criss-crossed the land? A priesthood must have been responsible for divining the most auspicious locations for each barrow or standing stone. Were these my ancestral predecessors? The maddeningly ambiguous image haunted me for weeks afterwards – my study was covered with every rendition I could get of him, my shelves with any book on the subject. But nothing can substitute for field research, although it wasn't until a month later that my own work allowed me time off to visit the giant in person.

I had been away for a fortnight and Maud was determined we should spend the weekend together, and so we compromised – she would accompany me on a visit to the Long Man. We would take a carriage out to the village and go for a good walk up on the Downs. Maud was tired and irritable for some reason, but this did not cast a cloud over the day.

It was a glorious summer's morning in late July – the fields were brimming with golden ears of wheat. We left our carriage in the grounds of the priory and followed a narrow track along the edge of a field, the giant looming large before us. It was difficult to take your gaze from him – his hollow outline drew you in – but fortunately I checked my step and narrowly avoided stepping on a snail crossing our path. Or were we crossing his? Perhaps it was some ancient snail-route, for here was the original Dod man, with his two horns – the namesake of the surveyors of yore, with their two sighting poles. And I was walking in their footsteps. This seemed auspicious at the time, although writing it down makes it sound ridiculous.

Yet before us was evidence that ancient people had taken the notion extremely seriously. It must have been a huge under-taking – the scale of it is incredible. He certainly is a giant. By the time we walked to his foot it was no longer possible to take him all in – only his legs were visible, stretching up the hill in sharp perspective. Up close his construction was discernible – his outline had been demarcated with yellow bricks. This was a shock – I had assumed he had been gouged out of chalk like the Uffington Horse or Cerne Abbas. Surely this was a recent addition – the ancient architects would not have done something so crude. The garish yellow paint, pale in the distance, was obviously a very recent 'contribution'.

I scrambled up the hill – following the line of his eastern staff up the slope, which must be at a thirty-degree incline. Regular footholds were provided by terracettes – ridges of earth that suggest farming, but evidently this hill was never cultivated. I resolved to return to survey him properly, but then I just wanted to get a scale of the man. By the time I scaled the two hundred and thirty odd feet I certainly could appreciate his vastness on a purely physical level. Breathless, I sat down above his head – it felt disrespectful to stand on him, and if every sightseer did so he would soon wear away.

The wide plain of the Weald spread out before me. This was what the giant looked down upon. To guard or to command? As far as the eye could see, this was his land.

Yet he seemed not to rule but to beckon – luring the traveller, encouraging the walker, a wise but silent guide. From a distance he seemed transparent – as though he was about to disappear into the hill. Or maybe he was silhouetted by a light beyond? Perhaps he was not holding staves, but holding open great doors – the doors to that other world, the doors between life and death? He certainly guards an ancient mystery.

I meditated upon this from my fine vantage point while Maud rested below. She had spread out a blanket and prepared our picnic. I waved at her, she waved back and it seemed alright to stay up there for a while – she seemed at peace, reading a book in the sunshine.

And I felt at peace on that sacred spot – the world stilled around me, my breathing slowed and I viewed the scene the Long Man surveyed. The dew pond at his feet was immediately obvious. Following the line north it passed through the Priory and church – surely not an accidental alignment. I decided to explore the buildings afterwards. What must the monks have made of this pagan effigy, constantly living in its shadow? Well, they not only tolerated it, but helped preserve it by the looks of things. We have them to thank for its survival.

Perhaps there was once a middle way between pagan and Christian. Sitting between the staves I thought of how important it is to keep everything in balance; the secular and the sacred, the inner and outer life, one's own goals and the needs of your loved ones, male and female – equal and proud.

I looked at Maud's tiny figure below, yet how large she loomed in my life. I stood up and shouted out, 'Maud, I love you!'

She sat up at this, and clapped her hands in delight. She called out something in reply, but the wind carried it away.

It was time to descend. I clambered down the other side of the figure, completing my circumnavigation of him. I ran the last bit and swept up Maud in my embrace, kissing her hard on the lips.

I was brimming with the magnitude of my discovery. My wife was bowled over by my enthusiasm. I seldom shared such moments with her, fearing her mockery. What must she make of my obsession? It must seem so ridiculous to her. But then I said, 'Oh, darling Maud – I am glad I can share this with you today! This place means so much to me. As do you, as do you.'

I slaked my thirst and dabbed my brow, flushed with excitement. She made me sit down and eat something, yet I could not relax.

I asked if she wanted to stay while I walked up to the top of Windover, but she seemed hurt, wanting to come with me. And so we packed up the picnic and we set of along the old chalk track. I was intrigued by what looked suspiciously like tumuli on the brow. We followed the track around – its depth suggested great age, the chalk and flint worn down by many pilgrims. The hill was broad and uneven, undulating with unnatural bumps and folds, evidence of man's activity here. We came upon a hollow, which could have been a quarry. Below was the chalk quarry and lime kiln, so this did not seem unlikely.

Higher up I was excited to discover a Neolithic long barrow, little more than a ridge now, and, more dramatically, a large Bronze Age barrow directly above the Long Man. We sat on this for a while as we got our breath back and enjoyed the majestic prospect. The southern side of the Downs looked out towards the sea – a blue haze in the distance, making me wonder whether the Long Man guarded this threshold of the English Channel. To the West stretched the line of the Downs, littered with other barrows – which I was determined to explore.

Perhaps the Long Man marked the end of a processional way. The way of the dead? Certainly, Windover on that tranquil summer's day seemed like an ideal place to be laid at rest, on the hills of peace – although in winter the story would be different. Then, only the dead would survive up here. Wild and windswept!

The white horse at Litlington was clearly visible on the neighbouring hillside. Are they related in any way? Were the makers of this Long Man connected by blood or belief to the makers of Cerne Abbas, or Uffington? Perhaps each tribe had its totemic hill figure, overlooking their lands as the chieftain would in death from his high-placed barrow. Maybe once the hills of England were scattered with these figures, giving rise to the many legends of giants in the land.

Whilst I idly speculated we lay there in the bowl of the barrow, and gazed at the clouds overhead, feeling content. Was this a taste of the ideal afterlife for those tribes – at rest in the Summerlands, the lord and his lady in each other's arms?

Yet we belonged to the land of the living and needed nourishment if we weren't to become ghosts ourselves, and so we headed down the hill again, light-footed, light-hearted and light-headed.

Casting a final glance at the Long Man we bid him adieu and headed to the Priory.

The church is dedicated to St Peter and St Mary, as if to emulate the duality of the hill giant. We looked around. The interior had a sturdy austerity, but little of note, except an inscription on one wall:

'I had rather been a doorkeeper in the house of my God, than to dwell in the tents of ungodliness.'

In the churchyard, on the south side of the church I noticed an ancient yew tree, forked from its base – an old flat stone lay entangled in its roots. Although this was on the side facing away from the Long Man, my estimates suggest it is in line with it, and perhaps originally offered a line of sight before the church was built in between. While I pondered this, the vicar noticed us and approached. Dressed for gardening, in a patched cardigan over his black shirt and grubby dog collar, he was a gentle old man with watery green eyes and a neck wrinkled like a chicken's. We shook hands and I introduced myself and my wife. His name was the Reverend Burrows.

'I see you take an interest in antiquities,' he commented, referring to the stone and the tree.

I explained how we had just visited the Long Man and that I was impressed by the ancient monuments on the hill.

'Ah yes. Windover ... There is a wonderful local legend about the origin of the giant connected with the hill. Would you like to hear it?'

Eagerly, I agreed, but Maud did not look so keen. He took us into the vicarage and over tea told us the remarkable legend of the Wind Smith, taking delight in a story he was obviously fascinated by himself: he had given talks about it locally. The vicar's parlour seemed like an incongruous place to be recounting such a pagan tale – but that paradox was the very nature of the beast. Drawing us in with his smoky voice, the curious old man settled into his story:

'When the monks of Wilmington had finished building their priory they set about their next task – to construct a windmill. For they had much good land thereabouts, and from it they reaped fine grain – and so they needed a mill to grind it, to make their flour, to bake their bread.

'The prior, who was a wise old man, thought it might be as well to invoke the offices of the Wind Smith, the surveyor of windmills. There was one who lived up on the Downs named Dru, who was a curious fellow – tall and thin, wearing a threadbare but clean white smock, a straw hat upon his head, wreathed with an oak garland, he wielded a staff in each hand, his sighting poles, and roamed the Downs, living off of beech-mast, berries and water from dew ponds. He was seldom seen, except when his services were required.

'At this the sub-prior, who was zealous and ambitious, cried out in anger. He condemned that vagabond of the Downs for not attending Mass, calling him idolater and one of the Devil's own. Now, the old prior practised the tolerance he preached, and thought it best to build bridges with those who walk other ways. But the sub-prior petitioned his fellow monks and with their support persuaded the prior to let him have his way.

'So the monks set about building their mill, sighting it without consulting the Wind Smith, and when it was finished they were pleased with their handiwork. All was in place, and so on the next windy day the prior made the sign of the Holy Cross and with loud cheers from the villagers the miller-monk struck home the striking rod. But the sails did not move, which was odd, for there was a fair breeze blowing. The monks tried to get them going by hand, but still the sails would not turn. The windmill was examined from top to bottom and everything seemed to be in working order. They were baffled and out of breath.

'Then the prior took matters in hand, sending a monk to find the Wind Smith. The brother returned to say that Dru would come in a week to ten days, which is an old English way of saying that he would come in his own good time! But, Dru had warned the monk there were to be no crucifixes or bells rung. "They upset my ears and eyes," he said.

'A fortnight later Dru the Wind Smith came striding down Windover Hill, and without a word set to work. He walked about the windmill, shaking his head, then started to pace back and forth across the hay meadow: plunging a staff into the soft soil here, then another one there – and sighting between the two. He would squint, tilt his head, stand on one leg, lick his finger, test the air, then start all over again. Dru did this all day long, until the sun was low over the Weald and the shadows were long. Then finally he found the spot – hung his oak garland over the staff marking it, and walked off with the other, back up Windover, not asking for reward.

'The monks ascertained from this strange behaviour that the new location had been dowsed, and so, with great reluctance, they dismantled their lovely mill, and rebuilt it, brick by brick and *beam by beam, on the spot marked by the staff and oak leaves.*

'The mill was finished, and on a windy day the striking pin was struck home – and this time the cogs span and the millstones ground together. Success! Quickly, the hoppers were filled with grain – which rattled down between the stones, coming out as good white flour. The prior ordered for the bells of Wilmington to ring out in thanks, but as soon as their peal was heard over the meadow the windmill ground to a halt. One by one the monks returned to the mill to see what the trouble was – and as soon as the ringing stopped, the sails started to turn once more.

'This was proof enough for the sub-prior that the windmill was indeed the Devil's work. But the monks needed their flour, and so a compromise was reached – no milling at High Mass. Thus, this extraordinary situation became the routine – though little it pleased the sub-prior – and so it was for a whole year, until the old prior, ill in health, passed away. The sub-prior took over his mantle, and he hated the sight of the windmill – it mocked him from the meadow, a symbol of Satan on his doorstep.

'One night as he tossed and turned in vexation he had a vision – of Saint Boniface, or "Bishop Boniface" as he was back then, famed for cutting down the pagan groves. He would send for Boniface, and the next day this is what he did. Seven days later a great ecclesiastical host was seen approaching from the west, and at their head was Bishop Boniface himself, in bishop's mitre, wielding his golden crozier. The new prior welcomed his esteemed guest, lavishing upon him the best food and wine from the stores. After dinner, the situation was explained in full, and Boniface said, "This shall require only a minor miracle – but first, we need to celebrate High Mass!" The new prior wanted to explain that the windmill would not work if the bells were rung – but he wasn't going to argue with a saint, was he?

'As the bells pealed across the meadow Boniface strode to the mill. "Strike home the striking rod!" he commanded, and struck it with his golden crozier. Immediately, the sails began to turn. Rejoicing, the monks poured their grain into the hoppers and out of the millstones came good white flour. They filled sack after sack, until the all the grain was gone. Then the striking rod was pulled out – but to their horror they saw that the windmill would not stop! The sails turned, the cogs span and the millstones ground together – scattering sparks on to the flour-covered floor,* *threatening to set the whole thing on fire! They had to keep the stones cool, and so a human chain was formed from the well in the Priory, and pails of water were passed along it to douse them. But the monks could not keep that up for ever! What were they to do? For once, Bishop Boniface seemed powerless.*

'Then from down Windover Hill came Dru the Wind Smith. He stood on the edge of the meadow, shaking his head. "Back, Devil's own!" warned Boniface. Dru just shrugged and watched as the line of water ran out. The well was dry, someone cried out. Red in the face, Boniface knew he had to ask for help. "Remove your curse!" Dru just stood there and smiled. The windmill was beginning to catch fire. "Remove your curse – and ask your price," Boniface spat in disgust. Dru watched him, impassive. Boniface was desperate now. "Remove your curse and I will make sure you shall be remembered long after we are all dust!" Dru seemed to consider this, but wavered. "You know I am a man of my word. By the cloth I do as I say!" Dru stepped forward, raising his staff – he looked angry in the firelight. Boniface flinched, but Dru ignored him and began walking backwards around the windmill. Three times he circled it, faster and faster, until he stopped dead and struck his staff against the mill. The stick split in two and the sails creaked to a standstill. Then a great gust of wind blew out all of the flames and the monks off their feet. Dru looked pale and shrunken. He gazed at them sadly with his grey eyes, then walked off, back up onto the windswept Downs – never to be seen again.

'After the mill was repaired and working once more, Bishop Boniface honoured his agreement with the Wind Smith. He ordered the monks of Wilmington to cut out his shape on the side of Windover Hill, removing the turf to reveal the chalk beneath. And there he stands to this day – remembered because of Boniface and the monks.'

The Reverend finished his story and we thanked him profusely, leaving Wilmington feeling like we had discovered a treasure hoard on our doorstep. What a place! What an intriguing tale! I was keen to get back to Eastbourne to write it down as well as I could remember. It seemed to encapsulate the need for balance and cooperation symbolised in my eyes at least by the Long Man – only by holding these opposing forces in harmony can good be achieved. Perhaps there is a message here for Maud and me. I need her as much as she needs me. We need to learn from each other.

Together we are greater.

The story has other resonances – it is another clue. The wind is the key in some way – if only I could work it out. The Wind Smith was the dowser – my antecedent! We have lost his secrets, but there are clues in the land, in these ancient places.

Yet is this mystery meaningful, or am I just chasing wind – looking for substance in these hollow pursuits? Is there something really there? A higher truth, nearly within my grasp?

Today I stumbled upon a secret hidden in plain sight – this giant will guide me to the revelation in the landscape, awesome and immanent.

Maud closed the notebook. She recalled that golden day at Wilmington with great fondness − such a contrast to the bleak February landscape sweeping by. Reading about herself was strange − but she was relieved to see herself mentioned for once! It appeared that Isambard was on his own journey of realisation as well. Yet why had he found it so difficult to share? Had she been that sceptical, that scathing? Yes, she had been scornful at times. Perhaps it was jealousy − at this pursuit that excluded her. Perhaps it was fear. A nervous reaction to what she did not understand and threatened her fragile construction of the world.

She would no longer be afraid, for she had nothing left to lose. Everything she had cherished had been taken from her. There was nowhere left to fall.

Through Isambard's words she could share his lost world vicariously. But that was not enough. Reading about it made her want to go out there and experience it herself − and with her husband's journals she had the best guide. Yes, by thunder, that is what she would do!

The gentleman opposite stirred, disturbed by Maud's exclamation. He looked at her with annoyance from beneath his bowler hat and black moustache. They were approaching Bristol anyhow − where she'd change for London.

And so she decided. She would have an adventure! Retrace her husband's journey, to honour his memory, and to understand what obsessed him so. Perhaps if she walked in his footsteps she could share with him what had been denied while he lived. His secret world would open up to her. Like his journals, she had stayed locked away for too long.

With his words she would walk out with Isambard one last time.

MAUD WALKS OUT

We shall all come tumbling down
To our old wrinkled red-capped town.
Perhaps the road up Ilsley way,
The old ridge-track, will be my way.
High up among the sheep and sky,
Look down on Wantage, passing by,
And see the smoke from Swindon town;
And then full left at Liddington,
Where the four winds of heaven meet
The earth-blest traveller to greet.
And then my face is toward the south
There is a singing on my mouth

'I have not brought my Odyssey', Charles Hamilton Sorley

The next two months were taken up with teaching, yet Maud did not stop thinking about what had happened to her.

Every night, after finishing her stack of essays, she read a little more of Isambard's journals – savouring every word, although at times there was nothing more than map coordinates, degrees and directions, and diagrams of alignments – marked with x's. Fortunately, most of it made far more interesting reading – and the vivid descriptions of her husband's walks gave Maud itchy feet. She decided on a route: it would be along the Ridgeway, that ancient road that passed through much of his research like a river. She began planning her Easter hike in meticulous detail; checking train times, booking guest-houses, making lists of what to carry and what not to carry. There were plenty of new books on the subject – hiking had become the latest exercise fad.

At the weekends she took Nubi on long rambles upon the Downs to limber up, and to practise with a Popular edition OS map and an

old compass of Isambard's. She would pass gangs of hikers all dressed
the same in cords and tweed, and she began to feel like she needed
to buy some proper 'gear' – for comfort if nothing else. She began
perusing outfitters on her way home from Lewes – but it took her a
while to pluck up the courage to go in. She used an extract from her
husband's journal from a walk he had done along the Wansdyke
across Wiltshire in 1902 as a basic equipment list, albeit with female
variations:

> *Dressed in my walking tweeds, stout shoes, and summer hat,*
> *wielding staff and carrying a little pack of provisions – water,*
> *bread, cheese, apples, and boiled sweets, plus my map, compass,*
> *spyglass, and ruler – I set off with light spirits, the sun shining*
> *upon my venture.*

Looking at herself in the dressing room in her hiking gear for the
first time Maud had to laugh. Was that really her – looking like
something from a leisure feature? She had taken the first step. Yet the
greatest obstacle was to be her family and friends.

She had seen Maggie every day back at school, but things had not
been quite so chummy since the night of the séance. It seemed her
dear friend had finally lost patience with her. But they shared their
tea over break time as usual, and the awkwardness slowly thawed with
the coming of spring and talk of the Easter holidays.

One lunchtime Maggie asked, 'So what are you up to, mystery girl?'

Maud looked blankly up from her sandwich. She had been
thinking about Fortune's 'green road of the soul', Watkins' 'leys' and
her husband's 'shining roads'. She was used to daydreaming and not
joining in the staff-room chatter.

'Easter – what are you doing for the holidays? Seeing a lover?
Eloping to Paris? Fighting pirates?'

'Oh, Maggie! Shush!' Maud blushed. 'You know I hate talking about
myself in public.'

'Beg your pardon – I'm only trying to make conversation. You
should try it sometime.'

'Sorry. Of course, with you, it's different.' She squeezed her friend's
hand. 'Dear friend.'

'Ah, you've remembered! And I thought you were going senile,'
Maggie joked. Maud loved to hear her Irish brogue.

'There's been times lately when I thought I was going doolally. So
I'm going on a long walk this Easter – to blow away the cobwebs.'

'A long walk — that sounds like my idea of hell. To where?'

'Along the Ridgeway — it's meant to be the oldest road in Europe, so I've read, but it's a kind of trackway across England over chalk downs. It passes lots of ancient monuments — hill forts and long barrows and the like.'

'Long barrows?'

'Ancient tombs — I can't remember if they're Stone or Bronze Age, but they come in different shapes: bell, disc, saucer...'

Maud stopped, seeing Maggie's expression.

'Sounds like a barrel of fun,' she said. 'You certainly know how to live it up!'

'And I suppose you'll be gatecrashing parties!' Maud teased.

'As many as possible — a girl's got to have a good time while she can. We'll all be ancient monuments before we know it — only open on bank holidays!'

'Maggie, you're incorrigible.'

'So, who are you going with. Some gorgeous guide? Tarzan of the Ridgeway?'

'No — by myself.'

'By yourself! Are you mad?' Maggie looked furiously at her friend.

'I'll have Nubi with me — and I'll be staying in guest-houses every night. They'll be expecting me.'

'So if you don't turn up they'll send out a search party. Great. Listen, I don't want you found dead of exposure up there, do you hear!'

'It's not that high up! Besides, it'll be late spring by then.'

'Yes, but I've known it to snow as late as Easter on the Burren back home — so you wrap up, girl.'

'I'm getting all the gear — walking jacket, boots, the lot.'

'Sexy, I'm sure. And what gave you this mad idea.'

'My husband. He — he told me about it once. Sounded lovely. I've been meaning to do it for years.'

'You're bonkers. As a March hare. But it's good to see you getting out and about — I haven't seen you this lively in years. Maybe you're not off to the knacker's yard yet!'

Her sister was not so supportive. Maud put off telling her for as long as possible, but Constance was beginning to arrange things for the holidays — and practically had her fortnight planned out. So Maud was forced to break the news. One day she just had to stop Constance in mid-flow.

'Constance, I'm not going to be around this Easter.'

Her sister was flabbergasted. 'But you're always around, sister.'

'And that's why I need to get away. I've been stagnating for too long.'

'Where are you going then?'

Maud explained about her trip. Constance's expression went from peeved to derisive.

'Maud, you're going mad – I've felt it for some time, but now I'm certain.'

'Mad – why? Because I don't want to fit in with your plans? It'll drive me mad spending two weeks with you – it was bad enough at Christmas.'

The clock ticked loudly on the wall.

'Bad enough at Christmas!' Constance boiled. 'You ungrateful minx! We're the ones who have to put up with you moping about – but we do it every year out of sympathy.'

'Well, I don't want your sympathy any more, sister. Keep it, and all your bloody hand-me-downs!'

'Get out! Get out of my house!' screamed Constance. Maud obliged and descended the stairs to the landing. 'Go on your sodding walk!' she shouted after her as Molly, looking embarrassed, gave Maud her coat. 'And do us all a favour and don't come back!'

A week later Archibald sent her a note:

'Dear sister-in-law,

Connie's in a right flap about you – I don't know what you said to one another, but I hope you can patch things up. Damned shame for family to fall out.

I was intrigued to hear about your proposed trip along the Ridgeway. Good for you! I enjoy country pursuits myself. If you need any advice or kit, let me know. I won't trouble you otherwise. I shall be worried for you – but I know you can look after yourself! Watch out for them wolves, Red Riding Hood!

Oh, but I forget – you're taking one with you! I'm sure Nubi will do his duty.

Good luck, take care and keep in touch,

Yours with love,

Archie xxx

Easter finally came and school broke up for two weeks. Maud reckoned on only needing a week for her trip, but it was good to have some leeway.

Maggie went with her as far as London – making the most of the excursion to go shopping in the West End. She waved her goodbye as Maud got on the Goring train. Bless her, thought Maud. A true friend.

Maud set off from Goring station in good spirits. She certainly looked the part, dressed in a double-breasted tweed jacket, with deep pockets, and belted around her waist, corduroy jodhpurs, laced at the side, thick stockings and stout shoes. She wore a broad-rimmed sun hat and wielded Nubi on his lead like Diana the Huntress. Only her canvas knapsack felt uncomfortable, but there was a certain satisfaction in carrying all she needed for the next few days – wash kit, towel, changes of undergarments, variations of wardrobe for hot or cold conditions, map, compass, Isambard's journal, and provisions. Also, at the insistence of Archibald, a whistle, an emergency bag of plasters, creams, pills, salt tablets and so forth. He had suggested she placed everything in two piles before she packed – of essential and desirable – then jettison all desirables. She'd appreciate it later, he assured her. Excess baggage soon becomes very apparent when you have to carry it all day, he warned. With typical will-power she had done this, although she kept Isambard's journal, a slim novel and her own notebook as concessions. Yet without her luxuries she certainly would be roughing it, even if she was staying in guest-houses along the way. She hoped they wouldn't mind her lack of appropriate attire.

Nubi wagged beside her, sensing the tang of freedom – this was to be an extra-long 'walkies'. She had some dog biscuits in her pocket and had checked there was water and feed available en route.

And so they set off – one woman and her dog, passing the mid-week shoppers – the ladies with their bonnets and baskets.

Maud strode and Nubi loped through the snug and smug streets lined by thatched cottages and mini-mansions trying to outdo one another. Yet all appeared well on that bright April morning, hazy with promise.

Here she was finally asserting independence – albeit in the footsteps of Isambard. She was going for a long walk by herself – against the wishes of her friend, sister and, no doubt, the memory of her mother. To hell with them! For once she was doing something for Maud – and it was giving her immense pleasure, despite the fact her stout shoes needed breaking in, and the straps of her pack rubbed her shoulders. Little discomfort for so great a freedom – and it paled in comparison with what her sisters had gone through in their struggle for emancipation – winning the vote through different kinds of efforts. Well this was her march of freedom. What had she done for the cause up until now? The protest movement had practically passed her by. She sent donations but found the constant campaigning exhausting and distracting.

She had lived in her husband's shadow and honoured his legacy far too long. Now she was at last attempting to stake her claim in male territory, even if it was in memory of her husband – in his footsteps, literally. As she crossed the Thames, she paused to mark the moment, reading the corresponding extract from her husband's journal entry:

August, 1903
Good to have a break from Eastbourne! Married life is good for the heart, but the mind needs nourishment too, and I think best on my feet. Caught the 9.22 a.m. to Goring. Took breakfast at a tea-shop and stocked up on provisions. Headed due west crossed the Thames bridge to Streatley, stopping to admire the boats issuing from the lock. As a coal-carrying barge passed under, pulled by a shire-horse. I thought of my Irish grandfather from Dingle – who had been one of the 'navigators'. He had cut these channels with pick and shovel like the henge-makers of old. As I watched the barge make its slow and steady way along the tow-path I contemplated how the coming of the railways had circum-vented waterfreight, as the canals had coaches – and before the roads had there been an even more ancient network of routes? I considered this as I stood upon the threshold of Old Father Thames. The original Ridgeway is in direct alignment with this crossing place, but instead the walker is forced to go right at the Bull Inn. Route detoured by landowners probably. There is something sacrilegious about that. In Ireland I hear how roads and railways have to be diverted if they threaten a fairy thorn, and buildings lose their corners if they overlap a fairy path. Were these alignments like canals of force – channelled and filtered by the ancient monuments, the henges, avenues and cromlechs? Like canal locks? If they were, I had passed through the first.
So I continued, passed pretty and extravagant houses with their own driveways. A well-heeled area indeed, this Arcadia of Middle England. A pheasant barked. I walked along an avenue of rowan, content, until I came to the turning for the Ridgeway and my

quiet was shattered by a passing automobile. Ghastly machines! The noise subsided into the distance, leaving only the wind in the trees. I set off up the track. The open road before me and time on my hands. My time. Cool cloudy day, slight breeze, perfect walking weather – mild and clement. Hiked out of the Thames Valley. Now high up as I stop to write this – feels like I've been walking in the sky. Peaceful vistas. Purple thistles. Horse dung and cart tracks. Flint and chalk underfoot. Bread and cheese for lunch. Watched a hawk overhead. Chiffchaffs chattered in the hedgerows. Solitude and bliss. All is well.

And so she followed in her husband's footsteps, but as she hiked out of Streatley and into the countryside, feeling the exhilaration of the open road for the first time, it was apparent she was doing this as much for herself as for her dear Sammy.

Maud stopped to catch her breath and take stock. Isambard's journal was in her bag, but she made herself not look at it now. She wanted to see this with her own eyes. Between the few remaining houses, the burgeoning fields spread out beyond the trees, bursting with spring life. Hills loomed either side, tantalisingly close, with promises of ancient sites, distant vistas.

The chalk track stretched up and up, along an avenue of trees – cloistered from the roar of the twentieth century – lost in its own time. Striking out, she would be beyond the help of a friendly neighbour, a bobby on the beat.

A woman rider trotted passed, making Nubi bark and Maud jump. She had to control him – as the haughty rider commanded – and her own fear. Taking a deep breath to calm herself, she set on up the stony path, silently fuming.

The rider had made her feel like a trespasser. The way she had looked down at Maud bridled her. She wasn't some errant serf! Yet she might well have been back in feudal England now – little had changed in those parts of the countryside clinging on to the past. Yet it felt unspeakably wonderful to cast off the yoke of her responsibilities, of teaching and endless marking, of families and well-meaning friends, if even for only a little while. Away from all the expectations and demands of life, the fields sang to her. Simply Nubi (who amused himself in the hedgerows, but always came back when called) and herself, and all of this!

Maud found a slim hazel stick by the side of the path. Remembering Isambard's Y-shaped staff she picked it up and tried it for size. It felt good in her hand – made her feel safer, stronger. It had broken off at four feet and left an angled ledge perfect for her thumb. With a smile she carried on – the stick giving her step an extra push. She measured her paces to its swing – three when she slowed, four at a brisk trot. At first, Nubi thought it was for him and she had to persuade him otherwise, finding a smaller stick to throw, which he carried along with determined pride. As she adjusted to the rhythm of the walking Maud remembered Isambard's entry about measuring the earth with one's stride:

> The Ride became a track paved by stones crossing open farmland between two fields. It headed towards a curiously sited clump of trees on the ridge ahead. As I crossed, no longer sheltered from the direct blasts of the sun, measuring the earth with my feet, I wondered whether the 'yard' was originally derived from this natural gait, the reliable unit of measurement for Stone Age man? His whole world would have been determined by how far he could have walked and meted out in stride-lengths.

Pushing ahead at a fair clip, putting some distance behind her now, Maud realised she had never been so far away from people in her life. Even when living alone these past few years, she had been crammed in by nosy neighbours, callers, passers-by, the omnibus that trundled by. And even in the privacy of her house there were the constant calls for attention of her marking, the telephone, the newspapers, the radiogram. It was as if reality did not want you to be by yourself – just in case you could hear yourself think.

A buzzard on a slanting gatepost suddenly took flight, spying Maud through a gap in the hedge. She watched it delineate a noble arc across the mother-of-pearl sky. It seemed to spell *Freedom*.

Maud walked on with feet of feather.

As she passed the hedgerows of rowan, elder and thorn, countless white butterflies were stirred and rose before her. A deeper-hued one danced before her, resting long enough on a blade of grass for her to see its three bands of black and yellow on each wing. Flame orange with a black frill – as if singed by the fire from where it stole its colour. Another she saw dead by the track-side. How brief its life must have been, yet it had danced in the heart of the sun. She felt the sentiment of the Romantic poets stir in her. She often had them ringing in her ears, but now she had an inkling of their meaning. Her one regret was not knowing more about botany — she wished she knew the names of the spring flowers, the shrubs, the birds. Nature was a book she had never been able to read — but now she looked at it with fresh inquisitiveness, imagining her own names for the simple wonders she beheld.

And so the time passed amiably away. No rush. No clock-watching. Being in the present, moment by moment she walked, adjusting to the rhythm — finding her pace. She no longer had to keep up with Isambard, or anyone. She would get there when she got there — distance measured by her gait, her feet a new kind of clock. Her husband's watch was in her pocket, still not working. The menders had tried everything to no avail — so she had collected it and kept it as a kind of talisman. She had a good sense of time anyway. Years of teaching had given her that.

Every half-hour or so she would pause to take a draught from her bottle — and offer a handful to Nubi with a biscuit. In the meantime the boiled sweets kept her from flagging, though she began to dream of the pot of tea and perhaps a small slice of Victoria sandwich waiting for her at the vicarage in Letcombe Regis — where she had managed to negotiate a night's accommodation with an old friend of Isambard's, a fellow antiquarian. Nubi devoured the dog biscuits and guzzled at a trough they came to — set aside for horses and hounds. While he slaked his endless thirst a solitary male walker approached. This was the moment she had feared. Her chest tightened. She tried not to look up, but she did not want to appear timid. She gripped her stick.

The man passed, tipping his hat. He seemed gentlemanly enough — perhaps a scholar on a literary stroll; in other circumstances they may have made acquaintance, but Maud uttered the word 'Hello' like a challenge or warning, glancing knowingly at Nubi — stroking his mane of grey fire. The man simply ambled by nonchalantly — lost in his own rêverie.

She carried on, reminded of her husband. Her mind went back to his journal:

Trusting my feet – letting my legs guide me, carrying me onwards, along tunnels of trees, edges of fields, flinty furrows, bridleways, byways, footpaths and tracks, old green lanes and Roman roads, up hill and down dale, towards the horizon, towards my destination – footloose and fancy free – servant of serendipity!

Well she could wax lyrical too! To amuse herself Maud began to make lists in her head – she loved making lists. The world was put in order when she made a list.

This was her first:

> <u>Different walking surfaces</u>
> Grass lines between the ruts.
> Flint scree.
> Hard compacted earth.
> Soft, freshly tilled soil.
> Dazzling chalk.

With hazel stick in hand she surveyed the land, like a Dod man she thought – measuring it out, yard by yard. In soft earth her staff was like a pea-stick, poking holes – on hard ground her rhythm counter, keeping time with a regular tap. And when there was a break in the clouds the stick was like a sundial, casting its shadow across her from the left – the sun was directly south, so she figured it must be midday, and nearly lunchtime. She was building up an appetite already.

Maud's physical universe expanded and contracted – while Maud's eyes were occupied with the widening view, of the vast sky overhead, she was increasingly aware of the weight she carried, and all her body's little aches and pains, its timbre and stresses.

Her gaze started to dip, and for a while she just noticed her left boot, then right boot, appear and disappear. Weary now, she had to keep checking her step so as not to stumble. To have a sprained ankle up here would be disastrous – potentially dangerous. How long would she have to lie there before someone found her – and what if they posed a greater threat?

Above, her sun-hat shielded the sky – its floppy corona above her brow like an eclipse of the sky. The straps on her pack seemed to dig deeper into her shoulders, and she had to keep pausing and hoisting them up. *And there's the rub*, she thought.

High up, out of the Thames Valley, out on to the open downs. Maud relaxed, rested by the wayside, among the thistles and meadow-grass, to take her lunch and take in the view – the rolling hills of Compton Down.

When she took the pack off she felt strangely weightless, yet her eyelids grew heavy, limbs leaden. She felt at peace – there seemed nothing malevolent in nature that day. She certainly felt safer than she did in the city. As her Sammy had said, all was well.

After a simple lunch of bread, ham and a boiled egg, she stood up, feeling stiff. The effort of walking with a pack had been a shock to her system. She heaved her pack back on, and it felt like it was full of stones. It wasn't a good idea to stop very often, Maud decided – everything seized up. She must keep on!

And so, sluggishly at first until her limbs loosened up again, she carried on – feeling every bit the Dod man snail carrying its home on its back.

Cows and sheep were her constant companions. As she passed she greeted them cordially – *like some mad old woman*. She lost count of the sheep she saw sweeping across the fields – keeping the Downs treeless and some would say bleak, although she found the austere beauty soothing. Here, the wind had few hurdles, but it felt purifying. It was an incessant whistling in ears, spring cleaning her mind. Yet, like spiders caught in a cobwebbed duster, she heard a word from the past: *hiraeth ... hiraeth.*

What did she long for up here? This was what she had awaited for two months, perhaps her whole life.

Maud smiled at the irony of walking on chalk, when she had so longed to get away from it, from the schoolroom. The Ridgeway stretched into the distance – a thin white line across a vast black board. Yet here nature was the teacher, and she was taking part in the longest lesson – the subject, her life. The further she walked, the deeper she went into herself. Memories, conversations, complications came back to her with the clarity perspective afforded. Walking on the ridge, Maud was confronted by two sides of life, in continual juxtaposition. They seemed to symbolise the choices she faced between accepting the courtship of Archibald and honouring her husband's memory – between life and death.

Coming to a sun-dappled glade along a shadowy tunnel of white-blossomed may trees, Maud sat down. Sitting by a cluster of bluebells surrounded by butterflies, she felt like she was in fairyland – or Goblin Market. She could almost hear the cries of 'Come buy', 'Come buy.'

Archibald was rather like a goblin, she thought.

Striking on through the afternoon as the sun tilted west, she passed through the Compton Hundred, where Alfred routed the Saxons in the Battle of Ashdown AD 871. His statue stood in Wantage, remarked the guidebook. She recalled the local rhyme:

Isley remote amid the Berkshire Downs,
Claims three distinctions o'er her sister towns,
Far famed for sheep and wool, tho' not for spinners,
For sportsmen, doctors, publicans and sinners.

It was the last lot that worried Maud. What if one of these 'sinners' was out and about? It niggled her as she walked along – like a stone in her shoe, working its way under her skin – making her jumpy.

Up ahead the path forked – fortunately it was sign-posted. A blue scarf lay abandoned in the bushes. Had it been blown off, or something worse? Her imagination began to accelerate into the worst possible scenarios.

Maud could now spot the tall landmark of the Lindsay monument. Relieved to see a reliable landmark, she struck out for it – and was surprised to soon reach it. From a distance it looked larger than it actually was. She inspected a stone column on a daïs of steps, about twenty feet tall, with a cross upon its top. Around its base were biblical quotes, a heraldic shield of a stag and eagle, and the inscription:

'Robert Lloyd Lindsay, Baron of Wantage, V.C. – K.C.B. 1901.'

Maud pondered it. It had been raised by dutiful wife, in memory of her husband – a Boer War hero, like Archibald. Isambard must have stopped here and thought that.

Was this walk a memorial to her Sammy then? Yet it was so transient. What would be left? Footprints in the dust?

Maud carried on walking until her feet felt like stones – the Ridgeway engraved upon them. It was by then a golden spring evening – the kind that draws memories to itself. The fat buttery sun gilded everything so that it was impossible to forget the kindnesses of nature. When Mother Nature smiled the world is glad, she thought. Enthused, she composed a new list:

Things to be glad about
   The freedom to find one's own way.
   Feeling warm outdoors again.
   Casting off winter's coat.
   New leaves on the trees.
   Birdsong in the hedgerows.
   May trees filled with blossom.
   Long shadows on the tall grass.
   Cobwebs shot with quicksilver.

Pony chewing on a nose-bag of hay.
The promise of a hot bath and soft bed.

Maud drank down the late sun like ambrosia, and, heady with light, she descended from the sky. *I will clamber through the clouds and exist*, she affirmed, recalling Keats.

Running on empty, Maud's legs seemed to carry her on with a mind of their own. She recalled her husband's journal, recording his descent into Letcombe Regis:

> *Comfortably weary, I descend to Letcombe Regis along an avenue of elder and blackberry bushes ready for the plucking. Like miniature bunches of grapes, these succulent fruits kept me going until I reached rest and repast. The Reverend Williams is an old friend of mine – we have shared much correspondence about antiquarian matters. It would be good to engage in conversation with another human being again after being alone with my thoughts all day. The mile detour down from the Ridgway will be worth it.*

The narrow road swept down from the Ridge along an avenue of white blossom and bluebells. Then around the bend she saw in the middle of the road a dead hare − it seemed frozen in mid-flight. The sight of the mangled corpse affected her worse than it should have done. The exhaustion is making me over-emotional, she told herself. Snap out of it! She shooed Nubi away from the hare, and hurried on quickly, feeling nauseous.

Ahead, two farm workers were swilling the road of spilt slurry. Inhibitions gone, but shielding herself from the stench with a lavender-scented handkerchief, she stopped to ask for directions to the vicarage. They were surprised to see a solitary woman walking down from the Ridgeway, and looked at her as though she was slightly barmy. Pointing along to the left, they carried on with their task.

Footsore, but satisfied, Maud entered the slumbering village. Letcombe Regis seemed undisturbed by the last millennium, let alone the modern century. Somewhere a dog barked like an old colonel lost in the memory of an old campaign. The little cottages were reassuringly quaint − but Maud felt wild in comparison. What a sight she must be! Feeling raw and ragged after fourteen miles on the road, she passed the Greyhound Inn and found the secluded old vicarage opposite – ensconced in its own leafy bower. She shuffled along the gravel drive, her feet dead weight. Here she would find sanctuary, a peaceful room and rest.

After Nubi was happily at rest in the kennel – weary from his long walk – Maud was shown up to her lodgings for the night by the servant, the Reverend being out on business. Scornfully, the young woman said the room was known as 'the old maid's room'. Was that what Maud had become – an old maid? Alone and unloved, a widow withering away?

Yet the room was not uncomfortable – in fact it was charming, although its approach was unpromising – at the top of a narrow flight of stairs, past copper pipes and stored bric-a-brac. Eight feet by ten wide this small but cheery room looked out onto abundant gardens, festooned with trees.

For some time Maud watched two white doves canoodle by the ancient dovecote. She felt content and heavy with fatigue. An iron burner stood in the corner for extra heat, next to the fireplace – both unneeded on this warm day. Little nick-nacks lined the mantelpiece, random pictures of birds and antique maps on marmalade striped walls. A single bed stood primly in the middle of the room, allowing narrow access either side – to a locker with a lamp on it and to a small table bearing a basin, jug and towel. Everything in the modest chamber spoke of decorum and comfort. If it was a hermit's cell, it was an agreeable one.

A sense of peace overwhelmed her. A carriage clock whirred and chimed. Outside the wood pigeons cooed. After washing and changing, Maud lay on the bed and was herself swept away by a deep tide of sleep.

Later, feeling ravenous, she rose and dressed for the evening. She met the thin-jowled vicar in his parlour for tea and sponge cake. He reminded her of an apologetic eagle, beak nosed but gentle-natured. He remembered Isambard's visit with great fondness – the long conversations they had. Her husband was a fascinating fellow, he recalled – full of earnest ideas.

'You must miss him greatly,' he said, hoary brows furrowing.

She sensed he wanted her to say something, to reach out for comfort, but she could not accept the consolation of his faith, or his humanity.

'Yes, of course I do,' she replied.

The vicar sipped his tea and changed tack.

'These have been difficult times for many. Have you found any strength in the Lord?'

Maud rose to this like a baited bear. Her walk had given her a new boldness.

'Strength? The only strength I have is in my limbs. Physics and physiognomy, Reverend. It is surely a cold mechanical universe.'

'Bu — but what of God, my child?'

'God is dead, so the modern philosophers say. He's been assassinated. We are all left marooned − on the naked shingles of the world, as Arnold puts it, without hope.'

The vicar choked on his Victoria sandwich, appalled by her disillusionment, her denial.

'My child, there is always hope − if you place your faith in Jesus Christ, our Lord. God is not dead; merely some people's belief in him. We cannot limit Deity by our whims and myopia. He is always there, whether you trust in him or not.'

Maud looked at him hard. 'Then where was he when my husband was taken from me − answer me that, Reverend?'

'Your loss was terrible. And I share some of that − Isambard was a dear colleague. A tragedy − shared by many. But when we suffer the loss of a loved one, we can find strength in our faith, not despair. Ours is not to question the will of God, but surely there is a greater providence at work than we can understand.'

Maud began to feel irate. Perhaps the fatigue of the walk had stripped away any pretence. 'So, you are saying it was God's will my husband died. And that is what I cannot accept. How can he let all this suffering happen? Why does he want us to live our lives in misery? If God is running the world, he is a cruel tyrant. And if it is a Hell of our own making, then God does not exist.'

'You will not find angels in logic,' concluded the Reverend wearily. 'Look into your heart for the truth. The Lord will come, if you let Him in. Good night, Mrs Kerne.'

He avoided her the rest of the evening as if she were a leper. Yet if she had made a pariah of herself Maud was grateful for the privacy. She dined at the Greyhound, enjoying her anonymity. After a hearty meal, which she struggled not to wolf down, her appetite so sharp, she tried to read her slim novel, William Morris's *The Wood Beyond the World*, but struggled to stay awake. A fatigue came over her that she could not resist − a weariness she had stemmed for many years. Now in this place she could finally rest − she had not felt such peace since Blackwardine.

She returned to the vicarage and slipped upstairs, flopping on to the bed with relief.

Sleep came quickly, but dreams stirred within her of a hunt, led by the Reverend on horseback, and she was the quarry. Frantically, she plunged through a thicket of thorns, torn and bleeding, until she plummeted into a chasm.

Feeling she was falling out of bed, she was startled awake. Shivering and breathing heavily, she looked around at her small room, confused, alone.

She had escaped — but not from herself.

❾

WHITE HORSE FOLLY

Before the gods that made the gods
Had seen their sunrise pass
The White Horse of the White Horse Vale
Was cut out of the grass.
GK Chesterton

The following day after a cooked breakfast in the kitchen, from which the vicar was notably absent – the maid explained that he'd left early on an errand – Maud set off, stiff from the fourteen miles of the previous day. It had been a shock to her body. She planned to do less today – about nine miles to Bishopstone.

It was a drowsy April morning – a fine drizzle bathed everything in a benevolent haze. Following the servant's directions she found the footpath leading up to the Ridgeway. Taking a stony track to a stile, she climbed over, leaving behind the safety of the village. The path led across damp fields that soaked her skirt hem – she wished she'd worn trousers again. Nubi raced ahead – devouring his freedom in greedy strides. Despite her protesting body and tender feet she found herself once more yielding to the rhythm.

Let's work off that breakfast, she thought.

Putting her back into it, she climbed up to the ridge. The tree-lined path passed through Sedgbury Camp – she caught a glimpse of the circular banks through gates halfway across. The path then intersected the Ridgeway and there she turned right, stopping at a stile that led down into Letcombe Basset: the village of *Jude the Obscure*. Even here in Berkshire, they were on the edge of Hardy's Wessex. She remembered with a shudder the graves of Jude's children. When she had read it as an English student, she tried to imagine the pain of such a loss. It would be too much to bear.

Yet life had brought her loss in other forms. Maud had not been able to have children, and Isambard had been taken away from her by the war.

While she mused on this and adjusted the straps of her knapsack, two lady riders passed by. They wished her good morning, seeming agreeable enough. She hailed them back, snapped out of her solitude. By herself, she drifted in thoughts like a phantom, disincarnate.

The mist began to burn off. Caressed by the soft rain, Maud carried on for an hour, feeling in a sombre mood. She watched the world wake up around her. In the surrounding fields horses pulled ploughs, guided by farmhands, but otherwise she didn't see a soul.

Further on, the country opened up, sweeping away to the right. Maud sat for a moment looking towards the combe of the Devil's Punchbowl — defined by a promontory ending in a clump of trees. The place seemed bleak even in spring.

The world was sombre this morning, subdued. Yet Maud felt at peace with herself, and replenished; 'inkwell refilled', as her Sammy would have said.

And that's when she saw the figure watching her.

At least that's what it looked like to her — although it could have been a stump, an old gate-post. It was a good quarter of a mile over the valley to the Devil's Punchbowl — and the visibility wasn't particularly good, so her eyes might have been playing tricks. Yet she swore it was somebody — yet if they were spying on her, why stand there in plain sight? If it had moved, she would have had her fears confirmed. But its stillness was beguiling. Was she imagining it, her dormant paranoïa projecting onto the landscape what she half-expected to see, like Isambard's 'shining roads'? She was becoming more and more like her husband every day.

Rattled, she quickly hurried on — but if this was an assailant then he could easily cut her off before she reached the road and Bury Down beyond. Her heart raced, but she tried not to walk too quickly. *Just keep walking*, she said to herself. *Don't look.*

Maud made it to the empty road and crossed quickly, fearing to turn around. She called Nubi to her, but he seemed more concerned with the hedgerows. If there had been anyone near, he would have sensed it. She did not feel safe until she was on Bury Down — its wide thoroughfare was less conducive to ambush. Yet no assailant manifested and Maud felt foolish for imagining the whole thing.

Chastised, she continued, resisting attempts to look over her shoulder any more. Besides, she had Nubi with her — enough to make any man think twice.

Was she just jumping at her own shadow? What was she scared of?

The wind? Or the ghosts in her mind?

Admonishing herself, she tried to shake off the fear. With a deep breath, she ploughed on. The chalk track rolled beneath her stout shoes – she built up the pace, got into her stride.

Maud climbed all morning, and by noon the land spread out to her right – the Vale of the White Horse, green and hazy in the April sun, stretching to the horizon. She remembered a phrase from the journal:

'Walking so high up makes you feel like a giant striding across the land – like the Long Man himself!'

'Or the Long Woman!' Maud called out in joy, making Nubi bark. With stick in hand, she strode ahead, feeling she could walk across the world.

The miles rolled by effortlessly, until the turning for Seven Barrows made her hesitate – uncertain of the direction her husband had taken at this junction. Maud flicked through the journal to check. She was right. Isambard would typically have taken the eight-mile detour to inspect the line of burial chambers, if he had not noticed the sign for the Blowing Hole inn, named after the Blowing Stone, situated a little further along:

Intrigued, I walked the 800 yards down the Blowingstone Hill to look at the mysterious Blowing Stone in the garden of a cottage. Evidently the inhabitant was used to a curious passerby examining the standing stone that resembled Swiss cheese. If one blows into one of the holes that pierce the stone, a deep trumpet-like sound is produced. A local belief is that King Alfred put it to use during the Battle of Ashdown. What interested me more was the sound that stone was capable of producing. Would not the wind whistling through a narrow-necked barrow create the same effect? And did such sound have any significance, or was it merely coincidental?

Maud's stomach was making interesting noises too. By the inviting pub sign, offering Maud the last chance for a decent lunch, there was a poster advertising Uffington Fair, a lively occasion by the look of things; with coconut shies, an Aunt Sally, heavy horses, Mighty Smith the strong man, merry-go-round, barrel organ and tug o' war. Maud recalled the reference Isambard made in his journal as he had approached the hill fort:

They used to hold fairs up on the Trendle, as the old fort is known locally – coinciding with the annual scouring of the white horse, when the chalk figure was cleansed by the villagers.

Imagining the high spirits of the fairgoers, whilst I walked along I started to hum an unknown melody and a ballad came to me;

> *I'm on my way to Uffington Fair,*
> *I hope to find my true love there.*
> *For many days I have wandered,*
> *And many nights I have squandered.*

Whether it was old, or of my own invention, it became my marching song, and I imagined bodhrans and whistles making the feet light. Light-footed, like my namesake, Kerne – my father's ancestor – a 'light-armed Irish foot soldier', as I remember reading once in a book of family names.

She imagined the countless feet that had passed before – Neolithic traders, drovers, warriors, outlaws, soldiers, surveyors. Was she following in the wake of *her* ancestors? She would be one herself if she didn't eat soon! Nubi was looking ready for a biscuit as well. She ploughed ahead, determined to reach the hill fort for lunch.

Growing sluggish with hunger she slowly ascended to the highest point of the Ridgeway. Her path became a bone-white line. She paused for breath and pulled out the journal once more. Isambard's words carried her along like the ghostly strain he had heard or fancied – a line of song stretching across the land:

> *I imagined the Ridgeway stretching to the East, all the way to the Icknield Way, the Fens and the North Sea, and west it carried on to Lyme Regis – the greatest road in England!*

Maud made Uffington Castle at noon, breathless and weak. The Ridgeway skirted its flank, and she crossed a field to get closer. It didn't look much of castle, she thought as she approached – just another grassy bank. Climbing the rampart, she could see the fort was circular, like Segsbury, and of considerable size – it took her a full ten minutes to walk around the steep defences. Only then did she get a true feel of the size of the thing.

On the west side she glimpsed a bouquet of lilies tied with black ribbon and a handwritten note reading 'In memory of my father'.

It seemed she was not the only one walking with the dead.

Maud sat down by the head of the white horse, had her sandwiches the vicar's maid had prepared for her and enjoyed the view that looked twenty miles north. The Manger, scooped out of the hillside, dropped dramatically below − formed by the thawing of a glacier, according to Isambard's journal.

Cheek by jowl to this was Dragon Hill, squat and conical at its tail, supposedly scarred with dragon's blood where Saint George slew his dragon. Beyond, the village of Uffington lay − with its thirteenth century church tower forming a possible alignment with the chalk figure, her husband had speculated. Certainly Blackheath Clump on the horizon seemed to align with hill, horse and fort. Maud read a little more of his notes:

> *I was presented with a map of the past. Everything was fitting into place around me – from this high place it all made sense. The signs were everywhere. Secret folds, proud ridges – enticing, guiding. Map and compass were quite unnecessary – it was all laid out for the pilgrim to follow.*

The vast panorama of fields and villages spread out like a tapestry at her feet. Maud watched trains pass from east to west, west to east. She recalled being on that train to Glastonbury four months ago after her harrowing experience at Paddington. The shell-shocked man leered at her still, but she stifled his features. Was it *him* she was expecting to leap out at her, or the ghostly figure on the Tor? She had almost forgotten about that apparition − or had tried to − the thin cloaked figure, seemingly holding two staves, like the Long Man.

Lead grey clouds rolled above, darkening, promising rain. The wind threatened to blow her hat off, so Maud tied it around her head with her scarf, self-conscious because of the many visitors traipsing up to the ancient monument. At least the day-trippers made her feel safe, if a little isolated. To be surrounded by the families and courting couples made her feel lonelier than when she had been walking along the Ridgeway. Yet, as she watched the figures with a detached melancholy, she remembered when she had first seen the white horse, with her husband at Faringdon.

It had been a restless autumn day − the last of the old century − when they were still courting, and Isambard had swept her up from Banbury amid the swirling leaves to take her in his horse and trap to Faringdon, the charming little village in the Vale of the White Horse with its ancient market cross and sleepy streets.

Isambard had important news he wanted to share with her – but no amount of teasing would get so much as a clue out of him. She knew he was hoping for a promotion – but she had to wait until 'after they had tiffin' for the revelation.

They stopped for tea at a delightful little tea-room – all doilies and dried flowers, ceramic ornaments and pictures of dogs. Thawing out by the fireplace, they looked at each other with eyes dancing with light. They had cream tea, taking sensual delight in applying the damson jam and clotted cream on to the still warm scones. Over pots of tea they chattered about all and nothing. How carefree they had been back then. Maud's heart sang like a bird – almost bursting its cage in joy. Here at last was someone that she could share her hopes and fears with! Isambard was so knowledgeable yet oddly naïve, with visions of changing the world.

Maud saw in him the same frustrated passions as in her father, the same furrowing brow and earnest statements. She wanted to hold him to her then and there – he had such fire!

Whipped by the gust spiralling down the chimney breast the fire swirled and sputtered in its hearth – like the emotions fluttering in her bosom.

They agreed to get a dog when they were wed, settle down in a little house by the sea – perhaps somewhere on the south coast – and take their pet for walks everyday along the cliffs.

Isambard finally shared his news – he had been appointed chief surveyor for the GWR.

Maud hugged him, delighted. A new world was opening up for them. Isambard was following in the footsteps of his father and his namesake. His work would take him far – but he promised to take her with him as much as he could – no more buying train tickets with the first class staff pass!

The future seemed full of giddy promises. What the new century would hold, who could say? But that day they felt immortal.

After tea they walked up to the folly – the tower on the hill, surrounded by trees like a wizard's citadel. The fresh wind rattled the grey-limbed beeches, stripping them bare. The copper scales whirled about them. They kicked the piles formed by the eddies. Light-hearted, they had leaf fights, laughing, until ruddy-cheeked and breathless. Suddenly they were holding one another. Maud lost at sea in his dark gaze – like looking into the night sky, she thought.

Then they kissed and her whole body trembled – as if she had waited all her life for this spark to her kindling.

'Come look at this!' Isambard suddenly pulled her after him – gloved hands tight. He led her through the grove to the edge of the trees. There he pointed out across the misty vale to the line of hills opposite.

'There.' He directed her gaze with his finger.

Six miles distant a graceful chalk figure could be discerned – elongated, stylised, like a signature in white.

'The White Horse of Uffington.'

'What is it? I've often seen it and wondered.'

'The oldest chalk figure in Britain, probably pre-Roman, although recut by King Alfred after his victory over the Danes. Perhaps it was the totem of a tribe of horse warriors or worshippers of Epona, the horse goddess of the Celts. Godiva of Coventry and Banbury's cockhorse may be remnants of her worship.'

Horse warriors! Maud imagined them for a moment, galloping towards her to sweep her away. She held Isambard's arm tighter, shielding herself from the wind within the folds of his coat. He would protect her now – she had her champion.

'Above it is Uffington Castle, an Iron Age hill fort. Behind it runs the Ridgeway – a Neolithic trackway, some say the oldest road in Europe. One day I want to walk it.'

'How long is it?'

'Forty-three miles from the Thames at Streatley to Avebury, Wiltshire, though some say it stretches from the East coast to Dorset. Ivinghoe beacon to Lyme Regis!'

'Crikey – sounds a bit far for me! But I'll walk it too if it means I can be with you.'

'Oh Maud – may we always be together like this. There is so much I want to show you, to share with you. The adventures we could have!'

Isambard gripped her with both hands, towering over her like the folly. His enthusiasm infected her, despite her not usually caring for ruins and folklore. This was now, this was here, this was real.

And the future belonged to them.

The wind brought her back, rolling across the Vale of the White Horse and breaking like a wave on the flanks of Uffington, making Maud shudder out of the past.

The elemental surroundings of Uffington reinforced themselves –

the wind hissed around her, buffeting the grass. A small boy leaped over the sinewy chalk lines, yelling, 'Look at me!' Another, slightly older, crashed a kite, making biplane noises. The parents looked on indulgently. The sight of young children always made Maud feel edgy, bitter even. Her rêverie broken, she continued on her way – back across the fort to the seclusion of the Ridgeway, dragging her shattered dreams with her.

10

THE BLACKSMITH'S SHADOW

We shoe the horses of the sun,
Harness the dragons of the moon;
Forge Cupid's quiver, bow, and arrows,
And our dame's coach that's drawn with sparrows.
Till thwick-a-thwack, thwick, thwack-a-thwack, thwack,
Make our brawny sinews crack:
Then pit-a-pat, pat, pit-a-pat, pat
Till thickest bars be beaten flat.

'Song of the Cyclops', Thomas Dekker

Across the vale a smear of shadow rolled in, obliterating details, smudging the sharp lines of the villages. Rain was the last thing Maud needed. She felt exposed on the hill fort. Already she preferred the shelter of the Ridgeway, though the day before it had seemed like the Devil's road. But as she waded through the grass to the line of trees marking the track, she spotted a dark figure on the far side of the field. The stranger lurked on the edges of the woodland, as though unable to come out into direct sunlight. Maud tried not to panic. He could just be a solitary walker – a botanist perhaps, examining the hedgerows.

Nubi's ears pricked up and he slinked against the ground – watching carefully. Then he bolted. 'Nubi!' The lurcher shot across the hillside like a whip crack of lightning. She wanted him to stay with her – now she was defenceless! Her heart pounded like the thunder in the sky. Nubi disappeared into the thicket.

What should she do? The lurcher did not reappear. She plucked up courage and began to approach, shouting the dog's name, a challenge and a plea.

'Nubi! Nubi!'

There was a rustling in the undergrowth, a struggle. Had Nubi caught something?

Then the dog burst from the bushes, nearly knocking Maud over. He chased a stick thrown from the trees, caught it in his slavering jaws and, grinning triumphantly, paraded about with it.

Maud stared at the trees.

'Hello?' she called out nervously.

There was a sound like the whinny of a horse, but the wind distorted it, making it almost demonic.

Nubi dropped the stick before her and sat down – waiting for her to play.

Maud did not want to touch the stick, but was both intrigued and terrified. Who had thrown it? Who was in there? She was not going to pick up the black and slimy branch, but Nubi didn't seem bothered. If it had been a deer he might have emerged gory and swaggering with victory. Whoever it was had got off lightly. Then it occurred to her: was it someone they knew?

Maud tried her best to compose herself and attempted to carry on. What else could she do? Skirting the lane, she joined the Ridgeway over a stile. It stretched before her – a double-edged sword of light and shadow. By the wayside a thrush cracked a snail shell on a stone. The unexpected violence of this action played upon her already taut nerves. In a panic she walked quickly along the naked track, constantly looking over her shoulder. Her heartbeat raced. She could walk really fast when she needed to. Or even run like rain.

Gobs of rain spattered around her – the storm had caught her up. It mixed with the chalk, making it slippery and semen-like. Maud skidded about and was glad of her hazel staff.

After several frantic minutes she felt that she had left the stranger behind, but a twinge in her side warned her she was developing a stitch. Her walking shoes slid and her knapsack seemed incredibly heavy – she wished she could just throw it away. She resisted the urge to look back, but the sweat was already turning her into a pillar of salt. Just keep going, keep your eyes fixed on the horizon, she told herself, imagine yourself there, like swimming a length.

A sharp pain flashed up her leg and she stumbled – twisting her ankle in a tractor rut. She bit her lip so as not to cry out, but her eyes watered. Nubi licked her exposed ankle. Damn, she thought. Things suddenly had become a lot worse.

She needed to hide, to find cover! Get off the track, her instincts screamed. She was visible for a hundred yards in each direction.

To the right there was a gap in the hedge leading to a clearing surrounded by tall trees. This looked promising, she thought, and she hobbled to it, seeing that it was a beech glade dominated by the grassy mound of a long barrow faced by four enormous stones. A freshly painted Ministry of Works wooden sign read 'Wayland's Smithy'. It stirred a memory in Maud, but she was too distracted to recall it properly. No time to daydream – she had to hide!

Darkness never bothered Maud – daylight worried her more, being exposed, vulnerable to the sky, to calamity. The shady opening called to her, offered sanctuary. She was not superstitious. What did she have to fear from an old mound? Her husband had taught her long ago that the bones found in them were so ancient that all bacteria had been stripped from them – as the barrow had been stripped clean by tomb-robbers over the centuries. Yet she suddenly remembered reading that an excavation in 1920 had discovered the skeletal remains of eight bodies jumbled up. Maud quelled her disgust, crouched down and limped inside, finding the cool shade delicious, the mustiness reassuring. She slipped into a side-chamber and crouched in almost a foetal position, breathing heavily.

Her heart knocked against her ribs. The stone walls pressed down on her. It was like being inside a cadaver. As her senses adjusted to her new surroundings, a frisson of fear sent a shiver through her. Was this to be a dead end? she joked to herself, her throat dry.

Rain dripped down the sides of the antechamber. She hissed at Nubi to get inside too – he might give her away. The lurcher hesitated, seeming unsure about the barrow. He sniffed and whined, scratching the threshold.

'Nubi!'

The lurcher responded to the urgency of her voice, loyalty transcending fear. He rushed into the antechamber and cowered with her, ears lowered, tail between legs. She gripped his fur for reassurance and wrapped the lead around her wrist.

The pounding in her head seemed to get louder – became harder, like metal striking metal, like a hammer striking against an anvil. She now recalled the legend of Wayland's Smithy she had read in the journal, 'If a traveller on horseback wanted his steed shod he had to leave it here overnight with coin – and it would be done by the morning', supposedly by Wayland himself, the Saxon smith-god. Yet Maud had scoffed at this when she had read it in Isambard's journal. Surely it was more likely to be local employment for tinkers living in the hedges?

Yet the thudding sound seemed very real and was getting louder.

She was trapped by a paroxysm of fear. Should she run and face real danger, or stay and face this new unknown terror?

The sound was like a hammer on her heart. Distorted by the white noise of rain and the walls of the barrow, it resolved itself into the familiar, if still troubling, sound of horse hooves on a stony track – a rider was approaching, but how far away it was impossible to tell.

The lurcher growled. Maud held his lead tight.

Shlip-shlop, shlip-shlop – the sound was slurred by the sucking of mud. Then the horse hooves stopped. A snort. Heavy feet landed, then footsteps approaching – one dragged slightly.

Nubi bared his teeth, growled – the fear of his current predicament forgotten. At least she had him. Whoever it was would have Cerberus to contend with.

A shadow fell across the entrance. Nubi went wild, barking before she could stop him.

Too late – whoever it was knew she was in there.

A voice rang out, calling her name – like an executioner's summons.

Her bones turned to water, like chalk in the rain.

Again the stranger called to her. She could hide no more.

'Maud?' the disembodied voice rang out.

God, he knew her name! She panicked and Nubi wrenched from her grasp and bolted out of the barrow – knocking the figure flying. A man's curse. Growling, scuffling.

Maud listened on tenterhooks, awaiting the outcome of this battle.

The barking turned from anger to excitement, then, unexpectedly, there was laughter.

'You're a devil, aren't you? You terror! Nubi, who's a big bad boy?'

It was a voice she recognised.

She ventured a look – and gasped. At first thought it was her husband. Isambard playing rough and tumble with their old dog. She blinked, rubbed her eyes, looked again. No, he was broader, with a big moustache – it was Archibald! He was dressed for riding and was raising his crop – apparently to strike down the dog who had dirtied his jodhpurs and jacket, but when he saw Maud looking he pretended to throw it instead, teasing him.

'Fetch, Nubi! Go on, boy! He's still as strong as ever – sent me flying!' He wiped his grinning face. His clothes were splattered with mud.

'Archibald! What are you doing here?'

Maud was livid with rage and relief. She went to slap the man who had scared her witless. Instead a surge of pain shot up her leg and she stumbled – collapsing before him.

This was the final straw and the floodgates opened. The terror of her experience overwhelmed her, but, perversely, she began to laugh hysterically. Archibald strode over and helped her to her feet, hugging her close.

'It's all right, Maud – I'm here. Nothing to worry about.'

At that moment she was unable to offer resistance. She yielded to his embrace and found herself comforted by it – much to her disgust.

'There's a man out there – a stranger, following' she blurted, confused, dismayed.

'It's okay now, Maddy – you're safe now.'

Archibald lifted her on to his horse and covered her legs with a blanket. He swung himself up behind, and holding her tight, dug his heels into the palfrey.

'Fly, Pegasus, fly – carry my princess to safety!'

The horse whinnied and took off.

'Nubi!' Maud cried out.

'He'll follow, I'm sure,' Archibald grunted.

If it was Archibald's intention to lose the lurcher he had no luck, for the ruts of the Ridgeway prevented his stallion from going faster than a canter without risking a broken leg – and Nubi, half greyhound, had no trouble keeping up with them. In fact, he seemed to enjoy the exercise.

The trees sped by in a blur as the rain stung Maud's face. This was her walk, her time – and it was being snatched away from her! Was she being rescued, or abducted? Archibald held her tightly around the waist. He had a strong grip and a stronger will.

Maud was in no position to resist, or to think of a strategy. The incessant rhythm of the horse rocked her into a daze – reminding her of her childhood rocking horse. *Ride a cock-horse to Banbury Cross.* Yet now they approached the ramparts of Barbury Castle. The Ridgeway pierced straight through the middle of it. She felt like Guinevere abducted by Melwas. Where was her Lancelot?

She tried to persuade Archibald to stop but he pretended to mishear her and sped up, until they had left the trees behind and were out on open farmland – the bleak hills of Fyfield Down loomed, littered with grey wethers. Twisted hawthorns rose like strangled cries from the broken rocks.

The rain had cleared, leaving a soft haze. Avebury spread out to the right, the hub of a gigantic wheel of hill forts, barrows, avenues, standing stones. On the skyline the Wansdyke loomed, Knap Hill to Morgan Hill. To the right Cherhill Down with its obelisk and horse. The conical mound of Silbury Hill rose and fell behind Waden's Hill as if a ship on a stormy sea.

Their path was intersected by another track heading at a right angle down to the village of Avebury. 'This is the Herepath,' shouted Archibald, 'though some call it Green Street. I wish the locals would make up their mind!'

Yet her brother-in-law was making up her mind for her, and she was too weak to resist. Instead of her travelling the Ridgeway to its terminus at the Sanctuary – which had been Maud's intention, the climax of her journey – Archibald deprived her of such an achievement, and stormed down the track, into the huge stone circle, stopping only when they reached the Red Lion at its heart.

Horse-shoes sparked on cobbles. Leaping off, his limp strangely absent, Archibald barked for a stable boy to come and give the steaming palfrey fresh hay and a rub-down, then he turned to Maud and, bowing, offered his hand.

Shaken, she mustered what dignity she could and climbed down by herself, though it pained her ankle.

Archibald smiled rakishly. 'Ah, you've always been an independent woman, Maud – that's what I've liked about you.'

'I was a married woman for thirteen years – not that that stopped you behaving outrageously! You've always been a rogue and that's what I don't like about you.'

'Oh, Maud! How hurtful!' Archibald rejoined, looking like a beaten dog. He pulled off his riding gloves. 'Admit you have a soft spot for me – even just a little one.'

Nubi had caught up, looking lithe and feral, and frolicked playfully about Maud, who tousled his hair. 'I've more of a soft spot for this fellow than you!' But she couldn't help smiling.

'Well, forgive me for rescuing you! Come, let me make amends and buy you a sherry.'

Maud realised how shaken she was. Still unsteady on her feet, she begrudgingly accepted Archibald's offered hand.

'Don't be smug, Archie – it's almost unbecoming of you.'

Yet her guardian could not help but feel triumphant as he escorted

Maud into the smoky low-beamed interior. There was hardly a soul in sight. He took her to a window snug, made a great show of pulling back her chair, then he went to the bar. The landlord was nowhere to be seen, so Archibald rang the bell on the counter. Not a stir. So he rang it again. With much muttering and the creaking of steps the landlord appeared from the basement, looking like a disturbed mole.

'Bessy, where the bloody hell are you, gal? You're meant to be keeping an eye on things!'

'A decanter of your finest sherry, my good man.'

The fox-haired mutton-chopped landlord winked knowingly. 'Right you are, sir. Will you be wanting anything else?' He cast a surreptitious glance at the lady in the corner.

Archibald turned and smiled at Maud. 'I'll let you know, Mister Chives.'

He sat back in the seat next to Maud.

'This is one of my favourite haunts.'

'So it seems.'

'A tavern inside a druid circle − can you imagine anything more romantic? Thought it would be of interest to you, since you're taking an interest in Sammy's old hobby.'

Maud was thrown. Did he know about the journals? The thought made her blood run cold. 'Please, leave him out of this. I will not have him mocked in my presence.'

'Apologies − I would not want to insult the name of Saint Isambard.' He nudged her. 'A joke; it's a joke!'

Her stony stare did not fade.

'Listen, Maud, you've got to lighten up. I thought the walk might have blown some of those cobwebs away.'

'It was − until you interrupted!'

Just then the barmaid, a rosy-cheeked girl of flaxen curls, brought over a silver tray with the decanter of sherry, placing it before them with excessive flamboyance.

'Thank you, Bessy. And how's the belle of Avebury today?'

'Well, Master Kerne.' The girl blushed, curtseyed, taking a sly look at Maud and giggling. She turned in a rustle of skirts and sauntered off − her swaying hips followed by Archibald's gaze.

It made Maud flinch to hear her husband's surname spoken − and by a barmaid. The whole situation seemed seedy.

Archibald poured the sherry. 'May I raise a toast in honour of your husband to make repair?'

Maud looked hard, then sighed, acquiesced. The experience had taken more out of her than she had realised. 'Very well.'

'To Isambard.'

'To Isambard.'

The sherry took effect and combined with the fatigue and aftershock to make Maud feel very light-headed. Yet it made her sink into her seat at the same time.

No one else was in the bar at that time of day – mid-afternoon. Dust motes floated in the sunbeams. A cat stretched and yawned on the bar. The pendulum of the grandfather clock swayed tipsily.

They looked at each other suspiciously. Who was going to make the first move?

Archibald swirled his sherry in its glass.

'So how was the walk? Must have been strange walking on your own?'

'It was delightful – until I was disturbed. Someone appeared to be following me.' It seemed foolish saying it. But there it was, the bold fact.

Archibald laughed gently. 'But Maud, that's absurd! I followed you. There was no one for miles: came that way – didn't see a soul.'

'Then it – it was you that was scaring me witless! No wonder I thought I was being followed!'

Archibald looked almost sheepish, but smiled wolfishly. 'I – I was worried about you. A woman walking alone. It's not right. After you left Eastborne I decided to track your whereabouts – just to keep an eye on you. Your guardian angel. I kept a respectful distance – just near enough to keep tabs. I hope you don't mind.'

'Mind? You frightened me half to death! What were you doing, lurking in the bushes?'

'Ah.' Archibald went red. 'I was caught in a tight spot, like you. Nubi soon sniffed me out. I felt terribly foolish – couldn't reveal myself without giving the game away. So I threw the stick!'

They both laughed at this, and Archibald breathed with relief, topping up their glasses.

'If I offended, then please accept my apologies. Truce?'

Maud frowned. Was it all in her mind? Perhaps she had been the foolish one. She shrugged – glad for this mutual opportunity to save face.

'Truce.' Their glasses chinked and the action seemed to signify more than it should.

The minutes whittled away with small talk.

'You're going nowhere with that ankle – I suggest we book a couple of rooms and stay the night. There'll be omnibuses tomorrow to Swindon, where you could see a doctor.'

Maud was taken aback – alarm bells were ringing.

'I don't think that would be a good idea.'

'Why on earth not?'

'It would feel unseemly. I had not planned to elope with you, Archibald Kerne! I was intending a solitary endeavour.'

'Oh Maud, you have to jolly up! You're on holiday aren't you?'

'It's not a holiday – it's a—' She did not want to phrase it in front of him, he'd only mock. 'Pilgrimage,' she uttered quietly, realising for the first time that's what it was.

'A pilgrimage – to where? You're not making sense, Maud. You have to get over this. You have to let go.'

The clocked ticked loudly.

'I think it's time for you to leave, Archibald. If you do not, I will.' She pushed the sherry glass away.

'Maud, listen to yourself – you're in the middle of nowhere and would have been stranded by that bloody pile of rocks if I hadn't found you. I'm trying to help – but all you want to do is turn me away. I'm trying to help!'

'I don't need your charity, Archibald! I'm quite capable – you have old-fashioned ideas about women. Read the magazines. These are modern times!'

'I know, I know. But don't start chaining yourself to railings, whatever you do! You don't strike me as a modern woman Maud – you're the one living in the past...'

As soon as he said that, Archibald regretted it.

'What do you mean by "living in the past"?'

'Maud, it's been nine years. Nine years! You have to let go sometime, you have to move on. Isambard is not coming back. You've got to accept it sometime. He's dead.'

Maud pursed her lips. She stroked Nubi, her hand shaking.

'I think you should "move on", Archibald,' she said through gritted teeth. 'You've said enough. Go, now. Before I start screaming.' Her voice was low and threatening. He could see in her eyes that she meant it.

Archibald tried to think of something to say but he knew it was hopeless.

'Go!'

He needed no further prompting. Sighing heavily, he stood up and hobbled to the bar.

Leaving a coin on the counter, he limped out, a wounded beast, shaking his head in disbelief and disappointment.

'Boy, bring me my horse!' he roared, striking his riding crop on his boot. He glared over at the mullioned window where Maud sat. Somewhat reluctantly – having earned its rest – the palfrey was brought out. Archibald leapt upon him. There was a clatter of hooves and he galloped off, leaving Maud alone in the Red Lion.

She glanced at a newspaper and realised what day it was – Good Friday. Once, it had meant something – before Isambard had been taken from her. Now, the only death of significance to her that day was of her dream of freedom, freedom from the ties of her life. She had buckled and given into a man – worse, to Archie. He had revealed his true colours. She knew what his game was and she wasn't going to play it. She would not be bent to someone else's will! The more they tried, the more stubborn she would become. Life was forging her into something altogether tougher – if she did not break in the process. She tested her ankle: it throbbed in agony. First she needed a room, a place to heal.

11

SANCTUARY

I want to see you rise
From my brain's dry river,
I want your lips of wet roses
Laid over my eyes.

(...) Let me return at last
to your fertile wilderness,
to sleep with the coiled fernleaves
in your heart's live stone.

'The Wild Trees', Laurie Lee

The journal of Isambard Kerne

9th September, 1906

Made it! Approaching the Avebury complex from the North-east along the Ridgeway puts the whole thing into context. By the time the pilgrim reaches the Sanctuary after a four-or five-day walk he is in an exhausted and emotional state. The rhythm of the walking is trance-inducing and the elation of reaching one's long-sought for goal is akin to religious ecstasy. These ancient roads are temples in time as well as space – one is changed along the journey. Are such processional routes designed to alter the state of consciousness in the pilgrim? Thirst, heat and fatigue certainly made me start to see things differently – vividly, like in a Celtic dream.

I entered Stukeley's Sanctuary as a devotee, the veneer of my English reserve stripped away. I knelt and kissed the earth to thank the Great Architect and lifted my arms to praise the sky. The skies have been kind – today was the hottest day, yet it was good to raise a sweat, to purify myself. I took off my shoes and socks and walked tenderly upon the temple – the grass felt soothing to my blistered feet. Despite this place being little more than post-hole markers by the roadside, it had gained a whole new significance through my undertaking – the mundane had been transformed into the divine.

The thrill of seeing the banks of the Henge and Silbury as I approached from Barbury was unspeakable – I let out a whoop of delight to the sky. The continued view – close but far away, as the Ridgeway veers by it south to the Sanctuary – increases the sense of awe and anticipation, heightening the drama of this divine mystery.

People going past in carts and cars faded into the distance – as if they belonged to the distant future. I was present in the past, participating in a rite with others, four-and-a-half thousand years ago.

I walked along the Avenue, following its snaking curves as it approached the Avebury Circle. Its serpentine path puzzles me. Why not build in a straight line like the Romans, whose road crosses its base? Perhaps the earth's current flows like water, like a meandering river in places – elsewhere, a fast-flowing stream. There are no straight lines in nature – so what am I doing trying to impose them upon the land with my alignments? A typically male thing to do. I've been walking a phallic line – now I enter the circle, the feminine goddess centre. Here I am, in her sacred centre, the navel of the world – I have finally come home like a prodigal son, learning humility and patience along the way. Any walk outside is a journey within.

Perhaps I needed to become lost in the labyrinth to find my truth.

Easter Saturday, 1923, Avebury

After an evening spent reading her husband's increasingly esoteric journal and nursing her ankle, Maud slept late. It was an overcast day, warm and humid with the threat of rain heavy in the air. She was feeling shaken after her encounter with Archibald, but was determined to reassert her independence. She had booked herself into a guest house after he had left – with some assistance from the landlord. Her injury had made it painful to walk. In the confusion of her 'abduction' her hazel stick had been left behind at Wayland's Smithy. It occurred to her then how much it had contributed to her feeling of security. It would have been useful last night!

Instead, she borrowed a gnarled blackthorn stick from the porch, and, wrapping her shawl about her shoulders and carrying a little basket of food and drink – a simple relief from her knapsack – she struck out, Nubi at her side. *Like an old witch,* she laughed bitterly.

Her ankle was still tender from the fall and she put her weight on to the stick, feeling connected to Isambard, imagining him walking this landscape with stang in hand.

She first did a circuit of the stones, walking along the massive henge ramparts that encircled the gigantic ring of megaliths. The village that had sprouted in the middle of the ancient complex seemed incongruous and imposed, the road that slashed through it, desecrating. Omnibuses and old charabancs chugged along it, disgorging Easter tourists, while farmers and other villagers went about their business stoically, like the cows mingling with the time-worn stones, rubbing against them, licking them or using them for windbreaks. They seemed as indifferent to the sacredness of the stones as the stones were to all the activity around them. Maud watched it all from the vantage point of the earthwork, feeling distant, removed, as though gazing back over the centuries.

How transient it all seemed.

Picking a page skipped by the acceleration of events, Maud read some of the journal:

> *Barbury Castle: View from the ramparts to SE stunning. Warm, cloudy day with sun breaking through. Watched the day-visitors – father brought son to park without bothering to show him actual castle. As a nation we seem to be suffering from collective amnesia. These ancient sites serve as landscape mnemonics. We honour our ancestors by visiting them. Here, I salute the Celts who raised this mighty earthwork in the sixth century BC. I can see them in my mind's eye, standing proud and fierce in their plaid and woad, hair stiff with lime, holding leaf-shaped spears, flashing gold ornament, a torc around the chieftain's bulging neck, sky blue eyes scanning the land, circles within circles – father and son, mother and child, tribe and land, gods and ancestors – the chain of life, unbroken.*

Maud reflected on this – the chain of life *had* been broken with her, childless, barren. Yet she felt no less a woman because of it. First and foremost, she was a human being. Wasn't child-rearing just another role prescribed to her sex by society? For surely, as Maggie would say, she did her share – with her Lewes girls. But that was aptitude more than instinct, wasn't it? Her ability to teach English had come from her enthusiasm for the subject, but maybe it was also borne of a deeper need to pass something on to the next generation. So the past would not be forgotten.

All we can do, Maud decided, *is remember and honour what was.* There was no point regretting what never could have been.

'Come on, Nubi.' Getting up, Maud brushed down her skirt and carried on her perambulation. Passing through a gate and across shadowy Green Street, where the day before Archibald had brought her down from the Ridgeway, she entered the next quarter of the circle.

Awkwardly, Maud clambered up among the cataract of roots flowing from a clump of giant beeches. Nubi sniffed about, chased a squirrel, then loped off – looking for less agile prey. Here she sat for a while to give her ankle a rest and to take a sip of elderflower cordial, cool in its stone bottle bought from the local store. The smooth grey trunks of the trees offered comforting shelter. It was like being held in the arms of a giant.

It reminded Maud how her Sammy used to hold her. She felt close to him here, in this circle of stones. In truth, he had never left her. She did not just carry his words with her. He was inside her. It was as though she saw through his eyes now, even thought his thoughts. Yet that intimacy and influence could easily become smothering. Indeed, it had stifled most of her adult life. Perhaps it was time to extricate herself from the giant's embrace – and find her own way in the world. The men in her life had shaped her more than the women. Her father had towered over their family, though always cut down to size by her mother – until he had become a shrunken man. Isambard had replaced him. Daddy's girl had to grow up one day.

Leaving the shadow of the beeches, Maud followed the curve of bank around to where it terminated in another grove – and the road. She descended into the circle, passing through two massive stones facing the avenue. It felt like a threshold – leading into the heart of the complex. Finding a single low stone, she sat on it and caught her breath – still weak.

Here she was at the centre of a giant hub, going nowhere. Whose journey was she on? Following in the footsteps of one man, being chased by another, where were her choices? Straight lines – journeys with a fixed itinerary – were such a male thing. Here, in this circle, she felt safer, in her power. Why? Surely it was just a bunch of old stones. Was she starting to think like her husband as well? She felt too tired to 'think straight' – yet did she want to? Wasn't that just another male metaphor? Even the words she spoke belonged to men. She needed a language of her own.

She took out a hot cross bun from her basket, bought from the little grocery store in the village, and for the first time noticed its ancient symbol. The cross in the circle − quartered, like Avebury had been by roads. On a whim, Maud broke the bun into four pieces and laid it on the stone − a silent offering, to what she could not say. Let the birds have it, she thought, embarrassed at this subconscious gesture. As quickly as her ankle could carry her, she walked off, shouting for Nubi. The lurcher appeared from a thicket, looking guilty. He raced over and circled around her.

'Where have you been, you terror! Stick close next time!'

What is this place doing to me? The stones were powerful in their silence − sentinels of a mystery beyond comprehension.

Maud spent the day wandering around them, touching them, resting against them, listening to the wind, the distant murmur of people. Figures moved around her, from another century. She was lost deep in herself, outside time. The world carried on, careering through space, but here all was stillness and peace, a sanctuary from the storm.

Overhead, the sky was mute and dark, laden and leaden − long grey clouds capping the dark towering stones like a trilithon waiting for a sunrise.

12

THE WINDLASS

Where had I heard this wind before
Change like this to a deeper roar?
What would it take my standing there for,
Holding open a restive door...
'Bereft', Robert Frost

As the darkness gathered, Maud, feeling subdued and heavy of heart, spent the evening in the guest house, resting her ankle and reading some more of the journal.

25th July, 1907
Inspiration! I visited Caen Hill locks today while passing through Devizes for work. On a sweltering August day I sought the cool air of the canal-side and walked the mile and a half to the top of the extraordinary flight of twenty-nine locks – sixteen in quick succession down the hill. They enable barges to ascend or descend the hundred or so feet: a remarkable feat of engineering and ingenuity! Each lock on the slope has its own winding hole – a rectangular basin for the barges to turn in. The black beams with white ends reminded me of a magician's wand. Through this slow magic a process of change occurs. Indeed, the whole flight of locks seems to resemble a gigantic water clock, measuring time, filtering and funnelling it. Too much in one burst would be more than most could bear. We have to sip tiny draughts of this strong liquor, one moment at a time – otherwise it would drive one mad, I dare say.
With the decline of the canals as the chief mode of freight transport, they have fallen into dismal disarray – the paint peels away, the wrought iron rusts for want of care. It is a sad state of affairs, considering the colossal time, finance and effort that went into their construction, as my grandfather knew only too well. Their heyday only lasted a generation – forty years before the

railway began to take over.

One is reminded of Shelley's 'Ozymandias' – 'Look on my works, ye mighty, and despair!' Are all my efforts to be in vain? What am I doing, wasting my life away surveying railways that may never even be built – and if they are, will they be supplanted by a newer, faster, more competitive mode of transportation in a few decades? No doubt.

Is the endless inventiveness of the Victorians merely lines in the sand? Civilisations have risen and fallen before us – and they all thought themselves immortal. The might of Rome crumbled. Even the glory of Egypt did not last – yet the Egyptians prepared themselves for the transience of life better than anyone. And their great treasures remain as clues – like the chambered barrows of our chieftains. Osiris, their Lord of the Dead, journeyed through the underworld belly of Nut, passing through twelve gates each night, to be reborn at dawn – resurrected as Ra, the sun. These gates have been likened to water-locks. Do we have in our canal system a metaphor of this? Are the barges like those pharaonic funeral boats? They are certainly coffin-like. Osiris himself was sealed in a resplendent coffin, tricked by his brother Set, the first Cain (Caen Hill?), and cast adrift on the Nile!

If the barrows, cromlechs and sacred places of the ancients are doorways to the Otherworld, then is the passage navigable? If so, then how are the gates opened? By Death alone?

I can imagine my own Set, Archie, mocking my inquiries. 'Balderdash!' he would scoff.

Watching the catspaw on the winding hole below, I sat outside the lock-keeper's cottage. The lock-keepers are forced to make tea for passers-by to make ends meet in these threadbare days – not much passing traffic now.

Yet some people remain nomadic – it's in their blood. I saw a wiry gypsy boy pass, leading a giant shire horse pulling a barge loaded down with coal. The horse was given some hay while the boy waited for his father to see to the first set of gates. Wielding the iron windlass, the swarthy man looked at me from beneath dark brows, suspicious at my presence. I waved an arm in greeting. He grunted back and set to work. Sleeves rolled up, neckerchief about his thick neck, face smeared with black dust and sweat, the coal-merchant winched up the sluices of the gates with his windlass as though he was turning the very wheel of fortune itself.

Suddenly it struck me. A windlass! That is what I need to find!

The rusty sluices relented and let the dun-coloured water pour through, filling the middle of the lock. Eventually it will be the same level as the outside, and their vessel will be able to pass through – descending, step by step, to the lower plane. An afternoon's descent to the Underworld – or the Summer Country, as the Celts thought of their afterlife. The Somerset plains stretched out to the hazy West, golden with promise.

Find the windlass to the ways of the dead and it shall unlock the mystery of what lies beyond! And like Osiris I shall travel between worlds!

Maud awoke to the sound of bells. Confused at first, disorientated by her surroundings, she saw that she lay in a nondescript bedroom – as characterless as only a cheap guest-house could be. Turning in the thin sheets she felt a twinge of pain from her ankle and remembered where she was: Avebury.

The journal slipped off the bed, making her start. She had fallen asleep reading it. She had slept deeply. The ardour of the last few days, weeks, months, years had finally caught up with her. It had been a sultry night and the windows were half-open – letting in the exuberant peal of bells. Disgruntled, she picked up the precious tome and pulled on her dressing gown, hobbling to the casement. She looked out on to the village, ready to complain about the noise. To God himself if need be!

The sky glared down at her. In the fierce shards of sunlight villagers in their Sunday best were making their way to the small parish church opposite. Then it dawned on Maud what day it was – Easter Sunday. The bells rang out, celebrating the resurrection of Christ.

Yet she felt like death. After washing and dressing, she made her way slowly downstairs, testing her foot on each step, and found a note from the landlady on the kitchen table, saying she had gone to church and Maud should help herself. Very trusting of her – but it was obvious that Maud wasn't going to run off!

She had no appetite that morning. Contenting herself with a cup of tea, she took some dog food out to Nubi instead. She hated seeing him in a kennel, but as a paying guest she had little choice – she was lucky to find one that would take them both in. The little village was not used to visitors who stayed more than a couple of hours.

She fed and fussed the lurcher, then put him on his lead. 'Come on, boy – let's go for a ramble!' Fetching her hat, stick and her basket, she wrote a note to the landlady explaining she had taken some provisions but would be back later to pay for them and her lodgings. Putting a blanket and some bread, cheese and plums in her basket, she filled her stone bottle with water, a whiff of elderflower still in it, and set off – determined to make the most of the solitude, before the day-trippers descended.

The stone circle was deserted – everyone was at church in that God-fearing district except her, it seemed.

Feeling frail and frustrated, she decided to set out for the Sanctuary – to finish her Ridgeway walk properly. Archibald be damned!

Leaving the circle by the south road she followed the parallel line of standing stones called the Avenue towards Overton Hill and its post-holes. If ever there was an ancient processional route this was surely it. The tall stones were like a tree-lined avenue, leading her onwards. The pain of her ankle became a dull throb. Nubi raced ahead. It was already getting hot. The unseasonal heatwave had to break soon, but the sky brooded with its burden – dark against the bright fields.

The grass simmered before her. The mile and a half seemed a lot longer – the avenue telescoping into a wavering infinity. She steadied herself on a cool stone, hugging its shade, and the megalith seemed to give her strength. Gripping her stick, she carried on until she came to the end of the Avenue – or rather to where it petered out on the roadside, the rest destroyed. Ahead, there was a junction. Maud crossed the road and made her way along the old Roman road to the Sanctuary.

After such an effort to reach it, the circle of post-holes was an anticlimax. The way her husband had waxed lyrical about it belied its mundane appearance. Yet at least she had made it at last – by herself. But now she felt empty.

Looking back across the Sanctuary she saw Silbury Hill squatting in its ditch of water. It looked like an enormous pregnant belly and perhaps that was intended. The farmland thereabouts did seem exceptionally lush. The conical mound mocked her with its fecundity, contrasting her own barren belly. King Sil was said to have been buried within upon a golden horse, according to Isambard's research. Yet she was hollow inside – hollow as Glastonbury Tor was said to be. And she carried her ghost with her.

Nubi sniffed around the posts, leaving his scent. It did not seemed like sacrilege – the cows must do the same, and worse. How else would the grass be so lush?

Across soft dew-wet fields Maud headed towards the hill – finding it strangely magnetic, but as she drew nearer a sign for West Kennet Long Barrow caught her eye. Scanning the skyline, she saw the barrow on the brow of the hill to the left – a mound shaped like a sleeping figure.

Deciding to visit this less dominating monument, Maud walked up the narrow track between two fields – the one to her left was burgeoning with spring wheat, the one to the right, ploughed and fallow. Were these the choices that faced her? The path of life – or the path of death? Archibald or Isambard?

Or was there another way – a third route? Maud's way?

The long barrow rose before her, huge flat stones guarding the entrance. In all respects, except scale, it was similar to Wayland's Smithy, but this barrow seemed like a palace in comparison. There was something grander about it. She felt compelled to enter, to find sanctuary again.

Careful with her ankle, Maud stepped behind the massive entrance stones, but Nubi lingered outside, whining, unwilling to enter.

'Oh, stay there then, you great coward!'

Taking a deep breath Maud entered, bending down instinctively to do so, although the ceiling was not that low. She was worried about hitting her head, and at first she reached out her hand, groping her way along. But as her eyes adjusted to the twilight she could see as well as feel the smooth sarsens lining the passage. She was impressed by how well constructed it was. It must have been to have lasted so long. Five thousand years old, if she recalled correctly from Isambard's notes.

A ray of light at the far end drew her deeper into the passage. Maud passed three sets of openings on either side, which provided access to the smaller chambers. These looked too claustrophobic to consider, so she continued until the end of the tunnel, which opened out into the largest chamber. The gloom was pierced by the daylight – blinding now in comparison. It came from a tiny aperture in the roof – caused by the tomb-robbers at a time when the entrance was still blocked off, Isambard had surmised. The light cast a cathedralesque shaft into the inner chamber.

Here, Maud spread out her blanket and food and began her picnic with the dead. She imagined Isambard being there and laid out his share of the meal. This seemed the natural thing to do. Maud was surprised to discover herself performing in such a superstitious way. Who was she fooling? Nobody was there, were they? Yet here she was, down among the dead men.

She looked at the uneaten bread, cheese and fruit, and the pointlessness of it struck home. Nothing could assuage that endless yearning, her hungry ghost. The stones seemed to whisper *hiraeth ... hiraeth.*

What was she doing with her life? Where was she going? However far she went, she would never be able to escape the past or find peace in the present – until she had laid Isambard to rest. Why had it all gone wrong? Her life had died. Were these the last rites for her husband or for herself?

In the absolute emptiness of the tomb a wave of grief surged up from the depths and overwhelmed her – she let out a howl of pain and crumpled as the storm broke inside. All the tears she had never shed reached saturation point, all the grief denied – not just for Isambard, but for her own wasted life. What had she done wrong? Why? Why her?

Wave after wave of sorrow broke. Her heart cracked, splitting wide, releasing its petrified feelings. Maud wept for the woe of the world, for the slaughter and folly, the vast tragedy of it all.

And her weeping became keening, as the tears ran dry and the only way to exorcise the pain was to scream it, to give birth to it, to howl as the storm raged about her, and to surpass its fury. Blind with wrath, Maud vented her anger on the forces that had thwarted her, tormented her, taken her husband, stolen her life, and finally on herself – she beat her head and tore at her hair, rocking back and forth like a mad woman. Then the keening became a low droning, a guttural groan, ragged and raw. Until all that was left was a tenderness, a delicate frail flame – and Maud began to sing, quietly at first, a whisper against the softening rain. A child's voice, cracked and pure:

In Fleet Street, in Fleet Street,
The people are so fleet;
They barely touch the cobble stones
With their nimble feet.

The lads run like a windy day,
The lasses run like rain,
From Temple Bar to Ludgate Hill –
And then run back again.

The atmosphere thickened, as if the stones themselves were listening – or the dead. Maud continued, her voice growing in confidence:

The lads run like a windy day,
The lasses run like rain.

Again, the tightening in the air ... Was that whispering she could hear? Or the wind whistling through the cracks?

Then it dawned on her. Something Isambard had said – had written in his journal. The great mystery that had obsessed him all his life – he had been searching for something ... for the key! Yes, that was it: searching for the key that would unlock the gateway between the worlds.

Maud's song echoed around the chambers of the barrow, of her mind: *lads run like a windy day ... lasses run like ... wind ... lass! Wind lass!* That was it! Her singing was the key – *she* was the wind-lass!

'*I held in my hand the key-plan of a long-lost fact.*' Watkins words came back to haunt her, to mock them both.

The secret was within Isambard's grasp all along – but because he did not share his search, he never found the answer at his feet. Maud could have unlocked the worlds for him.

Could she do it now?

Maud tried singing again, consciously and conscientiously this time. Listening to the sound she was making and the silences between. The acoustics of the barrow seemed designed to enhance the music's quality. No longer using words, she intoned, raising the pitch and the stones at the far end seemed to soften and shift. A corona of light filtered around the edges, poured out of the gaps.

She felt alone no longer.

There was a blast of wind, a rumbling, and the end wall seemed to roll back.

And in the void was silhouetted the figure of a man, a tall man wearing a hooded cloak and holding one staff, or two – it was hard to tell in the vortex of light. The howling wind whipped his cloak around him like wings, and turquoise fire crackled into the chasm beyond.

Maud fell before him, stricken with fear – but when she looked beneath that hood she gasped, seeing a face she recognised, and loved.

'Isambard! You've come back to me! You're alive!'

The phantom lowered his hood, revealing a gaunt face. His eyes gazed as though across a fathomless gulf. He spoke in a voice sounding like a faint radio broadcast, distant and distorted.

'*Maud, my darling. Help me! I'm trapped. It's dark in here. So much screaming. Bodies pressed against me. Countless dead. Lost souls. Drifting in the mist. We fade, forget who we are. Drink the Lethe of oblivion. Who am I, Maud? You must remember me. Put the scattered pieces of my life back together. It's so lonely in here. Nobody knows your name. Nobody looks at you – everyone is lost in their own past. Trying to recollect, reconnect. The war shattered the natural cycle. All those sudden dead overloaded the system. It's pandemonium. The shock of a violent death – a soul doesn't know what's hit it. Confused. In denial. Angry – that's when they haunt a place, when they haven't been buried properly or let go of. Something keeps them earthbound. Yet something happened to me – there was a mistake. The angel gate allowed me to cross. My pilot was badly injured. Yet we were not killed. Somehow we survived, but were separated. I cannot hear Mallard. I lost touch with him as soon as we crossed. Maybe it's because I'm still trapped – perhaps he wasn't grieved over as I was. He wasn't held back by love.*'

Maud stared at her husband – feasting on his every feature. 'You are still alive!'

Isambard shook his head. '*I don't feel dead, but who knows what that feels like? All I know is that I am prevented from returning to the Earth of the living. Some doorways are one-way. I must pass on. I cannot go back.*'

'Why?'

'*Death is our ticket from this world – I have not the coin to pay the ferryman for my return, except by dying.*'

'You never died in my heart. Darling, you have not aged.'

Isambard looked out into the world. He tried to read the passing of time in Maud's face. He saw the ravages of time, of grief. '*How long has it been?*'

'Nine years.' Maud sobbed.

'*Nine years! It has been nine nights to me. You mourn too much, my love. Do not waste another day. Life is for living. Cherish every moment while you can. I can't taste, can't touch, but I can feel the cold*

– it's so cold here, Maud. I have lived among the dead too long. I want to see the sun again, to feel the wind on my face, the grass beneath my feet.'

Maud wept. 'Yes, yes. I have walked for you, my darling – followed your path.'

'You have honoured my memory, but now you must let me go. Let me pass on.'

'No! Never!'

'Maud, listen to me! I walk not along the paths of the quick. Nor does my spirit find release – your grief keeps me in limbo. You have to let me go. Only you can. Maud, you have found the key! You opened the way between – and you can close it.'

'No!' she sobbed. 'I love you too much!'

'Maud, you love me too much, while I did not love you enough … You were the wind-lass all along – if I had but eyes to see it. I should have shared the journey with you. But this time we can. The hollow road calls. Come with me. Meet me at the Long Man on Samhain – when the veil is thinnest. Then, with your song, you can set my spirit free.'

The figure began to flicker and fade.

'Farewell, my darling – for now.'

Outside the barrow, Nubi growled. The apparition shrank to nothing, as if down a plug-hole.

'Noooooo!'

The lurcher barked – and the spell was broken.

The wind died and the end-wall congealed into rock once more.

Maud was left in the empty barrow, curled up next to the blanket of withered fruit.

A shadow blocked the entrance. A man was entering 'What's the matter, Missy?' He looked like a farmer. 'We saw the lurcher running loose and wus worried...'

His voice faded as he saw the woman on the floor, shaking, dazed, frightened.

'Take me back,' she said in a cracked voice. 'Take me back home.'

13

A SHOOTING STAR AT GARSINGTON

Pillow'd upon my fair love's ripening breast,
To feel forever its soft fall and swell,
Awake forever in a sweet unrest,
Still, still to hear her tender-taken breath,
And so live ever – or else swoon to death.

'Bright Star! Would I were steadfast as though art', John Keats

Maud lay in her bed back in Bradford Street, adrift in time. The curtains were drawn in the middle of the day. Fuelled by a fever, the events of the last few days rose and fell before her like some magic lantern show – and she could not tell what had happened and what was happening before her at that very moment.

After she had been found in West Kennet Long Barrow by the farmer it had taken a long process of guesswork and questioning before she was returned to the guest-house. There she sat in numb bewilderment while the landlady searched her handbag and found an address book. With the assistance of the local vicar – whose telephone they used – help was summoned, in the unlikeliest of forms.

Constance had still not forgiven her for the outburst before her trip, and was unable, or unwilling, to help. She had 'her hands full with the twins'. Maggie was unreachable – still in Ireland seeing her family. And so late Monday morning, after a speedy drive across from London in his Silver Ghost, it was Archibald who came to her rescue. Maud was too weak to protest, but for once her brother-in-law shone through. He was in his element, taking care of everything – paying the landlady extra for her trouble, making a small donation to the church and tipping the farmer. He packed up Maud's things and put them in the boot, and even allowed Nubi to sit in the back with her – on a blanket. Hooting his horn, he drove out of Avebury and sped back with her to Eastbourne.

Despite his flashy driving he got her home in one piece. She would have to be grateful for that. Perhaps he wasn't a fairweather friend after all. Yet, she doubted his actions were entirely altruistic. He had leapt at the opportunity to prove himself useful to her, to redeem himself for his behaviour on the Ridgeway.

Throughout this time Maud had not managed to utter one word — she functioned in all other ways, but her mind was elsewhere. At first, Mrs Mulligan popped around to see to her needs and Nubi's. Then Maggie came back from Galway, and — distressed at what had happened to Maud, although what exactly no one was sure — she stayed over to nurse her back to 'the land of the living'.

The release of her grief in West Kennet had drained Maud completely. The effort of opening her heart again and the door between life and death — perhaps nine years of unshed tears had provided sufficient fuel — had left her raw and ragged. Yet her spirit was more tormented — for her precious paradigm had been shattered. The soul survived the body, and if there was a soul must there not be a Creator? Her husband had not perished — nor had he 'passed on'. He was trapped in Purgatory — and she was responsible!

Maud was inconsolable. Her friend did what she could. She visited Maud on the way to the grammar school. One morning, Maud finally spoke. 'It was my fault! It was my fault!' she howled. 'I would not let him die.'

Maggie had to leave or she'd be late again, but desperate to help her friend she lifted the silver cross from around her neck and gave it to Maud for succour. 'I find strength in the Lord Jesus Christ — who rose from the grave. May you do also.' Maud took it, as a symbol of her friend's love, if nothing else. When she held it she thought of Maggie, and felt safe, as though an angel were watching over her.

Throughout this convalescence Constance did not once visit. She sent her husband around with a 'get well' card and flowers. Embarrassed, Freddie explained how his wife was nursing the twins, who had gone down with mumps. Maud could imagine her saying Maud didn't have a 'real illness', that she was 'putting it all on,' wanting their sympathy, and thinking only of herself when others were in more need than her.

Archibald called by when he could, and was a darling — fetching anything she needed, seeing to the domestic bills, even doing a bit of gardening for her. She watched him through the window as he pulled up weeds. He 'enjoyed the exercise', he said. 'Better than sitting in a stuffy office.'

Yet she was still too feverish to feel anything but silent gratitude.

Her bedroom spun around her, the walls evaporating and congealing like the interior of the long barrow. She saw the spectral figure of Isambard manifest before her again – his words like a scratched record:

'I walk not along the paths of the quick. Nor does my spirit find release – your grief keeps me in limbo. You have to let me go.'

She had only wanted to honour her husband's memory. She had been the dutiful widow. Hadn't she? Had a day gone by without her thinking of him? Yet perhaps that was part of the problem. She had trapped herself as well.

'Maud, you have found the key! You opened the way between – and you can close it.'

Perhaps she had the means to release herself too.

'Maud, you love me too much, while I did not love you enough.'

Then Maud realised – perhaps the greatest act of love is to be able to let go of what you care for the most.

'You were the wind-lass all along...'

She was the key – it was her singing that had brought him back – and it was her singing that could release him!

'With your song you can set my spirit free...'

Yet only at a certain place, at a certain time.

'Meet me at the Long Man on Samhain,' Isambard had said. Maud tried to think clearly. The Long Man had to be the chalk giant of Wilmington. She had to rendezvous with him there – but when? He had said Samhain – pronouncing it 'sowen'. What was it? She had to look it up, but where? She needed the guidance of the violet lady from Glastonbury. Someone who knew about these mysteries – yet the psychic had been wrong about the figure on the Tor. It had not been Gwynn ap Nudd – it had been her husband. Of that now she was certain. Yet hadn't Isambard become a walker of the underworld now? Isambard was not dead, or fully alive. She'd trapped him in limbo with her love.

'You have to let me go,' he had pleaded. But her memories were all she had. She was trapped too, in the past – a ghost to the present.

How had they first met – what strange fate had brought them together? If she could work out how they had become entangled, then perhaps she could unravel the knot.

While her surroundings blurred, the memory unravelled before her with absolute clarity.

It was the shooting star that clinched it, that night at Garsington, when they had first met.

She was a prim nineteen; a precocious student of Somerville College, Oxford, where she had rubbed shoulders with the silver spoon set and made friends with fellow student Lady Ottoline Morrell, society beauty: 'Otty' as Maud knew her. Maud had been invited to a soirée at Garsington – the Morrells' country house. She had felt underdressed and out of place from the start – the tuxedos and evening dresses swished and rustled around her, and her ears were filled with laughter and piano music. The conversation was pretentious and full of private jokes. And she felt like one of the jokes – Ottoline's little blue-stocking friend. Maud had been greeted with enthusiasm by the hostess, and introduced to a circle of old Somerville school friends – 'You'll have something to talk about' – but not to the élite. Gathered in Garsington's plush grand hall was the great, the good and the beautiful – but Lady Ottoline outshone them all in her recherché ball gown, made famously by her own fair hand; she was like some fairy queen, gracing the realm of mortals for one night. Yet here she was in her element as society hostess, and Maud definitely was not. Her old Somerville friend had recently wedded – and her Midas of a husband acted the indulgent monarch, giving into the whims of his formidable queen. It was she who held court, like the Queen of Hearts. And Maud felt like Alice, fallen down the rabbit hole – taking care not to lose her head.

It was the final fling of the Naughty Nineties. The spirit of fin de siècle was in the air, but it seemed back then that the party was never going to stop. Maud was buffeted by the phantasmagoria of it all, *The Yellow Book* decadence. Beardsleyesque ladies glared down at her from high heels like gorgons in ball gowns. Salome-like, Ottoline swirled about her guests, scene stealing, fatally stunning. Servants with silver trays offered exotic dainties, dangerous cocktails. At any moment Maud expected to see the head of a poet brought in, the fickle muse's latest victim.

Becoming faint, Maud stepped out for some fresh air. It was a lingering Indian summer's evening, when the day's light seemed to cling to every leaf and flower, like heat from sun-warmed rocks. A warm breeze wafted over the Arcadian garden, enveloping her like mulled wine. The heady fragrance of a magnolia bush filled her nostrils, mingling with the cloud of perfume from the French windows. Silky white blossom floated to the floor.

The crunch of gravel under heel made her start. A cigarette hissed, snuffed out.

She noticed the shoes first – white uppers with black spats. Following the satin seam on the trouser leg, the crimson cummerbund, her eyes came to rest on a man in his early thirties, ill at ease in his tuxedo.

'Disgusting. Habit, that is. Smoking,' the man apologised. He gestured to the smouldering cigarette butt in the gravel.

'I would hazard a guess you came out for some fresh air,' he smiled.

'Oh, it's quite alright.' She pulled a loose strand of auburn away from her flushed face. 'It was getting a little stuffy in there, I have to say. But I'm glad I came out.'

'It's such a fine evening, is it not?'

'Yes, it is,' she sighed. It was certainly improving rapidly.

The man seemed to be making every effort not to look at her. He was gazing down the garden, which stretched into sharp perspective.

'Makes you want to just run along it, doesn't it?'

Again, that curious inversion, which she was beginning to find endearing.

'You mean the garden walk?'

'Mm, along the Chase – but if you did you'd end up falling off the Ha-Ha, of course!'

The both laughed at this, and the man nervously caught her eye. His were opalescent orbs beneath dark brows, unruly black hair making his taut skin seem paler.

'And your name, sir? Or are you a famous athlete, and I foolish?'

'Apologies. I do run ahead of myself, but I'm no sportsman. I'm not famous yet either – but my namesake was. Please don't laugh.'

'I wouldn't dream of doing so. A man's name is everything to him.'

The man reached out to clasp her gloved hand lightly, and bowed. 'Isambard, Isambard Kerne, at your service.'

She restrained herself, but when she saw Isambard turning red, she burst into peals of laughter with him.

'Oh, forgive me, sir,' she said, wiping her eyes.

'No, please – forgive my parents. My father was a great admirer of Brunel. He works as an engineer himself for GWR – and that seems to be my destiny also.' He said this with some gravity, making Maud subdue her smile.

'Does this destiny not please you, Mister Kerne?'

'It is what I can do – surveying. I am lucky to have a profession awaiting me. And yet — '

Maud looked closer and saw the tension in his posture, the clenched fist. He seemed to draw in the night.

'Yet — we all want to choose our own path, do we not?' he said.

'Some of us have no choice, Mister Kerne. Some, no voice even.'

Isambard snapped out of his fug.

'I have been most remiss,' he said. 'Lost in my own world as usual. And what did the gods deem to call you?'

'Maud Arkwright. My father was a miller from the North. He moved to Banbury when he met my mother.'

'Ah, Banbury, not far from here — on horse.'

She blushed at this, unsure whether the connotation was intended.

'And where do you hail from, good sir?'

'The Malverns, originally. A little village you wouldn't have heard of and will never probably visit.'

'Who is dictating fate now?'

Isambard looked somewhat abashed at this.

'Would you care for a stroll around the grounds, Miss Arkwright?'

Maud hesitated. From an open window came the tinkle of piano and the clink of champagne glasses raised in toast, the murmur of conversation punctuated by occasional guffaws of laughter.

'I would be glad to accept,' she said, holding out her arm.

Isambard hooked it through his own, and, a little awkwardly, they began their walk.

The sounds of the party faded, though snatches of music were borne on the breeze.

For some time they walked in silence, taking in the beguiling maze of topiary and statues, semi-animate in the shifting twilight. Then the conversation came, first as a trickle, then as a flood. They both felt out of place, out of their league. Among the luminaries present that night were said to be Huxley, Russell, Lawrence, Woolf — or was she confusing it with Otty's later bashes? Maud had been invited less and less often, as the A list had grown and the Somerville crowd dwindled. But Isambard didn't fit in either — he had only been there because of brother — just back from the escalating Boer War with a shrapnel wound and a medal. Many gathered around the 'famous' Archibald, eager to hear news from the front. His loud voice carried on the night air — bragging, vulgar, drunk. He would be humoured by the inner circle, for now.

They wandered along colonnades lit by Chinese lanterns, avenues of white blossom in the thin moonlight.

Isambard pointed out the new moon in the purple sky – you could see the circle it embraced. 'The maiden in the arms of the crone: *earthshine*.'

They paused at a gazebo. There was a growing chill in the air, making them both shiver. She wanted to be held by him then. 'Just for warmth,' she reasoned with herself. 'It makes sense.' But she hesitated. Why give into animal instincts, to his musk?

Then they saw the star. It shot across the sky, and they caught its fiery tail. At the same moment they turned to one another and found themselves holding hands in delight.

'That was a beauty!' said Isambard, looking fully at her for the first time.

'It was a sign!' said Maud, breathlessly.

'Of what?'

'Oh, I don't know – the future,' she said, embarrassed. 'It just makes me feel optimistic.'

'I – know what you mean. It feels like we have our whole lives ahead of us. A new century is around the corner. Unmapped, vast and unknown. We need any guides we can get to help us navigate through the uncertainty – like bonfires on beacon hills. May the stars light our way.'

Maud couldn't believe what she was hearing. She sensed the Romantic spirit in Isambard, which she had always dreamed of meeting. As an English student the works of Shelley, Keats, Coleridge had set fire to her heart – she longed to share that heat.

They huddled in the gazebo, drawing closer and closer.

They talked of their beliefs. Maud was brought up dutifully as Church of England, but her faith was mostly lip service. She could not accept it as a literal truth, though she felt there was something between the lines – while Isambard had straddled the Catholic through his father of Irish descent, and the Non-conformist through his Welsh borders mother, not fitting comfortably in either shoe.

Looking up at the stars, Isambard began to quote: 'There are more things in heaven and earth—'

'Than are dreamt of in most people's philosophy,' Maud completed.

They looked at one another and smiled, but only their teeth and eyes were visible now. Night enshrouded them in its violet satin. It was so still, so serene, as if the world were holdings its breath, waiting for the future.

How could they guess all that would transpire in the first two decades of that bright new century?

All that mattered was in that moment, that place. The powerful connection between them was undeniable – it was like some new energy, a magnetic current charged with unspoken desire.

The darkness made it impossible to glean expressions any more. Disembodied, all that was left was voice: hers reserved but full-bodied, rich and clear; his low-timbred, as if each thing he said emanated from a deep source, like water from an underground spring – emerging in a cascade; rash, but decisive.

Only as dawn unveiled them, layer by layer, could they discern features once more. By then the enchantment was total – she had fallen in love with his voice, with his soul.

Far away, a cock crowed and the spell of night was broken – but its effect did not diminish. That night at Garsington was never forgotten. The shooting star was an auspicious one, for over the coming months their romance bloomed as the old century died.

Suddenly, the telephone rang, snapping Maud back into the present. For a moment, she lay there in bed, the blankets tangled around her, wondering where she was.

She recognised her bedside cabinet, with the photograph of Isambard in its gilt frame. The black telephone trilled next to the art nouveau lamp. Maud looked at it as if it were an exotic bird, raucous and annoyed. Distantly, she knew she should pick it up, but what use was the present? The door of time had been ripped off its hinges and could not be put back on. She was the wind-lass and she had to let the winds blow through her until they blew themselves, or her, out.

14

HANDFAST POINT

BREATHLESS we flung us on the windy hill
Laughed in the sun and kissed the lovely
grass.
You said, 'Through glory and ecstasy we pass;
Wind, sun, and earth remain, the birds sing
still,
When we are old, are old...''And when
we die (...)
We shall go down with unreluctant tread
Rose-crowned into the darkness !'...Proud
we were,
And laughed, that had such brave true things to
say.
- And then you suddenly cried, and turned
away.

'The Hill', Rupert Brooke

Maud lay back in her sickbed, and put the book of poems down, sighing heavily. Even her favourite books could give her little comfort, the way she was feeling. Her skin felt like parchment, each wrinkle a calligraphy of care. When was the last time she had been touched in tenderness? Held by strong gentle arms? Maud felt like a stranger in her body. She had not always been. Isambard had always been a considerate lover, breaking her out of her shyness, making her yearn for his touch. Blushing, she remembered their first night together as husband and wife. Until then she had known only chaste kisses. The shock of sex had split open her world.

It was on the Isle of Purbeck, midsummer, and the first day of their married life. Despite being exhausted from the big day, and the long night in each other's arms, they woke at sunrise, trembling in the strangeness of their status, beholding one another like Adam and Eve in the London hotel room. The apple had been bitten into; its juice stained the sheets. Yet they did not feel fallen, but reforged. Into one life.

With the daylight, Maud's shyness returned. She covered herself and scurried into the bathroom. They did not have much time, if they were to catch the morning Holiday Line to the Isle of Purbeck. When asked about their honeymoon destination they'd had to explain countless times that it wasn't really an island, just a rounded piece of Dorset jutting out into Poole Harbour. Still, it seemed world away from the noisy streets of the city.

After dressing quickly, taking breakfast, a frenzied packing of presents, a dash to the station, and the tipping of porters, the newlyweds were ensconced in their own compartment, arm in arm, enjoying the changing view as civilisation was stripped away from the land in their progress west, until only cows and church spires remained.

They passed through the Vale of the White Horse, running parallel to the Ridgeway, and Isambard pointed out the elegant Uffington giant. 'That's horse-power,' he joked, in good spirits.

The rhythm of the carriage rocked Maud to sleep, the franticness of the last few days catching up with her. Finally, she and her husband could be at peace. When she next awoke they were trundling through a richer landscape, the dells of Dorset.

Isambard had been making notes, but put away his journal when he noticed his bride stirring. 'Nearly there, darling.'

They steamed through the rolling chalk downs in style – first class, with her husband's staff card. A horse-drawn carriage took them to their hotel along the meandering lanes to the eccentrically turreted Manor House Hotel by South Beach. There they mingled with bright young things in tennis whites, drunken uncles, sullen veterans and loquacious dames. The hotel was full to the brim and stuffy with opinions. They were glad to get away.

After arranging for their lunch to be packed as a picnic, they set off like adventurers – eager to explore this first day of wedded life. They decided to walk along the coast west to Old Harry Rocks, or Handfast Point, as it's also known – as if there had been a difference of opinion on the matter. They joked about this: Maud preferred the reliability of Old Harry, Isambard was intrigued by the mysterious Handfast Point. Laughing, they strolled along, hearts as light as the day.

The chalk track shimmered in the June heat. They walked arm in arm across the cliff-tops – entering a tunnel of trees that followed the horn of the bay, veiled in green shadow between the shards of sun. Occasionally, through the trees they would be treated to views of the wide harbour, where white boats bobbed, their sails like seagull wings. The sea was almost turquoise beneath the clear blue sky, calm except for the whitecaps left by boats in their wake.

Conversation faded. They felt shy, strangely awkward, like young lovers courting, not a married couple. Maud did not have to pinch herself. The ring did that, it changed everything. It had chafed her finger at first. Yet it was heavy, cool and solid in the ethereal summer's heat. The two circles of their lives overlapped. They now belonged to one another, body and soul. Did this make them wary? It was as if they had to reconsider how they treated one another.

Isambard was acting the gentleman, being sweetly over-formal and protective. Now they had to behave like a respectable couple – as if they had done anything otherwise before. Their forced small talk was like a rehearsed script. They passed other couples and nodded to them in polite conspiracy, and, yes, she might have actually blushed. The memory of the previous night came back to her vividly.

After a mile the trees thinned out, and suddenly they were there – the cliffs plunged away beneath them, a hundred feet to the wave-pummelled rocks. And where the land yielded, the stacks of Handfast Point loomed, bone-white sides, topped by a flat layer of grass. They walked to the isthmus where the footpath dwindled to nothing. Beyond – a sheer drop a hundred feet to the sea. He held her hand tightly and insisted she did not walk too near the edge.

'I don't want anything to happen to you,' he said, holding her close. 'If you died, my world would end.'

They embraced. It felt like a beginning.

Other tourists were approaching, so they moved around the cliff-edge for a little seclusion.

'Here', said Isambard, squinting beneath his sun hat and pointing. 'This is the best view.' Maud admired her husband first – he looked so resplendent in his cream summer suit, hair sleek and black, beard trimmed; a handsome man of thirty-one, ten years her senior.

He showed Maud the natural arch in the central stack – through it the pellucid water shimmered, like a gateway to another world.

They laid out the picnic things. Isambard spread out the chequered blanket, a courtier before his queen. She felt like royalty that day in her new summer dress, shaded by her little parasol against the fierce sun. The tangy breeze cooled them, teased her thick russet locks. She scanned the horizon. The sea stretched almost right around them – on the other side of the point was a deeply carved cove and beyond, fin-like pinnacles lancing the sky and the vista of Swanage in the distant haze.

The gentle humming wind scoured all worries from them. Far below, the waves lapped like a thirsty dog. Seagulls keened and wheeled. The newlyweds ate their picnic of cucumber and cold ham in contented peace, then Maud lay against Isambard, the long grass swaying around them, and sighed.

So this was married life. This was how it was going to be from now on. Yet the honeymoon would not last for ever. When the mead runs out, what then?

A cormorant, black-winged, yellow-beaked, crossed their field of view – a needle threading the horizon.

Isambard suddenly became animated, stirring them from their rêverie. An idea had struck him. He sat up, staring at the cliffs. 'Our grip on life is so tenuous,' he said. Maud was confused at this sudden leap of logic. She had been daydreaming of a home, a garden, a family to fill it. She looked at her husband, puzzled. There he goes again!

'What on earth do you mean, dear husband?' The words were so delicious in her mouth that she said them again: 'Dear husband.' Yet his mood was at odds to hers and, sensing her playfulness, he withdrew his urge to share his serious reflection.

'Oh nothing. Just the ramblings of a fool.'

'Really? Come on, I would like to know. Honestly.'

Isambard brooded. He looked deeply at his wife, as if to gauge her sincerity. She tried her best to look serious, an earnest student. Her husband's attitude shifted slightly, like continents drifting. He took a sip of the dark wine, the colour of his eyes.

'The way there is this thin layer of life over all the dead matter,' he said, pointing at the stacks, the slither of grass over the bulk of chalk. 'Life is so precarious. Yet it clings on with such tenacity. Look at those gulls nesting. What if a chick fell? What if one of us fell?'

'Oh, Sammy,' she chided. 'Such morbid thoughts – on such a beautiful day! Our first day of marriage! I hope you aren't going to be doom and gloom all the time!'

'But Maud, it's not morbid – it's the way of things. The great cycle. Nature regenerates. Nothing is lost. All those sea creatures became the very land we stand upon, the soil we farm, the minerals in our food. We live on the bones of the dead.'

Maud made him stop that line of thought – it was making her uncomfortable. How could he think such things on that glorious day? A shadow had been cast over it for her – however slight. It should have been perfect, yet nothing ever was. She watched a fly embroil itself in the preserve. Its buzzing was like the annoying thoughts, the niggling doubts, crawling around in her brain. She tried to smile and brush them off, yet her brave face was a kind of rictus.

Isambard put his arm around her and kissed her brow, smoothing her hair. In his journal he called such moments – when awareness of life's fragility and impermanence gave it a bittersweet edge – 'death-in-life'. 'Does not the midsummer sun, at its zenith, know of its own demise?' he argued. 'The shadows are darkest in the bright sun, are they not?'

The next day Isambard insisted they walked up on to Nine Barrow Downs – he wanted to 'take some measurements'. Maud did not mind where they went. She was happy to let him indulge his quaint obsession – to begin with. And he obliged her by letting Maud indulge hers when they passed a bric-à-brac shop; a weakness of hers. She could not pass one without going in. It was obviously someone's house, overtaken by an obsession for the old and obscure. 'Foss's Antiques' read the peeling sign above the front window – although the authenticity of the 'antiques' was questionable.

The couple stepped inside the dark, cool, musty interior, crammed with all manner of curiosities: stuffed birds, stags' heads, a gathering of grandfather clocks (all telling different times and defiantly sticking to their version), a collection of clay pipes, albums of cigarette cards, foothills of books, a stack of 78s, wax cylinders, a new gramophone, horse-brasses, fire pokers, knife sharpeners, cabinets with tiny drawers like Chinese boxes, massive trunks, an escritoire, swords, African spears, grotesque masks, huge gilt frames and miniatures, fish-eye mirrors and a witch-ball reflecting everything back at them like an Escher drawing. The shop was so cluttered with the past that there was hardly any room for the present. They had to squeeze past the packed aisles, and felt like they were trespassing in history.

Isambard muttered something about it being a glorified junk shop, growing irritable as he waited for his wife to finish browsing. Then something caught his eye.

It was an old milk churn full of canes. Isambard admired them one by one – the elegant black and silver evening cane, the coarse cudgel, a tall hunting staff, riding crops and whips, sticks with horn handles. He weighed them one at a time. All were too fanciful, except for a simple unadorned longstaff with a Y-shaped prong that fitted his thumb perfectly. It was just the right height, coming to his shoulders – the canes felt too short for his frame.

'This would be perfect for walking with,' he commented. Then he caught the face looking at them through the tangle of antiques.

'Has sir found something to his liking?'

The odd voice startled them both. The man stepped from behind a bookcase and shook their hands.

'Foss at your service,' he said with a West Country twang. 'Bill Foss.'

He was an old man with a chancy gleam in his eye, dressed in a collarless shirt and the waistcoat and trousers of a Sunday suit. His hair was a white corona around the brown sun of his face.

'You look like a man who knows his sticks, sir,' said Foss, winking.

'Yes,' replied Isambard, trying to gauge the honesty of the remark, or whether it was mere flattery. 'I just want a good honest walking stick.'

'Can't get more honest than that, sir – honest as the day is long. It is what it is and nothing else, although –'

Isambard smiled at Maud, who joined him on his arm.

'Madame, if you would excuse the folly of the old, I would like to share a local superstition with your good husband.'

'Of course, I know he has a weakness for them.' She nudged Isambard in the ribs.

'Well, sir. You have in your hand a *stang*. It may look like just another walking stick to you, but in the West Country these fellows mean something else entirely.'

'What are you getting at?' Isambard's curiosity was aroused. Maud looked on in amused detachment.

'Here in the West we cling to our old ways longer than most.' In a whisper: 'It is said cunning folk hereabouts use them for divining.'

He had uttered the last word with respectful awe. It resonated around the room. All the artefacts seemed to sit up and listen. Dust motes swirled in the sunbeams, stirred and settled.

'Divining?' queried Isambard, finding it difficult to maintain the reserved manner of a buyer wanting to strike a bargain.

Maud scoffed at this – surely it was just some tourist bunk. But it excited her husband and he had inquired further. After ascertaining Sammy's genuine fascination and knowledge in those mysteries, the old man told him in hushed tones how to use it — by placing it on the ground you want to divine and resting the 'Y' against your temples.

Then, somehow, you could feel if there were water there, or 'other currents', he said with a strange inflection.

Kerne thanked him profusely, paid the bumped-up price without question, and strode off with the staff. The old man called out, 'If you're going up on to those Downs, watch out for the wight!'

Unnerved, Maud struggled to keep up. She was relieved to leave that fusty shop. She hadn't found a bargain after all. Back in the light again, she gulped down the clean air. With dismay she noticed her husband racing ahead — trying out his stick. He was eager to get to open land to use it. With the staff in hand he stormed ahead.

Maud caught up and grabbed his arm. 'Hold your horses! You're like Stevenson's *Rocket!*'

He apologised and made a joke about how his namesake, Kingdom Brunel, had a famous walking stick, which he'd had specially made so it could be used as a track gauge as well. It was revered by the GWR as a sacred relic, a badge of office passed down with pomp and ceremony to each successive chief civil engineer. Kingdom Brunel had his stick, Sammy would have his stang, like the chalk giant of Wilmington — striding over the land, measuring the ancient roads with rod.

With provisions they had set off out of the village, following the track up to the Downs. Passing Ballard and Ulwell, they crossed the Swanage road up to Nine Barrows. It was hot walking weather, and they stopped to take a draught of lemonade.

Isambard wiped his brow with his monogrammed handkerchief, Maud flickered her fan. Hiking was unheard of back then and a holiday wardrobe was ill-prepared for such excursions.

The Purbeck coast spread out below them. The sea was a rich blue. It looked cool and inviting. But they turned their attention inland and struck out across the shelterless hill. Thick grass basked in the sun. They walked among buttercups and dandelions. A skylark hidden in the undergrowth sang like its heart would burst.

The ridge stretched from Swanage to Corfe Castle, Isambard explained, and placed upon it in an irregular row were at least nine Bronze Age burial mounds, sunken but still massive.

'It may take a village to raise a child,' he said — paraphrasing his

Boer War brother, who had learnt some African sayings during his brief time in the Transvaal – 'but perhaps it takes a village to bury the dead as well.'

'Sammy, don't speak of such things. Remember what that odd man said. Watch out for the witch, or some such. I've got the creeps.'

'Wight. Foss said "watch out for the wight". As in the Isle of Wight. Wight being a particularly nasty kind of ghost – these mounds are said to be haunted.'

'Splendid! Now you tell me. You know how to reassure a girl, don't you!'

Isambard held her hand. 'Fear not, my bride. I am here. Quicker than the dead.'

When he looked at her like that, with his coal eyes, all concerns melted.

'Come on!'

He enthused about the barrows as they raced up and down each one, counting them. He was intrigued why people had buried their dead up here. Who were these individuals, to have such prestige? The chieftains of the tribe, the priests or the warriors? Why barrows in a line? Were they a blood-line? Or did they rule the area over generations and were buried up here to keep on eye on the living, or to be closer to the gods?

Isambard would have walked all the way along the Downs – three miles to Corfe, but Maud wanted to head back, she wanted to be human, she wanted to do normal things married couples do. They hadn't even been down to the beach yet. Everyone was bathing those days.

'It's getting too hot!' she complained. 'How about a half shandy at the Bankes' Arms, overlooking the bay?' *Let's be human, let's be real, let's be with the living, not the dead*, she thought.

Her lack of enthusiasm took the wind from Isambard's sails.

He leant upon his staff, pressing it against his temples. Brooded in his own shadow. She could feel him debating, gauging which way his path lay. He yearned to follow the call of the road, but his wife pulled too. Duty or destiny?

Yet weren't their paths aligned? Wasn't their destiny a shared one?

He scanned the landscape below for some clue. How did everything link up? He couldn't think straight now, his train of thought was derailed.

A mournful whistle blew from a passing engine in the fold of the valley.

'You're right, my dear, of course. How remiss of me. It is hot. Let us return. Forgive my selfishness.' Isambard looked disappointed, although he masked it with bluster. He went with Maud like an admonished schoolboy: to be the dutiful husband, to do what was proper.

From that point on he rarely spoke of his obsession. And, surely, it was in that moment the seed of their marriage's doom was sown. Yes, Maud was certain that was where the rift had started: right there, on Handfast Point − a hairline crack. And the fissure had widened on the Downs. And stayed with them. A secret meridian − inexorably dividing them − stretching through their lives.

Like the natural arch slowly being gouged by the bitterness of the sea, the gateway had been opened and would grow wider with the tides of their difference.

In her sickbed, Maud silently wept. And that was how Maggie found her. She had let herself in after school − calling around to see to her patient and to make her some tea. Seeing her friend in distress, face flushed with tears, she rushed to her side and cradled the shaking form shuddering with the after shocks of grief, rocking her gently, holding her hand.

'There, let it out. You're not alone. I'm here. You'll be alright now. Old Maggie will look after you.'

1 5

WATERSMEET

The fountains mingle with the river,
The river with the ocean.
The winds of Heaven mix together
With a sweet emotion.

Nothing in the world is single,
All things by a law divine,
In one another's being mingle —
Why not I with thine?

'Love's Philosophy', P B Shelley

May Day was fast approaching, and, although Maud was oblivious to the quickening of spring outside, the regenerative forces were quietly doing their work within. Yet she was still not quite right as rain, as Maggie would say. After two weeks 'cooped up in that poky house', as Archibald indelicately phrased it, who would be? She needed some fresh air and exercise — and he had just the ticket.

'I ruined your holiday, so how about another? Allow an old fool a chance to redeem himself.'

Her brother-in-law still felt guilty about what had happened at Avebury, and she still felt sore about it too.

'What about one last jaunt before the summer term? Consider it compensation.'

Maud resisted the idea at first, but she knew she needed it, to get her strength back and to blow away those damned cobwebs.

Archibald arranged everything. They were to stay at the Shelley Hotel in Lynmouth. Maud was in no position to refuse — she was too weak. All the fight had gone out of her. She had sunken inside herself — within a carapace of taciturn immobility. The dilemma had crushed her — whether to accept Archibald's advances or to carry on mourning her husband. Life or death — her choices were no less stark.

The school was appeased. Nubi was given to Mrs Mulligan again.

And they set off.

She spent the journey in Archibald's Silver Ghost in a daze, not taking in the rolling scenery as it transformed from the chalk Downs to the lush vales of Dorset and Devon, and on to the bleak beauty of Exmoor. Stumpy ponies appeared in the foglights. Maud fretted they were going to knock one over – or break down and be at the mercy of the elements. Even in her blanket the damp clung to her bones like a ghost seeking warmth.

'Don't worry, Maud – the old lady hasn't let me down yet. Touch wood.' Archibald tapped the dashboard.

Maud was relieved when the car finally descended between the folds of the coast into a tree-lined gorge, which the narrow road followed down precipitously to the tiny fishing village of Lynmouth, almost Alpine in its dramatic setting, looked over by its less frivolous cousin, Lynton, on the cliffs above.

Archibald had booked them adjoining rooms in the homely surroundings of Shelley's Hotel. The manager was keen to point out that the poet and his young bride had stayed there on their honeymoon.

'Harriet – his first bride,' Maud noted coolly. Whatever Archibald hoped, she would never marry again.

After they had refreshed themselves from their long drive and settled in, they enjoyed a Devonshire cream tea, which they walked off along the quayside bustling with May day visitors. They marvelled at the water-powered lift up to Lynton, and agreed to experience it themselves the following day – after Archibald had taken her 'somewhere special'.

Maud did not want to appear ungracious and complain – because although some peace and privacy wouldn't go amiss, this little break in such a beautiful place was just what she needed. The very air seemed charged with energy, revitalising her. It was indeed the charming place Archibald had promised it would be – she had to give him some credit, and that evening over a dinner of fresh sea bass she acquiesced to his infectious good humour and played the agreeable companion.

The sky was overcast when they set out in the morning, but this didn't dampen Archibald's spirits. He was positively beaming, an excited schoolboy eager to share his secret discovery. The place he was going to take her was very special to him – although he did not say why. It would 'spoil it' for her. He wanted Maud to experience it pure – without any connotations. And walking along the riverside between the towering banks of trees it was easy to imagine a primordial innocence. Beyond the village it could have been a scene from the dawn of time.

The sides of the gorge rose higher and higher, festooned with languid growth – trees sagging with gravity, draped with creepers, writhing from moss-covered rocks. Maud and Archibald followed the riverside path, picking their way among the boulders that punctuated the banks. For a while they walked in silence, overwhelmed by the majesty of the scene – as though tiptoeing past giants. The whispering of the river and the wind through the trees was sufficient. Maud began to feel at ease, feeling the burden of the last few days begin to lift.

Archibald had been struggling on valiantly, but now stopped and mopped his brow, gesturing with his cane like a tourist guide, or a magician with a wand who had just conjured it all up.

'Magnificent, isn't it?'

'Yes, it's lovely. Are you alright there? Would you like a hand?'

'Oh, that's kind of you. This leg still plays me up. Take pity on an old war-horse, eh?'

He reached out an arm and she hooked hers through his, a little awkward with the contact, but knowing it would be churlish to refuse – war-wound or no. And it had to be said, though she felt uncomfortable to acknowledge it, he had been a generous and often considerate companion.

Together they ambled up the riverside path in agreeable silence. Now and again Archibald would stop and point out some feature – a tree twisted like a Rackham dryad, or a rocky pinnacle shaped like a face. It seemed the whole forest was eavesdropping upon them, and Maud became increasingly agitated that someone was watching them. Archibald noticed her discomfort and paused.

'What is it?' His brows beetling, a slightly peevish tone in his voice.

'Oh, it's silly.' Maud brushed her fears away, suddenly foolish under his scrutiny.

'Come come – something's up. I can sniff it. I would hate for anything to be bothering you.'

Or him, Maud thought.

'Well, it's just that I feel someone's watching us.'

Archibald nearly guffawed, but stopped himself. 'Fear not – I will defend you!' he joked. When he saw her flush with embarrassment, his tone changed, became conspiratorial. 'You know, I felt the same thing in the jungle but in that case there usually was someone watching us, with a gun, a spear or a poison dart.'

'Stop it, Archie – you're making me nervous!'

'Then hold tight, my sweet sister-in-law. You're in no danger with me around. This old soldier still has some fight left in him!' He challenged the trees with his cane. The noise startled a heron perched on the other side of the river – it had been so still they had not noticed it. Thin and silent, it took wing – flying around the bend in the gorge, upriver.

Maud was startled for a moment – first by the movement, then by the sight of the heron. She had seen that bird before, only she couldn't place where. It was an omen. Was it warning her, or did it want them to follow?

'That was the culprit. I wish I had my old Winchester to bag it.'

Maud bridled at the thought of this, stopping in her tracks in protest, arms folded. She could not articulate what the bird meant to her, but she knew it was not game for Archie's gun!

'Come along, my dear – we'll never make it back for lunch at this rate.'

Over-riding all concerns was the state of Archibald's stomach – his actions were dictated by how full or empty it was, and all had to toe the line.

Maud sighed. The river eroded her brittleness. So on they carried, following the windings of the gorge – the river a gigantic serpent that they pursued to its lair. The roaring grew louder and more ominous as they made their way along the precarious footpath which rose and fell through the layers of the wood – sometimes the river frothed at their feet, other times it was a hundred feet down and one slip and they would meet it. Maud found herself holding on to Archibald more and more for her own support and safety. Despite his lame leg, her guide was sure-footed and showed no fear – in fact he seemed to be thoroughly enjoying this 'jungle trek', as he called it.

Her edginess grew, until she jumped at the slightest sound.

At one point she slipped, grabbing his arm just in time, but dislodging a rock. They watched it tumble down into the gorge below, where it vanished with a splash.

'Watch your step.'

'Thank you,' she replied, shaken, for once grateful he was there.

'Would you like a sip?' Archibald had produced his hip-flask and offered her a drop. 'It might steady your nerves.'

'But not my feet. No thanks.'

'Suit yourself.' And he took a swig.

So they continued for half an hour, the sky darkening above, threatening to break at any moment, casting an oppressive pall over the whole gorge. The pressure on Maud's temples grew and she knew a migraine was coming on.

'How far is it?'

'Nearly there — just around the next bend. It'll be worth it — believe me.'

They descended a sloping track until they came to a stout wooden bridge crossing the narrowing river. The water flowed faster here — they were nearing the source — the 'birthplace of the Lyn' as Archibald deemed it.

And then there it was — up ahead the gorge split and from both channels flowed the rivers, which merged where two bridges met.

'Watersmeet,' declared Archibald.

On the left bank a Tudor-style hunting lodge sat snugly beneath a sheltering cedar. Walkers sat on the balcony, taking tea.

Archibald waved at them and led Maud across the narrow bridge to the arrowhead of land between the rivers — a steep promontory of rock.

'This is amazing,' said Maud.

'What did I tell you? Splendid, isn't it? And here we stand, between two rivers — where the waters meet.'

Maud gazed down into the co-mingling waters — trying to discern the point at which they joined. There was something magical about this place — just standing there one imbibed its alchemy.

'Thank you, Archie! This is —' Words failed her. She climbed down to the water's edge and placed her hand in the fast-flowing current — cupping it and holding the shining water aloft. Two rivers merged and made a third. This young river was their unruly child — one could almost feel its childish tantrums and infectious energy. Maud's senses tingled. Her headache seemed to clear. She had never felt more alive.

'Wait until you see the waterfall! Follow me.'

Archibald wanting attention again — but her curiosity was aroused — she loved waterfalls, ever since as a girl she used to play in Langley Beck when taken to Macclesfield by her father.

Lifting her long skirt, she climbed back up to the path — taking Archibald's hand as he hauled her up. With a gleam in his eye he led her around the rock edge where the roaring was loudest and there they beheld a sight that made Maud gasp in delight. A waterfall cascaded down a tumble of rocks in a rainbow-filled dell. What little sunlight there was seemed caught there in a pool. Perfect for a water spirit, thought Maud. She could just imagine one sitting on a little rock ledge, cooling her legs, clothed in a veil of fine spray.

'Archie – this is delightful!' Maud suddenly felt like a little girl again, and scampered up the side of the cataract before her guide could stop her.

'Be careful – it's dangerous!' warned Archibald.

'Oh don't be such an old maid! I would play in a place like this as a young girl without a second thought.' And she did indeed look naturally agile and in her element on those rocks. For the first time in longer than she could remember a broad grin spread across her face and she felt impishly young at heart.

There was a break in the clouds. A shaft of sunlight pierced the gorge. Then she saw the heron above the waterfall – sitting to one side, looking at her. Maud had to steady herself. She froze and gazed upriver, to a wood bathed in a summery light, like another world. The river must flow straight off the moor – wild open country, not at all like the secluded mystery of the dell. Its untamed expanse called to her.

The heron looked enigmatically at Maud – forming a question mark with its body. What was it asking? Maud wanted to understand it. Archibald was rattling on, but his voice merged with the white noise of the water. All that mattered was Maud and the heron. What was its question? Did Maud have to make a choice? Was that it? Two rivers, two lives – which one did she choose? A new life with Archibald, or a living death with Isambard? Companionship or honour? Was she going to spend the rest of her life mourning and following her husband's ghost – or was she going to take this second chance offered her, and enjoy life once more, rejoin the human race? Her migraine returned, as the pressure in the sky built. She rubbed her temples. If only she could think straight – but the roaring of the waterfall, the chatter of Archibald prevented her.

'Maud, what is it? What's wrong?' He seemed a million miles away – small and ridiculous. And Maud could finally see clearly what his game was: he had brought her here not to help her recover, but to seduce her. He had failed at Avebury but here she was at his mercy. He had cornered her, hunted her down while she was weak. It would be so easy to go with him now – to walk hand-in-hand back down the river. But what if she went against the flow? What if she went *up* river?

The waters did not have to meet.

The heron took off and flew along the green tunnel of light. Maud watched it diminish into the distance. Her vision telescoped, her head throbbed – but she knew what she must do.

'Maud? Come back – I can't reach you up there.'

She would go where he would never reach her again. Maud decided her path – she wanted her own way. She did not want to be forced into making such choices. Why did everything have to be about what the men in her life wanted? Perhaps there was another way.

She would leave him tomorrow – she would let him take her up into Lynton on the lift, then she would arrange her own transport. Where could she go? It did not matter – she would find somewhere, deciding in her own time, on her own terms.

'I want to go back, Archibald. I want be by myself for while.'

16

THE SEA HARP

And what if all of animated nature
Be but organic harps diversely framed
That tremble into thought, as o'er them sweeps,
Plastic and vast, one intellectual breeze,
At once the soul of each, and God of all?
But thy more serious eye a mild reproof
Darts, O belovèd woman! nor such thoughts
Dim and unhallowed dost thou not reject,
And biddest me walk humbly with my God.

'The Eolian Harp: composed at Clevedon', S T Coleridge

The sea breeze scoured all cares from her. Its sad tune ebbed and flowed like the waves it summoned, expiring with a desultory sigh as they were abandoned, again and again. The tide was withdrawing, leaving slimy rocks, strewn with seaweed and ship-litter. The rain rolled in from the leaden waters of the Severn estuary, grey and windswept on this Saturday in May.

Maud walked along the promenade, passing the determined holidaymakers, ignoring the drizzle. Excited children with lollipops, grandmothers and young girls, courting couples, veterans proudly parading with their medals, or being wheeled along in Bath chairs, limbless, hollow-eyed, drooling. A brass band played on the octagonal bandstand; people nodded off in deck-chairs under umbrellas to the torpid tunes.

A chapbook seller stood in the rain, talking of God: 'Jesus said, "Here I am!" I stand at the door and knock. If anyone hears my voice and opens the door, I will come in and eat with him and he with me.' Seeing Maud, the man handed her a piece of coarse paper with these words badly printed on them:

As the hart panteth after the fountains of water, so my soul
panteth after Thee, O God! When shall I come and appear before

the face of God? My tears have been my bread day and night,
while they say to me daily: Where is thy God?

Maud read the words and wandered on alone, the phrase 'Where is thy God?' haunting her. The screams of the seagulls seemed to accuse her. *Where? Where?*

Further on, a young man took a long drink from the gothic drinking fountain, wiping his lips and dabbing his face under his straw boater with a handkerchief. He looked up and Maud looked away. She could not catch anyone's eye that morning – in case they saw her pain.

Although leaving Archibald in Lynmouth was the right thing to do, she was feeling drained and vulnerable. Each encounter with him had worn her down, leaving her more naked and exposed. The sea-spray rubbed salt into her wounds – but felt good, cauterising them – making her wet, cold and numb.

This would not do, this would not do at all – she had to sort herself out! She picked at her thoughts like a beachcomber. What was the best thing to do? Which way should she turn? She walked along the promenade, seemingly a casual visitor, but she was just going through the motions. She wasn't really alive – so why should she be with the living? It was she who was the ghost.

Maud's absent-minded wanderings eventually brought her to the famous pier – an elegantly ornate wrought-iron structure, delicate in comparison with the stodgy buildings.

Paying thruppence, she walked along the wooden boarding that swarmed with well-dressed visitors walking arm in arm, rubbing shoulders with fishermen in their rough wool sweaters and sou'westers, who were impaling bait on hooks, gutting and slicing fish, weighing their catch, smoking pipes. The stench of fish and tobacco made her cough – but a fresh gust from the sea replenished her lungs.

Maud passed a young lady in a red hat sitting and watching the world go by in a demure manner, nodding and waving to people occasionally. Young men noticed her and offered her cigarettes, but she was scornful of her suitors – she could pick and choose, the world at her feet. 'Annie Cord! Annie Cord!' they called out, like some incantation, hoping she would grant them a boon.

Engraved beneath the lamps that marked the pier at regular intervals was the inscription '1868, RJ Warm & JW Grover,

Engineers'.

A year before Isambard was born.

From the end of the pier wafted jazz music. It reminded her of the time Isambard had brought her here on a second honeymoon, attempting to revive the romance. They had danced on the pier then, young and foolish things.

Maud watched a young couple on the corner of the pier, by the telescope. The man placed a coin in the machine and allowed his lady to look through – as she did so he produced a small box from his pocket and displayed its contents in front of the telescope – the young woman shrieked in delight as she realised what it was. The suitor knelt on one knee and murmured something to her. She fluttered a handkerchief, blushing and faint, but nodded. The man leaped to his feet and hugged her close, then stepped back and slipped the ring onto her finger, kissing her again. The audience who had gathered for this drama now clapped and the couple realised they had been observed by the people in the tea-room above. The young man bowed and proudly presented his fiancée, who held her ring aloft in delight.

The band suddenly struck up 'Here Comes the Bride' and the couple were persuaded to dance. Maud tried to ignore the celebration and fixed her gaze on the horizon.

To the left the two tiny islets of Steep Holm and Flat Holm could be seen, guarding the entrance to the estuary like the Symplegades. A flag snapped on its pole in the brisk breeze, keeping its own time. Barry Island and the smoke stacks of Port Talbot could be discerned through the haze on the other side of the estuary. Wales was a dark line along the horizon. The wind whispered to her, *hiraeth ... hiraeth ...* yet what did she long for? A lover? Solitude? Independence? Peace? Death? Or rebirth?

She did not want Archibald, but she did not want Isambard either. What did she want? What did she want?

Then it came to her on a sea breeze:

Her own way.

She wanted to choose her own path. Not to be dictated to by men. Not to walk in their footsteps or in fear of their shadow. She wanted her own path, her own life, a freedom to choose her own destiny like the Suffragettes, her sisters in the struggle. Yet should she have to chain herself to railings to be free? Was there another way?

A scruffy young boy, perhaps eight years old, was watching an

approaching paddle steamer with great excitement; following its
progress to the end of the pier, where it would disgorge and pick up
passengers. It was *Ravenswood*, he called out excitedly to one of the
fishermen. Of P&A Campbell's White Funnel Fleet, Maud could now
see as it gently nosed into position, a stately old queen of the Severn,
steam billowing from its two tall funnels, a hooter sending gulls
outraged in its wake. 'That's right, Tibbs,' replied the fisherman with
a slow eye. 'Same as usual, the 5.30 Severn cruise, regular as
clockwork.'

The urchin carried on up the pier, scrounging titbits from the
fishermen, who ruffled his hair or tolerated him, only to shout out as
he ran off with something, their anger soon melting into laughter and
the shake of a head, white-bearded like the waves crashing in.

Maud felt that the whole structure was unsteady and would cast
adrift at any moment – or was it her own legs which seemed weak?
She felt light-headed and had to sit down for a moment, the ground
rocking beneath her – she could see the swell of the tide through the
cracks of the boarding, which made her feel even more nauseous.
The world reeled around her and the seagulls screamed.

'Are you alright, dear?' a kind-looking lady asked. 'You don't look
too well.'

'I'm fine, really.' Maud took a gulp of air. 'I just need to sit for a
moment.'

'Come and have a cup of tea – out of this wind.'

Maud nodded, and the lady guided her.

At the end of the pier a bowler-hatted jazz band bravely played
'Sunny Side of the Street' in the stinging sea breeze. Holidaymakers
huddled in the shelters with their cakes and tea. Maud was led up
some steps to the little enclosed tea-room – a glass box out of the
rain with lead light panels high up and a view overlooking the little
bay embraced by two arms of rock. It was good to be out of the driving
rain.

'Here, take a seat and I'll get you a cuppa.'

Maud watched the old lady walked to the counter. It could have
been Martha. It should have been her mother. But she was alone in
the world and had to sort things out for herself.

The hooter blasted out and the *Ravenswood* pushed off, heading
upriver, making its own way against the flow – as she would do,
determined to forge her own destiny.

There, on the end of Clevedon Pier it was decided. Maud would face her problems head on – she could 'run like rain' no longer. She had reached the end of the line. She would deal with Archibald, and exorcise the ghost of her husband once and for all. She would not let him suffer any longer.

She had never felt more resolved in her life. It was as though she had been asleep until that moment. Maud vowed then and there – to the cold grey sea – that she would free her husband's spirit, and her own. She would be played by others no longer.

17

The Lordly Ones

Come away, O human child!
To the waters and the wild
With a faery, hand in hand,
For the world's more full of weeping than you can understand.

'The Stolen Child', W B Yeats

After Maud's return to Eastbourne, life got in the way of her plans. After her prolonged absence from school she had a lot of catching up to do. Yet she felt refreshed and determined. Her recent experiences had stripped her down – revealing a core of rock-like conviction. She had found her centre again. Yet many things remained a mystery. Her entire world had been shaken to its foundations by the encounter in West Kennet.

Death, it seemed, was not the end. Matter was not all. Spirit inhabited flesh, and persisted in some form after its destruction. If there was a spiritual dimension to life – then what of a creator? Perhaps God had not died after all.

Her husband had somehow survived – yet it seems she was responsible for keeping him on this plane. Her inability to complete the grieving process properly and let him go had trapped him in the No Man's Land between life and death. She had to release him, she was the wind-lass Isambard had searched for – through the key of her song she could lock or unlock the gates. All she had to do was be at the Long Man at Samhain. If she could find out when or what Samhain was! So many questions ...

She wasn't going to find any answers in Eastbourne. The local library yielded no results, and after a couple of weeks of fruitless efforts Maud nearly gave up hope of ever finding any clues. In the fever of end-of-year exams it all seemed like so much fairy dust.

Then one day Maud noticed an advertisement in the *Evening Standard* for a talk by Sir Arthur Conan Doyle, the famous author, on 'The Coming of the Fairies' at the Theosophical Institute in London.

It was a promotional event for the book of the same name, released late the previous year, and Maud imagined him preaching to his converted fans. The whole Cottingley photographs affair seemed no more than a nine-day wonder to Maud, yet interest in it and the 'little people' did not seem to want to go away – it had tapped into something, a consoling fiction in times grim for most. In the aftermath of the Great War, and with the economy flagging, people were trying to find any consolation they could.

In the Whitsun holidays Maud caught the London train and headed to the Theosophical Institute on the Strand. It was a dreamy sun-dappled June day.

The city was brimming with the usual hustle and bustle, but the sunshine made everything like a great dance. She passed a theatre where J M Barrie's *Peter Pan* was playing, and in the hazy light of the afternoon it was easy to imagine even the plane trees of London crowded with otherworldly life, like Blake had envisioned as a child. Medieval monks questioned how many angels could fit on the end of a pin. Was it a merely theological conundrum? Such infinitesimal angels seemed no different than fairies, yet they seemed of another order entirely. Certainly Maud's vision of otherworldly life conflicted with the twee images that had caused so much controversy.

The large hall was filled with people – housewives, widows, critics, mystics, veterans, admirers, hecklers, Sherlock Holmes buffs in deerstalkers, and fey middle-aged women in colourful scarves.

Maud sidled along her row, reminded of the séance in Eastbourne. She had to suppress a smile.

Either side of the stage on billboards were adverts for the book *The Coming of the Fairies* in big letters. There was movement at the back of the stage and the hubbub died down. The lights were dimmed and the spotlights flooded the stage. To everyone's disappointment, Gardner, the Secretary of the Theosophical Society, appeared – an excitable balding man with no stage presence. He was delighted to see so many visitors. Eager to seize the opportunity to proselytise, he went about explaining the tenets of theosophy in a workmanlike way, reading from crib cards. He concluded triumphantly: 'In this twentieth century there is promise of the world stepping out of some of its darker shadows. Maybe it is an indication that we are reaching the silver lining of the clouds when we find ourselves suddenly presented with actual photographs of these enchanting little creatures – relegated long since to the realm of the imaginary and fanciful.'

After a murmur of excitement from the auditorium, he said, 'It is my great pleasure to welcome our esteemed guest, the finest ambassador of theosophy in Britain, Sir Arthur Conan Doyle!'

To rapturous applause Doyle finally appeared − immaculately dressed in a tweed suit, a middle-aged man with a well-groomed moustache and silver head of hair. He had a dignified presence and a commanding tone.

'Of all the teachings and philosophies in Western lands I know none save that ancient teaching now called theosophy which has any place in it for elemental forms of life, or what are commonly known as "fairies". With the Cottingley photographs we have at last proof of their existence. That is my conviction, and experts have stated they can see no trace of forgery in them. As Holmes says "Improbable as it is, all other explanations are more improbable still." But let us examine the evidence, so you may draw your own conclusions.'

The audience hushed in anticipation as the curtains were drawn and the lights were dimmed. This was what they had come to see. Doyle nodded to Gardner, who operated a photographic slide projector − dust and cigarette smoke swirling in its beam like minute forms of life.

The first Cottingley photograph appeared, dating from July 1917. It showed the younger girl, Frances, a garland of flowers in her hair, standing against the bank of the beck − the waterfall flowing twenty feet behind her to the left. In front of her danced a cluster of six 'fairies'.

The audience gasped or guffawed. They seemed so blatantly fake to Maud that it was absurd − something one of her Lewes girls would do. In fact, it might make a good art activity. She admired the skill and enterprising spirit of the two friends. Apparently, they were the first photographs they had ever taken.

The second one from September in the same year showed Elsie in a long white dress seated on grass on a September day playing with a 'gnome' holding tiny pipes. The plate was badly exposed and produced more sounds of incredulity. The faithful kept silent.

The third showed Frances again, three years later, in August 1920, with a 'leaping fairy' caught in mid-flight. The face of the girl was blurred but the fairy was in sharp focus.

The penultimate one was even more theatrical, showing Elsie in her late teens, with make-up and Pre-Raphaelite hair. She looked more like Isadora Duncan than a Yorkshire maiden, thought Maud. It was a mid-shot from the waist up. Light streamed from behind into the wooded glade. A 'fairy' hovering before her offered Elsie a posy of harebells. One had to admire the skill of this, and the audience murmured in appreciation.

The final one was built up to be the most remarkable, but the slide was a grey smudge. It was apparently depicting a fairies' 'sunbath' – 'where they recharge themselves', Doyle explained. However, it was too dark to make anything out other than foliage. It could have been any sunny day in a forest.

The gentle strobing of the slides lulled Maud into a semi-hypnotic state. She started to drift off and found herself thinking about her own childhood. The images of the two girls' rural idyll reminded her of her own blissful days playing at Langley Beck when she had visited Macclesfield with her father. Had she felt a presence then? The place was certainly magical to the impressionable mind of a young girl – butterflies dancing in the sunbeams. A lonely child – having no companion to play with there – she made up imaginary companions such as a talking squirrel called 'Tosky'. She had been told not to stay late – otherwise the fairies might catch her. She recalled a time when she had stayed later than usual – dusk had fallen around her. Then with a thrill of fear, she had thought, *The fairies will catch me*, and in that moment she felt certain they would. A doorway seemed to open – yet nothing had come through. Maud went home and never felt anything like it again. She grew up as a good Christian girl, married and led a normal modest life on the straight and narrow – until God died that day her husband was taken from her. Surely she was in the same boat as everyone else in this hall.

The lights were raised and the curtains opened, flooding the room with summer light. The phantoms conjured were banished, made absurd again in the clear light of day. Maud felt she was not the only one awakening from a rêverie, a summer's day dream.

In a cut-glass stentorian voice of one used to giving lecture tours Doyle began to draw his conclusions: 'I must confess that after months of thought I am unable to get the true bearings upon this epoch-making event. Yet one or two consequences are obvious. The experiences of children will be taken more seriously. And these little folk who appear to be our neighbours, with only some small difference in vibration to separate us, will become familiar. The thought of them, even when unseen, will add a charm to every brook and valley and give romantic interest to every country walk.'

Maud suddenly riled at this – stood up and to everyone's consternation, interrupted Doyle.

'Ridiculous! Try being charmed or romanced when a six-feet spectre appears before you! They are not little people – it is *we* who have diminished!'

A gasp of surprise and disgust, followed by jeers and heckles.

'Sit down, woman!'

Maud nearly collapsed under the onslaught of withering looks, sniggers, and journalists scribbling. The room spun about her. She fell back in her chair, but a hand with silver rings was there to assist her.

'Well said. Here, take this.' A soft Irish voice from behind, reminding her of Maggie. She turned around and saw her ally.

The presence of a man with green eyes reassured her somehow. He was smiling at her and offering his handkerchief. It smelled of lavender, and cleared her head.

'Thank you,' she said weakly.

Maud looked at the man, and his strange eyes. Who was he? Yet the noise was too great to converse at length. The ensuing clamour threatened to end the proceedings, but Doyle appealed for calm.

Like a skilled politician, the writer spoke in an appeasing tone – seemingly agreeing with Maud's point of view. 'Mr David Gow, editor of the theosophical journal *Light*, first formed the opinion that fairies were simply human spirits, seen, as it were, at the wrong end of a clairvoyant telescope.' He tried to catch her eye across the crowded room.

Maud conceded the point, not feeling capable of matching the master orator in debate. It was possible, if any of it was. Yet the spirit of Isambard had not looked diminished. If anything, he appeared larger. But it was a good enough sop for the audience and so, warming to his subject, Doyle delved deeper.

He talked of amphibious creatures 'who may dwell unseen and unknown in the depths of the waters, and then some day be spied sunning themselves upon a sandbank. Something of this sort may exist in our psychic arrangements. One can imagine that there is a dividing line, like the water edge; this line depending upon what we vaguely call a higher rate of vibrations.'

Doyle paused to let this sink in. Some people looked slightly bemused, but were too embarrassed to ask for elaboration. Many gazed on admiringly.

It was like a room full of acolytes, thought Maud; unquestioning of the wisdom of their master. Perhaps the more sceptical were just giving Doyle enough rope to hang himself with. They waited in the wings, ready to swoop with acerbic sarcasm.

Doyle seemed oblivious. A man in love with the sound of his own voice, he continued: 'When Columbus knelt in prayer upon the edge of America, what prophetic eye saw all that a new continent might do to affect the destinies of the world? We also seem to be on the edge of a new continent, separated not by oceans but by subtle and surmountable psychic conditions. Might those little creatures suffer from the contact and some future Las Casas bewail their ruin? If so, it would be an evil day when the world defined their existence. But there is a guiding hand in the affairs of man, and we can but trust and follow.'

There was a wave of anticipation, as if Doyle himself were a guide leading them to a lost world.

'Are you Professor Challenger?' sneered a reporter from the back.

There was an outburst of laughter, jeers and catcalls. Gardner stood up and appealed for calm.

'Would the gentleman reserve his queries – however ill-founded – until the end!'

Doyle looked down on them like a headmaster, his glare of contempt reducing the hall to silence once more.

The pall of cigarette smoke was making it intolerably stuffy. Maud was finding it difficult to breathe. She twisted on her seat in discomfort. She would not be able to leave without causing a fuss. People were jammed in right to the doors. She hoped the talk had almost finished. At any moment she would surely faint.

'The recognition of the existence of these creatures will jolt the material twentieth-century mind out of its heavy ruts in the mud, and will make it admit that there is a glamour and a mystery to life.'

Thunderous applause drowned out the hecklers. Doyle bowed slightly, smoothed his moustache and sat down by the lectern, taking a sip of water.

Gardner appeared again. 'We thank our esteemed guest speaker for his fascinating talk. There will now follow a session of questions and answers, followed by a chance to purchase a signed copy of the book.'

A weasel-faced journalist stood up and asked Doyle what he thought of the fact that the older girl, Elsie, had worked in a photographic studio – retouching photographs!

Doyle sighed heavily. 'To accuse these innocent girls of such subterfuge is more indicative of our cynical times than of their guilt. These photographs have been scrutinised by experts in the field, and none can detect any trace of forgery or trickery. To suggest so would imply these girls are cleverer than the finest minds of the Empire. Yet it is their very innocence which has made them suitable recipients for such a manifestation. They had no intention of sharing the photographs. Initially they were taken only to prove to their father the veracity of their claims.'

Another journalist asked, in a mocking tone, whether all spiritualists believed in fairies.

Doyle responded to his accuser with a caveat: 'Let me emphasise that this whole subject of the objective existence of a subhuman form of life has nothing to do with the larger and far more vital question of spiritualism. I should be sorry if my arguments in favour of the latter should be in any way weakened by my exposition of this very strange episode, which has really no bearing upon the continued existence of the individual soul. The fairy question is infinitely small and unimportant compared with the question of our own fate and that of the whole human race.'

'Mr Doyle, may I make an observation?' Gardner interrupted, looking very agitated.

Doyle nodded.

'On Slieve-na-mon, one of the sacred hills of the Emerald Isle, I have observed ranks of elementals ranging up the slopes in increasing order and size. But the space around the summit is sacred to the great green angels who have watched there for more than two thousand years, guarding one of the centres of living force that link the past to the future of that mystic land of Erin. Taller far than the height of a man, these giant forms, in colour like the first new leaves of spring, look forth over the world with wondrous eyes that shine like stars.'

Gardner became aware at last that the room had grown very quiet and his voice very loud. In an apologetic tone, he muttered, 'One realises very fully the power and importance of the hidden side of things when one beholds such spectacle as that.'

Awkward silence ensued. The secretary sat down.

'Thank you, Mr Gardner. Now may we move on? Next question.'

A fey-looking lady asked if Doyle thought the appearance of fairies was a sign from beyond.

Doyle nodded. 'We have had continued messages at séances for some time that a visible sign was coming through.'

A smart journalist stood up, and twirled his pencil. 'Sir Arthur, would you say the tragic loss of your son to pneumonia five years ago was instrumental in your conversion to spiritualism?'

There was an awkward silence. Doyle visibly subdued his rage, and in a controlled tone answered, 'Those who conjecture, sir, need to establish the facts first! Kingsley was taken from us in 1918 – two years after my so-called 'conversion'. My turning to theosophy was not a Damascus-like revelation, or a seeking for consolation, but a logical process, based upon the available evidence. If, having eliminated all the possible explanations for the life of the soul, only the impossible remained, then that is the only answer there is. In my book I am not talking of spirit return, where seventy years of close observation has given us some sort of certain and defined laws, but rather of those fairy and phantom phenomena that have been endorsed by so many ages, and still even in these material days seem to break into some lives in the most unexpected fashion.'

The audience applauded, and even Maud thought this was a salient point and calmed down.

'The matter does not bear directly upon the more vital question of our own fate and that of those we have lost – but anything that extends man's mental horizons, and proves to him that matter as we have known it is not really the limit of our universe, must have a good effect in breaking down materialism and leading human thought to a broader spiritual level.'

More challenges from the floor – from journalists:

'Sir, some of my readers may wonder whether the author of the great detective has also slipped into opium addiction like his fictional creation! Could this explain such fanciful notions?'

'My soul is filled with a cold contempt for the muddle-headed indifference and the moral cowardice that I see around me! It almost seems to me that those wise entities who are conducting this campaign from the other side, and using some of us as humble instruments, have recoiled before that sullen stupidity.'

Supportive applause erupted from Doyle's fans, drowning out the journalists until, like Moses parting the Red Sea, Doyle gestured and the wave of noise subsided.

'Victorian science would have left the world hard, clean and bare, like a landscape on the moon; but this science is in truth but a little light in the darkness, and outside that limited circle of definite knowledge we see the loom and shadow of gigantic and fantastic possibilities around us, throwing themselves continually across our consciousness in such ways that it is difficult to ignore them.'

This received a standing ovation and Doyle ended the session there with a curt bow – while the advantage was his. In dramatic fashion, he swept off the stage. As chairs scraped and the audience chattered the secretary attempted to announce Sir Arthur would be signing copies in five minutes time.

As fans began to form a queue Maud headed for the exit. Journalists milled about the refreshment table. It was difficult to squeeze by the swarming crowd. Maud sensed the lingering hostility from some of the faithful, who had taken offence at her remark. She was just about to leave the hall when a man tapped her on the shoulder. 'Begging your pardon, madam.'

His swathe of thick black hair reminded Maud of her husband. Yet there was something otherworldy about him, as though he had stepped from another age. He wore a velvet jacket and a cravat, and leant upon a silver-tipped cane. She recognised him from earlier as the man who had lent her his handkerchief.

'My name is George Russell, although I like to be called "AE" – that's my nom de plume.'

Maud eyed him suspiciously. Not another crank, she thought.

'I'm a writer – a poet.'

Was she meant to look impressed? She tried to get by, but failed.

'I agree with what you said about the gentle folk, the *sidhe* as we call them in Ireland. They are in fact the Lordly Ones – the Tuatha De Danann, the aboriginal aristocracy, who were subsumed by later régimes and went underground. Into the hollow hills. The threshold of the Many-Coloured Land.'

Maud looked about, wondering if anyone else was hearing this. She felt uncomfortable talking about such things in public. She kept moving, but the man kept up with her. Outside, there was a little park to one side, with benches around a small fountain. It was an immense relief to be in the open again, and Maud gulped down the fresh air.

AE encouraged her to sit down. Something about his ardent manner and magnetic green eyes made her do so. Although she did not believe everything he was saying she felt that here was a kindred spirit reaching out to her.

Maud sat down on the bench. There were plenty of people about.

It felt safe enough. As pedestrians streamed past, she sat back and listened – aware of the bird-filled trees, the sunlight on the bubbling water.

AE spoke again: 'Sometimes lying on a hillside with the eyes of the body shut as in sleep I could see valleys and hills, lustrous as a jewel, self-shining, the colours brighter and purer, yet making a softer harmony together than the colours of the world I know...'

The fountain trickled soothingly. Starlings swooped down, splashed in its water.

'There, too, in that land I saw fountains as of luminous mist jetting from some hidden heart of power, and shining folk who passed into those fountains inhaled them and drew life from the magical air. They were, I believe, those who in the ancient world gave birth to legends of nymph and dryad. Their perfectness was like the perfection of a flower, a beauty that had never, it seemed, been broken by act of the individualised will which makes possible a choice between good and evil.'

Maud looked around her at the garden in a new light, sensing a numinous quality of the pollen-heavy roses. She liked the sound of the stranger's voice. His soft accent was reassuring. Were not Isambard's ancestors Irish? What was it that drew her to the Celtic? Was it a yearning to reconnect with the magic withdrawn from England's shores? Yet was not such magic there with them at that moment, even within the confines of a municipal park?

'Such a beauty begins to glow on us as we journey towards Deity, even as earth grows brighter as we journey from the gloomy pole to lands of the sun; and I see that glow upon you now!'

The haunting green eyes burned into her, and Maud felt that she herself was the seeker. But she had turned from the Divine. Only half a year ago she would have scorned such a statement. Yet had she not spent all of that time seeking?

And her quest was not over. She had to get to the Long Man at Samhain. She suddenly was inspired to ask this mysterious AE about it. Perhaps he would know.

'Do you know what "sowen" is?'

'Ah, a curious question. Samhain is Hallowe'en – or All Hallows' Eve. When the veil is thinnest and spirits, both mortal and immortal, can pass through.'

When the veil is thinnest – that was Isambard's phrase!

'It is a dangerous time to be abroad!' AE warned. 'The day after is the Celtic New Year — rebirth from the gate of death. Yet in Gaelic belief the souls of the dead do not perish, but journey to Tir na Og, the Land of the Ever Young. To one who lay on the mound which is called the Brugh on the Boyne a form like that the bards speak of as Angus appeared, and it cried, 'Can you not see me? Can you not hear me? I come from the Land of Immortal Youth!"

Maud got up to leave. AE took her hands and looked into her soul.

'The Golden World is all about us and that beauty is open to all, and none is shut out from it who will turn to it and seek for it.'

She thanked him, and left. Crossing the road she saw him still standing in the sun, looking up into the sky with a wide smile on his face, eyes closed in bliss.

Deep down she felt he was nearer the truth than Doyle. A year ago she would have felt otherwise.

Who was away with the fairies now? She had an appointment with one: *at Samhain*. So she had found her answer — but many more questions besides.

Maud walked along the Strand, trying to pull together the threads of her unravelling universe.

19

CURSUS

Yet, if you enter the woods
Of a summer evening late,
When the night-air cools on the trout-ringed pools
Where the otter whistles his mate,
(They fear no men in the woods,
Because they see so few.)
You will hear the beat of a horse's feet,
And the swish of a skirt in the dew,
Steadily cantering through
The misty solitudes,
As though they perfectly knew
The old lost road through the woods...
But there is no road through the woods.

'The Way Through the Woods', Rudyard Kipling

Back in Eastbourne Maud was determined to make sense of it all. In her husband's study she scoured the journals for reasons, explanations. What road had led her to this strange place? What had fascinated Isambard so much? If Maud had gleaned his method correctly, Isambard had decided that the correlation of four or more ancient landmarks designated an alignment. He marked them with crosses on his maps and drew lines between them.

Yet to Maud it seemed tenuous to connect sites from different eras just because they happened to be in a straight line, such as a Bronze Age barrow, a church, an ancient oak and a drovers' road – unless the alignments stretched through time ...

Could not the same principle be applied to their lives? Do we not weave a narrative from the seemingly random episodes of our life history? Telling the story of our selves – to ourselves – to make sense of the world.

Maud thought about the significant events in her life with Isambard: their meeting at Garsington; the day at Uffington; the proposal on Glastonbury Tor; the honeymoon at Old Harry; married life in Eastbourne; their first visit to the Long Man. Could not events, memories be landmarks, making an alignment through time?

So where did it start to fall apart?

Maud picked up the penultimate journal, dated 1913. The last year of peace ... Browsing, she stroked the pages, letting her fingers linger over the handwriting. These precious final entries were all she had left. The summary of a life.

She came across the entry for their trip to Stonehenge, and her blood went cold. *That was the day the shadow fell.* Bracing herself, Maud made a cup of tea and took it with the journal to the small garden out the back of the house. It needed some serious work. The grass was long and littered with flowers and weeds. At her side Nubi gnawed a bone contentedly.

Sitting in her sunchair, Maud began to read with a sense of dread:

21st June, 1913, Salisbury Plain
We parked up the old Bentley where the Wessex section of the Ridgeway intersects the Wincanton road, having set off from home at midnight. It was 4 a.m. and already the shortest night was ending – the darkness yielding to the steel of dawn. Yet all was still grey around us – and we looked like phantoms in the twilight in our long woollen coats. There was a chill in the air, worsened by the damp fog – and by Maud's mood. She had not relished the prospect of this field trip and had been sullen all the way in the car. Yet, with the coming of sunrise I hoped her spirits would lift. Even she must appreciate what we were about to behold. I let Nubi off his lead to let him have his run. He seemed more excited than Maud. As soon as he was free he bolted into the field of fog, to suddenly reappear in a different place as he ran in wide arcs around invisible obstacles. Then in the mist the mounds loomed. We were by the Winterbourne Stoke Barrow cemetery. Maud was slothful, but I insisted we got moving. It would warm us up, I said. Besides, we had our flask ready. Grabbing my stang, and my wife by the arm, we set off. I did not want to miss that sunrise!
We walked into the dew-strewn field, and immediately our legs became soaked. Only Nubi's tail was visible, wagging ahead like a guide with a brolly. Salisbury Plain stretched to our right, but the Stones were still not visible in the sea of fog. Using my

compass, I navigated us to the start of the cursus. A cluster of barrows marked its beginning. It was not much to look at, to be honest, but once we stood within its dip the channel became apparent. Nubi's tail had vanished, and now we could see why. He greeted us with a wet nose and shining eyes, then raced ahead in bounds.

As we walked along in a south-easterly direction I explained to Maud how the antiquarian Stukeley discovered the cursus in the middle eighteenth century. He thought it was a Roman racetrack, and so gave it the misnomer 'cursus', from 'circus'. Later thinking suggests these features are far older – one stretching across Dorset covers six miles. This one was far more modest, but its setting was more spectacular. As we walked along the mile-long groove we could finally see to our right, emerging from the mist, the tall grim ruin of Stonehenge. The morning fog erased any trace of the twentieth century. We could have been Neolithic pilgrims who had just traversed the Ridgeway and, after a weeks journey, finally arrived at our destination – to make offering to the gods on the real Midsummer's Day: the solstice. It was a thrilling sensation.

Maud was reminded of the climactic scene of Hardy's 'Tess of the D'Urbervilles'. Was she to be my sacrifice? she joked dourly.

With half an hour to go, we quickly made our way to the end of the cursus, feeling the quickening of dawn. In the trees of Normanton Down the birds sang their chorus. We walked along the line of beeches towards the Avenue – where we would make our final approach to the Stones. Among the trees, which Nubi inspected assiduously, were more barrows, and I was reminded of the exhibits I had seen in Devizes Museum that summer I walked the Wansdyke; exhibits from the Cunnington and Colt-Hoare excavations of the area.

What excited me the most was the so-called 'Bush Barrow Man' from Normanton Down itself – an extra-ordinary discovery, the richest Bronze Age grave burial in Britain! The man of high rank was buried with a gold diamond plate upon his chest, a gold buckle, a bronze axe, two large daggers, a mace of rare stone with zigzag bone inlay and a round milk-white stone, among other rings, flints and beads. It is suggested he could have been the engineer of Stonehenge – he is contemporary with the first phase of its construction, circa 1600-1500 BC.

I climbed on to a mound and imagined it was his very grave. I placed my stang respectfully on the ground and rested my brow against its Y – paying my respects to this man of vision. Then I gasped as a wave of déjà-vu came over me. I had been here before in another time, another life.

In a flash of revelation I felt I had found the missing piece of the puzzle of my existence. The millennia peeled as I realised: I had been that man! I was following in my ancestor's footsteps, surveying the land – ostensibly for the railway, but actually more and more for myself. Why else was I drawn to these ancient places? Not only to them; but to measure and map them? Finding alignments – perhaps not just over the land, but through time! How far back does it go? To Egypt? Atlantis?

The hollow roads – open to those who know how to navigate the locks.

I must find the key to this mystery. All this time I have been searching, yet still no success. I wanted to share my revelation with Maud, but she had walked ahead – oblivious of my discovery.

The Stones beckoned – we had to make it to the Hele Stone for sunrise. I descended the barrow, to Nubi's barking, and caught up with Maud. She had reached the gap in the trees formed by the Avenue. It is another processional route – this one taking us straight into the Stones. As soon as she ascertained that was my intended route, she struck out that way.

My mind was racing. I had to share with Maud my revelation.

'Maud, I've just had the most remarkable experience. I – I felt like I'd been here before. In a previous life … That perhaps I had been one of the architects of Stonehenge itself, or at least there at the time of its construction!'

She stopped dead.

'Reincarnation?' She looked at me incredulously.

'Maud, darling – we're going to miss the sunrise.' I implored.

She seemed not to hear me. It was as if she were looking at a stranger.

Shaking her head in disbelief she said, 'Isambard Kerne, if I didn't know you better I would think you were mad! But this latest hare-brained notion of yours really does take the biscuit.'

I challenged what she meant by 'hare-brained notion'. I did not like her tone at all.

She took a deep breath. Somewhere, a crow cawed.

If she had not been so cold and irritable perhaps she would have brushed it aside – 'Oh nothing, it doesn't matter' – but she had had enough. There, in the shadow of Stonehenge, she revealed what she thought of my 'ridiculous theories': 'Oh, insufferable man! You see lines on the land where there are none; look for meaning in nonsense.' She scanned the mist, then looked upwards. 'And what of God? Isambard, you're going down the Devil's Road – and it is a dead end.'

I tried to explain, to elaborate – but Maud cut in: 'There you go – rambling away on your hobby horse. What about me, Maud, your wife? I'm sick and tired of those straight lines – you impose them not only on nature, but on our life together.'

For some reason, Maud recalled our honeymoon. Apparently, that's when she first had her doubts.

'I knew I should have heeded the warning back then – trusted my instincts. But no, I stuck by you. All this time. Allowed you your indulgences and eccentricities. Even though I took second place to your obsession. But no more! You don't even remember our anniversary, do you?'

'Anniversary? What do you mean?' I could never follow her non sequiturs. Then I realised. Midsummer. Handfast Point. 'Oh, God. Maud. I'm so sorry. I knew it was a special day. Just forgot it was ours. Perhaps I am getting lost in my studies.'

'Lost in yourself! That's what it all comes back to, even when you realise you've forgotten our wedding day. That's why I agreed to come to this infernal place – hoping it was going to be an anniversary surprise. Something romantic. Not your bloody research!'

Nubi sensed the distress in her voice, our fierce body language, and began barking

Our altercation was interrupted by the sudden appearance of a figure in white – an old man in a chalky robe, wielding a staff. For the life of me he looked like a druid on that misty midsummer morning by Stonehenge. Then I saw the sheep manifest, like congealed clouds, around him – chaperoned by a sheepdog. They reminded me of the grey wethers on Fyfield Down. I noticed the man's staff was a crook. He was a shepherd. The Shepherd of Wiltshire Plain himself! We hailed him civilly, trying to act nonchalant about our argument, which he must have heard. There was no one else by the Stones that morning. I had heard druidic ceremonies took place at such times – but perhaps they were held in secret.

'Keep that dog of yours under control,' he warned in a Wiltshire drawl, but Nubi was more interested in the sheepdog than the sheep. He played a little with the other dog, then came back at my call. I put him on the lead, while the shepherd watched sternly. Then he nodded and passed silently with his flock into the mist once more.

Chastised by his graceful silence, we carried on awkwardly to the Hele Stone. When we reached it, we looked back along the Avenue to the north-east. The sun should have breached the horizon then, but if it did the mist obscured it. There was a sense of anticlimax, to say the least.

It should have felt a new day in Eden – instead it felt like the last. Maud walked off in disgust.

I leant on my stang in a brown study. It should have been a beautiful experience shared – instead it had turned into a nightmare.

I do not want such moments tainted by tantrums – I'd rather go to such places by myself than have them spoilt. Yes, from now on I will do just that.

Maud has had her chance. After thirteen years she still has not seen the light. She makes my research seem pointless, my theories worthless. Am I seeing lines where there are none? Yet what is marriage but a mutual act of make-believe? If you no longer believe in it, then the invisible threads that hold us to one another cease to be. If alignments are imaginary, then why not all of the ties that bind us? Isn't our whole world constructed of imaginary lines? Borders and rules, relationships and connections, ties and chains … All imposed by man, all artificial. One has to respect them all, or dismiss the lot. The world we have created is either meaningful, or meaningless. Like the Stones, it is a house of cards that could so easily topple.

Maud put down the journal. It was one of the last entries. After that he had withdrawn completely into his own world, becoming an obsessive recluse, not sharing anything of his internal life with her. He had kept it all for his precious journals.

They never really made up after that.

She wished she had said something – but it was her husband who had needed to apologise and he never did. The split was too deep.

Their love had died that day. On the anniversary of their marriage. The fault-line created at Handfast Point had finally spilt them apart.

And the next year her husband was taken from her before they'd had a chance to patch things up.

Nine years later she was still picking up the pieces.

Well, it seemed she had once last chance to redeem their relationship. At the Long Man at Samhain.

She had failed her husband in life, but she would not fail him in death. She had followed him this far. Now she would retrace his last journey – to France and Belgium. For nine years she had scrimped and saved. For once she deserved to treat herself. The last few months had stirred a wanderlust in her that she had not known she possessed. Yet this was no holiday. She owed it to Isambard. She needed to go to the places where he had last walked the earth, and to where he had disappeared. To see for herself, to understand and to accept. Perhaps there she would finally find an ending.

1 9

The Long Stones

When I set out for Lyonesse,
A hundred miles away,
The rime was on the spray,
And starlight lit my lonesomeness
When I set out for Lyonesse
A hundred miles away.

'When I set out for Lyonesse', Thomas Hardy

Maud stood on the deck of the ferry in the warm morning sunlight –
savouring the sharp lash of salt spray in her face. It was the end of
July and the beginning of the school holidays. She had decided to
visit the continent – retracing her husband's last steps from Brittany
to Belgium, and to give herself a sabbatical. Life had become so
serious lately. Truly, it had been for the last nine years, but she felt
she had reached a watershed. The problem had surfaced and she had
resolved to deal with it.

Standing a little unsteadily on deck as the ferry slowly rolled
forward, she knew she chartered uncertain waters, but at least she
was finally at the helm of her own life.

She remembered watching the *Ravenswood* from Clevedon Pier –
when she had made the decision to face her demons and to find her
own way. Yet the year was not yet over – she felt she needed to
retrace Isambard's footsteps fully for the exorcism to be complete.
Come November, if all went well, he'd be gone from her life for ever
– his spirit free at last. As she would be free. Already she was tasting
the tang of liberty. It would have been unthinkable for Maud to do
this even a year ago. She had grown bolder, more adventurous. Here
she was, on her way to France by herself, footloose and fancy free,
finding a joie de vivre long submerged.

She had kept the trip secret – especially from Archibald. She didn't
want any 'pleasant surprises'. This was for her as much as Isambard.
The end-of-term slog had taken it out of her more than usual. It felt
like her daily life as a teacher was a shadow of reality. She came alive

on the hill-sides, even amongst the dead places, the barrows and ruins that so obsessed her beloved. It felt as though she had one foot in this world, one foot in the next. And here she was, taking a ferry journey across a Twentieth Century Styx, which so many soldiers had passed over – never to return, including her husband.

Looking around her, she was relieved to see no Charon. The Captain looked like a far nicer man – resplendent in his uniform of black and brass, strutting about on the bridge like chanticleer himself.

Maud walked into the smoky bar filled with holidaymakers of all ages. While she wondered what to have, a man in a pale striped jacket and boater asked in French if she would like a drink. He had a black comma of a moustache and gleam in his eye. He seemed to have had a few himself already.

Even if Maud had not understood the gist of what he said, the tone of his voice was unmistakable. She blushed, unable to believe his audacity, or the fact it had happened – someone had made a pass at her. She sharply shook her head, and walked away.

She went to sit well inside out of the wind, and pulled out her copy of Tennyson's *Idylls of the King*, burying her face in it so as to hide her embarrassment and avoid eye contact with the Frenchman.

She'd understood him plain enough. Her French was better than she'd thought. She'd only ever used it to read and translate Gallic classics. Yet speaking it would be another matter. She'd had little opportunity to practise it in Eastbourne.

It was strange to be talked to in that manner. Perhaps for the first time in a long while she had started to feel, and look, like a woman again. Like clockwork, a literary analogy for her predicament came to mind. She thought of Tristan and Isolde – the love potion they had drunk on the boat between their respective realms. What if she had accepted the offered drink? Would she have been in the man's power? Would the drink have acted like the waters of Lethe? She wanted to remember, not forget. Her duty to Isambard demanded it.

After arriving at insouçiant St Malô, Maud made a beeline for Carnac, reaching it on 2nd August – the day of her husband's entry. It was mid-afternoon. The colour of the sea took her breath away: turquoise and translucent. And the sky – the sky was so full of light.

This was the furthest south she had been – a modest but personal triumph. She had reached the destination by herself. Her narrow world was stretching a little more each day.

She walked along the sea front, trying to guess which café he had sat at, but it was impossible. And so she chose one that felt right, sat down, ordered a lemon tea and a croissant and brought out her husband's journal.

2nd August, 1914, Carnac, Brittany

I sit here at a beach café overlooking the turquoise waters of the ocean in Carnac – the village that has grown like lichen on the back of the numerous alignments of megaliths called locally 'menhirs', literally long stones. It is late in the afternoon and the shadows are lengthening, and the shadow of war is upon us. I read the headlines with disbelief and amazement: Archduke Franz-Ferdinand and his wife assassinated in Sarajevo, Serbia and Austria-Hungary at war with one another; Russia mobilizing millions of troops, and Germany threatening to do the same unless they are sent back from the Frontier – but it's too late. The trains are rolling and cannot be stopped. The juggernaut of war lumbers into action – yesterday Germany declared war on Russia. Who will be next to be caught up in this madness? Will Europe survive?

The Foreign Office advises immediate repatriation of all British citizens. I must away. Only a couple of days ago this place was thronged with holidaymakers from every corner of Europe – Russians and Germans chatted side by side. Now they have all scattered because of the wind of war. Who knows who their enemy shall be tomorrow? Our destinies are at the whims of the powers that be.

How much are we in control of our lives? Sometimes it seems we are all railroaded down tracks we do not wish to explore. I wanted to pursue my research – but have reached the end of the line. I must go back. I cannot ignore the tide of death sweeping through the land. Yet it is unbelievably frustrating – just when I had discovered so much! What I had thought in my blinkered way to be a mystery unique to Britain is something that belongs to the world – here, in Brittany, there is vast evidence of that. And where else? I hear of tracks cut into the stone across Malta. Where do these mysterious roads lead to? Do they continue over the sea? Or even under it?

Here, in Brittany, there is the legend of the sunken kingdom of Kêr-Is – the sister of Cornwall's Lyonesse. Could they be the same thing: mutual folk memory of a civilisation lost to the sea between them? Where there were riches, now only a gulf.

And was this Lyonesse/Kêr-Is a remnant of Atlantis? Was that where the first alignment-makers came from? Mere speculation, but sitting here at this beach café, with thousands of menhirs around me, it is easy to imagine them extending into the sea, across the ocean floor – to other lands, or lost kingdoms. Which civilisation shall be next? The British Empire? What if the British Isles were to sink beneath the sea because of some unimaginable cataclysm. Coastal villages have already been consumed, even a city: Lethowsow; the Bottom Cantred of Cardigan Bay; Dunwich. In such places it is said you can hear the toll of bells from below the waves. Will one day Big Ben chime beneath Britannia's briny realm?

The alignments point to several mounds, the largest being the spectacular Mont St Michel: some say the mother of St Michael's Mount. Evidence of a similar culture perhaps – of a people who saw their high places as holy. I noticed one dolmen (a trilithon) had a cross upon it. Another Christianised pagan site.

Walking among the semi-circular cromlechs I came across the grand tumulus called Tumiac – it was from here apparently that Julius Caesar watched his fleet's victory over the Gauls in 56 BC – plus ça change. *Mighty Rome was to fall. Only the earth remains.*

Yet I cannot escape reality. It has caught up with me. I have to go back – duty compels. Archie will insist I sign up – to maintain the family honour or some such tosh. It seems my fate is not to be a mere railway engineer either. What destiny does the war hold for me, for us all?

And there the journal finished. Isambard had taken another, smaller one with him to war – and, according to the War Office, that had been lost with him in combat. And with it she had lost more than her guide.

In the dazzling light of morning Maud gazed one last time at the newly wrought waves. The sea stretched south – to Spain, to Africa. Another journey, another time, perhaps. Her husband's adventurous spirit was infectious. But now she had to turn east.

By mid-morning, Maud had left Carnac on the bus to Rennes, where she planned to catch the train to Paris. Feeling she had travelled a little closer to Isambard, she journeyed further on – beyond the edges of her world.

2⓪

HIDDEN SPRINGs

And then she follow'd Merlin all the way,
Ev'n to the wild woods of Broceliande.
For Merlin once had told her of a charm,
The which if any wrought on anyone
With woven paces and waving arms,
The man so wrought on ever seem'd to lie
Closed in the four walls of a hollow tower,
From which was no escape for evermore;
And none could find that man for evermore,
Nor could he see but him who wrought the charm
Coming and going, and as he lay dead
And lost to life and use and name and fame.

'Merlin and Vivien', Alfred Lord Tennyson

On the way north to Rennes, Maud decided to rebel from her husband's itinerary: to make a détour to visit the ancient forest of Broceliande – where Merlin had been enchanted and trapped by the wiles of a woman, whose name varies but whom Tennyson called Vivien in his version of the legend; one of Maud's favourite sequences from the *Idylls*. The prospect of visiting the setting of the famous scene was too irresistible – it would bring the magic alive, as had the journey following Isambard's journal. But she had followed in her husband's footsteps for too long. She would complete her pilgrimage, dutifully, but Maud wanted to do something for herself for once. As she stepped off the carriage and walked into the dark ranks of woods, she felt as though the trees themselves were watching her disapprovingly.

All that remained of Broceliande was to be found within the forest of Paimpont. The infamous spring, Font du Paimpont, wasn't that well marked, but Maud was determined to find it. It was here that, according to local legend, Merlin had taken his ardent pupil – to reveal his source of power. When he had done so the enchantress had trapped him with his own magic.

As Maud followed the narrowing forest trails she wished she had Nubi with her.

She had felt safe so far on her journey, but now she was alone – and nobody knew where she was. Maggie knew of her general itinerary, but Maud had decided not to tell her sister in case Archie found out and turned up unexpectedly.

Maud was alone in the ancient woods. The trees brooded in their own shadows. Some seemed to look down cankered noses at her with Gallic scorn. She imagined them indignant at a human intruder.

Instinctively she picked up a long stick for protection.

It was a hot summer's day, and she was looking forward to finding the spring. Her water was rapidly diminishing and getting warm and tinny in its flask. She came to a crossroad by a great gnarled hollow oak tree, and stopped to mop her brow and look at the map she had purchased.

She was grateful for the crash course in orienteering her husband had given her. All those rambles with Isambard had paid off. According to the map, the spring should be within a mile of where she stood – but in a wood that could be a very long mile. She tried to get her bearings and position the map and herself facing North, using the midday sun as her mark. When her shadow fell directly in front of her and over the map, she pinpointed her position and worked out the direction she needed to go in. She set off down the south-west track and, after quarter of an hour, was pleased and relieved to see a tiny wooden sign in the undergrowth pointing to the spring.

Through a thicket of hazel trees she came to a sun-dappled clearing. The spring bubbled up from a cleft in the earth. To one side was a slab of rock, and Maud thought of the 'Countess of the Fountain' story from the *Mabinogion*; another favourite of hers.

What would happen, she wondered, if she dashed some spring water upon the stone? Would a terrible storm strip the leaves from the trees and a black knight appear? It wasn't worth risking it, she decided. Not with how things had been for her this year.

And besides, it was so peaceful in the glade. She wanted to savour the solitude. This was her first time alone on the whole holiday.

Her body felt like the dry earth. Her skin dry and wind-burned, her bones aching. She felt like an old crone. Yet somewhere inside her was an untapped reservoir of words, of feelings, of strength. And these last few months had made her feel more alive than for a long time. Life was stirring in her again. But it would take a long time to fully surface.

The clear water gurgled up, and birds sang in the sun-heavy trees. The incessant trickling soothed her. She slipped into a rêverie, lulled by the sound.

The momentum of her journey stilled. The white noise of travel faded. What she had denied could be drowned out no longer.

Much to her surprise, she felt the music rise within her, and she began to sing. A pure sound issued forth, piercing the silence, yet expressing it too. Like light through a prism, this split into a spectrum of notes, modulating into tones, and a melody bubbled up – as if she were singing the spirit of the place. Feeling like a prodigal Vivien, Maud felt somewhere deep down as though it was her duty to free her Merlin. She had imprisoned Isambard with her grief and denial. Now she had to release him. Unbind her love.

With her pale bare legs dangling in the spring, Maud felt like a siren, like the Breton mermaid Mesuline. She felt suddenly the power of her sex stir within – her voice and her body becoming one, calling out, expressing her loneliness, her yearning.

Hiraeth, she breathed.

She felt the tiny hairs on the back of her neck tingle. A presence was close. Isambard? Had she opened the doorway again with her singing? Here she was in a threshold place – the spring was a potential portal. The glade was filled with a sense of the numinous, of imminent manifestation.

A twig snapped.

Maud went silent, sat bolt upright and scanned the foliage. Her heart was beating fast. Surely, she hadn't heard things. It had been a definite sound – too heavy for a deer.

Slowly, she stood up – feeling eyes bore into her.

'Please, don't stop singing. It was beautiful.'

Maud's chest tightened at the words in husky French. She turned to the direction of the voice and bit her lip when she saw a man step out of the shadows.

He wore a plain brown suit and brogues. His fair hair was smoothed sideways over his head with pomade. Baby-faced, but in his forties, he had a slight double chin and a piggish nose, with nasal hairs blending into a short moustache on his upper lip, which he licked quickly with the flick of a snail-like tongue.

'Whu-what do you want?' Maud stepped backwards.

'Just to hear you sing.'

The man stepped a little closer, holding out an open hand. The other was in his pocket. He seemed to be gripping something.

Maud glanced down. The man's tiny pig-like eyes flickered down and a cold smile spread over his face like mustard over ham.

'I like to hear women sing,' he said, staring at her, his gaze scanning the contours of her body beneath its summer dress. She had not been looked at like that for a long time. She did not like it.

Run, run like rain! her instincts screamed. She panicked, scrambled up and stumbled backwards on to the slab, slipping on her wet feet.

The man lunged forward and landed on top of her, smothering her with his flabby body. She kicked and screamed, and he tried to cover her mouth with his own — she tasted his saliva and felt his foie gras breath on her, glimpsing the pâté still stuck to his teeth.

'No! Please, for God's sake, no!'

Maud managed to thrust her knee between his legs. He doubled over in pain and she sprang to her feet, bolting for the trees. But he was up and running after her, a look of anger on his face. The under-growth tore at her dress, scratched her face. She held up an arm as she plunged through. Ahead, loomed the hollow oak. The crossroad lay beyond — she could outrun him on the open track.

But the man was right behind her and rugby tackled her, bringing her down. She banged her head on the oak and was momentarily dazed. The man was winded, and he crawled forward like a boar hunting for truffles. He lumbered to his feet, the whites of his eyes showing.

'Now I'll make you sing!'

Maud scrambled backwards into the hollow of the oak, but her assailant closed in after her, his girth blocking her only escape route. He was breathing heavily, and his collar was hanging loose, his shirt torn open, revealing the coppery hairs sprouting from his sweat-soaked vest.

Maud screamed, and the sound pierced the forest, shocking the birds from the trees.

The attacker tried to smother her mouth, but she bit his hand, drawing blood. He cuffed her around the face, but this only made her scream louder — her only defence. The man was taken aback by the sound, and he looked worriedly about the trees.

'Shut up! Shut up! I'll cut your tongue out!'

The pigman pulled a blade from his pocket and used his teeth to pull the leather sheath away, while holding her down with his other hand and the weight of his body.

Maud looked at the small blade, lethal enough to do its job.

Her scream died away, leaving an eerie silence, followed by the hiss of leaves. A wind rose around them, whipping branches. The great oak creaked in the sudden gale.

The man stopped – unsettled, confused. He stepped back, outside the tree. The fierce wind drove him back, driving his mouth open. A maelstrom raged about the grove, raking the forest with savage intensity. Above, a large branch split off and came crashing down in front of him, knocking him backwards.

A gash appeared on his forehead, and he put his hand to it, looking at the blood in disbelief. The wind howled about him, blinding him with its ferocity, as if the forest wanted to rid itself of some evil parasite.

'Mon Dieu!' He looked at Maud in horror. 'Sorcière!' he spat. Then in terror he turned and ran.

The whirlwind subsided, the leaves settled. Then there was peace.

It was some time before Maud stopped shaking.

When she was absolutely certain the man had gone for good she tentatively squeezed out of the oak, between the branches of the fallen limb.

Dazed, she wandered on to the crossroad.

Other people were coming up the path – Maud began to panic, until she saw that they were a family on a day trip – with dog and child. She did not want them to see her like this. She felt ashamed. Yet it was too late. They were upon her, looking concerned.

Shaking, sobbing, she blurted out what had happened in breathless English. They made her slow down. She took deep breaths and tried again, in French – her voice trembling. They had not seen him and Maud began to doubt her sanity. Had it really happened, or had she hallucinated the whole thing? Yet the state of her clothes, the bruise on her arm and the trickle of blood from the corner of her mouth testified otherwise. That unnerved her more than anything. After nearly a year of strange events, it seemed her life was built on quicksand.

The man tried to console Maud, but the wife looked at her suspiciously.

They led her back to the nearest village, where she recovered over a cognac. The family made sure she was okay, safely ensconced in a pension, before leaving. Composing herself, she thanked them and left.

What had happened? Had Isambard saved her, or had she saved herself? 'Sorcière' the pigman had called her. Had he thought it was she who'd summoned the wind? Was it just a coincidence or was she turning into some kind of sorceress? Perhaps she was just going insane.

So many questions ... If only her husband were here to help, to clarify. She was sure he'd have an explanation. Then she froze. She heard Isambard's voice inside her head: '*Maud, you are the windlass. The spring acted as a conduit of power, yet it was you who unlocked it. Your song opened the doorway...*' The surroundings returned into focus and Isambard's voice faded − if it had been his, and not her own fantasy. Was she just imagining what he would say? Speaking to herself now − great! Or was she just denying the truth? Something had happened at West Kennet Long Barrow. A power had been awakened in her, a deep power that shook her world to its core. It frightened her. Never again would she sing without caution − she had called a man to her with her song, but it had been the wrong man. The power was double-edged − a sword that could harm as well as heal.

Her scratches would soon fade, she could mend her dress and dust herself down, but something had been torn apart in that place. The stitches of the world she knew had been unpicked with every step of her journey. There was no going back now.

Chastened by her ordeal, Maud got on the next train for Paris, glad of the solid dependable reality of it. She looked at the men in the carriage with suspicion and fear, but her rational mind told her that the chances are they were fine. The veneer of normality was the unsettling thing.

It was the hidden motives that scared her the most.

She took courage from the fact that her mettle had been tested, and she had not felt a victim, but someone who could defend herself. Woe betide any man who challenged her again! She felt stronger, taller somehow.

Maud gazed out of the carriage window at the sombre Normandy landscape. A shire horse pulled a plough, cleaving a furrow in a fallow field. In another, farm workers scythed the wheat into stooks. She wondered how many other portals were out there − how many other places of power? While she was close to them she would, from now on, always feel safe. Again, she imagined Isambard's voice speaking to her: '*The world has hidden springs, doorways and channels, which access vast reservoirs of invisible energy. They are gateways to latent powers, to other worlds...*' She snapped back, hoping she had not been speaking to herself again. No one in the carriage seemed to have noticed. Relieved, she gazed out at the hypnotic patterns of fields and hedges rushing by.

Isambard had sensed this network, but Maud had unlocked it within her body, by finding her voice. She smiled feyly, catching her reflection in the glass. Had she played Vivien to his Merlin – finally seducing the cantrips from the old magician? She had strayed from the path and found her own power, whatever its source.

She would remain silent no longer.

All around the planet women were standing up and being heard, and Maud felt proud to be part of that long-denied cry.

21

THE NOCTURNE PAGES

Futile – the Winds –
To a Heart in port –
Done with the Compass –
Done with the Chart!

Rowing in Eden –
Ah, the Sea!
Might I but moor – Tonight –
In Thee!

'249', Emily Dickinson

Maud arrived in Paris at midday on the first Friday in August. It was searing hot and the city was all but deserted by the Parisians, who had escaped to the South in the annual migration. Only the work bound, unknowing tourists and ex-pats remained to endure the stifling heat. The station was like an oven, and Maud was glad to get out into the fresher air – even though it was still as warm as soup. Her dress clung to her body. She was ill-used to such a climate. The pell-mell in front of the station as cabs and carriages were loaded and picked up or dropped off passengers, made it worse. She hauled her luggage on to the pavement and caught her breath. After the arcadia of Brittany, Paris was a shock to the system.

The smog and congestion of London were worse, but the unfamiliarity of Paris made the experience of being in a city even more disorientating. Maud planned to stop over for a couple of days – to see the compulsory landmarks – but was already beginning to regret it.

A taxi driver offered his vehicle, a jalopy of former grandeur. He lifted her luggage into the boot, then opened the passenger door for her. With relief, Maud stepped into the dark interior. It smelled of warm leather and cigarettes, and was even stuffier than the station, – but as the cab coughed into life the air circulated around her.

She looked out of the open windows at the city she had read about so many times but had never visited. France's proximity to England's shores bred a certain blasé attitude in the British, even contempt − like the relationship between siblings. Indeed, the two countries were related more than they would like, from the Celts to the Normans. Yet they seemed worlds apart − like Maud and her sister. And like Maud and Constance, they should have got on better. Maud wondered what it would be like to have such sisterly support. After her experience in Broceliande she yearned for it more than ever.

The cab pulled up in Montparnasse, outside the Hotel Moulin Vert, where Maud had booked a room for a couple of nights. The driver helped her with her bags into the lobby, leaving his engine running. She thanked him, paid the fare and, when she saw his reluctance to leave, remembered the obligatory tip. She offered him a handful of small change and he left.

Maud checked in and the concièrge was amused by her French, but warmed by her efforts to speak it. He gave her the key and waved her to the lift. Her room was on the twelfth floor.

The room was just a little bigger than the bed, but at least it was clean and being twelve floors up, surprisingly quiet. She opened the sash window to let in some air. Outside, Paris was alive − a throbbing beast, and Montparnasse was its beating heart.

As she unpacked, Maud thought about her arrival. Her accent wasn't perfect, but lacking more were the Gallic mannerisms, body language, savoir faire. Maud felt especially English in Paris, stiff and formal and plain. All the ladies she had seen so far had looked so glamorous, so chic. She needed to do something about her wardrobe, she thought, as she hung up her clothes. She suddenly felt so old-fashioned. In the wardrobe mirror she saw herself − a dowdy widow. Sighing, she ran a bath and laid out her coolest summer dress.

After washing and changing, she felt better, and started to feel hungry. She would find something to eat and then explore.

Outside, it seemed that all of the population of Montparnasse was taking lunch − an enclave of Americans and English mainly, with some Russians, sitting at tables on terraces, smoking, drinking and devouring − insatiable for life.

Maud grabbed a Camembert baguette and ate it in the park, eager to soak up the atmosphere of Paris. In truth, she was still wary of men after what had happened in the woods. It was foolish, she knew − but an instinct made her wary. She looked at the couples walking arm in arm. Two young lovebirds were kissing on the bench, open in their passion. Maud tried to look away but found it compelling, and unsettling. When was the last time she had been touched like that, been made love to? Her body felt fossilised. Brushing the crumbs from her dress, she walked off, trying not to feel flustered.

Air – she needed some fresh air. She could hardly breathe in this city. The heat made her vision blur. Looking for an escape from the smothering heat, Maud decided to head for the wind-blown heights of the Eiffel Tower. Its fame was overwhelming – almost to the point of putting Maud off. But the prospect of all that cold clean air at the top of that tower was too much to resist. When she emerged from the nearest métro station and saw it for the first time she could not believe her eyes. As she approached, the awe did not diminish. Here was the tallest man-made structure in the world. The scale of it was beyond comprehension. Standing beneath its massive cast-iron arches, Maud expected it to come crashing down on her at any minute. A Tower of Babel baiting divine judgement. Yet in the endless queues all the languages of the world could be heard, it seemed.

Perhaps the Tower of Babel had already fallen. The war had toppled any illusion of a global brotherhood. And had left a god-shaped hole in the sky.

As she queued Maud read some of her guidebook. It was incredible to think the Eiffel Tower had nearly been dismantled in 1909 for scrap metal, only a couple of decades after its completion. All that saved it was its unexpected usefulness as a communications tower. How words could be transmitted through the air was mind-boggling to Maud. Such had once been the province of the gods, but Hermes had been circumvented by man's Promethean ingenuity. How far it could take him was limited only by his imagination, it seemed. Yet surely his arrogance would eventually receive its comeuppance? But for now, before the fall, all Maud could do was admire with the rest of the crowds.

The wait to get to the top was interminable, with two queuing stages, on the ground and two-thirds of the way up. At least up there she could breathe again – but when she reached the top her breath was taken away again as she stepped out onto the mesh-enclosed platform. It felt like being in the crow's nest of a gigantic ship. Maud was sure it rocked from side to side, having read on a plaque that the edifice expanded and contracted fifteen centimetres every year, with the heat and cold. It made her dizzy, and she had to cling on to the railings. She dared not look down, but the view out over the city was astounding. Here, spread out below her in every direction, was the city of light, built on an island formed by the confluence of rivers – with only bridges connecting it to terra firma, it seemed. Without them, it might float off into the sky.

Maud took deep gulps of air, and remembered her time on the Tor. She had to let the wind flow through her – not resist. Like the tower itself, designed to let the wind blow through it, a gigantic needle through which threaded the wind. Maud had to let go. She closed her eyes and let go of the railings.

For a moment, she found her balance and stood upright, feeling the cool wind hold her. Then a fat lady bumped into her, squeezing passed, and the spell was broken.

Maud descended, feeling proud of herself, if a little unsteady. She needed to ground herself, so she walked along the Seine – whose waters offered some coolness in the mid-afternoon heat. The cypress trees provided bands of delicious shade, as she walked slowly along the cobbled promenade.

On the opposite bank Maud passed the Egyptian obelisk in the Place de la Concorde. In the stark sunlight it cast a gash of shadow, like a giant sundial. It was just like the one on the bank of the Thames, she thought. Had it come from the same source? It made her think about Isambard and his ideas. Did it all lead back to Egypt, or beyond, as he had suggested? After Carter's discovery of the boy pharaoh, Tutankhamen, the previous November, Egypt-fever had gripped the West. Suddenly the ancient past had opened up as a living reality. The ancestors were closer than could have been possibly imagined.

Maud's riverside amble had brought her to the Île de la Cité Concièrgerie, the original settlement of Paris, of the Celtic tribe of the Parisi. Here stood the formidable edifice of Nôtre Dame, with its grotesque gargoyles and Trinity of intricate doorways. She marvelled at the exquisite carvings rendering the hierachy of heaven and hell in the symbolism of medieval cosmology. She joined the throng of tourists and entered the cathedral's dark embrace, and found some respite in its blissfully cool aisles, if not inspiration. It was a magnificent building, but did not move Maud. As she gazed up at the lofty vaults she imagined Quasimodo among the gargoyles above. The literary resonance excited her more than the architecture, and made her recollect something: an article she had read about an English-language bookshop in the Latin Quarter, opposite the cathedral, called Shakespeare & Company. She decided to hunt it down and left the sombre silence and shadows, blinking once more in the sunlight. Shading her eyes, Maud spotted the yellow and black sign over the bridge and made a beeline for it.

She now recalled how the bookshop – opened by an enterprising American lady, Sylvia Beach Whitman – had gained notoriety for publishing Joyce's magnum opus *Ulysses* early the previous year when nobody in Britain would touch it.

Maud looked through the lozenge windows and saw shelves stacked with books in a ramshackle manner. It looked like a genuine treasure trove.

In eager anticipation, she entered.

What struck her immediately was the atmosphere. Nothing like the austerity of a library. It had more the air of a bohemian côterie. The door-bell tinkled as writers, intellectuals, eccentrics came and went, chatting in the doorway or on the seats outside. A young woman with a Louise Brooks haircut looked up from the counter where she sat engrossed in a book, appraised Maud like the spine of a novel, smiled and resumed her reading.

Maud didn't know where to begin: there was such a feast before her. Yet there was also some order in the chaos. Sections were labelled with handwritten cards: biography, war, history, fiction. Maud's instinct was to go to the poetry section. There she found a worldly mix of 'unacknowledged legislators', as Shelley called them – rare volumes mixed with self-published pamphlets. She saw many unavailable in England. She picked up a copy of Eliot's *The Wasteland*, as well as Rousseau's *Meditations of a Solitary Walker*, Yeats's *The Wind Among the Reeds*, and Graves's *Fairies and Fusiliers*. She wanted them all, but she had to be careful with her tight budget.

She continued around the room, trying not to let anything indispensable catch her eye, yet savouring the temptation. Books were perhaps her only extravagance.

In the middle of the floor there was even a shallow well. It was dry but filled with a scattering of coins from around the world which customers had thrown in. She thought of the Font du Paimpont and shuddered. It was a shame her memory of the place was tainted. Surely many people had gone there without incident. Was she making her own luck? If so, could she change it?

On a whim, Maud tossed in an English penny, not sure of the wish she had made, except perhaps 'change'.

Either side of the counter where the shop assistant sat were two passages leading to the back of the shop. While deciding which way to go Maud noticed the book the nymph-like assistant was engrossed in: a thin dog-eared collection of poetry.

The young woman caught Maud looking. She gave her a quizzical look.

Embarrassed, Maud blurted, 'Can I leave these here?'

'Sure,' said the assistant in a mid-Atlantic accent, with a little shrug of her bare shoulders. She had the air of an initiate, her adopted Gallic mannerism a symbol of her elevated status.

Maud placed the books neatly on one side of the counter, and from the corner of her eye she noticed how the centre-parting of the shop assistant's black bell of hair resembled in negative the crevice of the book she read. A strong smell of jasmine and aniseed wafted from her simple cotton dress patterned with flowers.

Thanking the assistant, Maud continued her exploration. The place oozed with books. She squeezed past countless volumes, imbibing their musty scent, browsing rows of Russian and German books. The whole place had a worldly ambience, more than a bookshop twice its size in Britain. Cabinets housed curious relics, eccentric objets d'art. Underground magazines and pamphlets spilled from the sideboards and tables. Everything was weighed down with the sediment of centuries. Maud could almost hear the hum of words from the shelves, the books having conversations with themselves. The air was filled with the dust of thought.

Mirrors strewn with postcards and quotes lined the walls, but instead of creating the illusion of space, they made the rooms open up like Chinese boxes. Turning a corner, Maud came across a flight of narrow steep stairs. A young man with spectacles descended the staircase, clutching a batch of books under his arm. It seemed to lead to another floor, and so she climbed them, scanning the books on the way up. No space was left unfilled. Lowering her head, she emerged into another room. It could have been someone's bedroom. Indeed, in the corner a blond-haired boy lay on a bunk on his belly, engrossed in a book of pictures. He hardly noticed Maud, and seemed completely at home.

Opposite him, above another passageway, Maud read the legend in hand-painted black letters: 'Be not inhospitable to strangers, lest they be angels in disguise.'

What a wonderful place, Maud thought, smiling. It had been decorated like someone's house, and it certainly made you feel at home. She passed a cubby-hole made into a tiny study complete with a black Smith-Corona typewriter, fitted with a sheaf of white paper in case inspiration struck. Sitting in the chair was a fat black cat with a single white stripe on its nose, purring to itself.

Next to it a rusty tap dripped into a cracked sink, indicating that this had once been a utility room – now it led into a small reference library, bare-floored, but wall to wall with books. The only furniture was a couple of bunks piled with blankets.

This was book heaven. Here was the inner sanctum of a secret cult. And treading their ritual perambulation of the shelf-lined rooms were the acolytes in silent contemplation, looking for signs.

Maud sat down in the corner and caught her breath. Paris was exhilarating but exhausting. It was good to sit and be still for a moment.

She was delighted by her discovery. Here was something authentic, something not on the usual tourist map, but quintessentially part of the fabric of the city. It offered a doorway into the many kingdoms, the many minds engaged in redesigning the universe after it had been blown apart by the Great War.

Later she must visit the Arc de Triomphe, she decided. Only three years ago the body of the Unknown Soldier had been buried there.

She must remember what she came here for.

But for the moment this place was for her.

Maud imbibed in its heady ambience the perfume of philosophy, of struggle and challenge, of heated conversations, passionate endeavours. It made her want to be an earnest intellectual, to belong to the avant-garde, pioneers of ideas.

Suddenly, from a bundle of blankets to one side a man awoke and scratched his head. He looked at Maud in confusion, asked her the time in French. Instinctively, she reached for her watch. Then she remembered it was still broken, so she guessed the approximated time. He cursed, pulled on his trousers and dashed out.

It seemed some people really made themselves at home!

Amused, Maud descended carefully, and explored the other half of the shop. Here she came across a pile of new books – including the massive tome of *Ulysses*. So here it was – the infamous bête noire of books.

Maud had to buy a copy – it had been banned in Britain. She picked it up and was amazed by its weight. Here was a book that lived up to the impact it had created: a Bible for the new century. Gingerly, savouring the taboo, she turned its pages and scanned the dense text. It didn't look a light read – yet it was about only one day in Dublin. It was no *War and Peace* in terms of epic scale, but it was no less ambitious: the recording of consciousness, and the depiction of everything over twenty-four hours.

She handed it to the young woman, who nodded approvingly.

'That's one *Moby Dick* of book!'

'It looks it,' Maud agreed.

'I'm still reading it – a year on! I hope you have a long holiday!'

'Unfortunately not, but it'll keep me company.' Her eyes flicked to the book the woman was reading.

The American noticed and looked hard at Maud, searching for something.

'This one keeps me company.' Putting a slender index finger in-between the pages to keep her place, she showed Maud the cover. *The Poetry of Sappho.*

'I've never heard of him. Is he good?'

'She – the author's a woman. An ancient Greek. And the poetry is a full of light, heat and longing. You know when you find a book and it's like a long-lost friend?'

Maud nodded. *Mrs Dalloway* had been like that for her. 'Some poems are like that – they really strike a chord.' Her own words surprised her. Rarely did she show such enthusiasm in public. There was something about the girl that drew it out of her.

'You're not kidding. Sappho does it for me.'

'I'm afraid I don't know her.' Maud felt terribly ignorant all of a sudden, and she the English teacher. 'I like the Romantics myself.'

'Me too – Keats, Shelley, Coleridge. They were most fine.'

'Anyway, I must go – so much to see.'

'Your first time in Paris?'

'Yes, alas. I feel such an unworldly thing. And it's only on our doorstep.'

'Well, you've got a lot going on in London. But Paris is the heart of things these days.'

Maud paid for the book, and the poetry she'd selected earlier. The girl wrapped the novel in brown paper. 'Be careful taking this back across, won't you?'

'Of — of course.' Maud hadn't thought of that. She flushed. Caught with an obscene book at customs. The very thought of it made her blanche.

'You take care now. Have a great time!'

'Thank you.'

Maud walked to the door and turned, to see the girl cast one last look at her before licking her finger and turning the page.

The young lady was undeniably sweet, Maud thought, as she left the shop. There was something curious about her. Something strangely compelling.

As evening approached she headed off for one last tourist attraction — the Arc de Triomphe. She descended into the underworld again, with *Ulysses* as her guide. She felt like Aeneas, clutching his golden bough of mistletoe when he went to Hades to speak with the wraith of his father. The tunnel to the centre of the monument was dark and austere. Maud wondered whether this was intentional: to put the pilgrim in the right state of mind for the mausoleum.

Some graffiti scrawled on the wall in English changed the tone a little: 'Everything is erotic'.

Emerging from the métro, Maud was greeted by the formidable visage of the Arc de Triomphe. It straddled the Champs Élysées like a pair of giant thighs. Between it lay the gateway of life and death.

The body of the Unknown Soldier had been laid there in 1920. As a memorial to the war dead it seemed, at first glance, more impressive than the one in Westminster Abbey, which she had not visited but had seen newspaper photographs of. She made a mental note to visit it when she returned home.

Napoleon's folly, the Arc ironically became appropriated for the greatest folly of all — war. Yet it had a majestic dignity — the simple engraved slab at the centre of a vast mausoleum. She scanned the wreaths around it, the veteran with a limp and a chest full of medals guarding it. At the heart of it all, the eternal flame of remembrance flickered — emerging stronger in the dusk. And around it swarmed the traffic — the endless traffic, like a mistral of light. Horse and carriages struggling with automobiles, motorcycles, charabancs and lorries, in a fugue of horns. Yet what stunned Maud most of all were the roads — radiating out like spokes from a central hub. Like the hours of a gigantic clock, twelve avenues surrounded the Arc, with the Champs Élysées at four o'clock the grandest. At their centre, the Arc de

Triomphe – a powerful reminder of the debt owed, of death-in-life.

If Isambard could have seen it, he would have been ecstatic, for here was a grand convergence of alignments – designed into the very fabric of the city. Many cities, he had claimed once, had been built on geomantic principles. Here was sacred architecture – a meeting point between the worlds of the quick and the dead.

Paying her respects to the nameless fallen, Maud jumped on a métro train and returned to Montparnasse – making her way to her hotel where she freshened up. Along the Boulevard de Montparnasse already the cafés were coming alive, but this was just a prelude to the night. It seemed Paris came alive in the evening, after the hot languid day. As the skies cooled, the streets hotted up, the pavements retaining their warmth. A warm wind blew, spiced with the musk of another continent.

Even with the fan on full Maud could not stay in her stuffy room. She could hardly breathe. She showered for the third time that day and put on her thinnest dress, a pale cream silk number. Taking a light coat out of force of habit, she left to find somewhere to eat.

Rich smells drifted towards her. Her nose found her a busy bistro serving fondue.

Le Dôme seemed to have more than its fair share of English and American clients. Reassured by their accents, Maud sat at an empty table on the terrace and ordered a drink, feeling a little self-conscious sitting there by herself. She watched the earnest intellectuals and elegant women having animated conversations over coffee and cognac. Cigarettes perpetually burned – like the eternal flame of the Arc de Triomphe, or the sacred light of an inner temple – as acolytes appeased scornful goddesses. Maud only caught fragments of the debates, the rags of ideas wielded like battle-torn banners until the flag-carriers were shot down with a comment and cruel laughter.

Maud sat in the corner of the café, half-reading *Ulysses*, making sure she kept it open on the table without showing its cover, and imbibing the ambience. 'In the room the women come and go, talking of Michelangelo' she quoted to herself from Eliot's 'Love Song'.

And yet what am I doing? Measuring out my life with coffee spoons? She could not languish in cafés, however pleasant, indefinitely. She had to act, in the spirit of Bergson's élan vital – an idea in vogue around the coffee houses of the city.

Maud was about to leave, feeling out of place, when she spotted the young man by himself: bérèt pulled over his brow at a jaunty angle, wearing a shapeless Breton sweater and cords, he smoked continuously and looked very serious as he scratched into a notebook with his pen.

When he spotted Maud lost in her copy of *Ulysses* he called out: 'What are you reading?'

Maud was caught off guard by the question. She detected the ghost of an accent beneath the fluent French, but could not place it.

'Um, Proust,' Maud lied, in the same tongue. She didn't want to give him the wrong idea about her.

'How far have you got?'

'Um, not very – I only bought it today.'

The young man smiled knowingly.

'What's your name?' he asked, still in French.

'Maud Kerne.'

'Ah, Anglaise.' The young man offered a hand.

'Patrice Épine. Can I buy you a drink?'

Maud flushed, but felt like she needed some company. The city was overwhelming her. She needed to focus on one voice, one pair of eyes, otherwise she would lose herself completely in the endless ocean of humanity. The experience in the forest should have warned her away from men, but after what had happened she felt fearless – and the man looked a lot gentler than her pig-like assailant in Broceliande.

The lights were low, deceptive, like a magic-lantern show. Maud couldn't quite see Épine's face clearly. He had soft, refined features, and very pale skin – like alabaster – its luminosity enhanced by the black licks of hair around his cheekbones.

The young man stood up and pulled out the chair opposite him. 'Please, take a seat.'

'Thank you.'

Épine had a clean smooth face with arched dark eyebrows. He gestured to the waiter. The slim man in black and white weaved his way over.

'What would you like?' asked Épine.

'Oh, just some water.'

'Come on, you're in Paris! Live a little!'

'How about a glass of wine then? Yes, why not?'

'White or red?'

'Red.' Maud flushed, feeling as if she had broken some taboo.

The waiter nodded and left. He had a wry look on his face.

Épine had rather full lips, Maud mused. He was like a Caravaggio Adonis.

There was an awkward silence. Maud sensed the young man was ill at ease when she looked at him, in spite of his boldness. He scanned the room and pointed people out, seeming keen to distract attention from himself. What was he hiding?

'That's Modigliani doing some sketches!' Épine indicated with a turn of his head. 'He's always here at night — he seems to spend his life drinking wine and haunting the cafés. You wonder when he has time to paint! Last night, I saw Erik Satie doodling on a napkin. In the afternoon Ezra Pound and Ford Madox Ford can be seen playing chess out the front. I love this place! Cummings called it a "divine section of eternity".'

The waiter returned with a carafe of wine and two glasses.

'Thank you.' Épine poured, handed Maud a glass and raised a toast. 'To the Muse, may she grace us with tenderness and inspiration.'

Maud joined in the toast, uncertain how to take the way Épine looked at her so intensely.

It was she who wanted to change the subject this time.

'What is it you're writing?'

'Oh, nothing. Ideas. Illusions. I like to record the little epiphanies of life to save them from extinction. I'm a poet, or trying to be. I'm hoping some of the greatness gathered in this city will rub off on me. I'm just another one of the galaxy of minor bodies orbiting those celestial lights. There must be so many of us — and who's to know who will make it, who will perish in obscurity? The wheel of fortune, she is cruel, no?'

Maud's interested prickled. 'You write poetry? That's wonderful. I love poetry.' Perhaps she was gushing a little too effusively. The wine was already making her spill words out. 'The Romantics are my favourite. Who do you like?'

'I think the American poets have the edge these days — Auden, Eliot, Cummings. But if I had to choose an old favourite it would be Emily Dickinson. I have a soft spot for that girl from Amherst.'

'I want to hear one of your poems,' said Maud.

'Ah, I'm not quite ready to share my work. These are just notes really. But kind of you to ask.' It was time for Épine to look embarrassed. Maud thought she had never seen a man blush before.

Épine guzzled down his wine and refilled both their glasses from a small half-empty bottle by his side.

'Try this.'

Maud gingerly sipped a little of the green liquor. It tasted of aniseed. Her nose wrinkled and she grimaced. 'Crikey – that's strong!'

'Pernod. Everyone drinks it these days after they banned absinthe. Can't blame them – that stuff is lethal!'

Maud's head was reeling. The floor seemed to breathe in and out. She gripped on to the table as tightly as she could. The cigarette smoke was making her head hum.

Around her the phantasmagoria of Paris paraded in all its gaudy glory, Art Nouveau elegance bookended with crumbling tenements, streets full of dwarves and princesses, ogres in top hats and waif-like women dressed to the nines – it was an endless carnival, a collective work of art, a creation of genius and madness. She gripped on to the edge of the table, to stop herself falling to the pavement. Her world was spinning.

Épine stood up and offered his arm.

'Let's explore!'

'But it's late!' protested Maud.

'The night has just begun. Come!'

Maud would have hesitated if she'd had any doubts, but for some reason she felt safe with the young poet. Perhaps it was just the alcohol, but for once she threw caution to the wind.

The day refused to die. The light lingered in the sky in tatters – rags of clouds like feather boas strewn luxuriously across the night, drawing people down into the underworld of pleasure.

The city was a never-ending festival, always on the brink of collapse, yet somehow sustaining itself, like a drunk toppling forward, down the road of excess to palaces of illicit wisdom, nights of dark wonder.

They passed prostitutes flaunting their wares from red-lit doorways like music hall prima donnas rendered by Toulouse Lautrec, with gaudy make-up, basques of whalebone and satin squeezing wrinkled perspiring flesh into unnatural shapes.

A Negro band played on the street corner and people joined in, dancing with champagne bottles dangling from their hands, clapping and stamping, singing along with the popular songs. The night was intoxicating, and Maud was seduced by it, led by her guide, hand in hand, into Xanadu.

She realised how provincial her life had been, how white. It was fascinating to see the kaleidoscopic montage of North African,

Mediterranean, American and Northern European.

The throbbing beat of the city made her blood race. It was like some vast pagan rite, an invocation of ecstasy. The music, the dancing, the offerings of money, of morals, innocence, respectability – to the god of good times, to the Devil and his orchestra.

It was a danse macabre, dancing on the fallen of the Great War, dancing away the death, the shadows of horror. It was the exuberance of survivors, of the damned.

As they walked along a piss-stinking alley Épine talked excitedly of Dadaism, the latest art movement to dominate. Tzara's *Dadaist Manifesto* had taken the city by storm. Life is nonsense – madness. So why not art? Breton and his cohorts began creating art from the random collision of life. Newspaper headlines. Babies mewling. A politician's rhetoric. Planes bombing. Yet people needed dreams. The window of the imagination had been shut for too long. In the subconscious of Western minds a strange new landscape was being explored.

Maud suddenly felt dizzy.

'Please. I need to sit down somewhere quiet.'

The poet apologised. He had been thoughtless.

He lit a cigarette and offered Maud one. She shook her head.

'Do you like the movies?' he asked.

Maud nodded. In another life.

And so Épine led her into a picture house, where they were showing a DW Griffith production called: *Orphans of the Storm*, captioned in French. It was about two girls experiencing the French Revolution. The film was melodramatic but thrilling, and in the anonymity of the smoke-filled auditorium the new friends found themselves holding hands. It felt strange at first, but they had grown comfortable with each other's company. In the exciting bits they held on tighter, especially when the blind girl was abducted and adopted by a gang of beggars. They watched the beheading scenes from behind fingers, and left arm in arm, feeling closer.

In the light of the gas lamp Maud suddenly felt self-conscious again and pulled away.

She was trying to achieve some kind of clarity but her mind whirled.

'Wait, wait. What are we doing? What's happening?' Maud struggled to break through the fog of grogginess.

It was nearly midnight. The poet led her to the Vavin Métro. 'Come, before it closes.'

'Where are you taking me?'

'Back home.'

Maud hesitated. Should she follow? Her head was spinning. What if he tried to mug her, or worse? Yet she felt safe with him. And the alternative was a lonely hotel room. What did she have to lose? This was her last night in Paris. Who knew when or if she would ever return? And what a night it was! It was made for wild things. The stars had come out, offering infinite possibilities.

The young man took her past the sombre edifice of Nôtre-Dame, across the bridge into the Latin Quarter.

When Épine stopped in front of Shakespeare and Company and pulled out a key Maud was confused.

'Voila! Home sweet home.' He slid the key into the lock and twisted. What slender wrists, Maud thought.

The man turned and placed a finger to his lips. Such full lips ...

Then he took her hand and led her inside. Into the darkness.

She had suspected, but had denied it. She had wanted to play the innocent. To justify what was to transpire.

The poet led her to the back of the shop. Even in the darkness he knew his way, but Maud was blind. They came to the stairs and he led her up them. They creaked with fairytale insistence.

A low snoring came from the bunk in the corner. Maud was led through, past the dripping faucet, to the reference library − lit by the street lamp in yellow and black like a garish music hall poster.

Épine gestured to the bunk in the corner, while he fumbled drunkenly with a box of matches. He lit a fat stub of candle in the middle of the floor on a saucer. Its glow seemed to enlarge the darkness. The walls of books became vast battlements.

The poet looked at Maud across the light, its glow transfiguring them both. She recognised those opalescent eyes − a liquid darkness that drew her in.

'Glasses.' Épine seemed agitated, or excited. He rattled around for some in the sink, wiping them with a cloth, holding them up to the light, frowning. 'I'm afraid these will have to do.'

Maud sat mesmerised, frozen in fear and delight, at the movements of the poet. It was beyond coincidence that he lived here as well. She remembered the American woman at the counter − her smile.

Épine pulled the cork from the bottle and poured them both a drink, hands shaking.

'It is hot in here.'

The poet went to the window and lifted it up. The room was filled with the night-jazz of sounds, and the smell of a thousand feasts wafted in.

Then Épine tugged off his bérêt and threw it on the floor, shaking out a thick black bob.

The figure stood there, half outside the sphere of candlelight – ambiguous, uncertain, perhaps waiting for Maud's response.

'Come, come and sit by me,' she found herself saying.

The poet knelt down beside her, face illuminated by the candle light, almost ashamed to be unmasked.

'Were you the girl I saw at the counter?'

'Yes,' was the answer, in English, with a soft American twang.

'My heart knew what my head did not.'

'You should be the poet.'

'But you, you are poetry.' She looked into the dark mystery of the girl's eyes.

'What's your real name, Patrice?'

'Épine is my pen name, or alter ego. My real name is Rose Lamont.'

'That's a fine name. Don't be ashamed of it.'

'I'm not. Épine just gives me the freedom I need, on the page and on the streets of Paris. It's safer for me to go out at night. And easier for me to mix with women without being hassled by men ... Thorn by night, Rose by day. Poetic, non?'

Maud looked hard at her protean escort. 'Have you done this thing before then?'

Rose looked admonished. 'No, not really ... I've – I've never had the courage before to talk to anyone, but you seemed so gentle, Maddy.'

Maddy. No woman had called her that before. It seemed to melt something inside her, said in a New England brogue – as though she had been discovered on a distant shore and reinvented.

'Let us drink.'

Rose offered her a glass and raised her own.

'Salut.'

'Salut.'

The wine was warm and sour. Yet they drank it deeply, as if it were the very water of life itself.

Maud was sweltering and fanned herself with a copy of Le Monde. 'That must be hot.' She indicated Rose's sweater.

'It hides the woman beneath, what little of it there is,' Rose answered, shyly pulling it off, revealing a silk singlet underneath. It clung to a slender body, boyish and vulnerable.

'Why, you're beautiful.' Maud found herself saying, wanting to reassure Rose, yet it was she who needed help. She felt like she was on fire. Her thin dress seemed suddenly too heavy. She kicked off her shoes – the action made her hem rise above her knee.

Rose reached out and stroked her exposed calf.

'Such long legs.'

Maud shivered under the touch. A bead of perspiration trickled down her throat.

She breathed out and fanned herself with her hand. They shifted awkwardly on the mattress.

'Wait. I have just the thing. Don't move.'

Rose got up and went through a door to one side. Maud stared at the candle flame. It felt like a roaring fire.

Rose returned with a damp hessian bag. 'This should cool us down.' She pulled out a chunk of ice like a fat diamond. A drip descended on Maud's leg, stinging it like fire.

Rose held her gaze. Sensing a acquiescence, the young American placed the ice on Maud's thigh.

Maud gasped, but did not flinch.

Rose ran the ice between her legs, slowly, inexorably, towards the burning core of her being.

She could not believe what was happening.

How long had it been since she had been touched, touched in tenderness, touched *there*?

Maud lay back, let Rose pull down her skirt and reach into the silken folds of her drawers.

The room swirled about her. She was no longer on the bed, but floating in the sky, like a Chagall painting.

Rose had expert fingers, deft and nimble like a pianist's.

Maud felt like she was the blank sheet of paper upon which Rose Épine typed her poem. She cried out in stifled gasps, aware that others slept nearby. There were no doors. In the next room someone turned and coughed. Others slept downstairs. What of the young man she had seen sleeping in the library earlier? Where was he? For a painfully private woman, the sudden lack of privacy had a perverse frisson; the fact that at any moment someone might walk in and discover them in flagrante delicto, gave Maud a forbidden thrill.

Rose pulled off her baggy cords and singlet, and stripped off Maud's sodden camisole, so they were equal. Rose had small girl's breasts, a boyish torso.

Maud instinctively covered her chest, but Rose pulled her hands softly away.

'You have such a beautiful body. Don't be ashamed.'

Maud lightly stroked Rose's back and the younger woman slinked into position, kissing the inside of her thighs. Maud grabbed Rose's hair and ran her fingers through its thick black strands. Her body felt like a stranger. She looked down at it as if it belonged to someone else, as if this were happening to someone else.

Rose pulled away Maud's camiknickers, and buried her face there – her tongue like the candle-flame.

The smothering of their love-making made it the more intense. When the moment of ecstasy came, Maud bit the pillow, screaming inside. The explosion spread from her sex in spasms across her body. She knocked over the half-full glass, its red liquid forming a new continent on the floorboards.

It had been the first in a very long time. She wanted to cry out, to shout down the sky. Instead she let the books shout for her, imagining the chorus of countless words let out in one long sentence – lines of ink across continents, centuries, the contours of their bodies.

'Une petite mort,' Rose breathed. 'It is good to die a little – it makes us feel alive.'

They held each other, as waves of shivering subsided. Maud's skin felt on fire. The slightest touch set further explosions off.

'Oh, Rose ... '

Maud lay in an ecstatic stillness, feeling the shockwaves pass through her body. Doorways opened inside, gateways unlocking that had been closed for years. The defences of her fastness melted, revealing not a hollow land, but lush worlds within – echoing with the crashing of inner seas.

Then came a deep peace, a silent stillness. After all of the miles, all of the years, Maud finally stopped. Here, in 37, rue de la Bûcherie, was kilometre zero.

Maud felt the grain of the floorboards beneath her fingertips as she trailed her hand luxuriously over the floor. Above, a spider worked on its lattice of web. Flies offered themselves to its trap. The spines of books glistened in the half-light like tattooed skin. The beam of a motorcycle carved the shadow across the ceiling.

Paris buzzed outside the window, restless, insatiable, a black cat on the prowl.

Rose breathed into her ear, traced a nail over her flesh, leaving a wake of rippling shivers, like a pleasure cruiser on the Seine.

Maud felt split in two – with the river running through her. The flux of life.

It was as if she could hear the sound of Paris's thoughts, encompass all of its passions and pains. She felt stretched over the city – beyond skin, boundariless.

Paris was a woman and, tonight, Maud was that woman.

Rose sat up and lit a cigarette.

Maud admired the naked back, the braille of the spine, the violin curvature of the hips. Like the Man Ray photograph, she thought.

They stayed awake until dawn, talking, talking about their lives – their childhood, their dreams, their fears. Maud unburdened herself of nearly all that had happened – but held back from talking about the events at Glastonbury Tor, West Kennet and Broceliande. She found it impossible to articulate these inexplicable experiences without feeling ridiculous, or insane. Was that how Isambard had felt?

Maud wept with bittersweet joy – she felt had not felt so close to someone, so loved, since the earliest days of her marriage. It had been a long time, a long, long time since she had felt the touch of a human hand on her skin, received tenderness or affection.

She wept for all the years lost, all the denied feelings, all the yearning unheard.

Hiraeth, she sighed, exorcising a ghost. The longing had finally stopped. She looked down at her body like it was a stranger's no more. She had come home to herself.

Maud suddenly felt vulnerable, her soul exposed. But Rose reassured her, talked of her own background, told her secrets – so their intimacy was shared.

Hesitatingly, as if removing layers of make-up, Rose talked of her origins. She came from Providence, Rhode Island. Her parents were wealthy; her mother descended from French Jewish aristocrats, her father a hard-working, hard-drinking Protestant, something of a noise in the Big Apple. Rose had showed an aptitude for languages, and had an Ivy League education. As the only child everything was expected of her, including being the son her father never had. He had pushed her but had never been pleased. She had escaped as soon as she could, but her parents had wanted her to return, to marry, to settle down, to follow destiny – at least the one they had chosen for her. France had offered her a freedom denied her at home – here she could be herself.

Rose gazed at the flame. The candle guttered low in its saucer.

They held each other, shivering under the blanket in the first coolness of dawn. As the light grew outside, they came to know each other gradually, like photographs developing in a darkroom.

In the morning, as Rose showered next door, her wordless singing mixing with the gurgling and grinding of pipes, Maud thought of the last time she had made love — ten years ago, to Isambard before he left for the war. He had been frightened, tense. Their love-making had had a violent urgency about it, a rough desperation, as if her husband had known he was doomed. Afterwards he had whispered 'Thanatos ... Eros' bitterly to himself through gritted teeth, before falling asleep in her arms.

She had felt that she would never let another man touch her. It would have seemed like a betrayal of his memory.

Yet a woman's touch was a different matter.

That night the world had shifted in its axis...

'Come on, lazybones, let's get some breakfast!'

Rose was shaking her awake. Maud had nodded off. She wished she could lie in for ever. She did not want this to end.

But Rose was still there, full of life, drying herself quickly with a towel. Her joie de vivre was infectious. Maud quickly washed and dressed and hand in hand they went out, as silently as they had entered.

It had rained in the night and the streets were fresh. Rose took Maud to a nearby café, overlooking Nôtre Dame, where she ordered them warm pain au chocolat and scalding café au lait. They sat and sipped in silence, grinning at each other in the light of the new day, devouring the sight of each other — seeing each other fully in daylight for the first time.

Maud was ravenous. Suddenly she had an appetite for life again. Everything tasted so good. She even shared a cigarette with Rose afterwards. Her nose wrinkled and she coughed a little, but she liked its warmth inside her.

Rose leant against her. And Maud did not feel ashamed. It felt like the most natural thing in the world. They were girlfriends, able to display their affection in public far more easily than men.

'What would you like to do today?' asked Rose.

Maud sighed and shrugged. Here she was in Paris on a bright summer's morning. It felt like anything was possible. Her heart was so full it felt like it would burst.

'Oh, I don't mind – as long as I'm with you.'

Rose kissed her on the cheek. 'Come on then. Let's have some fun!'

Rose threw some francs on the table and grabbed Maud's hand.

'Where are you taking me?' Maud laughed.

'Wait and see.'

Rose led Maud down into the métro.

They emerged at Rocherau. Here, she was led down some steps into darkness. A bulldog-faced man was playing solitaire and smoking. He looked up from his counter with Gallic indifference. Rose paid, and led on.

'What is this place?'

'It's a scream. Here, you'll need a lamp.'

Rose handed her an oil lamp. Maud looked at it bemused.

Her guide led her into some low tunnels, damp and dripping. When Maud saw what the lamp illuminated she let out a stifled gasp.

'Skulls!'

'Yes. Thousands of them ... From the plague mainly – although they are perfectly safe now.' Rose stroked one. 'Here, touch it.'

Maud recoiled in disgust. 'Urgh, no!'

'It won't hurt you. You've got one beneath that beautiful face. Come on – there's miles of them!'

Rose led a somewhat reluctant Maud along the endless catacombs lined with bones – like dry stone walls. They held each other like they were on a ghost train, and made jokes, trying to laugh at death. But for Maud the truth was all too real.

'This place is giving me the willies. Can we leave now?'

'Sure thing! Worth seeing, though, wasn't it?'

It was a relief to be out in the bright sunshine again. Maud loved the sun on her face. She breathed in the air, still charged from the previous night's rain.

'You look like you've seen a ghost, Maddy!'

Maud began to speak about why she had come to Europe, the pilgrimage she was on to Mons. She talked about her husband freely for the first time, her loss, her grief, how her life had ground to a standstill, but did not mention how she had seen him that year, the inexplicable things that had happened.

'You're so pale. I think you need some colour! I know just the thing.'

'Where are you taking me next? To the Bastille?'

'No, silly! Shopping!'

Rose led her to the famous boutiques and insisted she tried on different dresses and hats. Until she bought something colourful, Rose would not let her go.

Shyly, Maud emerged in a chalk blue summer dress, with a lemon yellow chiffon scarf around her neck and a white cloche hat.

'That's better. Vive la Chanel!'

'Sorry for being so grumpy. Rose, you've done me the world of good. I don't know how I can ever thank you.'

'Buy me a meal – that'd be a start!'

'Okay – where shall we go?'

'I know just the place.'

They hopped on a tram and went to Montmartre. They sat at a table on the square where artists painted portraits. They had quiche Lorraine with a crisp salad drizzled with tangy dressing and crêpes Suzette, washed down with a carafe of chilled white wine. Maud wasn't used to drinking in the daytime, and was feeling a little dizzy.

It was midday and getting very hot.

'Can we go somewhere cool and quiet for a little bit?'

'Of course – we're in the right area. The Sacré-Cœur is just along the road. It's lovely. Sunday service should be over by now.'

The doors were impressively baroque. The two women entered in high spirits, bubbling with laughter, but Maud shushed her friend. She sensed the sacredness of the place, and respected it.

Finding an empty pew they sat in the delicious coolness of the cathedral. Maud detected in the circular designs of the building a sense of the sacred feminine. It felt like her world was turning faster and faster, but here she felt at the hub. While she kept her centre everything would be okay.

Afterwards, they emerged on to the steps, overlooking the city. Young people sat on the steps, chatting, playing guitar, laughing and smoking. Below, the city simmered like a summer field by Monet. Maud had wanted to see the Impressionists while in Paris but time was running out.

She did not know how to break the news to Rose.

Smiling, her new companion bought them each a lemon sorbet and they sat and licked them in the shade of a cypress tree in the park – like two Eves, joked Rose.

With the cold tang of the fruit upon their lips, they kissed briefly.

No one seemed to notice, or care.

Paris belonged to lovers.

Arm in arm, they walked across to the funicular railway, and took it down to the bottom of the hill. Maud could not remember when she had last done something 'just for fun'.

They emerged by an ornate merry-go-round.

Rose looked at Maud, her eyes gleaming. 'Shall we?'

'Why not?' Maud smiled, feeling frivolous, carefree.

Paris had seduced her. She loved its wise excess, its stylish flamboyance.

They climbed on the ornate horses, laughing. Maud side-saddle, but Rose straddled hers like a man, hitching up her skirt, much to the disgust of a prim mother with her fat boy. 'This is just like a rodeo,' laughed Rose. 'Ride 'em cowboy! Yee-haa!'

The music started and the wheel began to spin. The sun-dappled gardens swirled around them, the horses rising and falling erotically. The one constant was the gaze Maud fixed on Rose's laughing blue eyes.

Her heart was swirling. Was she falling in love? But this wasn't planned! She began to panic a little. It felt like she was being swept up in the momentum – things were out of her control again. Yet it was so wonderful, too wonderful. She felt like she did not deserve such happiness. It was not her lot. Her path was darker. She had a destiny to fulfil, a tryst with the dead. Before she could love and live again, she had this duty to perform.

When the merry-go-round stopped, they giddily got off, propping one another up. They collapsed on a bench and caught their breath.

'Woo-wee! That was a gas! I love this city. And there's so much more to show you.'

Maud had to break the news.

'Rose, listen. Be serious for a moment, please. I'm having the best time of my life, but I – I have to go.'

'What do you mean?'

'I've got to leave today.'

'Today?'

'Yes, I've got a train to catch at 4.30 to Brussels. I've got a hotel booked there. I'm planning to be in Mons tomorrow. And then I've got to go home.'

Rose looked devastated. 'You're going so soon? But we've started to get to know one another! I thought you were having a ball.'

'I am, believe me – but I have this one last thing to do.'

'What – visit a battlefield? Gee, that sounds really swell.'

'Rose, please – don't spoil it. He was my husband. I have to do this for him. Maybe one day...'

'One day, what? Maybe one day I'll have a husband, I'll understand – when I've grown up?'

Rose was red in the face. Her raised American voice drew the attention of onlookers.

'Rose, please, sit down. Don't make a fuss.'

'Don't make a fuss – that's so English! Stiff upper lip, take it on the chin – that's your problem. You don't let it out!'

'I know, but Rose – you're embarrassing me.'

'Embarrassing you, am I? Last night we were in each other's arms. You weren't embarrassed then, were you?'

Shocked looks from the people nearby. The prim mother led her child away, covering up his ears, giving them a scolding look.

Maud was mortified. She stood up, tight-lipped, and made ready to leave.

'Goodbye Rose.'

'Maddy, please, sit down. I'm, I'm sorry. Me and my big mouth ... Please – I didn't mean to hurt you – it's just that I'm hurting real bad. I – I love you.'

'Don't be foolish – we've only just met.' She couldn't meet Rose's eye.

'I know you feel the same. Don't deny it. You've been denying things for too long, by the sound of it.'

Maud didn't like this intimate judgement, but she knew Rose was right.

They held each other's hands, their defences collapsed, and they cried silently into one another's arms.

'Here.' Maud offered her handkerchief. 'You know, I never used to be able to cry. Now I can't stop.'

'Good, I'm glad. Oh Maud, I wish you didn't have to go so soon.'

Maud sighed heavily. 'So do I, but I have something I must do.'

'Then let me take you to the station at least.'

'Yes, of course. That – that would be nice.'

'We better get going then, I suppose.'

Together, they set off for the Gare du Nord. After the rush of picking up the luggage from the hotel and a sweltering taxi ride through the sticky streets they finally stood on the platform, breathless. Maud gazed around her in a daze. Steam rose in blue clouds like a Monet painting.

'Write to me!' Rose shouted.

'To where?'

'To the bookshop.'

A whistle blew with piercing finality.

The train began to move.

Rose ran alongside as the carriage shunted off. She caught up with Maud's compartment and thrust something through the window.

Before Maud could question her Rose stopped running, her chest fluttering like a bird's. She waved and blew a kiss, before vanishing into the veil of steam.

Maud sat down in the empty compartment and looked at what Rose had given her. It was the copy of Sappho's poems.

Maud held the book to her breast and the burning image of Rose in her mind's eye.

The wheels turned beneath her, faster and faster, taking her East.

Maud sat back and reflected on her time in France. How far she had come since leaving Paddington on that wintry morning! Her world had changed beyond recognition.

The train sped along – towards the place of departure, yet for the first time Maud wished her destiny belonged elsewhere than its terminus.

22

Vanishing Point

They were in one of the many mouths of Hell
Not seen of seers in visions; only felt
As teeth of traps; when bones and the dead are smelt
Under the mud where long ago they fell
Mixed with the sour sharp odour of the shell.

'Untitled', Wilfred Owen

Maud watched the landscape turn from Monet to Van Dyck as the train crossed into the flat fields of Belgium. Long straight roads intersecting the track at bridges and crossings disappeared into the haze of August. Only perpendicular lines of poplars broke the monotony. Telegraph wires rose and fell beside the track, and the parallel rails flickered and flashed like the end of a film reel. Hypnotised, Maud thought of Rose. Was she real, or a Fata Morgana? Maud's 'brief stopover in Paris' had turned into something more than she had bargained for! If it weren't for the additions to her wardrobe and the book she clutched, she might have wondered if it had really happened.

As the train passed through a shaded cutting Maud caught her reflection in the window – white hat, yellow scarf, blue dress. She did not recognise herself. It was not only the world that was changing.

From Brussels, Maud caught a local train to traumatised Mons, where she checked into a tidy but dull hotel. She was dog-tired after missing a night's sleep; despite freshening up after her journey she immediately collapsed on to the bed and was soon in deep slumber. The next morning she visited the small museum and bought post-cards of the famous 'angel'. The event had become incorporated into local legend. The memorials offered no more clues, except to the scale of the massacre. She had to visit the site itself. With the help of a local map, she set off for the battlefield.

Crossing over the canal, Maud followed the footpath – well trodden no doubt by others who had wanted to pay their respects.

The battlefield lay before her in the sunshine, tall with grass swaying in the sultry breeze. Poppies dappled the meadow. Maud walked carefully, as if over hallowed ground. And was it not? Had it not been sanctified, by death? Enough blood spilled, sacrifices made, so that one corner of it could be forever British, French or German?

Maud savoured the silence and space after the crazy hedonism of Paris. Her mind was still reeling from what had transpired. She tried to shake it off, to pretend it had happened to someone else. But it had happened to her – she could still feel the ghost of Rose's touch upon her skin. She carried the image of the young American in her mind as she scanned the fallow fields, a Demeter in search of her Persephone. She would not find her here. This was Hades' hunting ground.

The dry grass brushed her legs browned by the sun. The landscape seemed empty, bereft.

What was she thinking of, having a romance with someone half her age, a girl at that? Maud flushed with embarrassment. It was almost like running off with one of her Lewes girls – almost. Yet Rose was a young woman, not a girl, and an intelligent, independent one at that. Not the type to be forced into anything. The truth of the matter was that Maud had been the seduced, not the seducer. She was the innocent abroad, despite her years, whereas Rose was the sassy pioneer. What did she see in a frumpy old schoolmistress from Eastbourne? Maud wondered, scanning the fields. Then the bitter reality hit her like a mocking voice. Approval from a mother figure ... And what did she see in Rose? A surrogate daughter? So, she concluded, wanting to convince herself, the connection was maternal – and should never have escalated into anything else. Maud felt deeply ashamed, and wished she could turn back time, undo what had been done. Yet had it not been beautiful?

Among the sallow meadow grass, Maud spotted a nest filled with three eggs. Such a sight gave her an absurd sense of hope. 'Life-in-death', Isambard would call it. Then there was a slight parting of the grass, and an grey-scaled adder slinked into view – its zigzagged back eerily fluid, an organic geometry. Stealthily, inevitable as fate, it moved towards the eggs.

Maud, paralysed with fear, watched as the adder swallowed them, one by one. She felt helpless, but guiltily glad she was not the victim. Carefully she stepped back, out of its fatal compass. The snake, sensing her, recoiled into the grass.

She suddenly realised that she could have stopped it after all.

Upset, as much with her inaction as with the fate of the chicks, she wandered through the grass in a depression – dragging her own shadow with her.

It was so peaceful, she thought. Like any meadow in the summer. Yet here guns had split the sky and gouged the earth – hollows were still visible, like inverted barrows. Graves of the New Iron Age, Isambard would have called them.

Man-high saplings grew next to butchered stumps. Birds sang unseen in the branches. Such a sweet sound in so mournful a place. Like the birds of Rhiannon, Maud thought. Perhaps beneath one of these mounds the dismembered head of Bran entertained his war-weary company. But for Maud the forbidden door had been opened by the shell-shocked man in Paddington Station – and all the woe had come flooding back.

There would be no rest until her husband's spirit was set free.

Here, in the fields of Mons, he had vanished. It was impossible to tell where exactly. Yet in opposing lines ran the remains of trenches. Like the cursus at Stonehenge, she thought. A man-made line, carved from the breast of Belgium soil.

Was this the alignment you wanted to find? Maud thought bitterly.

A buzzing grew louder in the air. Maud looked up, expecting to see a biplane. Instead, she was surprised by a bee. She laughed. Drunk on pollen, it warbled over to a line of sunflowers – inspecting them like a fat general.

The exact circumstances of her husband's death were a complete mystery to her. All she had was the brief letter from Isambard's commanding officer. That was it. A life lost, another shattered, by a few words. She knew he had been in the Royal Flying Corps, that he was doing aerial surveillance. That he had gone missing in action on this battlefield in the first hours of the Battle of the Frontier was as far as the sparse facts went. After that, nothing – as if he had simply vanished into No Man's Land.

Yet he was not alone. How many soldiers fell in these fields? The place was tainted. That was the only way to describe it. On the surface it looked like a summer meadow – but it felt dark, cheerless. Maud sensed an invisible shadow. Before 1923 she would have ridiculed such a notion, but after what she had seen this past year, she had grown sensitised, and less sceptical, to such ideas. She had walked with ghosts – and now she stood in their graveyard. How many men had died here? The questioned niggled her. She dreaded to think. The visit to the memorial, to the war cemetery and to the museum had gleaned the cold facts. Yet she wanted something more than statistics. What she wanted to experience was the last place on earth where her husband had walked – or passed over. Had he been shot down, or just crashed? No one would ever tell her. The War Office was polite but unhelpful. Perhaps they simply did not know. In a mechanised war, death is such an anonymous business. No one could have kept track of the slaughter. Who kept records in a charnel house? Who could say exactly where Private So-and-so had been blown to bits? Where Officer What-not had been mown down by machine gun?

Maud wandered the killing field, wishing her Nubi was with her. Perhaps the lurcher could track down the last mortal remains of his master. Or had the trail gone cold? Who was she fooling? What did she expect to find here? A skeleton? A cromlech?

Isambard had taken his last journal with him to the grave. What his last thoughts were, in those first few days of the conflict she would never know. All she had was a censored letter home:

19ᵗʰ August, 1914

Darling Maud,

I'm stationed at xxxxxxxxxx. After initial rigorous training at RAF Duxford, flew to France. Preparations hurried, to say the least. Flying within a week, with my co-pilot, a chap called Mallard. We have to work close together. Camaraderie rather forced. There's a false bonhomie hiding the fear. Soon be at xxxxxxxxxx. Missing you dreadfully. Take Nubi for lots of walks. O, how I yearn for those lonely Downs. It is odd how things turn out. I had no wish to become a railway engineer. Now I have become a Surveillance Officer. Where is choice in this? Yet, for better or worse, I am here, doing my bit. I am sorry things did not turn out for the best. I wish it could have been better between us.

Will write again soon. TTFN.

With love, your Isambard

Maud tried to read between the lines. The fear, the loneliness, the tension ... Isambard had been a man out of his time. Forced into history.

She sat down and read a random extract from 'The Wasteland':

What is that sound high in the air
Murmur of maternal lamentation
Who are those hooded hordes swarming
Over endless plains, stumbling in cracked earth
Ringed by the flat horizon only.

It seemed to capture the mood of the place perfectly. It was as if the earth were silently screaming. She lay down against it and felt the pain and grief pour through her.

The tears came like summer rain. She wept for all those who had fallen.

For a long while Maud lay there, spent, silent. Then, aching, raw, she got up and dusted herself down.

Fortunately, nobody had seen this outburst. Raggedly, she sang 'Pack up Your Troubles in Your Old Kit Bag' to herself, her words falling like dead birds in the air. Scanning the mutilated land one last time, she whispered, 'Goodbye,' and turned away.

She was glad to leave the place. She made her way to the station, to catch the train back west. She would return to Britain with no clearer idea of how or why her husband had been taken from her − but at least a greater understanding of where. Now she had seen his place of departure it gave her some peace of mind. Another piece of the puzzle fell into place.

Every day, Isambard became more real to her. It was as if by manifesting him through memory she could finally release him. Upon her return there was one last port of call to complete the ritual − she needed to visit the grave of the Unknown Warrior in Westminster Abbey. It was the only memorial her husband had, as one of the countless missing in action. The Arc de Triomphe was impressive but did not have the same resonance to her. Paris had taken on another meaning.

Her thoughts once more turned to Rose. How gentler were the ways of women than those of men! Maud missed her − missed her voice, her vitality, her love for life. Would they ever see each other again? Not unless she did something about it − wasn't that the lesson she was learning this year? Nothing changes unless you take the initiative. Emboldened by her adventures, Maud decided then and there to seize the bull by the horns. To blazes with the consequences! When she got back to Eastbourne she would write to Rose at Shakespeare and Company. Perhaps they could maintain a correspondence at least. Yes.

There would be nothing untoward in that.

Hiraeth, she sighed. Yet for the first time her longing took on another form. What was this? Pull yourself together, woman! You have work to do. How could she entertain such foolish notions when she must return home and somehow release her husband's spirit? The vastness of her task threatened to overwhelm her. The sanguine porters loaded her luggage on to the train, but only she could carry this burden. She carried her husband's death like an unborn child. She would never be free to love, to live again, until she had freed his ghost. The engine whistle blew, the shrill sound of the trapped phantom within. The steam shunted the pistons into life and Maud moved towards her final destination: a rendezvous with the unknown.

23

The Unknown Warrior

Who but I knows the secret of the unhewn dolmen?
'Song of Amergin', Old Irish

22nd September, Westminster Abbey

Maud walked as quietly as possible through the pools of autumn light filtering through the stained glass, but her heels scraped on the flagstones and tombstones beneath, echoing about the vast cathedral. She remembered visiting the national mausoleum as a child on a school trip, but this was the first time she'd returned.

Of course, she recalled vividly the burial of the Unknown Warrior, with the grand procession witnessed by thousands of people. From the edge of Trafalgar Square she had watched the gun carriage, pulled by six black horses bearing the coffin of the anonymous serviceman – chosen by Brigadier General L J Wyatt from four exhumed from the battlefields of Aisne, Somme, Ypres and Arras. She had seen the King unveil the flag-covered Cenotaph for the first time. And as the eleven o'clock chimes of Big Ben died away she had stood in silence with the nation for two minutes to mark the Armistice. The effect of millions of people standing still and silent, of the restless city of London coming to a dead stop, was unspeakably powerful. It was as if those two minutes opened a doorway between the worlds of the living and the dead – a No Man's Land of time, brief, but containing eternity. The vacuum had stirred feelings subdued for too long. Maud had been unable to stay. In a panic, she rushed as best she could, through the crowds, back to the underground station – to escape the emotions threatening to overwhelm her. Grief was a private thing – it felt obscene to show it or share it. Her loss belonged to her, and nobody else.

Yet here she was, finally visiting the famous grave, three years later.

It was a weekday, and the Abbey was quieter than usual. Maud had come up to London for a training day, and had slipped away as soon as possible. Churches had made her nervous since she had renounced her faith – it was as though she were trespassing. A choir practised in the stalls, the strains of 'Onward Christian Soldiers' rising and falling. Visitors shuffled around, inspecting the famous graves, comparing what was before them with their guidebooks. A widow arranged the vases of flowers, the colours contrasting her black garb. Everything else was sombre, subdued, drained of colour.

Tentatively, Maud turned the corner of the nave. She was expecting a large tomb – so large had it loomed in the public imagination. But there it was on the floor – a black slab of marble bordered by poppies. She tried to swallow, her mouth suddenly dry. The nave was bathed in soft light. Visitors circulated around the grave and back out again. She wished she could be alone, but there was no option.

Carefully, Maud approached and stopped before it. The inscription, so familiar, etched as it was into the nation's heart, was there before her to read:

> BENEATH THIS STONE RESTS THE BODY
> OF A BRITISH WARRIOR
> BROUGHT FROM FRANCE TO LIE AMONG
> THE MOST ILLUSTRIOUS IN THE LAND
> AND BURIED HERE ON ARMISTICE DAY
> 11 NOV 1920 IN THE PRESENCE OF
> HIS MAJESTY KING GEORGE V
> HIS MINISTERS OF STATE
> THE CHIEFS OF HIS FORCES
> AND A VAST CONCOURSE OF THE NATION.
> THUS ARE COMMEMORATED THE MANY
> MULTITUDES WHO DURING THE GREAT
> WAR OF 1914–1918 GAVE THE MOST THAT
> MAN CAN GIVE, LIFE ITSELF,
> FOR GOD
> FOR KING AND COUNTRY
> FOR THE SACRED CAUSE OF JUSTICE AND
> THE FREEDOM OF THE WORLD.
>
> THEY BURIED HIM AMONG THE KINGS BECAUSE HE
> HAD DONE GOOD TOWARDS GOD AND TOWARD
> HIS HOUSE.

For several minutes Maud stood gazing at the inscription. She thought about her husband, who had no grave. Was this then his only memorial? She thought of the mighty tombs and barrows she had seen over the year, and on walks with her husband. How much more impressive they were, in the landscape, in their anonymity, than a few words on the floor – mere furniture for the 'house of God'! Was this what all those men died for? For 'King and Country'? To maintain the status quo? Justice and freedom? How much of that was in the world? Hypothetical abstractions. The hypocrisy and pointlessness of it sickened her.

'Not much, is it?'

Maud caught her breath, startled by the voice with its Cockney burr. She looked up to see a man on the other side of the grave. He was middle-aged, thin, with one eye. A scar ran down the left side of his face. Maud stared at the ruin of the eye socket, then purposefully looked away from it, noticing the details of his clothes – a cheap suit with medals pinned to it. He held a flat cap in his hands.

'Sorry, you startled me. What did you say?'

'The grave – not much to remember all those dead, is it?

'No. No, it isn't.'

'Lost your husband, did you?'

Maud blanched.

"Scuse me – no offense, like. But we're all in the same boat, aren't we?'

'Yes, I suppose we are. My husband. Isambard Kerne.'

'I'm sorry. What was his regiment?'

'He was an officer in the Royal Flying Corps.'

'Blimey, a flying man. Fair play. I was a sapper, meself. In the Fourth Middlesex. Went in with Frenchy's lot, the BEF, originally. What a bloody mess that was! Where did your husband buy it? Begging your pardon, miss. Don't want to talk ill of the dead, specially 'ere.'

'That's quite alright. It's better to talk about it openly, than smother it with euphemisms. "Passed on", "gone to rest", "no longer with us" – nonsense! They are always with us.'

The veteran was taken aback a little by Maud's passion.

'Of course, luv. Course they are. I – I still speak to me mates. The ones I lost. They haven't gone away.'

Maud looked curiously at the man. It seemed he understood.

'My Sammy went missing in the Battle of the Frontier.'

The old soldier went white.

'You – you mean Mons, Belgium? August 23rd, 1914?'

'Yes. You know your war, sir.'

'I should bloody do, 'scuse my French – I was there!'

Maud's eyes widened. She looked at the man with renewed interest. 'You were?'

'That's why I wear this, miss.'

The man pointed to one of the medals on his chest.

'Right old scrap, it were. The Hun had us outnumbered two to one, but we fought like the devil. We had the big fella on our side, didn't we?' He nodded upwards. 'At first, it looked like we were going to be wiped out – but then something strange happened.'

Maud was riveted by now. She was glad no one else was about. Their hushed voices held the silence, their words breathed like prayers.

'Now, you may have heard about this from the papers – but I was there. I saw it, with my two eyes – before a bit of shrapnel took one out. It was a scorching day. We'd walked seventeen miles the day before. We lined up along the Mons canal, all twenty one miles of it. My lot and the Micks – Second Royal Irish to you – we were caught between the Devil and the deep blue, at Mons itself, where the canal snakes east and north around the town. Mons, bleedin' grim place – old mining town, all slag 'eaps and soot.'

'I visited it recently.'

The veteran raised an eyebrow and looked at Maud in a new light.

'Did you, lady? That was brassy of you.' He hesitated. 'What was it like?'

'Eerily empty ... Everything had grown over, but it felt dead. It looked like a sunny meadow – but was full of unseen shadows.' Maud tried to find the right phrase to express the absence she had sensed there. 'It felt like a hole in the world.'

The veteran nodded, satisfied, and continued: 'I remember the mist that morning – like London fog. Yet it was boiling hot that summer, and the mist would soon burn off. And the strangest thing. The local church bells were ringing, as if it was any other Sunday morning, and we were off to church, not battle. All morning they tolled – p'raps the people were inside, praying for us all. We needed all the 'elp we could get. A hundred and fifty thousand of Kluck's lot were on the way.'

The veteran looked around to check they were alone. With a hunted look, he continued. 'The Germans came out of the mist and we opened fire. So began the "War to End All Wars". Until the next time.' He hacked into a handkerchief. 'Ciggies,' he explained, getting his breath back. 'Didn't start smokin' until the war... Now where was I? Oh yeah. The air was filled with fire and thunder, as if Old Nick himself was there, opening the gates of hell – welcoming us in. And we didn't have a snowball's chance. For many, meself included, it was the first time we had tasted combat. I was only just eighteen, but some were younger. Fresh out of boot camp – all arse and elbows. Some just froze stiff, but we cracked off a few good shots. I always 'ad a good aim. If we were going down, we were gonna take as many with us as we could. Four hundred we lost that day from my regiment alone. It looked like we were doomed. But then a miracle 'appened. A bleedin' miracle!'

The man crossed himself, and lowered his voice. 'Now, I know this is going to sound crackers.' He cleared his throat, looking nervously about. 'The sky opened up and...' The soldier looked up at the window, his eyes filling with light. 'There was the angel – shining above us. Michael 'imself came down, and rallied the troops. Suddenly it felt like we were in Agincourt, firing arrows instead of rifles. We felt fearless and fought like lions. No one had time to question what we had seen – it's like we were possessed, or something. The 'Oly Spirit was in us, and nothing could stand in our way. Then the light left and we 'ad to retreat – but not with our tails between our legs. We put up a good fight that day – we gave Fritz a taste of good English steel. Just so they knew what they 'ad coming. We weren't gonna roll over and give up the ghost for them.'

The veteran stopped, and suddenly became shrunken – the light fading from his eyes. Other visitors were approaching the grave. The man looked terrified all of a sudden and began to sidle off.

'Wait, what's your name?' Maud called after him.

With surprising speed the one-eyed man disappeared around the corner, out of sight. Maud tried to follow, but was forced back by a whole school party. By the time she managed to leave the Abbey, the mysterious veteran had vanished.

Maud was left reeling in windswept Parliament Square, the blodstained leaves being torn from the trees around her.

For years she had not known what had become of her husband, having been met with a wall of silence, but now she had a better idea – from someone who had actually been there. If she only knew his name, some proof of the conversation. It was slim pickings to hang hope upon – a rag, a bone and hank of hair. Yet it was more than she'd ever had. After visiting Mons and hearing the eyewitness account, at least she could visualise her husband's point of departure, if not the way he had gone. Something strange had happened that day, something beyond reason. Proof or not, it had taken her husband. He had crossed over, but somehow had not died. His spirit survived in limbo – thanks to her, she thought bitterly.

What this 'angel' had been who could say? If it had been merely a mass hallucination, then how could it have had such a significant effect on the battle and upon the morale of the nation and its army afterwards as the story of the 'Angel of Mons' spread like wildfire? Some claimed it had been triggered by a short story by Arthur Machen called 'The Bowmen' – but that had not been published until a month afterwards. Whatever it had been, its impact was real enough. Eyewitnesses had been found on both sides, but she hadn't spoken to one – until now.

If it were an angel, then would that not indicate the existence of God? It didn't seem God was dead after all. If anything, the world had become more supernatural. Had not Maud spent the year walking with the dead? And now she had a tryst with one – the Long Man at Samhain.

She sat on a wrought-iron bench and tried to centre herself. It seemed the ground beneath her feet was no longer firm. The autumn wind ruled, seizing everything not bolted down. Maud felt like she too was being swept off, at the mercy of invisible forces. Her sanity was on tenterhooks. She gripped the arm of the bench and tried to take deep breaths. Closing her eyes, she tried to focus on something solid, a vivid memory, as London roared around her.

She thought of Rose, her smile, her eyes, her accent, the texture of her hair, the crushed petals of her lips. Yet how real was she – her fairy lover? And if they were more than passing ships, then where, if anywhere, would it lead? Would the journey begun in Paris that one hot night ever continue? Or was it a one-off? How much of it was serendipity? If she hadn't gone on the pilgrimage she would not have met Rose, never had the experience in Broceliande, never found hidden talents, hidden tastes.

The significances telescoped around her, roads without end. By Westminster Abbey alignments of intent, chains of consequence, stretched out like wires, and she was caught in their cat's cradle. There was no extricating herself now. She had to go to the end of the line, to the Long Man.

2 4

The Bone Fire

Go now, beloved — but remember, past
The limits of terrestrial love or hate,
I, at the portal of the unknown vast,
Shall, silent, wait.

'Go Now, Beloved', Harold Monro

31st October, Eastbourne

Archibald rapped on the door, but received no reply. Well, he wouldn't be ignored any longer. Nobody ignored Archibald Kerne! It wasn't as if he had a shortage of admirers: 'lady friends', as he called them. One or two had even carried his children. But Maud was different somehow. She got under his skin. This time it had to be more than the thrill of the chase. Otherwise, what was he doing, standing in the cold in a god-forsaken back street of Eastbourne?

The sky cast a pall over the mean pinched houses. Dark at midday, Eastbourne out of season seemed as bereft as a widow.

'Morning.' A man passed, doffing his cap, casting a suspicious eye over the visitor.

Archibald had had enough of being cold-shouldered. Had he not done all he could have to 'be considerate'? She had avoided him all summer, and then buggered off to Paris after he had offered to take her there at Easter. The insult! She couldn't have hurt him more if she'd tried.

His hand was numb from banging on the door. Neighbours' curtains were twitching. Giving them a cold stare, he pulled out a key from his breast pocket and slipped it into the lock. Constance had lent it to him so he could go around and check on Maud – no one had heard from her in weeks.

'Hullo? Anybody home?'

His words fell dead in the air. The passageway was chilly. Flipping on the electric light, he could see his breath freezing before him. He was grateful that no Nubi bounded up to him, but slightly worried about the emptiness and silence. Where was she? You can't hide for ever, Maud.

Archibald explored the house. There was no sign of her in the parlour or kitchen. The house seemed hardly lived in, so spick and span it was – not like his bachelor hovel in Highgate. He climbed the narrow staircase and tried the bedrooms. What if he found her dead? he thought suddenly, his blood running cold. He pushed open her bedroom door, feeling uncomfortable about trespassing. The bed was made, the chamber neat and sober. A photograph of Isambard sat on a bedside cabinet. Archibald flinched from its gaze, and tried the other room.

Isambard's study lay undisturbed as a shrine, except for the opened escritoire. Archibald wandered around the small room, inspecting the accoutrements of his brother's private life. The maps and surveyor's apparatus did not surprise him – he begrudgingly admired his brother's expertise. Their father would have been proud of him, he thought bitterly. What did he have to make his father proud: a couple of minor medals, several debts and a dubious war wound?

Then he noticed the journals on the desk, and was immediately drawn to them. He picked one up and flicked it open. The handwriting was instantly familiar. He vaguely remembered Maud accidentally mentioning something about a journal. So they were Isambard's. The sneaky old cat – kept them to herself, hadn't she?

Leaning back in the chair, Archibald put his feet up on the desk and began to browse.

After attempting to read the scrupulous but obscure notes, his concentration wandered. Instead, he scanned for mention of his own name, flicking through the pages of detailed field observation. The diagrams and references to various place names around England caught his eye. So this was what Isambard had got up to. It was like catching up with a brother he never really knew. His opinion of him altered little. Useless dreamer, he concluded, snapping the final tome shut and tossing it back with the others.

Archibald went downstairs, rubbing his hands together. He went into the kitchen and put the kettle on. Scavenging, he found some Hunter & Palmer's to munch on. He checked briefly for any brandy, but could see none about. As he searched he noticed the wall calendar had that day marked on it with a cross. Beneath the date was simply 'Long Man' in heavily underlined letters.

Archibald tried to remember where he had heard of the Long Man. Was it something in his brother's journals? He had seemed to go on about it a lot. It gnawed at the back of Archibald's mind.

While the kettle boiled, he decided to ring Constance and inform her of his progress. Picking up the receiver, he noticed a telephone number scrawled on a piece of paper, beside it: 'Giant's Rest, Wilmington. Single room, 31.10'. The penny suddenly dropped. That's where the Long Man is. She must have gone there for the night. Tonight – the 31st October!

Instead of ringing his sister-in-law, he rang the pub.

A young woman answered. 'Hello, Giant's Rest, can I help?'

'I do hope so. Could you tell me, do you have a Mrs Kerne staying with you this evening?'

'I'm sorry, sir, but we cannot share details of bookings.'

'Damn it, woman, this is her husband!'

'Begging your pardon, Mr Kerne. Yes, your wife has booked a single for this evening. Is there a problem?'

'No. Well, yes. We had a bit of a tiff. I was worried as to her whereabouts, but I'm sure she's in safe hands. I shan't trouble her. Thank you.'

Bingo! Archibald put the receiver down. What on earth was she doing, going there on Hallowe'en? It looks like she's finally lost her marbles, Archibald concluded. I need to save her from all this foolish nonsense.

'Isambard, you're not going to drag her into the grave with you,' he shouted to the top of the stairs; 'not if I can help it!'

Maud gazed into the flames as they issued from the black crackling logs piled in the wide inglenook hearth. Like spirits eager for release, she brooded, over a brandy. The wind outside the Giant's Rest sucked up the sparks or spat them out, as if the chimney were clearing its throat like an ancient storyteller. What tale would be told tonight?

And what a night it promised to be – for a tryst with the dead. The thought chilled her blood. It was not a night to be outside, but she had little choice if she was to honour her husband's final wish. Tonight she would end it. Or it would end her. If she did not die of exposure, who knew what other forces would assail her on the night when the way between the worlds was open: Samhain.

Maud was glad she had booked herself a room in the Giant's Rest. She hoped she would make it back to enjoy its comfort. Nubi lay at her feet, gnawing on a bone thrown him by the landlord. Flames cast their flickering light on his coat. He noticed Maud looking at him, and glanced up, tongue lolling, eyes bright.

'Alright, I suppose we better take you walkies.'

The lurcher cocked his head at the mention of the 'W' word.

Maud downed the dregs of her brandy. It burned inside her and made her head seem heavier. Yet she needed some Dutch courage tonight. She had an appointment with the dead.

In the snug a gaggle of locals were listening to a ballad from one of their company – a mutton-chopped man with a red nose and a full tankard.

Maud only caught a snatch of the slurred chorus:

Whom Long Thomas has taken for his fairy leman ...

It was as if she were Long Thomas's lover. Or had once been ... But she had come a long way since then. Now her heart belonged to someone else.

The song ended and tables were beat with fists in approval, making Nubi bark. The sound seemed to snap the group out of their drunken rêverie.

As she passed them, one of the men, with a gap-toothed leer, called out, 'Where you be going on a night like this, missy?'

'I have to exercise the hound.'

'Be careful that's all you exercise,' he slurred, with a wink. 'Didn't you know that longshanks up there, on the hill, once had a wife? Until she ran away ... He's been looking for his Eve ever since!'

The group of men laughed, but a withering look from Maud shut them up. Perhaps they could sense that silent power within her.

The wind howled down the chimney.

'Good night, gentlemen,' she hissed through gritted teeth.

She shot them a cold glance and left, but felt humiliated. Why had they assumed that because she was alone she must be a disreputable lady? That it allowed them to talk to her in such a lascivious manner?

Maud wished Rose was there. That would shut them up.

Annoyed, she wrapped her winter coat around her and pulled on her hat and gloves. She was glad to be leaving the pub now, even its warmth and shelter. It suddenly felt stuffy and oppressive. Whistling to Nubi, she walked into the night.

The lane was dark and raked by the wind. The bare trees knocked against one another as Maud set off up the track, passing the stern silhouette of Wilmington Priory on her right. She came to a stile and passed over, into a field.

Before her was the familiar landmark, the vista transformed by the season, the hour, and the decade's distance since she had first beheld it with Isambard on that summer's day. The figure of the Long Man stood out on the flank of Windover Hill, etched in chalk by the moonlight. Clouds raced overhead, ragged shrouds across the crone moon. Wrapped in several layers Maud tramped up the footpath to the giant, glad to have Nubi by her side. The lurcher's eyes flickered lambent in the moonlight, air freezing off lolling tongue. Alert to presences invisible to Maud, the hound prowled covertly along the hedgerows lining the track. She gripped the stang tightly, feeling protected by its power: she was glad she had brought it with her – on a sudden whim she'd snatched it from the study where it had stood for nine years.

This was the night. Here, in this place, she would end it. *The Long Man at Samhain – when the veil is thinnest.* Here she would release her husband's spirit – once and for all.

It had been a long journey through the year since her first sighting of him on the Tor. Now, third time lucky, she would exorcise Isambard from her life – if not from her heart. It wasn't because she did not love him. Walking in his footsteps this last year she had learnt to understand him. And she had learnt something about herself as well. A wilful independence. She had found a strength within her she did not know she had.

The wind blew cold and dry, stripping the last leaves from the trees. The grass hissed. Maud pulled her coat tighter around her neck, although the cold seemed to blow right through her.

Before she would have been terrified: by herself, at night, in the middle of nowhere. But she had endured many terrors and wonders these last twelve months. At times it seemed she was more at home in the spirit world than her own. Work, family, even friends felt very distant, almost insignificant. There was little holding her to life in Eastbourne. Perhaps that's why she found it easier to make this final journey – to the threshold of death.

The track ended at the bottom of the hill. Before her loomed the Long Man, foreshortened out of recognition. She stood at the feet of a god.

Nubi ran wild over the hill-side, looping around the figure like a sheepdog.

The wind howled around the barrows. The Hills of Peace were

stirring: the dead were not at rest tonight. Revealed by the moonlight, the clouds were like fleeing ghosts caught by a photographic flash.

Maud walked up and down in front of the giant, trying to keep warm, wondering what to do. What the hell was she doing here? It was Halloween! Yet once it had been Samhain, the Celtic fire festival of the dead, as that fey poet in London, AE, had told her. And Maud wished there had been a great bonfire there right now.

Sensing the hush in the hollow of the wind, she instinctively began to sing, softly at first, a little embarrassed, but also wary of breaking the silence of the place. At first it was pure sound, a call of the heart. She called to her husband, called him to release him. She thought of all they had shared together, all that she had to let go of. With each memory the pitch modulated, from sorrow to joy, tenderness and rage. The wind seemed to echo her melody, a mournful contralto. Then, unbidden, the ballad of Isambard's mother came to her lips, arising from the seedbed of the subconscious where it had slipped in like a ghost all those months ago:

> *The twelvemonth and a day being up,*
> *The dead began to speak:*
> *'Oh who sits weeping on my grave,*
> *and will not let me sleep?'*

> *'Tis I, my love, sits on your grave,*
> *and will not let you sleep;*
> *for I crave one kiss of your clay-cold lips,*
> *and that is all I seek.'*

> *'You crave one kiss of my clay-cold lips,*
> *but my breath smells earthly strong;*
> *if you have one kiss of my clay-cold lips,*
> *your time will not be long.'*

The air about the chalk giant intensified. Maud felt the night grow aware of her presence. Chthonic forces were being summoned. She stifled her fear, and continued:

> *''Tis down in yonder garden green,*
> *Love, where we used to walk,*
> *The finest flower that e'er was seen*
> *Is withered to a stalk.*
> *'The stalk is withered dry, my love,*
> *so will our hearts decay;*

so make yourself content, my love,
Till God calls you away.'

The silence expanded, as if the hillside leaned closer to listen. The moon suddenly broke free of the clouds and bathed the Long Man in blue light. The chalk giant seemed to move, as if straining at what he held. And Maud realised for the first time that perhaps he did not hold staves, but held open a doorway. The white cracks widened, and a light blazed out, dazzling Maud. Nubi was going mad, howling and growling. A low rumbling from beneath her feet filled the air. Maud steadied herself on the stang, stopped herself from running. This was it. She had to face her destiny.

A swirling tunnel of light telescoped open from the middle of the chalk giant, and out of it stepped a cloaked figure wielding a staff. Pale but familiar features stared from beneath the hood.

'Isambard!'

Wind blasted her back, snatching her voice away.

She fell to her knees, holding on to the stang for dear life – the only thing keeping her from flying away.

A pounding dominated her skull, making her nose bleed. Then a voice echoed across the mouth of the maelstrom: *'Maud, my darling. You brave the edge of life. Do not fall now … You have opened the way. Now you must close it. Break the staff. Release me!'*

Maud tried with all her might, straining in the wind.

'Quickly, the doorway will not be open for long!'

'No,' she sobbed. 'I can't. It won't break.'

'If you cannot free me, then why not come with me? We do not have to be apart! What wonders we could discover together, Maud.' Isambard reached out, beckoning to her. *'What do you want to live for, Maud?'*

Her husband's voice sounded cold: was it mocking her, testing, or tempting?

Maud felt a fatalistic urge to join her husband – to leave the world behind. What did she have keeping her? Her family? Constance probably would prefer her dead anyway. Her work? She was replaceable. Maggie? Well, she did have a soft spot for her friend – but was that enough? She wouldn't want to hurt her. Yet why continue living to please someone else? What of Rose? Would she ever hear from her again? Rose had made her enjoy life, her body. But, there had been no word from her. No evidence to suggest it had been anything more than a fling. Whom had Maud been kidding? She had no hope, no ambition, no reason to continue ... but some instinct for life pulled her back. If it had been another year she might have been tempted, but something in the last year had made her love life again. Suddenly, life seemed unbearably sweet and precious. Its very transience made it even more important to cherish.

Yet Nubi could not resist his master's lure. Feeling the summons directed at Maud, or perhaps feeling her fear, the lurcher instinctively leaped forward – into the vortex. There was a howl of pain and the body of the dog was twisted in the wind, and dropped, crumpled on the hillside.

'Nooo!'

A firm hand gripped her – stopped her from rushing forward. She turned and recognised the face, but she was inconsolable.

'Archibald! How?'

'I followed. I was frightened for you, Maud. You've been acting so strange lately. Now I can see why. Although I don't know what the hell it is I am seeing.' Archibald gazed into the white inferno. From it poured an icy wind. 'Don't go further – for God's sake! Look at what it's just done to the dog, poor blighter.'

'Let me go! Let me join him!' Maud was beside herself, hysterical. She had finally succumbed to the death music that had played through her life – that had reached its crescendo here on this hillside. A doom had seized hold of her, but her brother-in-law would not let her go.

Maud looked at the lurcher's body, lying on the hillside, inert.

'Nubi!'

'Don't worry, Maud. Nubi could not pass over. He will roam these hills instead, where he was happiest. Loyal to the last, my faithful hound. Don't mourn him, Maud. His time had come. He had a good life. We loved him. He wanted to come on one last run ... but he cannot join me here. His spirit remains earthbound. Yet his death has paid for you to cross. Is that what you want, Maud? Instead of life? Instead of earthly love? Does not your heart now belong to another? Do not deny it – I sense it in your soul.' Before Maud could protest, Isambard said: 'But I see we are not alone any more ... brother, have you come to mock me, or to make a cuckold of a ghost?'

'Is – Isambard? Hell's teeth! Is that you? I – I don't believe ... What the deuce is happening? What are you doing to us?'

'Archie, I forgive you ... Find what happiness you can in that veil *of tears we've made of the world. Have Maud with my blessing, if she wants you. But perform one last favour for me – then you'll be free of me for ever. Break the stang – Maud cannot do it by herself. Do this and let us be at peace.'*

Archibald had heard the voice in his head, above the roar of the wind. He did not want to believe it — yet he experienced it. He had learnt to trust his senses. His soldier's instinct told him it was time to act. Only this would change things.

'Archie, you have to let go as well. You cannot always be my rival.'

Archibald reeled as if from a blow. His brother's words stung him to the core — because he could taste the bitterness of their truth.

Archibald sighed and let go of Maud.

'Here, give me the staff. Let it go! Do it, your husband commands!'

Maud handed over the stang.

Grabbing it with both hands, Archibald bent it over his good knee. He strained with all his might, the veins on his neck bulging.

'Aaargh!' The staff splintered and snapped. 'There. It's done.' He threw it to the ground, breathing heavily.

A sigh filled the night air, like the trapped air of an opened tomb.

The howling stopped and the portal of cold fire began to close.

'Thank you, brother. Peace to you … Maud, I love you. Live your life well. Be free.'

The figure of Isambard began to fade and flicker.

'I go beyond … the road does not end. I – I can see a door opening, Maud. I can see sky.

Farewell!'

The tunnel of light swirled to nebulae, to nothing, leaving only the distant glimmer of cold stars. The wind died and they were suddenly aware of the vast emptiness of night. The two tiny figures shivered on the hillside, holding one another. Maud wept for one last time. 'Goodbye Sammy,' she whispered. Then slowly she turned to Archibald. 'Thank you,' she said, her voice raw. Finally she composed herself and looked hard at the man next to her. 'I cannot be with you as a wife, but I hope we can be friends from now on. You have been a friend in need. I shall always be grateful for that.'

'Maud, I —'

'Please, Archibald. Don't make a fuss. You have behaved admirably. Don't spoil it now. Do me one last favour and help me bury this poor dog. He would want to be laid to rest here.'

Archibald struggled to restrain himself, but eventually he shrugged his shoulders. Her brother-in-law looked broken too. All the fight had gone out of him. 'As you wish, Maud, as you wish.'

And so he set to work digging a ditch with the broken stang, scooping out the dark soil with his hands and finally lowering the cold body of Nubi inside – the two pieces of the broken staff on either side. He let Maud say a few words, then he pushed the soil on top, laying the faithful hound to rest.

Above, Sirius shone at the foot of Orion the Hunter.

Bruised, shaken, they helped each other back to the Giant's Rest, to the healthy glow of humanity and to the real warmth of the fire.

25

GOD IN THE MACHINE

For the last blossom is the first blossom
And the first blossom is the best blossom
And when from Eden we take our way
The morning after is the first day.

'Apple Blossom', Louis Macneice

The day after, Maud woke on her forty-third birthday. She lay in the simple but snug bedroom of the Giant's Rest, stiff and numb from her experiences. She couldn't believe it was all over. She had done it: Isambard was free.

She gazed into the ashes of the grate opposite the bed – cold and grey. Her husband was laid to rest at last. Or was 'rest' the wrong word? Perhaps 'passed on' was a more appropriate euphemism. It would seem he carried on his journey. But what of Maud? The task had consumed her all year and now it was accomplished she felt hollow and purposeless.

And yet she could not go back to the way she had been.

The carriage clock on the mantelpiece chimed the ninth hour.

'Isambard, I will not waste another day.'

Maud picked up the fob watch from the bedside locker and held its coolness against her breast. The watch clicked open, and Maud glanced down. Blinked. Something was amiss. It marked the seventh hour. For the last year it had read 10.01 a.m.. She looked more closely. The second hand ticked around. It was working again! It must have started again when her husband had finally been freed at midnight. The watch had moved on nine hours since then. Time was no longer out of joint. She corrected the hands and clicked it shut. Time to get up!

Quickly she washed, using the sink in the corner, and threw on some clothes. It was a freezing morning – the windows were frosted over on both sides. She could see her breath in the room.

She made her way downstairs to warm herself by the still-smouldering fire while waiting for breakfast. There were sounds of movement in the kitchen.

Archibald was asleep in the inglenook with a blanket around his shoulders. He was snoring heavily. An empty brandy bottle lay kicked over by his feet.

Maud looked at him with fondness for the first time. Like a true friend he had come through in her hour of need. He had done something selfless for the first time in his life. Perhaps there was hope for him yet, although Maud had no intention of redeeming him.

She would accept his friendship, but not his love. Her heart belonged to someone else.

Maud gazed into the glowing embers and sighed, wishing Rose could be with her. She needed that human warmth now – more than ever. She had walked with the dead for too long.

Yet would she ever hear from her again?

She should have done by now. It had been over two months since she had written to Rose at Shakespeare and Company. Perhaps Rose had moved on too. Maybe she had gone home. Had it then been nothing more than fairy dust?

It made Maud's stomach knot just thinking about it.

Archibald stirred. 'Mmm, can I smell bacon?'

'Good morning, Archie. Sleep well?'

'Oh, Maud – there you are! Have you been watching over me like an angel?' He rubbed his eyes and temples. 'Oh, my head! It's okay – I don't expect any sympathy. It's all self-inflicted, as usual.'

Maud smiled. She knew he was only putting on a brave face. The way his eyes flinched from hers – she could see the hurt and disappointment in them.

'God, my throat's as dry as a birdcage. Is there any water?'

'Here.' Maud offered him a cup, and filled it from a pitcher.

'Crikey, that's cold – but good. Thank you.' Archibald tried to smooth back his hair but it stood on end, and his face was besmirched with fallen soot.

Maud had to laugh. 'You look a fright.'

'Charming! And have you seen yourself? You've got a white streak in your hair.'

'Have I?' She inspected her hair and shrugged. 'Well, I am an old woman now – it's official.'

Archie slapped his head. 'Of course, it's your birthday today! Silly me! Sorry, I don't know where my wits are this morning.

Congratulations! We'll have to make the most of it!'

'No, Archie – I don't want to have a party. I want to – reflect upon what has happened.'

'Of course ... I understand. You've been through a lot.'

'Yes. We both have ... Thank you, for last night.'

Archibald suddenly looked abashed. 'I had to help ... although what actually happened up there on the hill I haven't the foggiest. It's like a rarebit dream. And it's slipping through my fingers as I try to remember it ... Though my knee hurts like blazes for some reason.' Archie rubbed his leg, shaking his head.

'I know what took place up there – and I'll never forget.'

Maud scanned the embers. Among the ashes there was still life. Gazing into their dying glow she reflected upon what she had seen. When the portal had opened on the hillside she had glimpsed the Beyond. This world, it seemed, was not all. The body's house of flesh had a soul that survived death. Spirit inhabited matter and then returned – to where? Its source? And if the soul was forged before life, did that not suggest a Creator?

'*Dear Isambard – may you reach your destination,*' Maud whispered into the ashes.

Archie looked at Maud admiringly. 'My little brother found one hell of a wife. I hope I have someone to remember me ...'

'You will, Archie. You will.'

The landlord appeared with a tray of breakfast. Archibald rubbed his hands in glee and tucked in, his lust for life unabated.

After settling with the landlord Archibald drove his companion back to Eastbourne. The Downs were frozen white like a clean sheet of paper, Maud thought. She felt like the landscape – silent and cleansed, but content. She was looking forward to being home, to withdrawing and reflecting through the winter months.

Archie dropped her off and said he would be around Constance's if she wanted company. They parted with a polite kiss and a squeeze of the hand.

Maud entered her little terrace in Bradford Street and shut the door with a deep sigh of relief. She scanned the mat. Among the usual bills and catalogues there were a couple of birthday cards – a formal one from her sister, probably written by her husband, and a warm one from Maggie, encouraging her to go out for a drink in the evening.

Yet the one she wanted most was not there.

Maud pulled off her coat, and the dog chain fell from her pocket. She picked it up and held it tight, thinking of the lurcher. The house was empty without Nubi there, barking and wagging his tail. She walked into the kitchen and her eyes fell immediately on his bowl.

She automatically went to fill the kettle, but the pipes were frozen. She sat down heavily in the wicker chair and felt tears welling up – she let them come. She wept for a lost friend. Soulless or not, Nubi had been a blithe spirit who had brought a breath of fresh air into their lives.

Eventually, Maud gathered herself together and set about the household chores with an ardent thoroughness. She would cleanse the house from top to bottom, like winter did the earth. She had neglected the place and it had degenerated rapidly. Plates were piled up, dust lay thick on the windowsills and bookcases, cobwebs clung to the corners of the rooms. It was as if she had been the dead one.

Maud acquired some water from her neighbour. She lugged the pail back, trying not to spill any on the icy path. The cleaning warmed up her stiff limbs. It was good to be back in the land of the living, despite its toil.

As she dusted the study she recalled that day, what seemed a lifetime ago, when she had decided to read her husband's journals. Then, just as she noticed they had been re-arranged, there was a knock at the door.

The mystery would have to wait. Wiping her hands on her apron, then taking it off as she descended the stairs, she tried to scry the diffused shape through the frosted glass. The dark bulky silhouetted could be only one person. Archie! Wait until she had words with him! Peevishly, she undid the chain and opened the door. The visitor had vanished. Yet there was the Silver Ghost, incongruous against the working-class terrace. 'Archie?' she called out. The street was Sunday quiet. This was not the time for cherry knockers, Maud tutted. Suddenly it occurred to her with a sickening lurch – perhaps it was something else. Disconcerted, she went to slam the door, then she noticed movement below – on the doorstep was a cardboard box. It shuddered. Something was inside.

Gingerly, Maud pulled open the flaps and gasped with delight. Inside was a little grey-brown puppy. It leapt up and yapped, wagging its entire body.

Maud looked around. There was still no sign of her brother-in-law. What was that man playing at!

She leant down and picked up the puppy, which she could see now was a lurcher. It licked her nose and urinated onto her arms in excitement. Her mortification melted and she burst out laughing. He was a boy alright.

'You little terror! You're going to have to be better behaved than that if you want to stay here.'

Yet she held him to her breast. The poor thing was shivering. She crooned and cooed, stroking his head.

'Do you like him?'

Maud looked up.

'Archie!'

From behind the car her brother-in-law appeared arms behind his back.

'A little birthday present for you. Hell of a job finding one!' He approached − a little awkward with their new 'arrangement'.

'Oh, Archie .... You shouldn't have. That's so sweet of you. You're a darling! Thank you. Thank you.'

Maud leant over and kissed Archie on the cheek. The puppy barked.

'The little blighter's jealous!'

'He can't handle his drink either! I wonder who he reminds me of ...' She smiled. 'Would you like a cup of tea?'

'Yes, please − it's freezing out here!'

'I'm afraid it's not much warmer in here. The pipes were frozen, but I got some water from next door. The range is on, but I'm afraid it's not the Café Royal.'

'Oh, doesn't bother me. Perhaps these may cheer the place up a bit.' Archibald produced a posy of flowers from behind his back. 'I'm afraid they're dried − but they'll last longer that way.'

'Why, thank you! Let's hope this 'new you' lasts as well! What's brought all this on?'

Archibald shrugged. 'I don't know − maybe a wish for a fresh start.'

'Come on through. Let me find a vase.' A little overwhelmed Maud led her guest through the passage.

Archibald picked up the box and followed. 'There are some toys in here for him too.'

'I thought you didn't like dogs?' Maud called back.

'I can't say they're my favourite mammal − but I know you're fond of the daft things. You'll miss Nubi − and I felt partly responsible ...'

'Don't be silly. There's nothing you could have done. And you saved me from oblivion.' Maud remembered that cold fire, and shivered. She had been on the precipice. 'Here, take a seat by the cooker. Warm yourself.'

Maud put the puppy in Nubi's basket. The little lurcher seemed too small for it, but she felt it was right. Life had to go on.

'It's the best birthday present ever,' she said, kissing Archibald on the cheek again.

Well, the second best, she thought. But her life no longer felt so empty.

'What are you going to call him?'

Maud looked at the puppy sniffing his new surroundings. 'Sammy.' Yes, that seemed right somehow. Then she recalled the journals. She rounded on her guest.

'Archie.'

He knew that tone, and answered warily: 'Yes, my dear sister-in-law?'

'Tell me the truth — have you been in this house when I wasn't here?'

Archibald coughed. 'Ah, the game's up, I suppose. Yes, Maud — Connie and I were worried about you. She lent me the spare key to come and check if things were alright.'

'Tell me straight — did you go into the study?'

Her guest studied his fingernails. 'I'm afraid so, Maud. Sorry, it's in my nature to make a mess of things.'

'So, you've been looking at the journals!'

Archibald shrugged, began whistling. 'Maybe I should be going.'

'Stay right there,' Maud fumed. 'You're exasperating, Archibald Kerne!'

'I know, I know. Is this where the cat pays for his curiosity?'

Archibald avoided Maud's glare, looking guilty, waiting for the judgement to fall.

'You should respect other people's privacy!'

'If I hadn't called round and found the note on the calendar I wouldn't have found you at the Long Man. And Lord knows what might have happened then. It looked like I got there in the nick of time. And...' — Archibald looked honestly at Maud, 'perhaps I needed to make my peace as well.'

Maud had to admit Archibald's presence had been timely and indispensable. Perhaps, for once, she had to forgive his transgression. They all had needed to let go of something. It seemed Archibald had overcome his sibling rivalry at last. And he no longer saw himself as her suitor — she'd put a stop to that. He was finally being a friend.

Then the puppy jumped up on to his lap and spilled his tea. 'Oh blazes!'

Sammy's white-tipped tail wagged like a flag of surrender and Maud relented. We all transgress, she thought, and we all need forgiveness.

'It's alright, Archie – you can't help being the way you are, any more than Sammy here!' And they both laughed.

'No, I guess you're right – old dogs and new tricks, right? But I believe I've tried to move on – and you have changed too, Maud. I see it in your eyes, hear it in your voice. There's new life in you. It's good to see – even if it's not meant for me.'

Maud smiled demurely. 'That's sweet of you to day so, Archie. Here, let me get a cloth.'

While she went to the sink, Maud wondered *who* was it meant for. There was only one, but she dared not speak her name.

Normal life resumed once more, or, rather, Maud re-entered it with a renewed joie de vivre. She busied herself finishing the term, leading rehearsals for the school pantomime, decorating the classroom for Christmas, getting her girls to make delicate chains, stars and a Nativity scene. At home, the puppy made a mess – tearing everything up he could lay his teeth on. She had to leave paper out for him until he knew better. Although he infuriated her at times, his innocent expression soon made her heart melt. One day she took the puppy into school, to everyone's delight. And from then on, she did so every day – making her the most popular teacher in school. Her pupils saw her in a new light. She was no longer so stern. She had a sense of humour again. She introduced them to art activities, and the class-room became an explosion of colour and laughter. She joined in the school choir's carol practice, and impressed people with her voice.

Yet all the time she longed to hear from Rose.

November flew by with the business of living, and she had all but given up on Rose, when a small letter appeared on her mat. She managed to grab it just before the puppy chewed it up. It had a French postmark on and smelled of Chanel No. 5. Maud held it trembling in her hand, clutched to her breast, unable to open it.

Would it be good news, or bad? While in ignorance at least she had the memories – but as soon as the letter was read it would change everything. She could not live in limbo. She had to act.

And so she sat down at the kitchen table and slit open the letter with a cheese knife.

Carefully, she folded open the lilac paper and read:

My Darling Maud,

I am so sorry not to have written sooner. It's been madness here. Paris is a tide you cannot resist. I only managed to catch up with myself when I went south for a few days and visited my ancestral roots in Avignon.

My folks have been over, trying to get me to go back home. They have some frat boy lined up for me. I try to explain that I'm not interested, but it's difficult. They just don't speak the same language. And my mother never listens. I can never get a word in edgewise. I know they have my best interests at heart, but I need my freedom. New England would be suffocating. Hell, they don't even let you drink over there! A girl has got to have a good time while she can. There'll be plenty of time for staying at home in my dotage, not that I'm planning on being old – ever! Although you're a fine example for growing old disgracefully – if you don't mind me saying so. But don't be offended, I don't think of you as 'old' – you're younger in spirit than some people half your age. It was so brave of you to do what you did – I admire you, Maud.

Yet more than that, I am crazy about you! I've never forgotten that hot hot day! Or you ... You've done something funny to me, Maud, with your juju – you've made me care for someone more than myself. My life here seems superficial compared with what you have gone through. I want to be with you.

I can't be without you.

So, I've decided to come and visit for Christmas. I'll be over on Christmas Eve, and I have a cunning plan: to whisk you away from Eastbourne on my metal steed, and take you somewhere magical for a few days. How does Bath sound – hot springs in a cold season – I've always fancied going there? My folks gave me my money home – but I want to spend it visiting you and indulging us both.

What do you say?

Yours rowing in Eden,

Love, Rose

xxxxx

Maud stared at the small but bold handwriting. She was stunned. All her doubts and fears were banished. It was real – and Rose was coming to her!

Her mind whirled at the repercussions. Yet the details did not matter now – just the fact that Rose wanted her. It had mattered to her, she had remembered, she cared.

So love was worth believing in after all. What she cared for was not going to be taken away again. Maud's constant fear of losing what she loved was finally being exorcised.

She held Sammy in her lap and kissed him. 'Rose is coming! Rose is coming!' She laughed with joy. The puppy barked, swept along by her excitement.

The final few weeks of term could not go quick enough. Maggie noticed the impatience in Maud. One playtime, over tea in the staff-room, Maggie cornered her friend, who was checking her diary.

'What is it with you woman? Can't wait for Christmas? Normally you can't wait until it's over.'

'I know – but this year I'm not spending it with my lovely sis and her circus.'

'No? So what's the big secret that you're dying to tell me?'

Maud had been unable to speak directly about what had happened in Europe, but the changes were unmistakable. It wasn't just the more colourful wardrobe; it was the confidence, the unexpected passion, the new-found confidence.

'I've ... got a friend coming to stay.'

'Oh, have you now!' Maggie munched on a biscuit. 'You dark horse! And who's the lucky fella?'

'Shush, Maggie!' Maud blushed. 'It's not a man – it's a girlfriend I made in Paris.'

'That's great, Maud.' Maggie tried not to sound hurt, but it was difficult for her to hide her disappointment. She had always been Maud's closest friend.

'Don't worry, silly – you'll always be my number one pal!' She hooked her arm around Maggie and kissed her on the cheek.

'Anyway, what about you?' Maud said.

'Same as usual – back home to Galway, with the clan.'

'You're lucky having such a big family, Maggie. I have to make mine.'

'I know, I know. Must be hard, not having your parents around. And it's a shame you don't get on with your sister. But too many cousins, uncles and aunties can drive you mad as well!'

The two friends went for a night out together at the end of term, treating themselves to a meal, and going on to see an Ivor Novello movie: *The Man Without Desire*. The Byronic homme fatal was the heart-throb of both of them. They swooned together. It was just like old times – except now Maud could feel desire. She remembered sitting in the cinema in Paris with Rose and felt a little guilty, though she told herself that was absurd. Maud and Maggie felt they would be friends for ever, something that would endure the vicissitudes of life. Maggie was delighted to see Maud her old self again. For the first time in a decade she stopped worrying about her, but would never stop caring. They exchanged presents, and parted with not a few tears.

'Thank you, Maggie. Thank you for always being there for me. I hope I'll be a better friend to you in future.'

'Start by being a better friend to yourself.'

Then finally Christmas Eve came and Maud made sure she was packed and ready to go. She had never been to Bath, but had heard it was very pretty. She justified the decadence of the excursion by deciding to use it as an excuse to visit Glastonbury again, only twenty odd miles further. She was sure Rose wouldn't mind the addition to their itinerary. It would be strange returning there with a companion, but things had changed. It would no longer be an act of dutiful remembrance. This time she wanted to go for herself.

Maud finished her Christmas chores, sending cards and presents to all that she should. She had ordered a silver horse-headed walking cane for Archibald from Foss's in Dorset. For Constance she sent scented soap, her husband a telescope, the twins Arthur Rackham illustrated fables and colouring books. For Maggie she bought a copy of Yeats' *The Wind Among the Reeds*. The poet had just won the Nobel Prize for Literature. The only thing she hadn't sorted out was what to do with Sammy. He was just about getting house trained, but she wouldn't want to inflict him upon her neighbour. Sammy was too young to be separated from his 'mum', as she thought of herself with a smile.

Before she could decide, she heard a roaring down the street, the splutter and expiring of a petrol engine, then a brisk knock at her door.

She opened it and there stood Rose in a well-cut leather

motorcycle outfit, complete with boots and goggles. Behind was a motorcycle and sidecar.

Maud was speechless.

'Voilà – your deus ex machina! Well, aren't you going to invite me in?'

'Oh Rose, Rose – you don't know how good it is to see you! But of course, come in, please. Have a cup of tea before we set off, yes. You must have travelled far ... what an extraordinary machine you have!'

Rose pulled off her thick gloves and patted the saddle.

'My charger!'

'He's a fine steed, my knight errant ...Take off that silly hat and let me look at you!'

Rose peeled away her leather hat, and shook out her hair – a little longer than it had been.

'I remember the first time you did that – drove me wild.'

Maud shut the door and turned. They embraced and kissed in the hallway.

Over tea they caught up ... The events of the last two months spilled out over several cups of tea. It was just the minutiae of life but Maud loved hearing every word. She couldn't stop grinning. Maud didn't have much news on the domestic front – her life seemed so dull in comparison – apart from the night at Wilmington, of course. It wasn't the right time to talk about that, yet. It would come – she was sure of it – there didn't seem anything Maud couldn't talk to Rose about. Any half-formed notion or feeling. She had never been one for small talk, but with Rose conversation was a joy for its own sake.

Maud broached the subject of going on to Glastonbury. Rose instantly fell in love with the idea. 'Oh, wild – a girl from Providence in the court of King Arthur!' she clapped.

The puppy had woken up and Rose was introduced to Sammy.

'Oh, he's adorable. Bring him along too – if you don't mind him on your lap. You'll need a blanket. Wrap up. It's mighty cold out there. England is one heck of a chilly country, Maud – but maybe it's just appearances. Like you, when we first met.'

Maud shut off the gas and lights and locked the door – hesitating on the threshold.

'Come on, slow-coach. What you haven't got, we'll buy there!'

The luggage was strapped to the back. Maud squeezed into the sidecar, with Sammy on her lap. Rose kick-started the motorcycle into life on the second attempt. The engine growled into life like a lioness. Curtains twitched, but Maud didn't care.

'To Avalon, my knight of the rose!' laughed Maud.

'At your command, my lady.'

26

THE SUN ON THE HILL FORGOT TO DIE

The sun on the hill forgot to die,
The lilies revived and the dragonfly
Came back to dream on the river.

Yet half a beast is the Great God Pan,
To laugh as he sits by the river,
Making a poet out of a man.

And the True Gods sigh for the cost and the pain,
For the reed which grows never more again,
As a reed with the reeds by the river.

'A Musical Instrument', Elizabeth Barrett Browning

The journal of Maud Kerne

1ˢᵗ January 1924, Glastonbury
I begin this journal on New Year's Day with trepidation and
hope. For all of my literary interests this will be the first time I
have kept a journal. I am more eager to read others' words than
the whispers of my own heart. Yet no more shall I deny what's
inside. I have taken the green road of the soul.
I shall never forget you, Isambard. You have taught me much.
Your wisdom will linger. I will preserve your journals. But now
I shall write my own! I have found my voice. And my life again.
Rose is a revelation. She makes me feel alive. Who knows where it
will go? I just know things cannot go back to the way they were.
These pages stretch out before me, a world unmapped. For the
first time in a long while I can see the horizon. I can see a future.

Maud walked up the hill in the clear light of a new year. It was a stark
winter's day, the sky almost chrome blue. The sides of the Tor were
dusted with frost. The narrow steps snaked between the white spikes

of grass. Her breath congealed before her in clouds, as she rose into the sky – high above the Somerset Levels, beneath their sheath of ice. The air was sharp and thrummed around her, blasting away the last of the Christmas cobwebs.

Despite the indulgences of the last few days Maud felt more alive than she had ever done. The cold wind on her cheeks felt delicious. She took off her hat and let the wind tousle her long brown hair, with its streaks of grey. Silently, she ascended the white path. By the time she reached the tower she must have looked a right state, but she didn't care. No one was there to see her, for the moment.

Maud and Rose had arrived around midday, their cocktail hangovers blasted away by the bracing motorcycle journey across the snow-laden Mendips. They had thawed out in the only pub open – the George and Pilgrim, a twelfth century hostelry on the High Street. In a bookshop window Maud had spotted a display for *The Secrets of Dr Tavener*. She thought of Dion Fortune, remembered the encounter in the Assembly Rooms, and hearing her mention the book she had been working on. Have to look her up, Maud thought. She'd be interested in Maud's experiences of the past year.

What of Isambard's journals? What of his secrets? Maud felt protective of them. She would not want the memory of her husband mocked. They could never be published. Perhaps she would pass them on to a museum, to the local library – one day, but for now she wanted to keep them to close to her. They were all she had left.

The weak sun climbed to its midday peak, still far south, but growing a little nearer every day.

Rose came puffing up behind her – breathless, eyes shining. She led Sammy along on his trainer lead. The little dog tackled each step in a series of leaps.

'Wow – this place is something else!'

'They don't call it the "hill of vision" for nothing,' Maud quipped. She gazed out across the gleaming land, remembering what she had seen there last time, and what her husband had seen on the day he proposed to her.

'What's up?' asked Rose, huddling next to her.

'Oh, nothing. I'm just thinking of other times. The things I've seen up here.'

'You sure can see a long way,' observed Rose, scanning the horizon.

'Even into the past.'

Rose let her reminisce, deciding to explore the tower. Maud watched her disappear around the corner. She sighed and followed, only to be startled as her companion leapt out behind her.

'Please, don't – I've had enough surprises for one year!'

They hugged each other to keep warm.

'Cigarette?'

'Rose, have you no respect?' Maud chastised her.

'Only for you. I won't if it bothers you.'

'Well, maybe just do it outside the tower.'

'Yes, ma'am.' Rose saluted.

They stood in the lee of the tower as Rose struggled to light a Gauloise.

Maud remembered what had happened the last time she was here. And so much had happened in-between. Her world had changed. Even the littlest thing was filled with potential mystery, with a nascent sacredness. Before, God had been dead – now, now he was everywhere, in everything. Like her husband. Isambard's presence no longer haunted the tower, but his spirit permeated Maud's existence. She had released him by realising him within herself. The part of her that had been neglected or denied had now been awakened. She had walked between the worlds and had held them in balance, without being destroyed. The year past had challenged her to the limits of sanity, but she had survived. She was worthy.

And now life tasted so much sweeter.

Rose offered her the glowing cigarette and Maud pulled on its warmth, coughing a little as the acrid smoke filled her lungs briefly. She exhaled with relief, watching the cloud dissipate into the sky.

They gazed out over Glastonbury town and the Levels beyond. It seemed that all the alignments of the world converged on the Tor … Or started there.

'Where are we heading, Rose?'

'No one knows where the road will take you – until you take it,' mused Rose, taking a long draft.

'You're right. Life isn't a straight line. Just look at this hill – the path is a labyrinth, spiralling, looping back on itself. We can go full circle, but we're not the same as when we started out.'

'You're not fooling. I never thought I'd end up here, but it feels so right.' Rose looked straight at Maud. 'I'm glad I've begun the journey.'

'So am I, Rose, so am I.'

Rose stubbed out the cigarette butt with a quick twist of her boot; reminding Maud of the first time she had met Isambard. And now it was over − or was it? As she watched the last wisps of smoke curl and vanish, she thought − time does not run in a straight line. The past intersected the here and now, was ever-present. She saw her and Isambard in the tower, dancing in the wind.

'Come − you have to try this!'

Maud led Rose back into the tower. She stood in the middle of the tower and let the wind hold her. She raised her arms and leant back into it, feeling its strength support her.

And she sang, but this time she sang with joy:

And the lads run like a windy day,
And the lasses run like rain.

Echoing with song the portals of the tower gaped wide but her husband did not come. He was elsewhere. Not at rest, thought Maud. Still travelling ... exploring the greatest adventure of all. And for the first time Maud felt, with a glimmer of faith, she might one day meet him in the Otherworld − and they would talk of old times and new dreams. But in the meantime she would go her own way. Like many of her sisters, she had found independence at last. She was free, she was alive and she was ready.

Rose joined her and they danced in the air as one.

Maud took her companion's hand and they leaped across the threshold of the tower, into the light − the wind carrying them gently to earth.